BOOK TWO

A TALE OF RIBBONS & CLAWS

RACHEL E SCOTT

Bond-Mate, A Tale of Ribbons & Claws Book Two

Cover by Miblart.

Interior art by Rachel E. Scott

To all the people who come for the kissing. I tried not to disappoint.

<u>Also by Rachel E Scott</u>

Contemporary

The Grinch Next Door

Fantasy

Legends of Avalon: Merlin
Legends of Avalon: Arthur

A Tale Of Ribbons & Claws

Stale-Mate
Bond-Mate
Check-Mate (coming SOON!)

Plot Twist

Bonding With the Bodyguard (coming 2024)

Do you like to listen to playlists while reading? I've got you covered. Here's my personal playlist for
A Tale of Ribbons & Claws: Bond-Mate.
https://open.spotify.com/playlist/34JFKt09VgjsnsE7Ufif7D?si=5a7159ad648c
443c

Content Warnings

All of my books are clean reads, but here are some things to note before you begin reading:

- Age gap between love interests (10 years)

- Mention of death of past loved one

- Mention of cancer (past)

- Basic violence (nothing descriptive or graphic)

- No sex

- Kissing that stays sweet and swoony

- Mild innuendos (Ex: 'that;s what she said.' No vulgar jokes.)

Note: This book is the second in a trilogy, but by the end of the series, you will get a tied-up story with a happy ending.

Contents

Last Time on A Tale of Ribbons & Claws

F or the last three years, Caroline Birch has been playing vigilante to the city of Shifter Haven. As an Elf—a species extinct thanks to a centuries old civil war—she felt a personal responsibility to fight for the Shifters of her city. To end the Shifter trafficking, fraud, and drug rings that have gone unchecked for too long. And she was doing a good job of it.

Until Morgan intervened.

Morgan Hohlt, Chief of the Berserkers, had a reputation that weighed heavy on anyone who heard of it. As a species that can turn into large bears, a general respect and fear was allotted Berserkers. But Morgan has more than people's respect. Because of a string of murders containing the same killing method that he used to try and save his mom more than two decades ago, he has their terror. Which makes him the perfect scapegoat for the council to pin Caroline's vigilante work on.

Between Morgan's inability to bring down the Berserker gambling dens plaguing the region, and the Berserker Chief from centuries ago who was said to have killed the Alfar King—an act which started the civil war that decimated the Elves—the Shifter Council, comprised of one representative for each Shifter species for the western region, was quick to assume Morgan's guilt. So, he kidnapped Caroline, hoping to stop her heists.

Caroline and Morgan were enemies at first sight. But as the break-ins at the Shifter Alliance Building continued even without Caroline there to perpetrate them, they became reluctant coworkers and eventually friends. Along with Morgan's confidant Grey, his brothers Mike and Clint, and his best friend Logan, the antagonistic pair began to investigate Caroline's copycat.

But the combative duo quickly began to realize that what had started as a frame job was now an attempt to kidnap Caroline. It just wasn't clear if someone wanted her because they thought she would be good leverage against Morgan...or because they knew that Caroline was an Elf and wanted her magic for themselves.

A lead finally led them to break into the Dragon Queen's hotel. And by luck and pure stubbornness, Caroline and Morgan singlehandedly took down her entourage, and Morgan fought the Dragon Queen in his bear form. And won.

The heist was a success, but while Eileen had admitted to framing Morgan and attempting to kidnap Caroline, she insisted that she intended to sell Caroline to someone else. But Caroline and Morgan never found out who.

And just as Caroline was moving into the Berserker house and feeling some semblance of peace, she made a jarring discovery. Eileen the Dragon Queen had discovered that Caroline's parents were Elven royalty...*Alfar* royalty.

Then of course there's the mate bond between Caroline and Morgan...That Morgan *still* hasn't told her about...

The Shifters of Shifter Haven & Their Most Identifying Abilities

Alfar—Light Elves (powers unknown)

Berserker—can shift into bears.

Dragon—can shift into dragons.

Fenrir—can shift into giant wolves.

Firebird—can control fire.

Harpy—can control air.

Kelpie—can shift into black horses.

Mermaid—can read minds.

Minotaur—can shift into large, heavily muscled people with horns.

Nephilim—Dark Elves (powers unknown)

Pixie—can control nature.

Sphinx—can shift into large cats (lions, tigers, cheetahs, etc.)

Witch—can perform spells.

Wyvern—can shift into a wyvern.

Chapter 1

CAROLINE

As a dog parent, I recommend that all fur children be properly prepared for any environment. As a *spy* dog parent, that meant that Daisy Mae was trotting through the Shifter Alliance Building wearing little pink booties.

"I don't know why I didn't think of this earlier," I said, beaming at Morgan as Daisy walked beside us in her stylish dog booties. "She looks adorable, doesn't she?"

Morgan, in true Morgan fashion, glared at me. Because no, in the weeks we'd known each other, he hadn't lost his love of frowns. *I know, I thought my joyful—ahem, snarky—demeanor would've softened him too.* But no dice. In his defense though, he did wear a glare like a male model.

Not that I'd tell *him* that.

My sister might have been convinced that I had a thing for my best friend, but I knew better. I couldn't *allow* myself to have a thing for my best friend—and I had good reasons! (a) I was still being hunted by someone who wanted to *buy* me; (b) I was still an extinct species whose identity needed to remain secret; and (c)—most importantly—I'd had exactly one best friend in my life other than my sister.

Morgan. And nothing was worth losing that.

"She's the cutest thing I've ever seen," Morgan replied. Dryly. "That toddler outside Frank's the other day with the big brown eyes who was trying to down an extra-large hamburger? He has nothing on Maisy. Baby Yoda? *Half* as cute as your fur child. That little girl on *Despicable Me* with the stuffed unicorn? Doesn't even hold a candle to Mais."

I knew he was trying to be sarcastic, but the effect was kind of ruined by his usage of Daisy's nickname. Not to mention the adoring emotion I felt warming his chest.

"Careful Mor, your tone might be saying 'leave me alone', but your emotions are saying 'cuddle me, I need affection." And just because I knew I was getting under his skin, I latched onto his arm. Like an adorable, annoying leech.

"My emotions have *never* said such a thing," he grumbled, turning his attention back to the dimly lit hallway. We'd decided to break into the Alliance Building at night. Again. Why break tradition, right?

I shrugged, releasing him. "Alright, if you're so certain you don't want any affection, then I'll just—"

"Now hold on a second," he said, quickly grasping my hands and placing them back on his arm. "I may not necessarily *need* affection, but that doesn't mean you should move away."

"Why? Don't you want space for all your masculine energy? Where you can do your caveman grunts without my annoying femininity getting in the way."

Morgan shook his head, but when a smile tugged at his lips, I knew I was winning. "You're impossible. You know that, right?"

"Sure do," I grinned, snuggling a little closer to him.

"No," he warned as Daisy tried to lick his hand. "You're not any less frustrating than your mother, little miss. All you want to do is kiss—which would be sweet if your kisses weren't contaminated with poop."

"You are weirdly obsessed with French kissing, Mais," I agreed, chastising my sweet—albeit disgusting—brindle colored mutt. For a relatively small, forty-five-pound dog, she was a dangerous thing—especially when one considered what she ate.

"Did you just say French kissing?" Morgan sputtered.

I smirked up at him, pleased to knock him off center. All I needed in life to make me happy was French fries and an off-kilter Morgan. And maybe a milkshake.

"Oh, don't tell me that in all your married life, you never French kissed," I teased, tossing my long auburn hair over my shoulder. When he just stared at me, I tsked and shook my head. "You poor innocent boy, let me explain it to you. When two people care about each other very much, they press their mouths together and—"

"I understand the logistics of French kissing, Caroline," he growled. *Uh oh.* He was calling me 'Caroline'—that was never a good sign. "Not only was I married, but I also went to public school. We all knew what French kissing was by the second grade."

"Yeah, but back then we all thought it sounded gross. Now we know it's *not* gross."

Morgan, a much bigger prude than I'd realized, stopped in the middle of the hallway.

We were on the ninth and final floor of the Shifter Alliance building. Thankfully, we hadn't seen a security guard in ten minutes, so Mor standing there hacking up his lungs probably wouldn't be heard. *Big baby.*

"What is wrong with you tonight?" I asked, patting—smacking—his back as we started walking again. His emotions told me he was embarrassed, but there was something else there too. Something slithery and dangerous that I couldn't recall sensing in him before.

"Nothing," he insisted, coughing up the last of whatever awkwardness had come over him. "I just...I've never heard you talk about your romantic life before."

My romantic life. What a notion. As if I'd ever had time for one. Not that it would've helped if I did. The idea of having to lie to my boyfriend about my species hadn't exactly made me thrilled to try out the dating process.

"I'm not talking about *my* romantic life, I'm talking about Daisy Mae's," I said, pointing at her as she sniffed her way down the hall. "Maybe she needs a boyfriend. Should we get her a boy dog to kiss?"

"We?"

"Yeah. I'm living at your house, and you said that I'm a part of you guys—"

"You are," he agreed quickly, offering me a smile. "Our family is your family, and our home is your home. But *we* are not getting another dog."

And just like that, he ruined the sweet moment.

"Oh, come on. We could get an old cranky dog just for you!"

"Calling me old and cranky is not going to soften me up, Care."

"But you're calling me 'Care', so I must be getting somewhere."

He raised one threatening eyebrow, and I bit back a smirk. "You're going to get yourself in trouble. Which is your MO, so I'm not sure why I'm surprised."

"Rude," I pouted, lifting my chin. "And I do not get myself into trouble. You just shoot down all my ideas."

Morgan gave me an unimpressed look. "I take you to Frank's every time you ask me. I let you redecorate my library. I buy you whatever junk food you want. I never complain about how long it takes you to get ready. *And* you've talked me into no less than five bad mission ideas."

"I resent the implication that I have bad ideas when it comes to missions."

"Oh, I'm not implying it," he said, leaning his face close to mine, the blue ring around his irises almost flashing with his sassy attitude. "I'm stating it as a fact."

"Well maybe I don't want to live with someone who's so mean to me."

That did the trick. Mor grabbed onto my arm, keeping me close. "Oh no, you already moved in. You're not going anywhere." But then a twinge of insecurity lit inside his chest. "Unless you really don't want to live with us…"

Living at the Berserker house had been a big switch from living alone. I now had five loud, rowdy and ridiculous male roommates…but I'd come to really love having them around. The noise, the energy, the affection—I loved all of it.

And when Morgan insisted that I start calling the place home, I didn't mind. Because I didn't want this move to be temporary.

I liked watching TV and playing video games with Mike, Clint and Logan. I liked watching *The Bachelorette* with Grey and discussing which guys seemed crazy and which ones we wanted to save from winning. I liked seeing Morgan every day and finding new ways to bug him. I liked living in a house full of Berserkers who took every opportunity to tease me, cuddle me and make me feel like one of them.

It was a life I never thought I'd have. A safe space I hadn't ever dared to dream of before.

"Easy there, Bear Man," I teased gently, squeezing his bicep—totally necessary. For his benefit, not mine. Obviously... "I'm not going anywhere. Your casa es mi casa now."

Morgan nodded, mumbling a barely intelligible 'good'. And suddenly he seemed very interested in looking around the hallway. The *empty* hallway. But I felt the warmth in his chest. The pleasure, the affection, the peace. And part of me bloomed to know that I'd given it to him.

"I'm surprised you haven't done this before," he said, a not-so-subtle subject change. I let it slide though, taking pity on him as we turned a corner in the dimly lit hall.

The Shifter Alliance Building was empty at this time of night except for the security guards. During the day, they stayed at their posts protecting certain areas, but at night they roamed the building. Hence our presence.

"Done what? Snuck in somewhere with a boy?" I teased, shooting him a cheeky smile. "Who says I haven't."

"That's not what I meant," he complained. But then he glanced at me from the corner of his eye. "Out of curiosity though, have you snuck in somewhere with a boy?"

I grinned. "Yes. Junior year of high school. His name was Jake Jameson. We snuck into the pool next to the high school in the middle of the night. Made out for like two hours. It was fun until he got a little handsy."

"*What?*" Mor tried to stop again, but I tugged him along, knowing that his glare was burning a hole in the side of my head.

"Don't yell," I warned, listening for the telltale sound of footsteps.

"I didn't yell."

"No, but that was dangerously close, and I am not about to ruin my perfect record of never getting caught."

"I caught you."

I glared at him. "Not the point."

When I didn't hear any security guards coming, I picked up my pace. There was no telling when Morgan would start actually yelling. Especially with me around to provoke him.

"What did he do to you?" Morgan hissed, speaking quieter this time.

"What did who do to me?"

"Jake Jameson," he spat out the name like a curse. "You said he got handsy. Tell me you reported him."

I knew it was wrong to let him believe a lie—especially when he was getting closer and closer to ripping my head off. But how could I resist bugging him when a bugged Morgan looked *so* good?

All broody and angry, his thick brows low over his eyes, and his whole body poised to deck someone. Not to mention the faint white scar over his left eye and down his right cheek. *I should take a picture before he blows.* So, I did.

"Caroline," he warned as I shoved my phone back in the pocket of my black jeans. Again, with the 'Caroline'; he was really on edge tonight.

"Calm down, Mor," I said, settling my hands around his arm again. "Poor Jake Jameson didn't cross any lines. I was just kidding. You were being such a grouch and I wanted to have some fun. So, I embellished the story a little."

"You lied." The words may have been said with an angry tone, but the relief I sensed in him belied his jealousy. He was glad I hadn't actually been getting saucy in high school.

"Not entirely. Jake and I really did sneak into the city pool in the middle of the night. But we just put our legs in the water and talked about my sister—whom he was madly in love with, by the way. There was no kissing or groping—"

"Groping?" he exclaimed.

Cringing, I covered his mouth with my hand, but I was too late to stop his shout. "Seriously?" I hissed. "Do you want us to get arrested? Stop yelling!"

He pouted but didn't try to push me away as we stood there waiting for a guard to discover us. After a few moments, I decided the coast was clear and released him, urging us down the hall again.

"If you want me to stop yelling," he said, walking beside me, our arms no longer connected, "Then you should stop telling me fictitious stories about men kissing you while getting 'handsy', as you so sweetly put it. Also, please, for the love of God, don't ever use the word 'grope' again."

"Why? Because I'm too innocent to say such a dirty word?"

Morgan didn't respond right away. Instead, he leaned closer, and my entire body went on high alert. My nerves jittered, acting like they were on standby to launch. I told them to stand down, but they were too busy chanting in tempo with the increasing pace of my heartbeat. 'Closer, closer', they shouted. *I repeat, stand down!*

"No," he whispered, his deep voice drifting over me, simultaneously soothing and exiting my nerves. "I don't want you to have anything to do with the word again, because you deserve better than someone who doesn't touch you like you're precious. When a man is crazy about a woman, he doesn't 'grope' her like a monkey. He's gentle, simply skating by when he should..." I inhaled sharply as his hand skimmed the small of my back. "And pressing close when it's appropriate."

Then that same hand pressed snug against my hip, tugging me into his side.

Breathing. I should be breathing right now. But it was like his touch had sent every molecule of oxygen out of my body, leaving me stupidly breathless.

"Well," I stuttered, my voice wavering thanks to Morgan's moves—because apparently, he had *moves*, "I'll be sure to have you give my next date a crash course before he takes me out."

The comment lacked my usual sass and cheekiness, but it did the trick. Morgan's hand dropped away from my hip, and we walked on like the whole moment had never happened. *Back to the friendzone. The safe zone.*

Right where I needed to be.

"I'll give him a crash course, alright," I heard him grumble behind me. I smiled, glad to have him back to his caveman self. *Much safer than whatever he was a moment ago.*

"In answer to your original question," I said, getting us back on track, "I did sneak into the Shifter Intake Department on the first floor to check the database for mentions of my family—didn't find anything. I have not, however, snuck into the Restricted Records Department. Because until discovering that Dragon lady Eileen had somehow found information on my birth parents, it hadn't occurred to me that there would be anything about me on the restricted database. Now I'm thinking that there's a very good chance I might be a topic."

We paused at the end of the hall, peeking around the corner. Just as planned, there were no guards outside the double doors that led to the Restricted Records Department.

"Is that the only reason you haven't done it before?"

I glanced over at him as we walked up to the double doors. "What do you mean?"

He said nothing, silently watching me shift.

Magic slid over me, altering my face until I looked like someone with the security clearance to be here. I hated this part of my magic. It wasn't painful or difficult, it just really hurt my pride. Sneaking in like this always felt like cheating. Like I wasn't getting in on my own merit, but by playing tricks.

Bracing myself, I turned to face Morgan. "I think the reason you haven't snuck in here before," he said, his grey eyes seeing past my disguise, past my bluster and all my games, "Is because you knew you'd have to shift in order to do it."

I stared at him for a moment before turning to the biometric lock on the door. It scanned my eye, flashing green once it determined my fake identity. "Why would shifting keep me from sneaking in?"

"That's what I'm trying to understand. I know you don't like to shift because you think it's cheating, but it seems like more than that. This database could have answers, and I think you've known that long before now. Which begs the question, why didn't you try to sneak in sooner?"

I didn't answer as I plugged my USB into the lock to break the secondary passcode. It was none of his business why I hadn't snuck in before. None of his business why I hated shifting. We might be friends, but he had no right to go rifling through the private places in my mind. They were off limits to everyone—even him.

"You're not gonna answer me?" he prodded, and I took a deep breath before turning a glare on him.

"Nope." Then I put my USB back in my backpack and pulled one of the double doors open.

"You're so stubborn," Morgan mumbled, him and Daisy following me through the door.

"Pot meet kettle."

Mor grunted, unimpressed, but I ignored him. Up head, a desk sat at the end of the short hall; the roadblock between us and the archive room beyond it. Thankfully, there was no one in sight, only a takeout bag sitting beside the computer.

"That's what your DoorDash call was about on the way here," Morgan said, and I was surprised to see him give me an approving smile. "You knew that the guard would go somewhere else to eat the food."

"I hoped." I shrugged, moving past the desk to a door on the left side of the hall. I pushed it open to reveal the records room. "I ordered poutine and a pizzookie. Cheese loaded fries and a cookie baked like a pizza with ice cream on top seemed like food someone wouldn't eat around their work computer."

"Smart. Where does the guard think the food came from?"

I ushered Morgan into the room and shut the door behind us. "From their superior," I smirked, proud of myself. "I had a note added to the receipt that said it was a reward for a job well done."

"Well, aren't you clever."

"I know," I winked, turning to the bank of computers in the middle of the room. "But it's still nice to hear it."

He sighed—the kind that always accompanied a smile and a headshake—and I took a seat at the closest computer. The USB I plugged in had me logged into the database in no time. Meanwhile, Morgan went down the aisles of shelving where file boxes were stacked to the ceiling.

"Look for either of my last names, or anything on Alfar or Nephilim," I reminded him as I began to search on the computer.

"I know, Care." I smiled—he was using my nickname; his mood was improving.

My joy diminished though, as my own search in the database revealed twenty-seven other people with the last name Birch. And zero Ljosalfar—my birth parent's last name. *Well, that's not encouraging.*

I managed to find over four hundred documented reports on Nephilim and Alfar, but most of them were older—some even dating back hundreds of years. Dozens of ancient texts about supposed Nephilim sightings had been scanned onto the network from old parchment paper. And while the stories were interesting, none of them really told me anything I didn't already know.

"Nephilim are evil Dark Elves hell bent on destroying the world, yada yada yada," I mumbled to myself. If the world had put more energy into finding the Elves instead of spreading these stupid boogieman stories, then they wouldn't be so oblivious to my existence now.

One article seemed to be a little less subjective than the others, written by a Shifter agent in the forties. 'One would think the world would look more intently for Alfar than their combative Nephilim brethren,' the article read, 'But since the Nephilim had the distinct ability to alter their appearance, they would be theoretically easy to identify. The Alfar, however—a secretive group who valued diplomacy above all else—are much more difficult to claim, since no one quite knows what it was they could do. Alfar were known for playing their cards close to the chest, but what else they were known for—be it shifting into an animal or controlling the weather—we will likely never know.'

I sighed, letting my shoulders slump with my disappointment. I'd known that it would be a long shot to find anything about my birth parents and their identities. But I'd hoped to learn *something*.

Instead, I was leaving empty handed.

"Find anything?" Morgan asked, stepping up behind me.

"Failure, self-loathing, internal criticism and a computer that I swear is mocking me with it's insulting combination of zeros and ones," I whined shamelessly. "You?"

"I found a report about a Pixie King who was arrested in 1924 for painting the word 'ass' on the back end of a unicorn." He was teasing, trying to cheer me up. But there was no humor in his voice. There was, however, lots of worry radiating from his chest.

"Did you really?"

"Yep, took a picture for you."

"Thanks." I pouted as Daisy ambled over to us, finally done sniffing the place for food. I scratched her head, and she wagged her tail. Which we'd wrapped in fleece to help lessen the noise when she inevitably banged it against everything.

"Hey, we may not have found any answers tonight, but that's okay," Mor insisted, setting his hands on my shoulders. I felt him press a kiss to the top of my head before resting his chin on it.

"I think you and I define 'okay' very differently. The final season of *The Office* was okay. McDonald's burgers are okay. The month of January is okay. 'Okay' equals medium; nothing about this failure is medium. It's epic, Morgan. An epic failure."

Mor chuckled, the sound vibrating through me where his head touched mine. "Our definitions of 'okay' are the same, Care. Although personally, I can't believe you'd put McDonald's hamburgers on that list." I rolled my eyes, but he continued before I could argue. "But the point is that tonight wasn't a failure. Because your vigilante mission and your desire to know more about your birth parents isn't all your life is about anymore."

"That's true," I agreed with a sigh, "I also have this whole 'am I a Dark Elf or a Light Elf' mystery to keep me entertained. So that's fun."

"Care," he growled, tugging me to my feet.

"Yes Mor?" I said sweetly, my spirits lifting with every increase of irritation blooming inside him.

"I don't know why I like you." He shook his head, looking very vexed. It was adorable.

"Because I'm cute."

He snorted and tugged me toward the door, Daisy following behind us. "No. I'm too stubborn to be swayed by that. It's got to be some kind of Elf power. But my point was that you have things in your life that you didn't have before."

"An expanding waistline?"

This time when he growled, I tried to look a little contrite. Irritated Morgan was fun; angry Morgan was just annoying. "Sorry. Continue."

"Now, not only do you have your family," he said, one hand on the door, "But you have us too. Me, Logan, Mike, Clint, and even Grey. You're not alone anymore, Care; you don't have to hide or pretend with us. You're family, and you have a home with us. *That's* why it's okay that we didn't find answers tonight. Because we'll go home, regroup, eat, cheer each other up, and try again."

"I hate it when you're right," I complained halfheartedly, lifting his arm and draping it over my shoulder as I stepped into his side.

"But you're grateful for it." There was a smile in his voice as he squeezed me close.

"Maybe. But I'll deny it until the day I die."

"I'd expect nothing less."

Chapter 2

CAROLINE

"Morgan please! I will literally beg you on my knees," I whined from the passenger seat as we drove away from the Shifter Alliance Building.

"You act like I'm cutting off your arm or waterboarding you." Morgan shook his head and avoided my puppy dog eyes. Which was a shame because they were very effective manipulation tools.

"You might as well be. Do you know how often I go to Frank's after completing a job?"

"Too often. Which makes me wonder how you look like that and maintain this habit at the same time."

I paused, scrutinizing him carefully. "Look like what?"

He didn't answer, pretending like he hadn't heard me. But his body gave him away. His hands flexed on the steering wheel, embarrassment flashed in his chest, and a blush stained his cheeks. Morgan—the big scary Berserker Chief—was *blushing. Well, this is an interesting development.*

"I look like what, Mor?" I asked again, taunting him.

When we came to a stoplight, he glanced over at me, his grey eyes brushing me from top to bottom. Considering, calculating...appreciative. I felt my body go a little warm at his perusal.

"I don't understand how you can eat like a football playing frat boy," he said, his eyes finally making the trek back up to mine, "And still manage to be so lean."

I instantly deflated. Lean? What girl had ever dreamed of having a man call her 'lean'? Packages of hamburger in the grocery store were sexier than me.

"Did you seriously say that I look *lean*?" I demanded. Morgan nodded, unfazed, and I rolled my eyes. "Morgan, no woman looks forward to the day that a man calls her 'lean'. I feel like livestock. And you're wrong. I'm not lean. I'm five foot four and half of it is curves."

Morgan lifted one eyebrow, as his lips pulled into a smirk. "Point taken, but in my defense, 'lean' was the least dangerous adjective I could think of. And also, did it ever occur to you that you can be both curvy and lean at the same time? Because you are."

I didn't answer, because no, it had not occurred to me that a woman could be both lean and curvy. It was an oxymoron. A belief that had been proven by the parade of tiny women on every TV show ever.

Morgan shook his head and sighed. "Alright fine, I'll put it into clearer—but less platonic—terms. Care, you're a babe. You've got all the right curves in all the right places. You're small enough to hold tight, but there's also enough of you to hold onto. You're a man's dream, and I cannot reconcile that fact with the knowledge that you eat like a middle school boy who's been left home alone for the weekend. It's a scientific wonder. You're a real-life *Gilmore Girl*."

Thankfully, the traffic light turned green, and Morgan had to turn his attention back to the road. Which gave me the chance to react properly; jaw dropped, eyes wide, head pulled back, and triple chin on full display. Super sexy.

But all I could think about was how Morgan—my platonic best friend—had just described me in so much appreciative detail. I knew he was attracted to me—hello Elf powers—but it hadn't really ever registered in my mind how he *saw* me.

Like a woman. A woman he liked looking at. *Huh. I think I'll go spontaneously combust now.*

"You alright over there, Red?" he asked. I didn't have to look to know he was grinning.

"Red?"

"You blush pretty bright," he teased.

I groaned and dropped my head back against the headrest, completely mortified on top of being *starved*. "Oh, I'm just casually dying of mortification. And since my death is imminent and my blush is going to burn me to ashes in this seat, you should let me have a last meal of my choosing."

"I am not taking you to Frank's."

"But *why*?"

"Because Frank's is unacceptable breakfast food. No one eats burgers and fries at four in the morning."

"I do," I grumbled as I crossed my arms, refusing to look at him. No food, no eye contact. *Yeah, that's right. I'm a real cutthroat kinda girl. Deny me food and I'll shun you.* Dwight style.

A few moments passed in silence, Daisy peacefully passed out in the back seat, and Morgan feeling amused by my antics. *Amused. The nerve.*

"You know..." he began as we made our way out of town, "You're cute when you blush. Although I feel like we should come up with a different word, because that shade of scarlet is deeper than any blush I've—"

"Shut up," I snapped, reaching across the console to shove his shoulder. He laughed and I couldn't help but give in to a smile. "You're such a brat."

"But you love me."

"Nope."

"Like me?"

I squinted my eyes and pretended to study him. "I'll say yes if you feed me."

He laughed and I gave into a reluctant grin as we pulled down a darkened driveway. The road to the Berserker house was littered with tall trees and wildflowers, lit only by the small solar pathway lights along the edges of the road. The giant log house was just coming into view, a few lights on inside, when the vehicle suddenly slowed to a crawl.

"Why are you going so slow?"

"Because I have a question," Mor replied nonchalantly, "And I know you well enough to know that asking you while you're locked in a moving vehicle is the only way to get you to answer me."

Preemptively annoyed, I rolled my eyes and turned my body toward the window. "Then maybe you shouldn't ask it. Especially because you didn't feed me and I'm feeling particularly volatile."

"Why haven't you snuck into the Restricted Records Department before now?"

I sighed, turning my eyes to the darkness outside. I didn't want to see his empathetic gaze directed at me. Not when such an innocent question pricked at such a personal nerve. "Because I would've had to use magic and change my face to get past the biometric scanner."

"And?"

"And I don't like using my shifting magic if I don't have to." I shrugged, still not looking at him. "Because if I can get in, do my job, and make a difference all without changing my face, then I feel like..." I paused; all the words stuck in my throat as an explanation of my work somehow became an explanation of *me*.

In the past, I would use magic only to change my hair so the guards at the Alliance Building wouldn't recognize me. And it hadn't bothered me to do it, because I knew that anyone could've accomplished the same feat with a wig. Changing your face though, that was something only magic could do...

Morgan, sensing the gravity of the moment, reached across the console and took my hand. "You feel like what?"

I met his gaze, his eyes patient and yet hungry. He wanted to understand, to know the things that held me back. The things that hurt me. And for a moment, I let myself pretend that he could actually take all that hurt away.

"Like I'm proving something," I whispered. And as if he sensed the insecurity I was feeling, Morgan squeezed my fingers. "Like if I can succeed without the help of magic, then I can prove that I'm more than just some fragile, feminine girl who's too simple to do things on her own. Because I know that's what people see when they look at me. They assume that I'm dumb without even hearing me speak—that I'm helpless and desperate for attention. They think I'm weak. And I hate it."

Morgan didn't reply as he stared at me for the span of a few heartbeats. But those heartbeats stretched out as I tried to figure out what the emotions inside him meant. What the anger in him was directed at. But just as I was about to ask him, he sped down the driveway like the car was on fire.

"Mor?" I grabbed the door handle, holding on for dear life, and watched as the house came too close too fast. Within seconds, Morgan had the SUV parked in the garage. Then, without a word, he got out and slammed his door.

"What the heck is his problem?" I turned to Daisy in the backseat—who stood and tried to lick my face. She lost interest in me though when Morgan opened her door and let her out.

Then he slammed that door too.

"Maybe I'll just stay here—"

My door swung open, cutting me off, and Morgan stood there glaring back at me. I opened my mouth to tell him to go kick rocks, but he unbuckled my seatbelt and pulled me into his arms.

"Do you remember how you told me to prove them all wrong? That I should shock them with the truth of who I really am?" he whispered, his breath rustling my hair and his arms tethering me to his firm chest. I nodded, unsure what he was getting at. "Care, I spent years playing a role because I didn't believe that being myself would be enough. But you showed me that I was wrong..."

He pulled back, just far enough to look down at me.

"Try not to hit me when I say this," he teased gently. "But you spend so much time trying to prove to others that you're enough. That you're clever enough, strong enough, capable enough. But I don't know that you believe it about yourself, and I wish you would."

A little shocked, I flinched at his words. Was he right? Did I not believe in myself enough—give myself enough credit? I thought back to all those years spent feeling like I had to prove myself. Something I was still doing...

"You might be right," I said with a sigh. "Maybe."

He smiled, pushing my hair from my face. "I'm gonna let you in on a secret, Red. I'm always right." I rolled my eyes. "But really I just hate that you don't see what I see."

"And what do you see?"

Morgan looked at me so intensely that I struggled not to squirm under the attention. "I see a woman who's brave and compassionate. Who sacrifices her own happiness for others. Who's bright and fun and loyal and good. A woman who's so hard on herself even though she's the most impressive person I know. What I see is priceless, Care. And I just want you to see it in yourself."

I considered his words, unsure where to put them, but knowing that they needed to be kept safe and repeated often. Because as I thought about it, I realized that the entire foundation of *me* was built on the singular goal of proving people wrong. From the time in the first grade when the teacher had tried to tell me that girls didn't play kickball, to high school when all the boys thought I should be trying to get their attention and all the girls wanted me to fit into their molds of airhead or nerd, cheerleader or band geek. And now as a vigilante, I'd tried to prove that I was more than the stupid pretty girl. More than a Dark Elf. More than a *girl*. More than anyone could assume at first glance.

Proving people wrong was who I'd always been. And I wasn't sure who I'd be if I stopped pushing myself to break molds...

But maybe it was time to find out.

"Thank you," I whispered, kissing his cheek. "Maybe someday I'll get there."

Mor nodded and grasped my hand, giving it a squeeze. "You will. You're Caroline Birch. The most determined person I know."

"Why doesn't that feel compliment?" I teased, hoping to ease some of the levity from this conversation. I loved that Morgan cared, but there was only so much emotional heavy lifting a person could do in one talk.

"Because your determinedness has been known to get in my way," he said, winking before leading the way out of the garage. I sighed, grateful that he was letting the subject drop. For now.

We went through the connecting laundry room and out into the spacious dining area. It and the kitchen shared one large space, with two giant dining tables on the left to accommodate the dozens of Berserkers who *didn't* live here.

Why the house had been built for such a large occupancy when Berserkers tended to be more solitary creatures, I'd never understand.

The room was normally flooded with sunlight thanks to two sets of French doors—one set on the left leading to a home gym, and one straight ahead leading to the backyard. But thanks to our early wake up time, the world outside was all darkness. Only the kitchen on the right side of the room, with its big white island and ample pantry space, could brighten the room. And my spirits.

"Oh, praise God for food," I sighed, walking toward the kitchen with a sleepy grin.

But just as I took a step forward, Morgan moved in front of me and pushed me back toward the hall. "Nope, the guys are waiting in my office."

"Morgan!" I whined, looking fondly back over my shoulder toward the kitchen—and the food it contained. "Let me go."

"The food can wait, Care," he insisted, pushing me to the double doors that marked his office. "Please just go inside and I promise I'll feed you."

"You bet you will," I snapped, shoving his hands off with a petulant glare. "You're buying me dinner. My choice, and I'm ordering an obscene amount of food."

"As opposed to every other day?"

I paused with my hand on the office door and turned to give him the evil eye. If he'd been a dog, he'd have his ears flat against his head and his tail between his legs. But instead, he was just an annoying bear. "Sorry. Poor choice of words."

With the growls in my stomach mimicking the ones coming out of my mouth, I ignored him and stomped into his office. Mike, Clint, and Logan were already there, still dressed in pajamas. They all three greeted us from the assorted armchairs in the middle of the room, but I ignored them and faceplanted on the couch like a worm.

"What's wrong with you?" Mike asked in his usual, easy-going way. Unfortunately for him, I was too hangry to be nice this early in the morning.

"Your evil brother refuses to let me *eat* because he's a tyrant," I shouted into the couch. "*And* he manhandled me."

"He did what now?" Logan asked, an annoying smile in his voice.

"Shut up Logan," Mor complained, his voice coming closer. "I did not *manhandle* you, Caroline. I grabbed your shoulders. I've certainly done a whole lot more than that before."

"Say what?" Clint quipped. I heard a quiet thud, and the youngest Hohlt brother grunted. "Ow! What was that for?"

"For being an idiot. Now shut up," Morgan growled and the cushion in front of my head dipped as he sat beside me.

"I disagree. I don't think he's the one being the idiot today," I snarked, lifting my face from the cushion to make sure he heard me. Then I glared for good measure.

"Ah, you mean Logan?" Mor teased.

"No—"

"Mike? Because it certainly couldn't be me since I brought you a hot breakfast," he said, and I watched as he set a to-go bag on the coffee table.

Without bothering to ask if it was for me, I launched from the couch, and snatched up the bag. Inside there was a warm giant cinnamon roll and some milk in a to-go cup. "Oh my gosh," I groaned, clutching the treats to my chest.

"Happy?" Morgan asked, threading a finger through my belt loop and gently tugging me back down to the couch.

"You could have told me," I complained, a mouthful of cinnamon roll jumbling my words. What can I say? I was an easy bribe where food was concerned.

"But I wanted it to be a surprise." He shifted in his seat, setting his arm along the back of the couch where it grazed my shoulders. "Plus, teasing you was kind of fun. Until you turned against me."

"*You* turned against *me*," I snapped, pointing the fork at him. He looked at me with wide innocent eyes, and then slowly leaned forward and stole the bite of pastry from my fork. Enraged—Caroline *doesn't* share food—I shoved at his chest, but it did no good. *Curse your Berserker strength you big flea bag.*

"Fine. *I* turned against you by denying you your one true love. Food," he finally conceded with a mouthful of frosting. "But I swear that I'll never make you go without food for more than thirty minutes ever again."

"Good boy," I muttered, shoveling another oversized bite of cinnamon roll into my mouth.

Clint interrupted our banter as he clapped his hands against his thighs, smiling mischievously. "Well, now that you two are done—"

"Don't," Morgan barked, pointing a finger at his baby brother.

Clint grinned and ran a hand through his cropped dark hair. "I wasn't going to say anything inappropriate." He held up his hands in surrender, but the mischievous spark remained in his brown eyes. "I was just going to say that now that you two are done discussing food, we can get down to business."

"You guys can do whatever you want, just let me and my lover be," I moaned clutching the to-go container close to my chest.

"Should we leave you and the cinnamon roll alone so you can have some privacy to get to know each other better?" Logan teased, blue green eyes flashing with amusement.

"Would you?" I mumbled, smiling with a mouthful of cinnamon roll.

Morgan nudged my shoulder and nodded to my breakfast. "Do I have to go too? Or do I get special privileges since I'm the one who fed you?"

"Honey if you keep feeding me like this, you can do whatever you want. Heck, you can even have my first born if you treat me like this every day."

And just like that, the room went silent. Confused, I glanced around. Mike and Clint were avoiding my eyes. Logan wasn't even trying to hold back his silent laughter, his shoulders shaking. And Morgan looked like he wanted to murder all three of them.

"What's going on?" I asked, not sure what I was missing. But before I could force an answer out of any of them, Grey stepped into the room.

"Sorry to interrupt," he said, taking in the stilted silence, "I can come back—"

"No, stay," Morgan rushed to assure him, ignoring my glare. If I'd have been a Firebird Shifter, my look would've singed the short beard from his face. "What's up?"

Grey's head swiveled between us for a moment, the shallow wrinkles lining his face deepening as he considered. After a moment, he nodded and looked down at the clipboard in his hand. "Alright, I have news," he announced, and we all froze, poised with anticipation. "I couldn't find anything."

Rolling my eyes, I let my head lean back against Morgan's arm. As if on auto pilot, his other hand reached across his lap, and gave my wrist a reassuring squeeze. "Did you really have to phrase it that way?" I whined, taking a sip of my milk.

Grey just shrugged.

"Well, I guess now would be the time to admit that I didn't find anything either," Mike said sheepishly, shrugging his massive shoulders. The guy was so big, he could have been a stand in for Dwayne Johnson. If Dwayne Johnson was white and had hair. "I searched through everything you guys gave me from Eileen's computer. But I couldn't find anything on who she was trying to sell Care Bear to or who she hired to find the safety deposit box with Care's parent's documents in it."

I sighed internally, trying not to show how disappointed I was. It wasn't that I'd expected us to find answers immediately, but I hated being stuck in this same answerless, directionless position. It made me feel helpless.

Morgan somehow seemed to sense my frustration, and he grabbed a second to go cup from the coffee table—which I'd assumed was his—and handed it to me. Curious, I took a sip. *Tea.*

I sighed, side eyeing Morgan as I drank. He was up to something with these thoughtful gestures and comforting touches. I just couldn't figure out what.

"So, is *anything* fruitful going to come from this meeting?" Morgan asked, smoothly ignoring my scrutinizing expression as he gazed at the rest of the group. "Or did we all meet before the crack of dawn just to share our failures?"

"Easy there, prickle puss," Clint said with raised eyebrows. "No need to get snappy. We don't have answers just yet, but Logan and I are going to ask some subtle questions around town. Hopefully we can find something about whoever it was that wanted to buy Caroline."

"And I may not have had any luck with Eileen's files," Mike added. "But I'll take a look online and see if I can find anything about either Care Bear, her buyer, or Elves in general. And I'll check Craigslist to see if there are any new hits out or ones I might've missed before." Last time, my kidnapper had been hired via a Craigslist ad. Although it was doubtful, they'd use the same method now, it was worth checking.

Morgan nodded, and Mike, Clint, and Logan all stood, heading for the door. "Keep me posted on what you find," Morgan called after them. "And be careful when you go asking questions. The last thing we need is more attention."

The boys all nodded before slipping into the hallway—probably to go back to bed. There wasn't going to be anyone in town to question until daylight anyway.

"Well, that was unhelpful," I said dryly as I shoved a too-big bite of cinnamon roll in my mouth.

"I know it seems bleak but..." Morgan trailed off, stopping to glare at Grey. Who was still standing by the door. Watching us. "Don't you have something else to do, Grey?"

"No," the older gentleman replied, and I was shocked to see the stoic man smirk. In all the time I'd been at the Berserker house, I'd *never* seen Grey's lips so much as twitch, let alone smirk. *What is going on?*

The two men stared each other down, neither of them blinking. Morgan glared harder and I struggled not to laugh as Grey finally rolled his eyes.

"Oh fine, I suppose I could go organize some reports."

"Great," Morgan said with a cold smile. "Go do that then."

Grey shook his head, sent me a wink, and then turned to the door.

"Don't you dare watch last night's episode without me," I called after him.

"I make no promises," he shouted back as he stepped into the hall.

I smiled and shook my head, knowing he'd wait for me. Watching all things, *The Bachelor* was a ritual for us now. One I knew he enjoyed even if he wanted to pretend otherwise.

"So, how are you feeling? Do you want another cinnamon roll?" Morgan asked, his tone too soft and too eager. He'd gone from snapping at Grey to talking to me like I was an invalid in the span of seconds. *Something's up.*

"Why are you being weird?"

"What? Can't I be concerned about you and buy you food?" He looked down, suddenly interested in adjusting the pillow behind his back. "It's the number one tactic for a happy Caroline."

"There's something you're not telling me," I insisted as I set the empty food container on the coffee table and settled back against his side. "But honestly, I'm too frustrated with our lack of answers and too tired from getting up at one in the morning to figure it out right now."

Worry flashed across his face, and he studied me intently. I tried not to fidget as I sensed his emotions go from slightly nervous to fully concerned. "I'm sorry. I wish we hadn't come out empty handed today."

I shrugged, mindlessly tugging at a loose thread on the hem of his shirt. "I'm used to it. It just gets a little frustrating with all these partial answers. All we really know is that that my birth parents were Alfar royalty, which makes me Alfar too. Well...part Alfar. Because we also know that Nephilim were Elves with the ability to shape shift—which I can do." I paused with a groan. "But there's so much we *don't know.* Like which parts of my magic are Alfar, what happened to my parents, or who tried to buy me from Eileen. It's not the lack of answers that annoys me. It's the fact that we keep getting partial ones. Like we're being teased."

"I know," Morgan replied, gently tugging me closer to his side. Tired and hungry for affection, I kicked my feet up under me and leaned into him. He settled his head against mine, his arms curling around me.

"But we'll keep looking. Mike will keep searching online, Logan and Clint will pound the pavement, and we—"

"And we will do what?" I snapped, shifting my head on his shoulder so I could look up at him. "Keep chasing our tails while you try and distract me with food and cuddles?"

"Would that work?" he teased gently, his thumb rubbing my shoulder.

I bit my lip, but my smile escaped. "No. Not for very long anyway." He chuckled and we sat like that for a few moments; comfortable in the silence.

"I found an article in the Restricted Records room," I said finally, the heaviness of our real problems only pacified by sweet breakfast food for so long. "It said that the Nephilim have always been well known for their abilities to shape shift, but that no one knew what the Alfar could do. Which would explain why I have more than just the classic Nephilim abilities."

Morgan was quiet as he thought, and I found that I appreciated the way he weighed his words instead of blurting them like I did. "If you're both Nephilim and Alfar, then that means at least one of your parents was either full blooded Nephilim or part Nephilim. It also means that your ability to sense and manipulate emotions is probably an Alfar skill."

"Yeah, but unfortunately that doesn't exactly help us figure out who tried to buy me and what they planned to do with me."

"Maybe it does..."

"How so?"

He tilted his head to look down at me, a slight smile on his handsome face. "Because it's a reminder that we need to be playing to your strengths. By doing what you do best, Red. Breaking into places and fooling people."

"Did you just partially quote *Ant-Man* to me?"

"Did it work? Are you motivated now?"

"Promise me you'll buy me breakfast tomorrow too and I'll say yes."

He smirked and stole a sip from my cup. "Deal."

Chapter 3

MORGAN

It was the buzz of my phone on the dining room table that brought me back to reality and made me realize what I'd been staring at for the past...I glanced at my watch. "Twenty minutes? Wow, I'm pathetic."

I quickly skimmed Merida's text about the next Shifter Council meeting and hurried to reply. Then I turned my attention back to where it'd been for apparently twenty minutes.

On Caroline.

She'd been sparring with Mike and Clint in the backyard for the past hour. Which meant that in the last hour, I'd gotten next to nothing done.

The paperwork from previous council meetings still sat in front of me, untouched. And the stack of varying complaints from amongst the Berserkers had only thinned by *four*. I couldn't believe that in one hour, I'd read and dealt with exactly four of the forty-two *reports. I'm pathetic. Stick a beautiful, sharp-tongued girl in front of me and I'm hosed.*

But she wasn't just any girl. She was my mate. And that was becoming less and less of a problem for me.

Except when one considered the fact that I hadn't yet told her we were mates. *Yeah, that's definitely a problem.*

In my defense, I was only keeping the secret because I truly didn't think Care was ready for the information yet. It was only recently that she'd claimed me as her best friend. Between that, her moving into our house, and her working in a team instead of alone for the first time, it seemed like a bad idea to drop the whole mate bond thing on her right now.

Mate bonds were given to all animal Shifters as a way to recognize 'the one'. All someone had to do to recognize their mate was see their eyes—which would have a blue ring around the irises—or be in close enough proximity to begin sensing their emotions. So, really it was Caroline's fault that she didn't know the signs of the mate bond.

Not that Caroline would buy that excuse. And now that my brothers were teaching her to fight, she'd be well equipped to kick my butt herself once she found out I'd been lying to her.

"So, when are you going to tell her?"

I startled as Grey entered the room; his arms wrapped around that danged clipboard he always carried. I'd tried to buy him an electronic tablet years ago, but he'd adamantly refused. The guy liked paper.

Grey had been my Second—my right-hand man—since I became Chief six years ago. He'd also served as Second to our last Chief, Callen, before he retired. I'd gotten to know Grey well in the four years that Callen had mentored me before he retired to Florida, and I was voted in. He'd been a perfect Second to Callen, and he was a perfect one for me too.

I, by contrast, wasn't always sure I was a good Chief. Sure, I was responsible for making sure our people followed both the human laws and our own. I had to go through all the complaints Berserkers filed against each other, look through council meeting minutes, and research proposals that either other council members wanted to propose, or ones my people wanted *me* to propose. I did a lot of things as Chief, but that didn't mean I was any good at it.

"Tell who what?" I asked innocently, picking up the next Berserker complaint from the stack. It took me a full ten seconds to realize it was upside down. *Hm, so that's how stupid Caroline makes me.*

"I'm talking about the Mate Bond," Grey said nonchalantly. I tried not to show my panic as he walked around the dining table and sat across from me. But despite my best efforts, I felt my muscles go stiff. And thanks to the bond he so casually mentioned, Caroline sensed my sudden anxiety.

I watched as she turned from Mike—who'd been correcting her form—to look at me through the French doors.

Swallowing my nerves, I gave her what I hoped was a reassuring smile. She watched me for another moment, and I could almost feel her searching my emotions to figure out what had made me anxious. Finally, she dropped her eyes and let my brothers lead her through the next steps of their practice. I immediately relaxed. *That was close.*

The last thing I needed was Caroline asking questions about what Grey had said to make me so uneasy. Speaking of which.

"I haven't told anyone other than Logan. So how do you—"

"You haven't looked at anyone that way since Gen died," Grey interrupted, his tone gentle. "I didn't think you ever would. But the way you look at Caroline...it's like she's part of you—the good part. I haven't seen you this happy in years."

I scoffed. Happy was an interesting way to describe my life since Caroline had barged into it. The woman made me frustrated, annoyed, confused, and I'd never yelled as much as I had since I met her. But she did make me smile and laugh and feel known and safe and free in a way that I hadn't had...maybe ever.

Don't get me wrong, I'd loved my first wife Genevieve more than I knew I could. Before her, I hadn't realized how much affection could fit inside my heart—spoiler: it was a lot. But my mate bond with her was different than the one I now had with Caroline. The way I had interacted with Gen was different than the way I was with Care. And the person they each made me was different. Not better or worse, just different.

It was like Care had once said, 'I've learned that love is like ribbons. It connects us to people, tying us to each other. And it doesn't matter if someone dies, or willingly leaves us, because once the ribbon's tied...it's tied. The love is always there. But the really beautiful part about it all is that there's no end to the ribbon. There's no end to the patterns you can make and the people you can love.'

And now more than ever, I knew that to be true. I loved Gen; would probably always love her. But the ribbon I'd tied to Caroline was different than Gen's. They were different colors, thicknesses and textures, perfectly matching the women they were tethered to. And although Gen's ribbon would always exist in me, hers wasn't in color anymore.

Caroline's though, hers was neon. Vibrant, loud and a clear path home.

No one was guaranteed to find a second mate after losing their first. But here I was, mated for the second time. Once again, I had the privilege of knowing who 'the one' was. Once again, I had the opportunity to build an incredible love with the right person. I wasn't about to take that for granted.

"I get why you haven't told anybody but Logan," Grey said, no judgment in his eyes. "But you should probably tell *her*."

I sighed and turned my gaze back to Caroline. Mike was showing her a defensive move and motioned for her to try it out on him. But when she moved faster than he was expecting, my giant of a brother fell to the ground. Caroline grinned and pumped her fists in the air. She skipped around in a circle, her white cropped T shirt rising just a little over the top of her leggings as she rubbed her win in my brother's face.

"I can't," I admitted quietly. "She's not ready to think of me as more than a friend."

"You sure about that? Because she seems pretty obsessed for someone who just thinks of you as a friend."

I gave Grey an annoyed look, but he just motioned to the backyard. Rolling my eyes, I did as he insisted and looked through the French doors.

Caroline was laughing with my brothers as they began an impromptu wrestling match. But she kept glancing back at the house. Back at me.

Her emotions went warm and fuzzy when her eyes met mine, but what that warmth meant, I couldn't tell. Affection, attraction, jealousy, anger; I could usually identify them pretty easily in Caroline. But I couldn't quite pin this emotion down. Nor could I stop the spark of hope it lit within me.

"We're just friends," I defended weakly. But the words tasted bitter as I forced them off my tongue. Caroline and I weren't *just* friends. We weren't even just *best* friends. *But is Care actually interested in something more?* Had I read her wrong when I assumed she needed more time before she'd be ready for that?

"Well if you two are what friends look like, then I need to find me a friend or two," Grey quipped. I dipped my fingers in my water glass, flicking some drops in his face. He didn't even flinch as he continued speaking. "She lets you be affectionate with her, Morgan. *And* she seems to enjoy it."

I shook my head, turning back to the report in my hand. "She finds my touch comforting, not exciting."

"You don't know that; Berserkers can't hear heartbeats. Maybe hers kicks up when you touch, maybe that's what she's thinking about when she looks at you. The point is, she seems into you."

"Can't be. She's probably just reacting to my feelings. Or maybe she's figured out that I like her, and she feels bad for me—ow!" I shouted as Grey pulled a Severus Snape from *Harry Potter* and reached across the table to slap the back of my head. The guy didn't even look sorry. He just rolled his eyes at me.

"Would you stop trying to find something wrong with this? What you have with Caroline is a gift. You got a second chance at not just love, but a mate. So, stop looking for reasons to hide your feelings and just come clean about the bond already."

I growled and dropped my face in my hands. As grateful as I was that the mate bond had given me the chance to feel Caroline's emotions and pointed her out to me in a way I might not have seen otherwise, I also hated the bond. Because if there'd been no bond, then I wouldn't be lying to Care now. Even if it was by omission.

"I'm scared, man," I admitted quietly, the admission making me feel small. For years, I'd had the scariest reputation of anyone in the city, and yet here I was, cowed by the fear of a *mate bond.* And yet... "I'm afraid that if I tell her about the mate bond, she'll get scared and pull away from me. She's already made so many big steps in the last few months. She moved in, became part of a team and let me get past her walls. I'm not sure if she's ready to add one more big life change to her list and discover that we're mated...that I'm crazy about her. And after losing Gen, I couldn't survive losing a second mate."

I lifted my face from my hands and watched with dread as Care and the boys headed toward the house.

Being around her had become my own personal form of torture lately. Every touch, every private look, every bit of attention she gave me, I ate up. I was like a Golden Retriever, wagging my tail, following her around and begging for her affection.

But I was completely in the dark about her feelings for me. I felt her attraction, her affection; I knew how much I meant to her. But whether her feelings included romance, I couldn't tell. *I'm miserable and it's my own dang fault.*

Because Grey was right. I should've just manned up and told her the truth already.

"You won't know how Caroline feels," Grey added quickly as Mike reached for the French doors, "Until you show her how *you* feel. So, stop making assumptions and start making moves."

I flicked another round of water his way. He just smirked as the rest of the gang stepped into the dining room. "How was the workout?" he asked.

Care paused in front of the table, while Mike and Clint walked over to the kitchen. "Good. Although I'm wondering if the reason Logan hasn't been here to help train me in the last few days is because you told the guys to take it easy on me," she said, giving me a warning glance.

"Per your request, I'm not coddling you," I promised, raising my hands in surrender. "Logan just has an assignment that's been keeping him busy lately." I purposefully left out the details of Logan's 'assignment'. That info was on a need-to-know basis, and Care would read me the riot act if she knew.

"I'm going to ignore how cryptic that was." She turned her eyes from me as she began to struggle with the bracers strapped to her arms. "Because I can sense that you're feeling a little off today, and I'm too kind to push you right now. But don't think I won't ask you about it later."

I rolled my eyes and motioned her over, knowing that I'd have to bribe her with milkshakes and a *The Office* marathon, so she'd forget this conversation.

Care pouted, and though I knew she hated needing help, she came and sat on the bench beside me. I was just beginning to undo her left bracer when my phone vibrated with a text message.

Clint: $20 says my idiot big brother DOESN'T use this golden opportunity to flirt with his girl.

I quickly shoved the phone to the side so Care couldn't see it. Then I glared at my baby brother. My baby brother who I was totally going to pummel later.

Grey: I'll bet $25 that he touches her flirtatiously in the next twenty minutes.

When I glared at my Second, he shrugged. "I'm playing a hunch," he smirked.

"You okay?" Care asked. I turned, realizing that I'd stopped removing her bracer, and instead I was just gripping her arm. Tight.

I immediately loosened my grip and quickly removed the armor from both her arms. "Yeah, I'm fine."

I tried my best to ignore her attention as I worked, but it was pointless. It had somehow become my full-time job to be hyperaware of all Caroline's movements. All the time.

My senses were attuned to the feel of her eyes on me, the smooth brush of her skin under my fingers, and the heaviness of her breath, indicating just how hard she'd worked out. But worst of all, I was *acutely* aware of the way she was trying to read me by listening to my emotions.

I tried not to let my feelings give anything away as I set each of her bracers on the table. It was difficult though, with her sitting so close, her skin glistening with sweat, and bits of her auburn hair messy around her face. What was it about her being so disheveled that was so appealing? *I blame the pheromones.*

I glanced over at Grey, considering his advice. It was dangerous to be too honest with my feelings and scare Caroline off...But I could make some subtle moves and pay attention to her emotions. See how she responded to me in a more romantic mindset. *Let's hope I remember how to be subtle.* I was more than a little rusty.

"Turn around," I nodded, motioning for Care to turn her back to me. When she narrowed her green eyes, I sighed. My mate hated being told what to do almost more than I did. "Your shoulders look tense," I explained. "If you turn around, I'll rub them for you."

She raised her eyebrows and gave me a small, appreciative smile. "Well, if you're offering."

She turned her back to me, straddling the bench, and I moved her twin braids back off her shoulders. I was careful to focus on her emotions instead of my own as I began to massage her muscles. Which was probably the hardest thing I'd ever done, trying to force all the attraction out of my mind and only note her feelings.

Which honestly didn't help.

She relaxed so quickly under my touch, both her feelings and her body completely free of tension. Suddenly I realized how dangerous it was to have her relax so completely with me; *because* of me. It was intoxicating, knowing that I was able to bring her so much peace and comfort. Me, the man who was hated and feared by the public, was somehow Caroline's security blanket. I could get high on that feeling, knowing that right now, I was what she needed.

I tried to keep calm, but the Golden Retriever in me was ready to cuddle her, bring her tennis balls and scare away everything that made her afraid. *Keep it together, Hohlt.* Oh, who was I kidding? *Buy me a nice collar and call me Rover.* Because this girl pretty much owned me.

Clint walked back into the dining area, offering Care a glass of water, which she took gratefully. "Your girl is getting pretty good," he said.

"If by getting good, you mean I could get off the ground without assistance today, then sure, I'm doing awesome," Care said dryly before downing half of her water.

"Hey, at least you got up," Mike argued. "Clint laid on the ground and cried the last time Morgan trained him."

"I didn't cry. I was just really sweaty." Clint punched Mike in the arm, and Mike punched him back. Then them and Grey all three checked their phones and watches, glancing over at Care and me with too much fascination. *Real subtle guys.* The nuisances were all waiting to see who would win the bet. Waiting to see if I was going to make a move or not.

"Well, I'm certainly not going to judge you, Clint," Care sighed, setting her water on the table. "I didn't even have to endure the training tactics of Bear Man, and I still thought you'd have to call the fire department to get me off the ground. I feel so weak, I'm about ready to fall off this bench."

"Then lean back," I suggested immediately, tugging on her shoulders. That primal, masculine part of me was eager to meet her needs. And the curious part of me was eager to see how she'd react.

"Mor, you're not my personal back rest." She turned those defiant green eyes up at me, but in spite of her resistance, her body leaned back.

"For right now, I am. Just lean on me, Red."

"Fine," she breathed, and as her small frame came back to lean against my chest, I felt my body go tight while hers went lax. "Ugh, this is lovely. Thanks Mor. You're a gem."

Somehow, I managed to squeak out a 'you're welcome'. Even though all I could think about was the way her head nestled so perfectly against my shoulder, her hands coming to rest on my forearms where they sat on my thighs. *Keep calm, Hohlt,* I told myself when her fingers began to stroke my arm.

But my body wasn't listening to my mind anymore.

My heart was beating so hard I could feel it pressing against Caroline's back. And a delicious, torturous anticipation curled in my stomach, warming me from the inside out. My stupid body was interpreting every innocent gesture as a come on when I knew otherwise.

But maybe it was time for me to put Grey's advice to the test. Make a move and see what Care did. *Something subtle...*

I tried my best to focus solely on my affection for Caroline and *not* my attraction as I loosely wrapped my arms around her middle. She responded without hesitation, covering my hands with hers like it was the most natural thing in the world. Contentment radiated from her, bound up with affection and the slightest bit of curiosity.

So she *did* notice the shift in our relationship. I'd wondered if my increased physical affection toward her lately was having an impact. Apparently, it was. But she didn't seem bothered by it, just curious. *I can work with that.*

"Oh, Morgan," Mike said as he handed a few crumpled bills to Grey. I rolled my eyes at their stupid bet, but Grey just pocketed the cash. "Care Bear had a great idea that I think you should hear."

"Mike," Care hissed, kicking his shin. But she sounded more pained by it than he did. Poor girl was *sore.*

Curious, I glanced down at Care. "What is it?"

"Yeah, go ahead and tell him Care Bear," Clint prodded, smirking.

"I would kick you too, but the effort required is too painful to bother. Plus, I'd have to leave this very comfortable spot."

Clint and Mike exchanged a glance, grinning like idiots. And I didn't have to look to know that Grey was wearing a smug look of satisfaction.

"Ignore them," I said, looking only at Caroline. Wishing my moronic family would disappear. "What's your idea?"

Care turned in my arms but was slow to look up at me. *Uh oh.* I didn't think I'd ever seen her be shy before. *And it can only mean one thing.* She was going to ask me for something. Something I probably wasn't going to like.

"Well, I had planned to ask you this after plying you with tea and compliments and some of that icky health food you like," she began carefully, "But..."

"Yes?" I prompted when she'd gone quiet again.

She bit her lip, studying me. "Well, remember when you said that we should start leaning on my strengths more and break into places and fool people?" Man, how I regretted those words. "I think we should do some recon on the Shifter Council. Now hear me out. We know Eileen got her information about me from somewhere, and council members have access to a lot of information that they've been known to blackmail each other with. Eileen might not be the only council member who knows about me. So, I think we should spy on all of them and find out."

My brain seemed to short circuit at the idea of Caroline spying again. So many times, we'd laid traps for her copycat. And nearly every time, Caroline had ended up injured. I still remembered with perfect clarity the sight of her lying on the floor, blood dripping across the marble. I'd been completely panicked then, and I felt that feeling again now.

Caroline had no idea how terrified I was to lose her. Sure, she'd sensed my feelings, and she knew she was important to me. But she couldn't understand the origin or the depth of my fear. Because she didn't know I was falling for her.

"Hey," Care crooned, swinging her leg over the bench and turning sideways in my arms. "Look at me, Mor." I did as she demanded, mostly because I needed to assure myself that my memories were just that, and she was safe. "It's going to be okay. Neither one of us is going to get hurt this time. I promise, this plan is way less dangerous. We'll be okay."

"You don't know that," I argued, my voice quiet as thoughts of losing Caroline flitted through my mind. I'd already lost one mate, and it had been the most brutal experience of my life—even worse than losing my mom. But to lose Caroline? That would be worse. Because second chances were so rare, and I knew that Care was mine.

She wrapped her arms around me, holding me tight like I was falling apart, and she alone could hold me together. If only she knew how true that was. "This time, it'll be daylight," she insisted. "And I promise that I'll stay close by the entire time."

"Close by?" I did not like the sound of that. "Where exactly will I be?"

Caroline just smiled, and I silently cursed the mate bond. Because at this stage in the game, my feelings were too deep, and I knew I wouldn't be able to tell her no.

Chapter 4

CAROLINE

I strolled through the Shifter Alliance building—legally this time—a little sad to be here as a rule follower. I missed the adrenaline, the sweet satisfaction of getting away with something. But today I was just a boring old law-abiding citizen wearing a visitor's badge.

Morgan had told the security guards in the lobby that I was his assistant and insisted that I should be close by in case he needed me. And of course, the guards were too scared of him to do anything other than comply. The one guard even suggested that I walk the third floor so Mor could keep an eye on me through the windows.

"Idiots," I mumbled, recalling the way the guards had trembled when Morgan spoke to them. They were lucky I was too busy watching the Shifter Council meeting through the windows that ran along the inside of the third-floor hallway to lecture them about the good man that Morgan Hohlt really was.

Technically, as Morgan's 'assistant', I could've been sitting in the audience seating that lay on the far side of the council room. But since I'd only shifted my hair today, it was too likely that someone would recognize me.

"Imagine having to sit with them every month," Morgan's voice rumbled through my earpiece. He was rubbing a hand across his face to hide his mouth, his grey eyes pointed at me.

"Hey, you signed up for that when you ran for Berserker Representative. No one told you that you had to be the voice for every Berserker in the western region of the U.S.," I argued, offering him a fake smile just because I knew he'd hate it. "Now stop looking at me or you're going to give me away to the rest of the group."

He rolled his eyes, but acquiesced, turning his attention back to the meeting.

Every council member was present except for the Dragons since no one had taken Eileen's place after her arrest. Normally, Dragon leaders were automatically replaced by their apprentices, but Eileen had been too focused on her own greed to bother taking anyone under her wing—pun intended.

Which meant that for the first time in decades, the next ruler of the Dragons would be chosen by a tournament. It was a big affair that all the other Dragon kings and queens in the region had to plan. And once someone won the tournament and the crown, there had to be a vote to see which Dragon ruler would represent the species on the Shifter Council. Hopefully whoever won the tournament would be better than Eileen. *Shouldn't be hard.*

As if to remind me just how annoying council members could be, Drew the Firebird representative began speaking. "We'll only raise the dues twelve percent," he said with a shrug. I glared at his model-like face, emboldened since he couldn't see it. The man was an arrogant tool who expected his people to serve him rather than the other way around. He might even be worse than Eileen.

"*Only* twelve?" Parker, the Harpy representative interrupted, raising her dark eyebrows accusingly, blonde hair pulled over one shoulder. She was the youngest representative at only nineteen. And although she had the face of a cherub, she took flak from no one.

Obviously, she was my favorite.

"Relax little bird," Drew taunted, throwing a lazy grin her way. "Twelve percent is hardly going to break anyone. And it's not like I'm being selfish here. We need the funds if we're going to keep from going bankrupt."

"Why don't you use my accountant?" Lawrence, the Sphinx rep suggested in all his bearded glory.

Where Drew was sculpted like a runway model, with eyes that seemed to weigh everyone and everything with dollar signs, Lawrence was all masculinity. Just as sculpted and just as piercing as the Firebird, but with the added bonus of a well-trimmed beard, a few scars to give him some character, and an unimpressed attitude that came with a side of humility and a little bit of judgement. *Yummy.*

"I like Lawrence," I mused as I continued through the hall, watching the drama unfold below.

"Exactly how much do you like him?" Morgan growled, his jealousy bright and hot even from two floors away.

I rolled my eyes, unimpressed. "You're glaring." He opened his mouth to respond, but I cut him off. "Don't yell."

"I wasn't going to yell, and I'm not glaring. Lawrence just needs to make sure he keeps his attention where it belongs."

"And where is that?"

"Away from you."

I shook my head and returned my attention to the meeting. Drew was defending his decision to raise his people's dues, still claiming that the Firebirds were going bankrupt. Which was ridiculous, considering that his people paid the highest dues of all the Shifter species.

While humans paid taxes to the state and federal governments, Shifters paid a smaller amount in their regular taxes, as well as dues to their own species' leadership. The dues were meant to support their representative's income, help maintain infrastructure, provide upkeep for their buildings and other basic needs. But of course, the needs of someone like Drew were much higher than those of us peasants.

"If he's really that nervous about going bankrupt," Merida the Witch representative interjected, smiling so sweetly at Drew that I almost believed she actually liked the guy. "I'm sure King Drew would be more than happy to be mentored. Perhaps Alpha Lawrence could do it?"

Drew quickly sputtered an excuse along with a promise to fix his financial statement, and Merida lifted her hand to cover a smile. She was a trusted friend of Morgan's—just a friend. I'd asked...multiple times. I'd been intimidated by Merida when we first met, and who could blame me? She was tall and lean, with black hair so smooth it always shined, and bright blue eyes that were set off by her angled features. She was a deadly kind of beautiful. But now that I knew her, I just wanted to be her.

"I officially have a girl crush on Merida."

"A girl crush?" Mor whispered, rubbing his jaw to cover his mouth. "Should I be jealous?"

"Why would you be?"

"Because I don't like sharing your affection."

I laughed, ignoring the confused look I got from a man who walked past me in the hall. "Well, you have nothing to worry about. My feelings for you are *very* different than the ones I have for Merida."

"Good to know," he hummed, content.

But the meeting caught my attention again as Francine, the Minotaur representative interrupted someone. Shocker.

"I'm not so certain that Alpha Lawrence would be the best mentor for you anyway, King Drew," the middle-aged woman said, her calculating eyes sliding over to Morgan. "Although Chief Morgan might be a good choice. He seems to be pretty talented at getting his people out of just about anything."

Oh, how I wished I was in the room so I could rip the caramel-colored ponytail from her head.

Morgan growled, his anger unfurling like a lazy cat, trying to decide if it was worth the energy to get involved. "You know Francine, you should really learn to worry about yourself instead of sticking that big nose in everyone else's business. They never did find out if Eileen was colluding with anyone. So, if you make too much noise, they just might decide they need to investigate you. Glorified cow."

Minotaurs didn't actually look like the beasts from legend—who shared many anatomic similarities with cows. Instead, like all Shifters, they looked human until they shifted into their magical form. And even that form was only a subtle change. A change that included bull horns...

Francine rose from her seat, enraged. "What did you just call me?"

"Nothing you haven't been called before—"

"Enough!" Fitz shouted, cutting Morgan off. The mayor's voice echoed through the room, and even Francine was cowed by his authority—pun definitely intended. "You all seem to have forgotten that one of our own betrayed us just weeks ago. Or maybe the problem isn't that you don't remember, but that you'd like us to forget. Because maybe if we looked too closely at this council, we'd find out that there are more traitors than Eileen."

No one spoke as they shifted in their seats, eyes shooting accusingly around the room. A mixture of curiosity, anxiety, and fear wafted through the bunch, and it was hard to tell who might be guilty. Nerves were high and discomfort resonated through the whole group like the ringing of a bell.

"And at some point," Mayor Fitz went on, meeting the eyes of every person; a clear warning, "It might be necessary to start auditing council members to see who among us is above board, and who isn't. And if that doesn't sit well with you, then you need to ask yourself if you have any business being on this council. Because make no mistake, it is a *privilege* to be in this room. We *get* to be the voices for our respective groups. And if everyone doesn't start taking this job seriously, we will begin audits and guilty people will be removed from their posts. Don't forget that your position on this council and as leader of your people can be taken from if you prove that it's necessary."

Like a bunch of chastised children, the council sat silently in their seats. Fiddling with their thumbs, avoiding eye contact and their emotions clouded with both anxiety and respect.

Well, for some it was *attraction* and respect.

"Merida's *very* impressed with our mayor right now," I whispered into my earpiece.

"What do you mean?" Mor looked down at his lap, careful to keep his voice extra quiet in the silence.

"She's totally into him." I watched as a blush worked its way across the Witch's cheeks, her blue eyes glued to Fitz. "If he tried to kiss her, she definitely wouldn't stop him." When Fitz glanced her way, she quickly looked down to inspect her nails. *Aw, they're so cute. I totally have to ship them as a couple.* Now all they needed was a couple name. *Fitzida? Mitz?*

"She would *what*?" Morgan demanded, turning his head to stare up at me. Unfortunately, Gerard the Hunter representative clocked the movement and stared curiously at Mor from where he sat on Morgan's left.

"Morgan Gareth Hohlt, stop looking at me!" I demanded, resisting the urge to wave my hands at him. "You're going to blow our cover."

"Sorry," he mumbled, pretending to stretch his neck. Gerard bought the pathetic cover and flicked his attention back to the group. "But I don't agree with you," he said, *whispering* this time. "Merida and Fitz aren't a couple."

"No, but she wants to be. I guarantee you she's attracted to him."

"Attraction doesn't necessarily equal feelings."

"True, but there's more than just attraction going on. She also can't take her eyes off him, and she's blushing like a tomato."

Morgan seemed to mull that over as the meeting continued. More Council members gave reports on their faction's current standing, and for once, the group actually stayed on track.

"So, all that's required to be 'into' someone is being attracted to them and being physically affected by them?" Morgan finally asked. "I thought being 'into' someone implied deeper feelings."

He wasn't wrong. But I also really wanted to ship Mitz—Merida and Fitz's new couple name. "Okay, point taken. But technically feelings can be born from chemistry. So long as that chemistry is accompanied by mutual respect and interest, and at least a little base knowledge of each other, that's enough to be into someone." Granted, I didn't know if Fitz and Merida had those three things, but it didn't matter. I shipped them, and someday, they'd be together.

"That's all it takes, huh?" Mor asked, a strange note of curiosity in his voice.

"Yeah, that's all it takes."

His eyes flashed up at me again, but this time, I didn't chastise him. Partly because I was standing directly across from where he sat, so his attention wasn't so obvious. And partly because...I liked the look in his eyes. Warm, steady, and meaningful. Like he was making a silent promise.

By the time the meeting had come to the point where people could share new business, I'd become remarkably warm. Morgan had actually listened and paid attention to the meeting, but every few minutes, those grey eyes would flick up at me. What he was trying to tell me through that look, I didn't know. All I knew was that it sent a cozy, tingling feeling all the way to my toes.

"Chief Morgan, you said you had something to present today," Fitz said, snapping me out of my musings.

All eyes turned to Mor, who'd thankfully been paying much better attention than I had. "Yes," he nodded, sitting a little straighter in his chair. "I've had complaints from several of my people this last week about someone trespassing at their businesses after hours. Nothing was stolen, but they also said that once the intruder realized they'd been spotted, they turned into someone else."

The mood in the room suddenly went from bored to tense as everyone listened to Morgan insinuate that a Dark Elf had been spotted. The reports Morgan was referencing were all fake, fabricated to help us see if anyone was surprised by the mention of what could only be a Nephilim. Because anyone who already knew about me wouldn't be shocked to hear that a Dark Elf had been sighted.

"Nephilim?" Fitz asked hoarsely, his shock so thick it was almost palpable.

His surprise was reasonable given that Elves had been nothing but legends for centuries. Like dinosaurs, people knew they existed at one point in time, but it was a universal belief that they were extinct. So, shock—felt by the majority of the group—was a sensible reaction.

There were some people, though, who didn't quite seem so surprised.

Asher the Wyvern King could have almost been a statue he was so unphased by the news. And come to think of it, I didn't remember noting any of his feelings throughout the meeting. It was like he didn't feel anything at all. *Strange...*

Meanwhile Fitch, the temporary Pixie representative, was fidgeting nonstop. He was filling in since the previous king had been deposed—thanks to information I'd given to the mayor about the Pixie King's schemes on the magical black market. The king's daughter was set to take the throne, but she was moving from the Midwest, so Fitch was filling in until she arrived. But he was such a nervous man in general that it was hard to detect whether his nerves now were because he was guilty or because he was essentially a giant Chihuahua.

Other than the Wyvern and the Pixie, a few other council members also seemed off. Jack, the Kelpie rep was too smiley and calm for having heard such shocking news. Granted, he always seemed to be less stressed than everyone else, but that just made him all the more suspicious. Then there was Francine the Minotaur—an obvious choice—and Drew the Firebird, who were both way too anxious.

"Fitch is nervous," I commented to Morgan through our earpieces, scrutinizing each council member as they sat watching each other. "But I can't tell if that's just his natural resting state, or if he's guilty. Asher is giving me Bella Swan vibes; I can't tell what he's feeling. He's just a big vague beige wall of emotions. Jack the Kelpie is way too chipper right now, I barely feel any anxiety from him. And it should come as no surprise that Francine and Drew are both big balls of nerves."

"Guilt will do that to a person," Mor whispered back. Then he spoke up to the group, answering Fitz's question. "I'm not sure what it was that my people saw. It's possible that the witnesses didn't see the intruder's face clearly. If they'd gotten the shift on tape, then that would be a different story. But regardless, I just thought the council would want to know, in case the suspicions turn out to be legitimate."

Mayor Fitz thanked Morgan for sharing the news, though he probably wished Mor hadn't, and eventually the meeting came to an end. But as everyone headed out the door, whispering amongst themselves, Mor and I watched them go. Trying to find the truth in a sea of liars and posers.

Chapter 5

CAROLINE

"This is nice, Care Bear. Way nicer than Morgan's office," Logan said, looking around at my newly renovated office space.

When I'd moved into the Berserker house a couple weeks ago, Morgan had insisted that I make the library into my office. Then, because he's sweet but paranoid, he hired a contractor to come in and soundproof the space so it would be just as secure as his office.

Most girls got chocolate or clothes from their loved ones. Morgan gave me sound proofed rooms and weapons to practice killing people with. *Such a cinnamon roll.*

"Hey, my office is nice," Mor complained, looking around at my bright and cozy space.

The room was lined with floor to ceiling bookshelves, except for one spot where a window looked out onto the front lawn. I'd added some knickknacks and pictures amongst the books on the shelves to give the room some color. And of course, I brought all my own furniture, complete with a big, patterned rug, plush chairs and a periwinkle velvet couch.

Logan shrugged at Morgan. "Hers is more colorful, and her furniture is really soft."

"He's not wrong," I said, reaching around Morgan to set a tray of snacks on the coffee table. The boys immediately dug in, quickly making a mess of my pretty charcuterie board.

But Morgan just stood there, glaring at me with his arms crossed. "You know, you don't have to spoil them."

"Sure, I do. I'm slowly stealing them away from you, and food is a very effective strategy." I winked at him as I made my way over to my faded green, faux metal desk and sat in my fluffy pink desk chair.

"I don't think you can steal something you already own. Logan and my brothers are already enamored with you," he said, walking over to sit on the edge of my desk. I raised an eyebrow at his unwelcome behind, but he just shot me a smirk. "What? You always sit on mine."

"Fair enough."

"Hey Mike, how's the site coming?" he said, turning to his brothers.

"It's going well," Mike called out from the couch, his mouth full of cheese and crackers, "I think I have the database all set and ready. But we'll have to manually go through the info since a keyword tracker can only do so much."

Of course, with his mouth full, most of his words were garbled.

"Swallow man, you're not a marsupial," Clint teased, patting—AKA smacking—his brother on the back. Which just caused Mike to accidentally spit out some of his half-chewed food onto my carpet.

"You made me spit, idiot," Mike snapped, punching his baby brother in the arm. Clint flinched but tried to hide it by retaliating with a smack to Mike's thigh. Mike—practically a human tank—wasn't fazed.

The wrestling continued—with Logan shouting out bets and encouragement for more violence. Meanwhile, Mor sighed and rubbed his temples, looking like he wasn't sure if he should kill his brothers or himself. Amused, I grabbed a mini Reese's from my desk drawer and held it out to him.

"Here, this will help." But Mor just stared. Unimpressed. "Come on, just take it," I insisted, shoving the candy into his hand. He shook his head but dutifully unwrapped it. Then he ate the whole thing in one bite.

"What'd you do that for?" I demanded, slapping his hand. As if that could somehow stop him from completely destroying the euphoria of *savoring* a Reese's.

He snatched hold of my fingers, keeping them hostage on the desk.

"You mean why did I eat the candy you handed to me?" he asked, deadpan. "I'm honestly asking myself the same thing. I just willingly put processed sugar into my body. I blame your whole cottage core Barbie aesthetic. It's very distracting."

I took a breath, not sure where to start. "Okay, first of all, you didn't eat the candy. You *swallowed* it," I argued, flabbergasted to see someone enjoy sugar so little. "Second of all, my cottage core Barbie aesthetic? How do you even know what cottage core is?"

"First of all," he mocked, grey eyes light with mischief, "The toxic candy is now heading to my digestive tract, so I did eat it. I'll come find you later when it finally makes its exit." I smacked his arm. "Second of all, I know about cottage core because you used my laptop to search on Pinterest for 'cottage core outfits' and left the tab open." He shrugged, unapologetic. "Turns out, I like cottage core outfits. Especially with your Barbie spin on it."

I narrowed my eyes at him, unsure how to process the fact that he liked my style so much that he gave it a name. *A really cute name.*

I suddenly felt the need to start a blog titled 'Cottage Core Barbie'.

"You're being weird lately," I hummed, studying him. "Complimenting my style and my body shape. Being all sweet and snarky. I don't know what to think of it."

Mor went still, his emotions swinging from mischievous and affectionate to nervous and on edge. *Interesting...*

"I'm not being weird," he insisted, suddenly interested in a stack of sticky notes. "I'm being your friend. Friends complement each other and say sweet and snarky things. You've done it to me plenty."

I pursed my lips, unconvinced.

"Oh, come on. The weirdest thing I've done today is not eat the chocolate the same way you sugar addicts do," he said, tossing the crumpled Reese's wrapper in the tiny trash can beside my desk.

I took the bait immediately. "Daisy Mae eats slower than you ate that chocolate! And she once ate a pan of stolen brownies so fast that she ate the tinfoil too. Didn't even taste it."

"You stole the brownies or Daisy Mae stole the brownies?" he asked, glancing over at Daisy, who was fast asleep on her pink dog bed. I glared, but he just shrugged. "What? It wasn't clear who the thief was. And no offense, Miss. Spy, but stealing brownies doesn't seem out of character for you."

"I'll have you know that I've never stolen anything in my life. Breaking into places? Sure. Blackmailing? Absolutely—"

"Destroying property? She's all over it."

I rolled my eyes. "Are you ever going to get over the chair? It was one time!"

"You threw it against a door and broke the legs off."

"You kidnapped me and locked me in my room."

Morgan went silent. "Fair enough."

I smiled and glanced over at the boys. They'd almost finished off the charcuterie board—and officially made a mess of my coffee table. It didn't annoy me though. I was just glad to have them as surrogate brothers. Even if they were a bunch of pigs.

"By the way, did the chocolate help?" I asked, looking at Mor.

"No." He grimaced. "But you did," he added sweetly, giving my fingers a gentle squeeze. It was only then that I realized we were still holding hands.

Huh. *That feels interesting.*

We'd held hands before, even hugged and cuddled. Physical affection wasn't new for us. But this *felt* new. And the weightlessness that came over my arm, drifting out from where his skin touched mine, was *definitely* new.

"Okay I'm done now," Mike announced, and I jumped. Morgan raised an eyebrow at me, but I ignored it. It wasn't like he could read my mind or anything.

So long as I kept my poker face on, he wouldn't know about the weird thoughts swirling in my brain.

"I can now talk clearly like a big boy," Mike smiled, wiping his hands on a napkin while Clint wiped his on his pants.

"Can you?" Logan quipped.

Mike balled up a napkin and threw it at Logan's head. But Morgan got their attention before they could start arguing or wrestling. Which was good, because I was really attached to my furniture, and I was pretty sure none of it would survive their Berserker strength. "What were you saying Mike?"

"I said that I think the site is ready," Mike replied, shoving a hand through his thick dark hair, "We'll need to check it manually since a keyword tracker can only do so much. So we'll have to set up a system for who checks it and when, but that will also depend on how much the database gets used. If it doesn't fill up fast, then it won't take long to check it. But regardless, it's ready for tomorrow. I did set it up to note the words 'Nephilim' 'Alfar' and 'Elf', just in case people started hearing anything about Care. I also set it up to look for the word 'vampire'." Mike paused, rolling his eyes. "Because even all these centuries after the civil war, people still mistake Nephilim for vampires. Which is ridiculous, because we have tons of documented cases of Nephilim taking on the appearance of deceased people because they were harder to trace. Not because they were actually dead people brough back to life by drinking human blood. But do people want to think about the logic required to verify a story like that? No. They just want the Salvatore brothers to be real."

"Understandable," I shrugged. I wouldn't mind if the two *very* attractive brothers from the TV show *The Vampire Diaries* were real. *No, I wouldn't mind at all.*

Morgan scowled at me. Apparently, he disagreed.

"Point, bro?" Clint prompted, tapping Mike's knee.

"Right, sorry." Mike blushed, an embarrassed smile on his face. "Point is that the website is ready and set up to filter for both your needs and Caroline's."

"Perfect! You're awesome, Mike," Morgan nodded, smiling at his brother.

Mike sheepishly ducked his head and mumbled a 'you're welcome'.

"Alright, what about you, Clint?" Morgan asked, *still* holding my hand. Why I was so hung up on this fact, I didn't know. "Any luck in town?"

Clint shook his head, sitting back in his armchair. "Not yet. No one has any information about rumors involving the Nephilim. Although, I did realize something a little odd. We found out about the auction to buy the vigilante through Merida's black-market contact, but no one I've talked to has heard anything about it. Which isn't necessarily a shock since we know Eileen was the one to set up that rumor. But if Eileen didn't really set up an auction, then where did she find the buyer for Caroline?"

"Or did the buyer find her?" Logan asked, following Clint's train of thought.

In the penthouse, Eileen had said she had a buyer lined up for me. But the auction to buy the vigilante had just been a trap to get Morgan and I to the hotel. And no matter how many files Mike sifted through from Eileen's computer, there were still two people we couldn't find. Whoever it was she hired to locate my birth parent's safety deposit box, and the person who wanted to buy me. Both of which presumably knew not only that I existed, but that I was part Alfar royalty. *Such a comforting thought.*

"What have you been up to Logan?" I asked, trying to distract myself from the foreboding that had begun to settle in my stomach.

"Uh..." Logan mumbled, running a hand through his short blonde hair; strangely flustered. "Nothing much. Just doing a few undercover ops for Morgan. Nothing big, nothing to worry about. Just...stuff."

I raised my eyebrows. "Stuff?"

"Mhm."

"Well, that's not vague at all—" My phone cut me off, chiming about an incoming facetime call. I glanced down at the screen, my sister Ariel's contact picture smiling up at me. "We're not done with this conversation," I warned, pointing a finger at Logan before I answered the call. "Yeah?"

"Well, aren't you chipper?" Ariel quipped. She was sitting in her fuzzy purple armchair, her blonde curly hair thrown up in a bun. Half of it was falling out because it was too short and too chaotic to be contained by simple elastic, though she tried valiantly to tuck it back up.

"Sorry, I just witnessed Morgan completely disregard the magic of eating a Reese's," I sighed, shooting a sassy look at the Berserker Chief still sitting on my desk. He just winked and rubbed his thumb across the back of my hand.

"Beast Boy," Ariel 'tsked', shaking her head, "Haven't you learned anything? The way to my sister's heart is through her stomach."

"I buy her whatever poisonous foods she wants," Morgan defended, and I moved the phone so Ariel could see him.

"But it's not just about keeping your Caroline fed. You have to respect her favorite foods and treat them like the delicacy they are."

"Alright, why don't you just email me the Caroline Birch handbook so I can stop screwing up?"

"Honey there's not enough gigabytes in the world for a manual that size." Ariel laughed at her own joke, and if she were here in person, I would've smacked her. "But I will tell you one secret. If you're ever dealing with a particularly volatile Caroline and you don't know what's wrong with her, just take your shirt off. That'll shut her up and get her thinking about—"

"Okay, how about you say hi to the rest of the group?" I shouted, trying to cut her off before she could embarrass me—any more than she already had. I quickly switched to the back camera on my phone so she could see the rest of the room.

And suddenly my nosy sister didn't seem so flippant. I had a pretty good idea why.

Clint and Mike both said hi and Ariel returned it without issue. Then it was Logan's turn. "Uh...hey," he mumbled, his cheeks turning pink.

"Hi," Ariel replied awkwardly.

I eyed the two of them, confused. Just weeks ago, Logan had been interested in getting to know my sister, and now he seemed more uncomfortable than attracted. *What the heck happened?*

"Very verbose, guys," I taunted dryly. "Really, you should calm down."

"Hey sis, can you turn me around again?" Ariel pleaded. Somehow, she'd sunk further into her chair, now half covered by the long purple fluff.

I reluctantly switched cameras so she could see my face again. "Why are you being so weird?"

"I'm not being weird."

"You are."

"I'm not." She gave me a wide eyed, pleading look and I gave in with a sigh.

"Fine. How are things going there?"

"Eh." She shrugged. "I hate my boss, love my job, and I'm considering working in the office full time."

"You? In the office every day? But you've been working from home most days since you started at the publishing house." My big sister was a programmer, and she was dang good at her job. So good that the company pretty much let her do whatever she wanted. "See, this is why I'm self-employed."

"You're an heiress and a professional—unpaid—spy," Mor interjected, stealing a piece of cheese from the small plate I had set aside on my desk. "That's hardly what I'd call self-employed, Red."

"Says the man who lives in a log mansion that technically belongs to his people," I snapped, sliding the plate out of his reach.

"I still get paid to do my job. So technically I am employed."

I stared him down. "I don't like you."

Mor just smirked and leaned toward me until he was officially invading my personal space. "I don't believe you."

I was used to having Morgan in my space. He was a big guy, and he took up a lot of it. But this was different. There was an undercurrent that hadn't been there before. Some kind of energy I couldn't put a name to that had my pulse pounding, my face flushing, and this terrible yet pleasant swirling sensation in my gut. *What is that? Am I ill?*

Whatever it was, I'd never felt it before—I'd have remembered.

It was Ariel's loud whisper of, "That was hot," that shattered the moment.

"Shut up," I glowered, taking my time picking at a wrinkle in my shirt. "So why are you going into the office?"

"Tactful subject change, sis," she sassed. "I'm only going in one day a week. It's just...easier right now." Ariel shrugged, just as uncomfortable being questioned as I was. "We'll see how it goes. Now what about you? What did I interrupt? How's all the investigating going?"

I immediately deflated. "Not super great. Basically, we know that someone out there tried to buy me. But we don't know if Eileen somehow put out feelers to find a buyer, or if the buyer found her. Regardless, at least two people know I exist. We suspect someone on the Shifter Council might be behind some of it, but we need to do more investigating before we know for sure. So basically, we know nothing new."

"I'm sorry Care Bear," Ariel sighed. "Let me know if there's anything I can do to help. I mean, I know that's a dumb thing to say because there's literally nothing I can do. But I hate not being able to help, so—"

"Air?" I smiled, cutting her off. "I get it. And I appreciate the thought. I just wish there was a way to find better answers."

"Well," Mor interjected, a little hesitant, "There's going to be a Sleuth meeting tomorrow. It's just supposed to be a general meeting with the other Berserkers in the area, but I plan to ask a few questions that might help our investigation. I doubt anyone will know anything, but it never hurts to ask."

"At the very least, we can help people be more aware," Clint nodded, typing on his phone. "Let them know what to look out for and what to report."

Immediately Mike, Clint and Logan began brainstorming. But I couldn't quite focus on them or my sister—who was still listening—because Morgan was watching me.

"What?" I asked, sensing a random splash of nerves muddle his emotions.

"Nothing, it's just..." He sighed, turning his body to face me. "Sleuth meetings are usually private. We don't allow outsiders."

"Oh, okay. That's understandable. I can just wait upstairs—"

"But you're not an outsider anymore," he interrupted, "You're one of us...And you're important to me. So I'd like you to be there."

Oh. I didn't quite know what to say to that. I knew I was important to Morgan. But this felt different.

Because this isn't him stepping into your life, this is him asking you to step into his. And I knew how rare that was for Morgan. So rare, that I wasn't sure he'd afforded anyone this opportunity since Genevieve.

And I wasn't going to squander it.

"What do I wear?"

Chapter 6

CAROLINE

I don't know what I'd expected a Sleuth of Berserkers to look like. Maybe a little more...berserk?

For some reason, I'd envisioned a bunch of Hulks—minus the green skin.

Probably because Logan and the Hohlt boys were all varying levels of body builders ranging from The Rock to Steve Rogers. But the Shifters that filled the entirety of the massive living room in the Berserker house were just people. Some were bulkier like Morgan, but many were just average Joes with completely unassuming appearances.

A hum filled the room as everyone murmured to each other, eyeing their Chief. Morgan stood with Grey by the fireplace at the front of the room, the big, tall windows on either side letting in plenty of sunlight. Grey was holding his trusty clipboard and the two studied their stacks of papers, whispering.

"There's a lot more people here than I was expecting," I admitted quietly, toying with the ribbon I had tied around my high ponytail.

This meeting supposedly only included the Berserkers in Morgan's Sleuth, which spanned the city of Shifter Haven and all surrounding rural areas. And even then, only a handful of those people came to these meetings. Or so I'd been told. This didn't exactly look like a small gathering to me.

"Don't worry Care Bear," Mike replied, bumping my shoulder with his arm—the guy was like a foot and a half taller than me, "They're not even going to notice you."

"Knock on wood," I pouted. Don't get me wrong, I was honored to be invited to the meeting. It was a vulnerable, intimate thing for Morgan to have asked me. But now that I was here, it hit me that I was the only non-Berserker present. And I really hoped no one noticed.

Mike smiled and humored me, knocking on the end table in front of us. He, Clint, Logan and I were smooshed together in the entryway. The meeting was standing room only, so we'd claimed a spot behind a couch and end table where we weren't obvious, but we could still see Grey and Morgan.

"Well hello Miss. Caroline."

I turned at the familiar voice, smiling when I saw Mr. Wallace stepping up beside me. The old man had raised the Hohlt boys after their mom died and their dad left. And when Morgan had taken me to meet the older gentleman months ago, he was salty and sassy and far too blunt. I'd loved him immediately.

"Hi Mr. Wallace," I smiled back, reaching out to hug him.

He squeezed me gently before letting me go, his eyes twinkling and mischief flaring to life inside him. Although honestly, I kind of assumed that was just his resting state.

"So have you been keeping our man in line?" he asked, nodding toward Morgan.

I scoffed. "Have you met Morgan?"

"Fair point," he laughed, glancing between Mor and I with a calculating look that had me blushing. "He's different lately though. Happier. You're good for him."

I looked over at Morgan, and his ears must have been burning, because he looked up and met my gaze. He studied me for a moment, a small, mysterious smile lighting up his face. And I watched him right back, transfixed by the joy that seemed to flow out of him in rivers.

Grey finally had to snap his fingers in front of Morgan's face to get his attention, and I bit my lip to keep from laughing.

I glanced at Mr. Wallace, admittedly having forgotten he existed there for a moment. "I don't know if I'd go so far as to say that I'm good for him. I mean, I annoy him regularly and I'm definitely the cause for every single one of his grey hairs."

"No, I'm right about this," Mr. Wallace insisted, watching Morgan with the adoration of a proud father. "He was in a dark space for a long time. Between losing Gen and having lived most of his life as a feared man, he was in his Taylor Swift *Reputation* era."

I gave Wallace a disbelieving look and he shrugged.

"I might not be young, but I do know things. And that Taylor might not be the best person on the planet, but she has an album for every season of life. Morgan was in his *Reputation* era. But *now* he's in his *Lover* era."

"Oh, come on," I complained, shaking my head. "We're *friends* Wallace."

"And some of the songs on that album are about friends, or owning your reputation, or finding happiness. They're not all about romance. But the point is that he's happier now, and I blame you."

"Huh..." I didn't know how to argue with that. Because the truth was, Morgan *did* seem happier lately.

Mr. Wallace gave me a cheeky look and we both turned to listen as Morgan started the meeting.

I heard nothing Morgan said though, my attention completely eaten up by the sight of him standing there, commanding the room like a literal boss. He was wearing a grey Henley today, a shirt I'd seen him in a dozen times. But somehow, it looked different. *Does it fit tighter?* Because it seemed to highlight his shoulders in a way it hadn't before. And the way he had the sleeves pushed up to his elbows, the fabric all bunched up, drew my eyes to his biceps. And his forearms. *Blasted forearms.* They always got me in trouble. But could I really be blamed for that? Morgan was ninety percent muscle and one hundred percent alpha male. I'd have to be blind and missing a brain not to appreciate the sight of it.

Just as I was beginning to salivate like a dog—because I had zero dignity—Mor happened to look over and catch my eye. I froze, and immediately felt my cheeks go warm. Morgan must have noticed, because he sent me a small smirk before looking back to the listening crowd.

"As you all know, the Dragon Representative, Eileen, was arrested a few weeks ago," he said, all business. "She was the one framing me for the break-ins at the Shifter Alliance building. And now that she's been arrested, we hope that will restore some of our rapport with the public. But we still have a lot of ground to cover. Now I'm aware—painfully so—that I'm largely to blame for the way people see us. My reputation isn't great, and I've let it go unchallenged for too long. But with some help, I'm working on it."

At this, he sent me a wink. My chest warmed knowing that I'd somehow managed to get through to him all those weeks ago about his reputation.

It was humbling to realize that Mr. Wallace was right, Morgan was definitely in his *Lover* era now. Before, his theme song would have been 'I Knew You Were Trouble'. But now, I could practically hear 'I Forgot That You Existed' playing as he spoke. He wasn't bitter anymore, he was...confident. Self-assured. And it looked *good*.

"If we want people to start seeing us differently, then we have to get serious about *being* different. Most of you here aren't the problem. You're good citizens. You live your lives like everyone else; go to work, raise your families, contribute to society. The problem is the gambling dens. They've been the bane of our existence for too long and they've taken too much. But to get rid of them, we'll have to work together."

No one had dared interrupt Morgan so far, but at that last statement, a deep, sad silence took over the room.

I watched the faces of the Berserkers in the crowd and reached out to feel their emotions. I found no fear or resentment in any of them.

Empathy swept through the room, so deep and so clear that it rocked me where I stood. And the more I thought about it, the more sense it made. Morgan was ten when his mom was murdered and he killed her attacker in self-defense, and these people—this community—would have known about it. Would have probably taken turns babysitting him and his brothers when Mr. Wallace had to be at work. They'd probably watched him grow up and be mentored by the previous Chief. Seen Mor meet and fall in love with Genevieve. Then seen him lose her.

It had never occurred to me that while the majority of the city and the region thought of Morgan as a terrifying monster, most of his people would know him well enough to know better.

I liked them all the more for it.

"What do you need us to do?" Wallace chimed in, and I smiled at his pure devotion to his surrogate son.

Mor relaxed as others called out similar comments, eager to help. A few Berserkers here and there were a little reserved, but I sensed no hostility in the group. Then again, anyone who hated Morgan would be very unwise to show up and hate him in his own home. Even if they knew his reputation was a hoax. Morgan was kind, but he was still Morgan.

"I won't ask much of you. I'm your Chief and it's *my* job to protect you," he said, looking around the room at the multitude of people willingly handing him their obedience. He wasn't even using his natural leadership magic to encourage their allegiance. *This is all him.* And it was impressive. And kind of hot. "But I would ask that you report any suspicious behavior, rumors or people linked to the gambling dens, as well as any other shady endeavors like Shifter trafficking or magical products on the black market. Shifter Haven should be just that, a haven. And we're going to help get it there."

Then Morgan nodded to Mike, and Mike left my side to join his big brother in front of the fireplace. At first, his nerves were strong and bright, but the moment he started talking tech, he was totally fine.

"Alright, so, at Chief Morgan's request, I've built us an online system for sharing sensitive information. It can't be traced and doesn't show up in your browser history. You can access it from any device, and we have the URL in this week's email as well as on the website. The system is anonymous and completely incognito. We won't know who the information is from, and no one will know you sent it. Once you close the window, it's gone, leaving no trace."

Morgan nodded and clapped his brother on the back. "The system is a perfect solution to the fear I know a lot of you have about coming forward. The gambling dens, the Shifter traffickers, the magical black market, they're all dangerous. And your safety is something I would never ask you to compromise. So hopefully this system gives you the opportunity to come forward without taking such a big risk."

Morgan had Mike answer a few questions from the audience, and as I watched Morgan so effortlessly manage the room, it hit me. Mor hadn't been voted in as representative on the Shifter Council because people were afraid of him. Sure, his reputation was intimidating, but seeing him manage this meeting proved that it was more than that. Because somehow, Morgan had taken steps to fight back against the gambling dens, casually asked his people to be on the lookout for Shifter traffickers—AKA, my buyer—made a statement about improving his image, *and* given me credit for it, all in one big speech.

Goodness, the man could *lead*.

"If you don't stop undressing the Chief with your eyes," Logan murmured from behind me, "I'm going to have to go get the hose."

"Shut up," I growled, reaching back to smack him. He wasn't chastised, chuckling like the devil.

"We also have a guest today," Morgan suddenly announced. *Oh no.* I turned back to the meeting only to realize that somewhere in the few moments I'd been distracted, Morgan's eyes had shifted to me. Expectant.

I shook my head. *Nope, not happening.*

"Come on up here, Care," he said, waving a hand toward me. *No, definitely not doing that.*

"I'm good," I called back weakly, crossing my arms.

"Go on, kiddo," Wallace chuckled, shoving me into Logan—the old man was a lot stronger than he looked.

"Wallace—"

Before I knew what was happening, Logan was pushing me out in front of the crowd, and I froze as all eyes turned to me.

"Your turn," Mike teased as he walked past me to return to the group.

"Take me with you," I whispered, but he just chuckled and kept going. *Traitor.*

Morgan held his hand out to me, and I had half a mind to smack it away, but I took it instead. He was lucky I was nervous.

"I hate you," I whispered as he tugged me to his side.

"Liar," he whispered back. I would have argued with him—or maybe I would've just blushed and sputtered stupidly—but he began speaking before I had a chance. "Everyone, this is Caroline," he announced. "She's a very close friend of mine. She recently moved in here, and as far as everyone is concerned, she's one of us."

Surprisingly, *this* was the topic that got people talking. "Why?" a middle-aged woman asked. She wasn't annoyed or enraged by Morgan's declaration, just curious and...hopeful. *Interesting.*

But Morgan was already in defensive mode. His face shifted into a terrifying scowl and his magic stalked through the room, urging everyone to trust him. To submit.

"Mor," I whispered, squeezing his hand, "They're not threatening me. They're just curious."

His eyes snapped to mine, and for a moment, he just glared. But then his expression slowly cleared, and he reeled his magic back in. "Sorry, I just...I guess I'm a little sensitive when it comes to you."

Well...I really didn't know what to say to that. So instead, I just smiled reassuringly.

Mor looked back at the group, his expression much less severe now. "Let me put it this way, Caroline is a part of this Sleuth now. And any treatment you give her is given to me by extension. So, if you threaten her, you threaten me, and if you protect her, you protect me. From now on, she's a Berserker."

Everyone's eyes went wide, their mouths dropped open, and people turned to stare at each other in shock. Then, the woman who'd questioned Morgan looked at me with tears in her eyes and a tender smile on her face. "Of course, she is."

What the heck is happening? The whole room was looking at me like they'd found a unicorn—which was stupid because everyone knew that unicorns had a sweet-tooth and could be found hanging around any good bakery. 'Go find a real unicorn', I wanted to shout. But somehow, I didn't think that would make them stop looking.

And when Mor looked down at me, the affection in his eyes rimmed by a protective instinct, I melted. So, his people were treating me like some kind of long lost loved one. Did I love it? No. But I certainly didn't mind the caring attitude Mor was directing toward me right now.

And while some part of me whispered that my feelings were bigger than just 'not minding' his attention, I pushed them down and told them to leave me alone. Morgan and I were friends—best friends. He was the most solid thing in my life and that stability was more important than anything...

Liar.

Chapter 7

MORGAN

"Morgan, it's time to put on your big boy panties and start wooing Caroline. You need to stop being such a p—"

"Wallace!" I shot a wide-eyed look at my surrogate father, but he just motioned for me to continue hitting the punching bag.

He'd shown up an hour ago, all hot and bothered about my relationship with Caroline. When he realized I was just starting my workout, he insisted on training me for the day.

I should've tried harder to get out of it. The man had spent the last hour working every one of my muscles to failure as punishment for my 'stupidity'.

"I wasn't going to say anything bad," he shrugged innocently, arms crossed as he watched me exhaust myself with another set of hits to the punching bag that hung from the ceiling in the corner of my home gym. "I was going to say that you need to stop being a pansy where that girl is concerned. I raised you better than this!"

I rolled my eyes but continued to work on my right hook, knowing he wouldn't let up until he'd proven his point.

Was I forty years younger than him? Yes. Was I much stronger and bigger? Yes. Would I do what he said anyway? Yes. Because that man was the closest thing to a real dad that I'd ever had.

"I'm not being a pansy," I argued, panting and growing more sluggish by the moment. "I'm being smart."

"No, son. You're being scared."

I glared, but he wasn't bothered. "I'm not scared."

"You are, and I understand why more than anyone," he said, his expression softening as he tapped my arm for me to stop the workout. "I've had a mate before, Morgan. I know what that's like. How powerful that bond is. Being able to sense the feelings of the person you love is an intimate thing, and I remember the day it started for me. From the moment I met Gloria, everything shifted. My world had been spinning just fine on its own, but the moment we locked eyes, everything shifted. And although I was thrown completely off center, I'd never felt more on track. You know the feeling I'm talking about; that moment when you realize she's 'the one'."

I nodded silently. I didn't need to explain; Wallace had seen me fall the first time. Although I'd known at first sight that Gen was my mate, it took a week of dating for me to realize that she wasn't just my mate because the magic said so. She was my mate because she somehow filled the hole in my chest like she was made for it. That's when everything changed.

"I had that with Gloria for twenty-two years, and they were the best years of my life." Wallace paused and I gave him a moment to process his feelings. He never talked about Gloria, and she'd passed away before he took my brothers and I in, so I'd never really known her. "It sounds cliche, but life was brighter with her in it, even when it was hard. Then, when I lost her, all the color in the world went right along with her and all I had left was darkness."

I set a hand on his shoulder, remembering that feeling when Gen died. The way the room suddenly felt so vacant as her spirit left her body. The connection between us severing so that all I felt on the other end of the mate bond was silence. No emotions, no feelings. Because Gen wasn't there to feel them.

It was the worst day of my life, with my mom's death a close second.

And people were wrong, it wasn't easier to know in advance and have the time to say goodbye. Because with time came hope, the hope that she'd get better and the disappointment when she didn't. The pain of watching her suffer and seeing her fade. It didn't make it easier to be in the room and see her go, to have a final goodbye. Because in the end, she still left, and I still worried that I hadn't said it all, hadn't said the right things.

My wife had died slow, and my mom had died fast. I'd experienced both, and I hated them equally. Because death sucks no matter how fast or slow, no matter what you do or don't say. It always sucks.

"Like you," Wallace said, putting his hand over mine, empathy in his eyes, "I sat in that grief for years. I knew Gloria was happy and healthy in heaven, and that she didn't feel any sadness or regret, but I still had to figure out how to live life without her. How to somehow fill all the spaces she left empty. And I did a really poor job at it...So poor that I even let my second mate get away."

"You had another mate?" I exclaimed, so shocked that I staggered back a step.

For a moment, Wallace just stood there, looking vulnerable. He'd been a force to be reckoned with since the day he'd taken us in. He was the paragon of stability and routine, a person who was never rattled or intimidated. Yet here he stood, looking like he might break if I only tapped him with a finger.

"I met her at a grocery store on the west side of the city," he said quietly, no longer meeting my eyes. "She was looking for canned beets and I had to reach in front of her to grab some carrots. When she looked over at me, I dropped the can on the floor. She had the blue of the mate bond in her eyes, a bond I hadn't felt since Gloria died...The woman was friendly and tried to introduce herself to me, but I was so surprised that I practically ignored her. So, she walked away, and I stood there, caught between the decision to let go and move forward, or be stuck in the past. By the time I decided I wanted to try moving forward, she was already out of the store."

"You missed her?" I gasped. Mate bonds can't be broken except through death. Which meant that all this time, Wallace had been feeling all this woman's emotions, knowing he'd let her go. I couldn't imagine that misery.

Wallace shook his head. "I saw her getting into her car as I left the store. I thought about getting her attention, maybe asking for her phone number. But then I imagined what it would be like if it all worked out. If I went over there and we talked, went out, and eventually fell in love...But I knew that someday, I'd probably lose her just like I'd lost Gloria. And that terrified me because I didn't think I could survive that loss twice. So instead, like a coward, I watched her leave, knowing that if I never had her to begin with, I'd never lose. I haven't been back to the west end of town since."

"Wallace—"

"I was an idiot," he cut me off, and I knew he'd hit his limit for vulnerability today. "I lost my second chance because I was too stubborn to see that I was going to lose even if I didn't try. Don't be me, Morgan."

I sighed, unwinding the athletic tape from my hands. "You know this doesn't have to be the end for you though. You can still find her, your mate. She's out there somewhere, probably wondering if you're ever going to show up again."

"I don't want to—"

"Talk about it. I know. But as a fellow widower, I'm telling you that you can be happy again. That this doesn't have to be the end of your story, that you can love two people without diminishing that love for either of them." I sighed, remembering how fervently Gen had argued with me toward the end, insisting that I be happy without her—that I move on. "Part of the reason my feelings toward the mate bond with Caroline started shifting was because I know it's what Gen would have wanted. But it's also because of Caroline. Because until I met her and sensed her volatile emotions, I didn't know people could feel so strongly. Because although I still miss Gen...those spaces she used to fill aren't empty anymore. Caroline fits in them like she was made to. And there are new ones that she fills too, places I didn't know were empty until she swept into them."

I squeezed his shoulder, waiting to speak until he met my eyes. "I hear you when you say not to let fear control me, but I don't believe that it's too late for you to make that choice too."

Wallace didn't comment. But he didn't shove me away either. His eyes got a little glossy and he finally patted my hand before taking a step back. "I love you, you know," he mumbled gruffly.

I smiled, letting the tense moment pass. He was done entertaining my meddling. "I love you too, Wallace."

He nodded and then motioned for me to move to the incline bench. "Now back to you. If you're so excited about being mated to Caroline, then why aren't you doing anything about it?"

I groaned, wondering if I should try making a run for it. *No, he'll just get impatient and go to Caroline himself.* Which would be the worst possible way for her to find out about my feelings. I loved Wallace, but the man lacked tact.

"It's not that I'm unwilling to acknowledge her as my mate," I defended weakly, climbing onto the incline bench. "I just don't know how to pursue her when she's unaware that we're mates."

"Her not knowing that you're mates is not the priority," Wallace corrected as I began my sit ups. "The priority is showing her how you feel about her."

"I've been doing that. I'm flirting a little bit here and there, and I've been trying to find any excuse to touch her."

"That's good, but you need to amp it up. Caroline needs to realize that you're romantically interested so she can decide how she feels. *Then* you can tell her about the bond."

I mulled it over as I continued my sit-ups—as if my abs hadn't already been through enough today. What Wallace was saying wasn't all that different from what Grey had said. Although Wallace apparently wanted me to be as unsubtle as possible.

"Listen," he said, "Caroline is interested. She just needs to feel like you are too."

"How do you know she's interested?"

"I saw her watching you at the Sleuth meeting the other day. She just about ate you up on the spot."

"Attraction doesn't necessarily equal romantic interest," I argued, remembering Caroline's words when she spied on the council meeting. She'd said that people needed to have chemistry, mutual respect, a base knowledge of each other *and* interest. All of which we had. *Except for the interest.* Because I didn't actually know if Care was interested in me romantically.

"Which is why you need to make more of an effort," Wallace complained, flicking me in the chest.

"Ow!"

He rolled his eyes. "Oh, come on, you big scary bear Chief. I barely touched you."

"What do you mean when you say I need to make more of an effort?"

"I mean that you're playing it safe. You're too busy trying to be subtle and sly about everything. But what you need to do is just be obvious. Flirt without trying to cover it up with friendship, touch her without making it seem accidental or convenient. Pursue the woman with purpose! Then she can see how she feels in response."

I nodded, realizing that maybe he was right.

"Now can I ask why you haven't told her about the bond already?" he asked, and I grasped the top of the bench to give my abs a break.

"Because it's a big deal for Caroline to let me in the way she has. She's only ever had herself and her family to lean on. This is the first time she's ever trusted anyone enough to let down her walls." I loved that I was Care's one exception, but my insecurity was that if I pushed her too far too fast, she'd let hers get in the way. "But I'm afraid that if I tell her about the bond, she'll think that it means everything we've built is fake. That she'll doubt her trust in me. I know she cares about me, but I'm nervous that the gravity of the bond might scare her into pulling away."

"Hm..." Wallace rubbed the grey scruff on his chin, deep in thought. So I used his moment of distraction to escape the incline bench and grab my water.

"I think you're right," he finally said. "Caroline cares deeply for you, but if you tell her about the bond too soon, she just might push you away. *But*," he added, smiling mischievously, "If you show her how deep your feelings go; give her the opportunity to see what she could have with you, she might take the news a lot better."

"Okay...so how do I pursue her with more purpose?"

Wallace chuckled as he pointed me over to the weights. "Why are you asking me? I haven't dated in decades. You're the one with the most recent experience."

"Sure, but it's been years since Gen and I dated. And even then, I didn't have to convince her to date me, because she knew we were bonded. Which also meant that she was willing to stick around through my awkwardness. Because we both knew we were 'the one' for each other. Care won't have the same incentive, and I don't have any game when it comes to women. My vocabulary consists of four different ways to growl and three different grunts."

"Alright, fair point." Wallace grinned as I added weights to the ends of a barbell. "First of all, let's work on using your words."

"You sound like Caroline," I complained.

"Smart girl. So, step one is to verbalize more and grunt less."

"Okay, what else?"

"Smile."

I paused, glaring up at him from where I squatted on the floor. "Smile? Isn't that kind of a basic one?"

He shrugged. "You said you were bad with women. Step three is to start flirting in a more obvious way."

"Obvious?"

Wallace crossed his arms and watched while I picked up the weighted barbell. I didn't like the plotting look in his eyes. It meant I was going to hate whatever he said next.

"Give me an example of something flirty you've said or would say to Caroline."

I was right. I hated this. "No way."

"Morgan, do you want the girl or not?"

I glared at him, but he just smirked.

"Fine," I sighed, trying to think of something flirty and yet not completely embarrassing. "Uh...the other day she gave me a piece of chocolate because I was stressed. Then she asked if the chocolate helped. I told her no, but she did."

"Huh," was all Wallace said.

I stopped my reps, feeling personally offended by his singular grunt. "What? That's not a bad line."

"No...It's just not really all that powerful. I mean, I could say the same thing to you, and it wouldn't come across romantic. Here, ask me if the chocolate helped."

I stared at him. Deadpan. "No."

"Morgan Gareth Hohlt, I can only help you if stop being so stubborn. Now ask me if the chocolate helped."

Taking slow, deep breaths, I tried to imagine that I was anywhere but here. I also reminded myself that I couldn't hit Mr. Wallace no matter how many buttons he pushed. The man was way too old to take a punch to the shoulder.

"Fine," I bit out. "Wallace, did the chocolate help?"

"No," he smiled, reaching out to clasp me on the shoulder, "But you did." Then he stepped back and set his hands on his hips. "Now see how platonic that was? You're saying things to Caroline, hoping she can read the subtext. What I'm telling you is to stop relying on subtext and just be obvious."

Hm. I hated to admit it, but he wasn't totally wrong. I was saying essentially platonic things, relying on Caroline to realize that I meant more by them. Which was honestly stupid and a little cowardly.

"Alright fine, I agree. I need to be bolder."

"Yes!" Wallace exclaimed, raising his fist like a Boy Scout. "Now pretend I'm Caroline. I've just walked into the gym and I'm going to lift some weights. I say something very Caroline like..."

"Wow Bear Man, lift much," I suggested.

"Good! Now what do you say in response?"

This was hands down the most awkward experience of my life. How was I supposed to flirt with an old man pretending to be Caroline? Answer: I couldn't.

"Come on Mor," Wallace teased in a high-pitched voice that I gathered was supposed to be an imitation of Caroline's. "Flirt with me."

"Please never ever use that voice again."

"I'll stop once you start flirting."

I closed my eyes, trying to picture my mate and *not* Wallace standing there. "Why? Like what you see, Red?" The words were ruined just a little by my monotone voice, but I was not about to show my father figure what I actually sounded like while flirting with a girl. *Just kill me now.*

"Not bad," Wallace said, and I opened my eyes, reaching for the barbell again. "But that's still pretty subtle. You're teasing her, but you're not showing your interest in her."

"Okay...I think I see what you mean."

"Good, because the next step is to start dialing up the physical stuff."

I froze, and the bar almost slipped from my fingers. "*Excuse me?*"

"Come on Morgan," Wallace shouted, like he was coaching a football game. The man really needed a hobby. "You've got to make her think about romance. Now don't go in guns blazing and kiss her—I raised you to respect consent! But the trick is to make her *think* about kissing you. Get close and then pull away, let your fingers brush and then walk past. Find ways to touch her that don't cross the line, but also make her start thinking about being romantic with you. *That's* how you woo a woman."

I nodded, wishing I'd brought a pen and paper to this workout session. Wallace actually had some really good advice. Now if only he'd use it for himself.

"I think I can do all that."

"Wow," he sighed, batting his eyes like he might cry. "Would you look at that. My baby's all grown up."

I laughed. "Shut up, old man." He grinned and I went back to my workout.

I was in the middle of my fifth rep of dead lift squats when Caroline materialized, opening the French doors between the dining room and the gym.

Dang it, she looked good today. Truthfully, she looked good every day, but it hit me harder when I was holding five hundred pounds in my hands.

Wearing a cropped white sweater and a floral skirt with her pink converse, Care flounced over to us. Her hair was up in a bun today with a pale pink ribbon wrapped around it. Little whisps of hair framed her face and I had the urge to tuck them behind her ear and let my fingers skate down her neck. *Nope, you've got weights in your hands, dummy.*

"Hi Mr. Wallace," she greeted with a bright smile.

Then she turned to me, and her smile slowly disintegrated. Her lips parted and she raised one eyebrow, her gaze slowly following the lines of my body. *Oh.* Caroline was one hundred percent checking me out.

Attraction swirled around her like a pink cloud, thick and heady as she stared at me. I had a feeling that I could've waved a hand in front of her face, and she wouldn't have blinked. In her defense, I was shirtless, holding a weighted barbell, and my shorts were low on my hips. Had I known she was coming in here, I would have tried to dress a little more modestly.

A little. *I have to take every advantage I can get.* And apparently, my physique was doing me some favors.

"Hey Red," I teased, grinning.

"Oh!" she startled, cramming her eyes shut as her cheeks flushed. "Sorry, I just...Your nakedness is distracting." Then her eyes popped back open, and she looked between me and Mr. Wallace. "I mean, not that you're actually naked. Because you're not. Obviously. But you're...half naked...and I wasn't expecting. Um. I just came in here to..."

But then, her eyes found mine and she became distracted again. My chest warmed to know that this time it wasn't my body that had her attention. It was just me.

"I just came to talk about tomorrow..." her voice trailed off softly.

"Tomorrow?" Wallace interjected—loudly. Ruining the moment.

Caroline lit up with embarrassment as she realized she'd been caught staring, and I scowled at Wallace. 'Trust me', he mouthed. I shook my head.

"Um, yeah," Care babbled nervously, looking everywhere but at us. "I just wanted to double check about some of the details for tomorrow when we all go spy on different council members."

I opened my mouth to reply, but Wallace subtly motioned toward the barbell. Taking the hint, I began doing squats again.

"Um..." Care continued, her eyes tracing my movements as I squatted with the barbell in my hands and then stood, again and again.

"Care?" I prompted.

"Hm?"

"Tomorrow?"

"Right!" she squeaked, turning to sit on a weight bench a few feet away and swiveling so she faced Mr. Wallace instead of me. But that only proved that I was affecting her. "So, um...Clint and Logan are going to spy on Francine, Mike and Grey will take Jack, and you and I will watch Drew."

"Right," I nodded, struggling through the next rep. "This mission is just recon. None of us are going to interact with the people we're following. We'll just watch them for any suspicious behavior since they reacted strangely to the fake report at the council meeting."

"And you're actually going to let me go with you? Even though we'll be tailing a potentially dangerous Shifter representative?" she asked, standing from the bench. I couldn't exactly blame her for doubting that I'd be cool about her coming with me to spy on Drew. I'd been a bit of a bear about her safety since she got her second concussion—pun intended.

Then, feeling a little bit brave coming off the heels of Wallace's pep talk, I decided to test my rusty flirting skills.

"Sweetheart, you can go anywhere with me. As long as you stay close."

Care's eyes snapped up from where they'd dropped to my chest, and she furrowed her brows. "Did you just call me sweetheart?"

I ignored the bit of nerves flaring to life inside me and instead latched onto the feeling of curiosity I felt in Caroline. Setting the barbell on the ground, I stepped over to where she stood and crowded her space, forcing her to look up at me.

"Would you rather I call you Red?" I whispered, brushing a finger along the blush that tinted her cheeks.

Her green eyes went wide, and just for a fleeting moment, they dropped to my lips. *Yes!!* I wanted to fist pump, shout 'hurrah' and pop a few party poppers. For the first time since I'd met her, Care was looking at me not with passive attraction she could have for anyone, but with actual interest. I mean, it lasted for a single second, but it still counted.

"What's the matter, Red, cat got your tongue?" I teased lightly, letting my hand trail over to tuck her hair behind her ear.

"You're acting weird again," she whispered, her voice a little hoarse.

"Maybe that's just my new normal. Maybe you just need to get used to it." Then I hesitated, wondering if I'd read her wrong. "Unless it makes you uncomfortable?"

But she shook her head, studying me thoughtfully. "No, it just makes me notice how sexy you are."

I saw the moment she realized she'd said those words out loud. Affection, curiosity, and attraction all faded in the face of her embarrassment. I felt a little bad for her, but I was mostly pleased that she wasn't as indifferent to me romantically as I'd thought.

"You think I'm sexy?" I asked innocently, trying not to make it obvious that I was flexing my pecs. But I was totally flexing.

"Stop being so pleased," Care complained, smacking my arm playfully. "I also think Bucky Barnes and Damon Salvatore are sexy."

I opted not to point out that both those men were fictional and instead focused on the fact that she was staring at my bicep. The bicep that she was still touching—rubbing actually.

"Care," I whispered, leaning so close that my breath rustled her baby hairs. She didn't notice though, too busy ogling me.

"Hm?"

"You're staring."

Slowly, her eyes lifted to mine, guilty. Even as mortification swept through her, all I felt in myself was pleasure. Finally, I was getting somewhere with Care, somewhere far away from the accursed friend zone.

But because she was Caroline, she refused to admit defeat. "Am not!" She growled, spinning away from me and heading for the door.

I crossed my arms as I watched her go, wishing we were far enough along in our relationship for me to sweep up behind her and lock her in my arms. *Baby steps.* We'd barely crossed the threshold into 'friends who flirt'. And if I wasn't mistaken, this slightly bolder yet still respectful approach was working.

"See you tomorrow," I called after her, "Sweetheart." She scowled at me over her shoulder, but I just winked.

Laughter filled the gym in Caroline's absence, and I turned to see Mr. Wallace standing there, holding onto a weight machine to keep himself from falling over as he cackled.

"Well, that was telling," he finally said once he could fully breathe again.

"Do you think I pushed too far?"

"Are you kidding me?" he demanded incredulously. "This was just the tip of the iceberg, son. You laid some good groundwork just now, but you've still got a ways to go to convince her."

I sighed. He was right. This whole conversation had been very telling, and I now realized that Caroline wasn't as ignorant of our connection as I'd thought. I still had some work to do to get her to consider me as a romantic partner, but that was okay. *I can work with this.*

Chapter 8

CAROLINE

"Mm," I moaned, taking another sip of my pineapple brown sugar tea. "Say what you will about Pixies and their trust fund baby attitudes, but boy can they brew a cup of tea."

Pixies had plant magic, which meant that they could grow plants from pre-existing seeds, roots and bulbs. It also meant that they could use various plants to create potions that could affect the mind and body. Many of which were outlawed. But the most important thing that Pixies had a talent for was brewing the most flavorful teas in the world.

"Apparently our target would agree with you," Morgan replied, lifting his cup to cover his smirk. He failed.

"I saw that."

"Saw what?" He sat back in his chair, and the poor thing groaned under the weight of him. It was comical, to see such a big, masculine man in a tea shop like this. There were roses and greenery hanging from the ceiling, an eclectic assortment of chairs—not Berserker-proof ones, apparently—and benches placed at round tables, and an entire wall of decorative teacups. It was a much posher version of *Alice in Wonderland,* and my new favorite place. But it was a bit...feminine for Morgan.

"Your smirk," I said, tapping his calf under the table with my foot. "I know you're laughing at me on the inside."

"Laughing is a good thing. It means I'm *enjoying* you." Then, instead of tapping me back, he *tangled* his leg with mine, so that my ankle crossed over his.

Immediately, my face flamed, my ears went hot, and I found myself recalling the way he'd called me 'sweetheart' yesterday. That definitely hadn't been platonic.

And I definitely wasn't going to think about it.

"Having trouble formulating a thought there, sweetheart?" he smiled, nudging my foot where it rested against his.

I stared at him, wondering if I'd accidentally said my thoughts out loud. "Are you part Mermaid?"

"Why? Did I just read your mind?" he said, looking like the devil, and I swear his eyes got brighter. "Were you thinking about me?"

I stared him down but opted not to answer. Not when there was a strong chance that I'd end up blurting my very private, very stupid thoughts out loud.

I could see it now, I'd say, 'By the way, I think I might maybe possibly be just a teeny tiny bit into you'. And then he would stare at me, wide-eyed, our friendship crumbling beneath my feet. *Yeah, we'll just keep that thought inside our brain.*

But also...Was I into Morgan??

I let myself check him out, from his thick dark hair to his grey eyes, the faint white scar across his left eye and right cheek, the wide set of his shoulders. He was a specimen if I'd ever seen one. But I'd known that from the first time I saw him. And while I found a lot of guys passively attractive, there was something about Morgan, something deeper, that made me more aware of him. Something that took me further than just appreciating the sight of him, something that made me want *him*. In my life, in my space, in my brain, all the time.

Crap. Crap on a freaking cracker! I liked Morgan. Which was very bad! *Wait, why is it bad?* Oh, how I wanted to slap myself. *Because if I act on this, I could ruin our entire relationship!*

That is, unless he likes me back...

But as I watched him, studying every shift in his expression, I didn't know what to think. It wasn't clear whether or not he reciprocated my feelings. *And I don't even know if I want him to.* Because at the end of the day, I wasn't sure whether or not I was willing to risk what we had...

"Red? Did I fry your operating system with my smolder?" Mor teased, a lighthearted smile on his face.

"Oh look! Drew's finally ordering," I announced dumbly, desperate for a subject change.

We'd learned from Clint's contacts in the city that the Firebird representative got his tea here every day at ten. Honestly, I was surprised that pretty boy was up before noon. But I supposed that corrupt people probably had a lot to do in a day.

Drew was standing by the counter, tapping his foot and checking his expensive watch every ten seconds. His brown hair was perfectly styled as usual, and today he wore a grey suit that I assumed cost more than my entire wardrobe. He also had on a pair of thin, black-framed glasses that I'd never seen him wear. Though they did accentuate his angular features nicely. *But I bet they're fake.*

"He could've been nicer to the barista," I complained, glaring at Drew even though he wasn't looking at us. "She was trying to flirt with him, and he completely shut her down. I get that he's not interested, but she was being really brave talking to a pretty stranger like that."

"Pretty?" Morgan scowled, his hands tightening around his teacup.

Knowing the strength of a Berserker—especially an angry one—I removed the cup from his hands. We'd gone unnoticed so far because Morgan sat with his back to the counter and wore a baseball hat to keep Drew from recognizing him. *Which he should definitely start doing more often because it's totally working for him.* But shattering ceramics would definitely get us noticed.

"Yes," I said, setting the teacup aside. "Drew is pretty, like a model."

Morgan growled. "A model?"

"Oh relax, Bear Man. Drew is one of those people who has great bone structure and a winning smile, but his overall aesthetic does nothing for me personally. He's pretty, but I like my men a little more..."

Mor leaned forward, hanging on to my every word. "A little more what?"

"Masculine. I prefer my men more masculine."

Morgan hummed, thoughtful, and I silently chastised myself.

I might now be aware that I liked Morgan, but I definitely didn't need him knowing that. I barely knew what to do with it.

"Masculine huh?" he smirked. That smirk was dangerous. It made my puny cavewoman brain think that Morgan might be interested. *But he's not. And I don't need him to be.*

And if I were Pinocchio, my nose would've grown three inches.

"Oh look, he's on the move!" I scooped up mine and Mor's teacups as Drew's to-go order finally appeared on the counter. Drew, of course, snatched it up without so much as a 'thank you' to the barista, then grimaced when he tasted it.

"Ugh, I take it back," I said. "He's not pretty, he's ugly. He's a big fat ugly troll."

Mor chuckled and we waited for Drew to get to the door before we stood from our table. I took our dishes to the bucket by the door and followed the Firebird out onto the street. The afternoon crowd immediately swallowed us all up, and we watched Drew from a few paces back.

"I'm glad to know that you're officially turned off by him," Morgan said, setting his hand on my back as we stepped around a pair of businessmen in suits. "Means I have one less man to compete with."

I spun to face him. "*What?*"

But Morgan just winked and then looked straight ahead.

I wanted to grab him by the collar of his shirt and demand that he tell me *what the heck that meant*, but that would give away my investment in his feelings. And giving anyone the upper hand emotionally just seemed like a bad idea.

"I'm surprised he didn't bring a bodyguard or a personal assistant," Morgan hummed thoughtfully.

"I think he's a little too arrogant for a bodyguard," I replied, thankful that he hadn't somehow guessed what I was thinking. "And something tells me that he can't keep an assistant to save his life. I can only imagine what a terror he'd be to work for."

"Fair point. Or it could be that he doesn't hire guards or an assistant for the sake of privacy. If I were someone doing bad things, I wouldn't want anyone on my payroll who could find out about it."

"Hm, that too. I wonder—"

I stumbled a little as Morgan slipped an arm around my waist and tugged me into his side. Then, as if my brain wasn't already overworked today, he kissed the top of my head.

The man was treating me the way I treated the last Reese's in the bag: with complete reverence and adoration.

"Is this okay?" he asked, a little worried when I remained mute.

"Mhm. Yeah. It's fine. I mean, we're under cover so…This is probably less conspicuous than just…walking normally." And since I couldn't be trusted with basic human functions like speaking, I bit my lip.

"This," Morgan whispered, gently squeezing my side, "Is not for Drew's benefit. This is just because I wanted to."

I turned to gawk at him, but he pointed down the street. "He's heading for the bank."

Sure enough, Drew was standing at the crosswalk across from the bank. And as he stood there waiting for the signal to change, he took a drink of his tea and smiled. *Smiled.* Like that cup of tea was the best part of his day, even though he'd acted disgusted by it in front of the barista at the tea shop. *Ugh, what a jerk.*

"Since he's apparently on his way to being bankrupt, I'd imagine he's looking for a way out of it," Morgan commented as we watched the crosswalk signal turn green.

"Remind me how he got voted in? He's absolutely terrible."

"His dad was heir to a timber empire—"

"They have those?"

"Yeah, but not long after Drew's dad inherited the money, he went to prison. Can't remember what for, but he's been in for at least a decade now. The money went into a trust, but a lot of people believe that Drew's dad is still in control of that money from prison. They even believe that he supposedly used it as leverage to get Drew voted in as regional representative."

"So why isn't Daddy bailing him out now if he's some kind of loan shark?"

Morgan shrugged and we watched as Drew crossed the street to a large, ornate office building. Once he disappeared inside, Morgan sighed, disappointed. "This isn't going to be much of a reconnaissance mission if we can't hear what he does in there."

"Well then it's a good thing your partner comes so well prepared," I smiled, pulling us over to a bench in front of a furniture store that faced the bank.

"Why am I not surprised?" he said, shaking his head as I pulled a bulky piece of tech from my crossbody bag. "Do you have snacks in there too?"

I held up a mini can of Pringles and he chuckled.

I smirked. "I packed them just for you. And as for Drew, I planted a listening device in his pocket, so we can hear what he hears." I plugged in a pair of headphones to the listening device and handed one earbud to Morgan.

"Have I told you lately that you're impressive?"

"Hm...No. But now that you say it, I think I'd like to hear it daily." Then I turned on the listening device.

"*Mr. Hoffman,*" someone greeted from the other end of the transmission, "*Nice to see you. Can we get you anything?*"

"*A solution. That is your job, is it not?*" Drew snapped.

"*Of course, sir. Uh...please have a seat and we'll take a look at your financials.*"

"*You haven't prepared for this meeting? Honestly, this is supposed to be a professional institution. I expected better.*"

Mor and I both rolled our eyes as we listened to Drew be a complete jackrabbit. *As usual.*

The poor man running the meeting was so flustered by the Firebird's rude behavior, that he kept stumbling over his words as he summed up Drew's financial issues. Which basically showed that Drew had spent more money than he owned, and without a line of credit or some very shady banking help, he and his people were indeed going to go bankrupt.

"Quick, someone get this man a Dundee for being the least frugal person ever. He could even beat out Kelly Kapoor," I said, leaning back against the bench. "I'm disappointed in Drew. He's single handedly affirming the stereotype that people can't be both smart and pretty."

"The irony is that he proves the stereotype, and you're always breaking it."

"Flattery will get you everywhere, Bear Man." But just as I began to smile, the expression slipped away. The hairs on the back of my neck stood up, and I was suddenly overwhelmed by the feeling of being watched.

Uncoiling my magic, I let it slink out around me, telling me the emotions of those in our vicinity. Adoration, attraction, joy, misery, irritation—they all pinged off of different people. But each emotion came and went as people moved along the sidewalk.

All except one.

Behind me, just at the edge of my awareness, I felt a cloud of intense ambition. It was a combination of competitiveness, focus, and cruelty, and I would have been an idiot not to assume that it was directed at us.

"We're being watched," I whispered, grasping Morgan's hand.

Mor tensed, and immediately began scanning every bystander that passed. "How can you tell?"

"I sense it. There's an emotion that's not moving along with the crowd. It's focused and cruel. I think whoever it is, they're here for us."

Morgan didn't argue with me about the reliability of my abilities. "Where are they? Can you tell?"

"Behind us. Maybe in the alley? It's hard to say without going over there."

He froze, his fingers gripping mine tighter. "You want to go after them." It wasn't a question.

"We've been at a disadvantage lately," I pleaded, shoving the listening device and headphones back in my bag. "We don't know who Eileen was working with.

We don't know who tried to buy me or how they knew about me. We need answers, and if we can surprise this stalker, then we might be able to find some."

Mor didn't respond at first. He flexed his jaw, jiggled his leg, and watched the people on the sidewalk like each and every one was a threat. I tried not to breach his privacy by reading his emotions, but it was useless. His emotions were the only ones I never had to reach for.

"I know you're worried," I whispered, sensing his fear and apprehension. "But you don't need to be. We've got each other's backs. Plus, you can shift now without losing control. And saving a girl from abduction would probably be really good for your image."

Morgan scowled, not amused.

"Right, sorry." I grimaced. "Listen, the best-case scenario is that we catch the stalker unprepared and take them home to question them. And worst-case scenario, we end up having to fight. Which is fine because we're prepared. So, there's nothing to worry about."

"I can think of at least ten things to worry about in either of those scenarios."

"Come on, Mor. Don't you want answers?"

He sighed and pulled me up from the bench, grasping my shoulders as he leaned down to look me in the eyes. "You will stay safe," he commanded gently, "No matter what."

I nodded and threw my arms around him. He hugged me back tightly, as if I might disappear if he let go.

"Morgan," I squeaked, his hug growing tighter, "Can't breathe."

"Oh. Sorry." He released me. "Okay, let's do this. Once we get to the alley, you distract them, and I'll shift?"

I nodded and he took my hand again. "Deal."

Wearing fake smiles and feigning unbothered happiness, we turned down the alley next to the furniture store. I leaned my head on Morgan's shoulder, trying to sell the idea that we were just two lovers taking a shortcut.

"You know, one of these days we're going to go somewhere," Morgan whispered as we passed a dumpster, "And nothing exciting will happen. It'll just be you and me doing something completely mundane, totally uninterrupted."

"Now what would be the fun in that?" I teased, grinning up at him.

Amused, he kissed the tip of my nose. The action was so quick, I didn't have time to react or process my feelings before he was looking ahead again.

"I should know better," he said, "Of course, you'd need a few bad guys here and there in order for life to feel interesting."

I felt the attacker before I saw them, spinning around just in time to see a metal pipe fly past my head. The attacker—a lean man with a narrow face and an intense scowl—snarled and turned to strike at Morgan.

Mor may not have been fast like me, but he was strong, and the metal pipe had nothing on him. He blocked it easily with his hand and tore it from the attacker before flinging it across the alley.

While the attacker was distracted by Morgan, I kicked the back of his knee. He stumbled a few steps and let out a few curses as he spun toward me. *Well, I've got his attention.* Hoping the training I'd had would be enough to fend him off for a few moments, I pulled my knife from its hidden sheath.

Morgan had already begun his shift, his body starting to morph from man to bear. I'd seen the transformation before, but it was hard not to watch as his body stretched and thickened, fur rising across his skin.

But my attacker had no problems getting my attention. He sprung toward me, a knife now in his hand, and I knew by the way he moved that I was outmatched. *Thank God I'm fast.*

He swiped at me a few times, but as good as he was, I still managed to slip out of his reach at the last moment. He'd missed me for the fourth time when he growled and pulled a travel sized spray bottle from his pocket.

I had no idea what he had in the bottle, but it couldn't have been good. Darting close, I kicked at his hand, knocking the bottle to the ground. He snarled at me, and for a moment, I thought he might tackle me.

But then he fell forward, landing on the pavement with a grunt.

And standing behind him was Morgan, in all his Berserker glory. He was beautiful as a bear, with silver fur, beige paws and a matching snout. He was as terrifying as he was magnificent. He towered above me, his sides heaving and rage swirling inside him like a hurricane.

"Nice timing," I smiled, spinning the knife in my hand. Then I dropped it. *Of course.* "You didn't see that," I insisted, pointing the knife at Morgan.

"You told me we could follow this idiot because we were prepared," Morgan growled, setting a paw on the man's back as he began to crawl away. The man squeaked and I gathered that Mor was putting a little more of his weight into it than necessary.

"And we were prepared. I mean, we took out the bad guy in less than..." I checked my watch. "Three minutes. Go team!" I held up my hand for a high five, but Morgan just stared at me. "Come on, don't leave me hanging."

"I am not high fiving you. We shouldn't have done this. You could have died."

"Excuse me? I didn't even get any injuries!"

"You were lucky, Caroline."

Now that made me angry.

"Alright, let the man up and I'll show you just how *lucky* I am." I glanced down at the attacker under Morgan's paw and realized that he'd reached his hand out just far enough to grab his little spray bottle. "Crap, no!"

I reached out to take it from him, but he sprayed it up at us before I could reach it. To my surprise, the spray was pink, floating through the air with a sweet, sugary scent.

"Is that waffle cones I smell?" I turned my eyes from the pink fog back to the attacker, but he'd pulled a mask up over his nose and mouth, watching us with mirth in his eyes. "That can't be good."

"Care..." I turned to Morgan, who was blinking rapidly, his big head bobbing like he couldn't hold it up. Then his whole body began to sway, and he fell to the ground.

"Morgan!" I exclaimed, kneeling beside him. "Mor? Talk to me."

"I feel...funny," he said, his voice heavy with sleep.

"Funny how? Whoa..." I shook my head as a wave of dizziness came over me. "Care?"

I was vaguely aware of Morgan's voice saying my name, but it was hard to focus when the world was tilting around me. Then the next thing I knew, I was lying on the ground, looking up at the bright June sky.

My head felt thick and heavy, like it'd been stuffed full of cotton candy. And everything still somehow smelled like sugar.

I tried to sit up, but my body was just too heavy, and my vision was warped and fuzzy. So, I laid there, weak and vulnerable as our attacker stood and made his way over to me.

"Go away," I mumbled, blinking up at the man with heavy lids. "I don't...like you."

"Feeling's mutual, your Majesty," the man said through his face covering. I got the impression he was scowling.

Then he squatted beside me and took out a handful of zip ties. Something about that felt ironic, but I couldn't put my finger on why.

"Not my ma..." Morgan groaned, his paws twitching. He was faring better than me; I couldn't move so much as a finger.

"Shut up, I'm not here for you," the man snapped, snatching hold of my wrists.

I wanted to stop him, to fight back, but I couldn't move. Even my magic seemed to be out of reach, kept from me by a thick wall of pink fog.

"What do we have here?" a new voice said from somewhere behind me.

The man with the face covering quickly stood. Apparently, he didn't think I was much of a threat at the moment. He wasn't wrong. I was still trying to wiggle my big toe.

"This doesn't concern you," the original attacker warned the newcomer. "Be on your way."

"Hm..." the other man replied, and I finally managed to tilt my head and catch a glimpse of him. He wasn't wearing a face covering like the original attacker, but he was dressed in all black. Black jeans, black boots, a black T shirt and a black leather jacket.

"I think I'll stay," he said, smirking. He was handsome—as far as I could tell in my drugged state—with a dark short beard, black hair and sharp features. He kind of looked like Ben Barnes as the Darkling. *Oh, I love the Darkling! He definitely deserved a redemption arc.*

Pay attention Caroline. Right.

The original attacker approached the Ben Barnes lookalike, and I wanted to warn Ben about the spray bottle of waffle cone drugs. But I couldn't quite find the energy to yell.

Turns out, I didn't need to.

The attacker raised his hand to spray the drug, but Ben was *fast.* He snatched the bottle out of the other man's hand and slid it in his back pocket. "I'll take that, thank you."

The attacker seemed a little surprised at first, but then he launched out at Ben. Most of the fight was too blurry for me to follow, but from what I gathered Ben was a good fighter.

The original attacker had to be a Shifter. Because when he hit Ben in the side of the head, Ben staggered and dropped to his knees, blinking rapidly.

"Come on," I pleaded quietly, wishing I had the energy to use my magic and help Ben. I didn't know if he was a good guy or not, but he hadn't drugged me so far, so I was on his side. "Get up, Ben—"

A growl cut me off and I turned my head to see Morgan struggling to his feet. He was still in bear form, and even without access to my magic, I could tell he was pulsing with fury.

As he faced the attacker, the man abandoned Ben, judging Morgan to be the bigger threat. *Smart.*

Mor was so big that his head stood above the other man's, and his sheer bulk was enough to make anyone run in terror. But the man wasn't cowed, and he walked toward Morgan with confidence.

Morgan reached the attacker and swung his head toward the man like a wrecking ball. But the attacker was prepared. He ducked under Morgan and whipped his arm out, knife in hand. I cringed as Morgan let out a muffled cry.

But if I thought Mor had been angry before, he was vengeful now.

He swiped a paw at the man's legs, and when the man dodged it, Mor was ready.

He leaned back onto his hind legs and swiped the man's legs out from under him with his other paw. The attacker hit the ground, groaning. But he refused to stay down, crawling a few feet away to stand.

But as he turned back to face Morgan, a slightly off-balance Ben darted forward and swung the discarded pipe at the attacker's head.

Surprised, the attacker barely stepped back in time to avoid the pipe and turned to throw his knife at Ben. But a silver blur plowed into the attacker's side, and I heard the crack as his head hit the pavement.

Trying *not* to think about the man whose skull had been crushed by the blow, I closed my eyes. *Deep breaths. Do* not *vomit while lying on your back.*

"Care?" Morgan shouted. I opened my eyes to find him cornering Ben against a brick wall. "How you doing over there?"

"I..." I paused to swallow. "Better, I think."

"Can you move yet?"

Unsure, I tried wiggling my big toe. When I successfully moved my entire foot, I tried sitting up. But Morgan quickly shouted for me to stop. "I don't want you to fall over and get hurt. Can you get to your phone and call the guys?"

"Sure." I fished my phone out of my pants pocket and called Clint's number.

"Hey Clint," I said as soon as he picked up, "Can you or one of the guys come down to the alley beside Pinewood Furniture?" I glanced over at Morgan, who was still cornering Ben Barnes. "We've got something to bring home."

Chapter 9

MORGAN

"Are you sure it was smart to bring him here?" Logan asked beside me as we stared at our houseguest.

"No," I admitted. "But I couldn't let him go. We're lucky no one seemed to notice the fight, but we can't involve the police since I'm positive that he knows...about Care." I didn't dare explain exactly what I thought he knew about my mate. Not while the man was in the room.

The man who'd helped save us in the alley might have been intimidated by me when I'd been in bear form, but he was completely unbothered now.

He sat on the couch in my office, spread out in the middle of it like it was *his* office and we were the captives.

The whole thing felt shady to me; he was too unfazed. Even when we'd taken him from the alley and asked for his address so Grey and Logan could go grab some of his things, he complied without issue. *Whoever this guy is, he has too much confidence for a captive, and I don't like it.*

"Well, technically, pretty much everyone's seen the fight," Clint pointed out, standing behind one of the armchairs. No one seemed to want to get close to our visitor, unsure just what kind of person we were dealing with. So, we all stood around the room, watching him like he might Hulk out at any moment.

"What do you mean, *everyone's seen it*?" I demanded with a gut full of trepidation.

"Mike posted the security footage on the internet." Clint pointed at Mike, and I turned my attention to the second-born Hohlt brother. And if someone didn't explain quickly, there wasn't going to *be* a second born Hohlt brother.

"Caroline made me do it," Mike hurriedly defended, pointing at my mate, who stood beside me in front of my desk. Looking deceptively innocent.

As per usual.

"Caroline Felicity Birch, explain," I growled, crossing my arms. "Now."

Care fluttered her green eyes at me and wound her arm around mine. Against my better judgment, I felt myself begin to relax. *Freaking mate bond.*

"Listen, it's not like the whole fight is up online," she pleaded, her voice too saccharine to be genuine. "I asked Mike—"

"Coerced," Mike corrected.

Care rolled her eyes. "Whatever. Point is that Mike stole the security footage from the furniture store so no one would see the fight. And then I had him take the most flattering clip of you and post it on the internet to boost your image." I glared at her, and Care smiled sheepishly. "Did I mention that you are now trending online? As is the phrase 'Chief Hohlt hero bear'."

I glanced at Mike, and he nodded. "She's right. You are trending, and people do seem to be referring to you positively for once."

I wanted to be mad at both of them, but one look at Caroline and all thoughts of frustration fled. *I'm so whipped.* And I so didn't care.

"We'll discuss this later," I whispered.

But Care wasn't fooled. "You mean you'll give into me later."

"While your improving reputation is important," Grey interrupted, "We still have the houseguest to deal with. What do you intend to do with him? Are we just collecting stolen people now? Because you're kind of making a habit of it."

I scowled at him, but he just shrugged. I mean, he wasn't wrong. This was the second person I'd kidnapped. Although in my defense, this time it had been a group effort.

"Alright, start explaining," I sighed, turning back to the man on the couch. "Who are you and why were you in that alley today?"

The stranger with too much hair product smiled. "Well, to answer the first part of your question, my name is Volund. And as for the second part, I've been watching *her* for a few months," he said, nodding at Caroline. "When you two were attacked, I thought I ought to step in."

Care released my arm and stepped toward Volund like she meant to attack.

"You've been *watching me*?" she hissed, and as much fun as it would have been to see her tear into him, I latched an arm around her waist and tugged her back. I didn't want the creepy stalker's hands anywhere near Caroline. *My* mate.

"Not like that," Volund hurriedly defended, leaning forward to rest his arms on his knees. "No offense, but you're not really my type. I prefer brunettes."

"A narcissistic fantasy, no doubt," Care quipped, not softened by his defense. And rightfully so. Stalking is disturbing, even if there isn't any vicious intent behind it.

"I mean, I wouldn't say no to a woman with dark hair, dark eyes, and incredible taste," Volund smirked.

No one returned the expression.

"Wow, fun crowd," he sighed. "Listen, it's not like I've been watching you for years or anything. I don't have photos of you, and I didn't watch you in your home or anything like that. I just kept tabs on you for a few months, trying to figure out if you were like me."

"Like you?" Logan demanded, taking a small step away from the wall where he stood. Volund eyed the movement, and I felt gratified to know that while this man who'd been stalking Caroline might be dangerous, my mate had five Berserkers ready to defend her at the slightest provocation.

Volund turned his eyes back to Caroline. "An elf."

Well, shoot.

"But that's not..." Mike stuttered, each of us trading varied looks of shock and confusion. "He can't be...Can he?"

I wanted to say no, but when Care leaned back against me like she couldn't quite hold herself up anymore, I knew Volund wasn't lying. She would've sensed it if he was.

"What kind of Elf are you?" Caroline whispered. She was anxious about his revelation, but beneath the stress, I sensed a twinge of hope. And I understood it. Care had been the only one of her kind for twenty-two years, and now she'd just discovered that she wasn't alone after all. That she didn't have to carry the burden of her species by herself. And while I liked that she had this sense of hope and possibility, I despised that Volund was the one giving it to her.

Volund didn't answer her question though, smiling wide. And in the blink of an eye, he wasn't Volund anymore.

His face morphed so smoothly that I almost didn't see the change until suddenly I was staring at myself.

"I'll let you guess," he said, my voice coming out of his mouth.

"You're Nephilim." Care was a mixture of awestruck and disturbed as she stared at Volund, but I was just disturbed. The guy was wearing my face like this was *Mission Impossible.*

"And you're part Nephilim," Volund nodded, casually dropping another bomb about his knowledge of Caroline.

She stilled against me, unnerved, and gave him a murderous look. He visibly swallowed.

"Easy there, I'm not going to tell anyone," he said, raising his hands in surrender. "I'd be stupid to out her. All it would do is send people on a hunt for Elves—which would be bad news for me since newsflash: I'm an Elf."

Clint gripped the back of the armchair in front of him like he was preparing to toss it at the Dark Elf—I wouldn't have minded if he had—and stared Volund down. "Alright Mr. Unearned Confidence—"

"Unearned confidence?" Volund demanded incredulously.

Clint ignored him. "How did you even know to watch Caroline? What made you think she might be an Elf?"

"I know a lot of things," Volund said, sporting a knowing smirk that made my blood boil. "I know that Caroline has been outing council members and other Shifter leaders for their bad behavior. I know that Morgan kidnapped her and yet...you two seem much more comfortable with each other than a prisoner and a warden. Caroline, you do know that Stockholm syndrome is real, right? If you need help escaping, blink twice."

If Volund's smirk was unsettling because I didn't know what was driving it, Caroline's was terrifying because I did. "How many times do I have to blink to erase you from the planet?"

"Once," I said, leaning closer to her, my chin brushing her temple as I stared at Volund. "I'll have him gone in one blink if you want it, Red."

"Hm...tempting," Care hummed, her eyes zeroed in on Volund.

"Okay, Fine. I'll behave," he conceded, though since he still rolled his eyes, I took the words with a grain of salt. Thankfully, the doorbell rang before the Dark Elf had a chance to further test my patience.

"Oh look, it's the coroner here to take care of your dead body," I taunted, with a Cheshire cat smile.

"I'll get it," Grey offered, but he paused in the doorway and glanced back at Volund. "You have about ninety seconds to convince him not to kill you. Use it wisely."

Then he disappeared into the hall. Volund stared at the open doors for a moment before turning his eyes to me.

"So, I don't suppose there's anything I can do to get on your good si—"

"No." I shook my head.

Volund narrowed his eyes and studied me for a few beats. "But you're not really going to kill me...Right?"

"Give us a good reason to keep you alive and we'll consider it," Care sassed sweetly.

Volund opened his mouth to speak but was interrupted by a female voice—and it wasn't Caroline's. "Oh Morgan, really, another one?" Merida sighed as she stepped into the room, Grey trailing behind her. "You really need to stop kidnapping people."

"You do have a problem, man," Logan nodded. I glared but he just winked at me.

Meanwhile, Volund shot an arrogant smile at Merida. "I don't mind being kidnapped, so long as beautiful women such as yourself are present."

"No!" I pointed a finger at the Dark Elf. "Don't even think about it. Both women in this room are off limits to you. If you want to keep possession of all your appendages, you won't flirt and you won't stare. Got it?"

Volund pouted and fell back against the couch, silent and sullen. But when I raised an eyebrow at him, he muttered a petulant agreement.

"So, I assume you need another binding," Merida said, crossing her arms.

"Unregistered bindings are illegal, you know," Care teased, referencing the last time I'd called Merida over here to bind someone. At the time, she'd bound Caroline to me so Care couldn't leave the house. How ironic that she now lived here of her own volition.

"And willingly moving in with your captor is a sign that you need professional help, you know," Merida sassed back with a smile.

Caroline laughed. "Touché."

"Alright, so who am I binding and why?"

"He's Nephilim and he knows that Caroline is part Nephilim," Clint explained, not so subtly checking Merida out as he looked her way. Thankfully, he was smart enough not to hit on my only non-Berserker friend though.

"Ah." Merida sighed. "I guess I can see the need for the kidnapping then. What exactly are you thinking for the binding?"

I motioned for her to step into the hall, and Caroline and I followed, leaving Volund in the care of my brothers, Logan and Grey. All of whom took a step closer to him, crossing their arms in unison. The Dark Elf was rolling his eyes when I shut the doors behind us.

"If we just throw him in the dungeon, then we get nothing," I said, turning to the two women. "He's never gonna talk as a prisoner; he's too arrogant."

"Ha!" Care exclaimed, pointing a finger in my face. "You called it a dungeon! I told you it wasn't a basement."

Instead of answering, I kissed the top of her head. Then I let her squirm, smirking when her emotions flashed with nerves and a blush lit her face.

"So, then what do you want me to do?" Merida asked. "Bind him to you like I did to Caroline?"

"No, I don't trust him like I trusted Care. But we need him to think we're giving him a chance to earn our trust. Let's bind him to the house so he can't leave, that way we can let him roam like a guest. Hopefully, he'll get comfortable and spout some bit of truth by accident. I don't think he's a psychotic murderer, and he did save us today, but he's hiding things and I don't like it."

"I agree," Care nodded. "From what I sensed, he wasn't lying about anything, but he's definitely hiding something."

"Which brings me to my next request." I turned pleading eyes to Merida. "How're your emotions today?"

She eyed me skeptically, blue eyes narrowed, and lips pursed. "I had a meeting with the other Witch houses this morning and they treated me with the same condescension and dismissal they usually do, so I'm a little irritated...Why?"

"I'm wondering if you can manage both a binding and a curse."

Merida seemed to mull it over, looking from me to Care. Then finally, she nodded. "What did you have in mind?"

Relieved, I quickly made my request. "I'd like you to curse him so that he can never hurt Caroline."

"What?" Care demanded. "If we're going to curse him, we should be clever about it. Curse him to always tell the truth or keep him from ever betraying us. We can't waste this opportunity on me, Morgan."

Taking a step forward, I met Care toe to toe. Her green eyes widened but she didn't budge, meeting my stubborn will with a fierce one of her own.

And that right there was what she didn't understand.

"I'm not wasting anything, Red," I whispered sternly. "If Volund lies, I'll find the truth. If he betrays us, I'll hunt him down. But if he hurts you or kills you...I don't have a solution for that." At the thought of losing her, my voice trembled. She might have thought this curse was an unnecessary precaution, but that was only because she didn't realize what she meant to me yet. "Let me do this. Please."

Caroline watched me silently, her empathy and affection outshining her frustration. "Fine," she groaned. "We'll do it your way—but only because I suspect that whatever Volund's planning has to do with me. I'm not just giving into you because you pouted. You're cute, but you're not that cute."

I smirked and kissed her cheek. "I knew you liked me." Caroline blushed, sputtering as we returned to the office.

"Alright," Merida said, flipping her dark ponytail over her shoulder as she waltzed up to the couch, "Here's the deal. I'm going to bind you to this house, which means that you can't leave—not so much as a fingertip. Then I'm going to curse you—which works for me because I've got some frustrations to let out."

"What will the curse do?" Volund asked calmly, seemingly not alarmed by the threat of being bound to our house for the foreseeable future.

This was a question I was happy to answer. "It will keep you from ever harming Caroline."

"I mean, it's all a little unnecessary," the Dark Elf shrugged. "I've never planned to hurt her, but I get it. Until you can trust me, I'm a threat. So go ahead and bind and curse or whatever."

No sooner had he finished his sentence than Merida latched a hand onto Volund's arm, her other hand tracing invisible patterns through the air. Within seconds, her appearance shifted, her thick black hair changing to a glowing pearly white, her eyes turning from blue to an inhuman shade of gold. And then her skin began to shimmer, becoming slightly translucent as she seemed to glow from the inside out.

"I don't think I'll ever get used to this," Care said, waving her hand at Merida.

"Me neither," Clint replied absently, his eyes a little unfocused as he stared at my friend with a lovestruck expression.

"I want to know if there's any females under forty that you wouldn't moon over," Mike teased, smacking the back of Clint's head.

"No." Logan shook his head. "He's too desperate for attention to turn anyone down."

"Ha ha," Clint complained, rubbing his head. "You laugh now, but I'm the only one here who's never lonely on the weekends."

Mike rolled his eyes. "You're also afraid of silence, so I'm not sure you're the best measure of success, bro."

Clint stuck out his tongue and I gladly turned my attention away from my adolescent brothers and back to Merida and Volund. I couldn't tell if Merida was still working on the binding or if she had moved on to the curse.

As I watched her draw the invisible design, part of me wanted to know what loophole she'd woven into the curse. All curses required one, and Witches usually chose something that the person being cursed would never do.

I could only hope Merida chose something too humbling for an arrogant man like Volund to willingly do.

When she finally finished, her appearance shifted back to normal, and I clapped her gently on the shoulder as she stepped away from Volund. "Thank you so much. I owe you one."

"Please," she scoffed, "You owe me like fifty. But that's okay because I'm keeping a running tab. And someday, I'll come to collect."

I chuckled, but my good humor vanished when Volund opened his big mouth. "So, what's the deal now? Do I get a room or just the couch? Because I'm a fan of spreading out and this room isn't all that big. Also, what are the rules about going outside? Because I may be a Dark Elf, but I'm pretty pale and I like to get a good tan, so I'm gonna need access to some sunlight."

Feeling well past my window of tolerance where Volund was concerned, I stepped so close to him where he sat on the couch that he had to crane his neck to look up at me.

"The deal," I hissed, "Is that you're under house arrest. We don't know you; we don't trust you. And until we do, you'll be bound to this house. So, I'd recommend you start being more forthcoming—and quickly. Your usefulness determines your freedom, and right now you're just a pain in the backside. Now get out of my office and find an empty room upstairs to 'spread out' in."

Volund smirked at me before standing and heading for the door. Then he winked at us over his shoulder. "You got it, roomie."

Anger made my body go hot, the rage only barely cooled by the touch of Care's hand on my arm. "I already hate him," I grumbled. And something told me that wasn't going to change anytime soon.

Chapter 10

CAROLINE

*G*ood *news Miss. Birch,*

The sale has officially closed, and your house has been sold! Congratula-
tions!

-Harry Hamilton

I sighed at the email from my realtor, not sure if I should be jumping up and
down or sighing with disappointment. Despite the fact that my old house had
been a little bit of a fixer upper, with a screen door that never stayed closed and AC
that didn't work, I was still going to miss the place. I would miss Mr. Finch and
the big window in the back where the hummingbirds hung out and the kitchen
drawers that never closed all the way. It hadn't been much of a home, but it had
been mine and I would miss that.

Not in the mood for a pity party, I closed my laptop and stretched out on my
bed. Daisy Mae sighed beside me, and I absently petted her as I pulled out my
phone to facetime my sister.

"Please tell me you're calling me to announce that you and Beast Boy have
finally given into your heart's desires and made out," Ariel begged dramatically
in leu of a greeting. She was sitting in front of her office wall, which was decorated

with illustrations from comic books, *Lord of the Rings*, and a bunch of other geeky things that I couldn't identify.

"Do you ever do any actual work?" I asked, instead of answering her question.

"Yes. In fact, I just finished an entire project and sent it off to my boss, so I have the rest of the day to do whatever I want." She smiled mischievously and I groaned. "Oh, shut up, it's my job as the big sister to annoy my baby sister."

"You're older by eight days. That hardly makes you my big sister."

"Oh, just humor me. Now what's wrong Care? You sound off."

I sighed and leaned back against the headboard. "I sold the house."

Ariel was quiet, her blue eyes watching me. Between her glasses, her short curly blonde hair and her small stature, she gave off a very innocent and unassuming vibe. But I knew better. My sister was stubborn and too inquisitive for her own good. If it hadn't been for her aversion to violence, she totally could've made it as a C.I.A. agent.

"Well," I complained after a few moments of silence, "Say something."

"Why does it bother you so much that you sold the house?"

I shrugged. "It doesn't."

"It does."

"It doesn't."

"Caroline Felicity Birch," Ariel commanded, pointing a finger at me, "Answer the question. Why does it bother you that you sold the house? You have a new home with Morgan and the guys, so why are you upset to get rid of your old one?"

"I don't know," I whined, rubbing the tension from my forehead. "I guess because even though my house wasn't a home, it was mine and I knew where I stood. But here at Morgan's house, I don't really know what I am. Am I a guest? A renter? A friend? What is my place is here?"

"Oh Care..." Ariel sighed; blue eyes filled with empathy. "Your place is with Morgan."

I rolled my eyes and willed the blush to leave my cheeks. Thank the Lord, I was the one who could sense Morgan's feelings and not the other way around.

Otherwise, he would be wondering why I was so hot and bothered. "Morgan and I are just friends."

"I hate to ruin this delusional world you're living in, but guys don't ask girls to move in with them out of a sense of friendship. They also don't take on a woman's problems and put her needs first if they're 'just friends'."

I ignored Ariel's jab, not interested in hashing out my very new and very confusing feelings for Morgan with my sister. I barely knew how I felt, I wasn't about to vocalize it to anyone else. Especially not Ariel. She'd be *way* too excited to find out that my feelings for Morgan weren't one hundred percent platonic.

"So, are you lonely without me?" I asked in a pathetic attempt to change the subject.

Ariel opened her mouth—to tease me, I was sure—but then snapped it shut as her eyes focused on something beyond the camera.

"What?" she whisper-yelled to someone off screen. "Yes, you don't have to ask me."

I could vaguely make out the sound of someone whispering back to her, but I couldn't quite hear who it was.

"Oh, for crying out loud—" Ariel froze and turned wide eyes back to me. As if she'd almost said the name of whoever it was she was talking to. *Interesting...* "Um, sis, I gotta go. The uh...housekeeper needs some help."

"Housekeeper? Since when do you have a housekeeper?"

"Uh, it's pretty recent. Hence why they need some help," she mumbled, eyes flicking from me, back to whoever else was in the room with her. "Okay, I really have to go now. I love you sis. And remember, if you decide to man up and kiss Morgan, you have to give me details! It's my sisterly right. Okay, bye!"

She hung up before I could say a word, and I sat there, certain I'd been lied to but unable to do anything about it since my sister was too far away to corner, and I couldn't risk going to her house right now.

"Well, that wasn't as comforting as I'd hoped," I sighed, shoving my phone into the pocket of my sweatshirt. Daisy lifted her head to look up at me and I scratched her chin. "Yeah, Aunt Ariel loves to stir the pot and then run away laughing. But don't worry. We'll get her back for it. For now, let's go find a distraction."

Anything to keep my mind from circulating on my weird and inconvenient interest in Morgan. *Because when all else fails, ignore your feelings until they go away.* Now whether or not that worked was another story ...

Daisy and I wandered down the hall, hoping one of the boys was nearby for me to bug. I sensed Morgan in his room and pointedly ignored the fact that he was the only person I could identify by emotions without even trying.

Weeks ago, when I'd asked him why he was the only person I could sense no matter the distance, he'd insinuated that I would be embarrassed by the answer. *Maybe he clocked my interest in him before even I did?* I shook my head. Lord, I hoped not.

Only one bedroom door was open as I strolled, and I gravitated toward it, hoping for company. The room was similar to mine, but where I'd added personal touches and my own décor, this room was rustic and masculine just like the rest of the house.

"How's the unpacking going?" I asked, leaning against the door frame.

Startled, Volund nearly fell over where he'd crouched in front of a duffle bag on the floor. I covered a grin with my hand and feigned a yawn.

"Laughing at my misery, are you?" he complained as he stood. "Rude."

"Such a drama queen. You're staying in a mansion, that's hardly misery."

"It is when your idiot friends only packed me *one bag* of clothes." Volund scoffed and shoved his dark hair from his face in a move that seemed way too practiced. "Thanks to them, I only have a week's worth of clothes and a very limited variety of pieces. I can't just re-wear the same outfits for however long I'm stuck here."

I really wanted to give him a hard time, but the truth was that I also highly valued my wardrobe. "I could probably persuade them to go get some more clothes for you."

Volund narrowed his dark eyes at me and crossed his arms. "In exchange for..."

"Some honesty. I have three questions and I want you to answer them honestly."

Volund rolled his eyes and watched as Daisy trotted through the room, sniffing as she went. I could have warned him of her...temperamental attitude. But it was much more fun to watch him ignorantly try to pet her only to have her snip at him.

"What a lovely demon dog you have there," he said dryly, holding his hands close to his chest where Daisy couldn't reach.

"Oh, come on, Daisy's an angel. She just needs a chance to warm up to you."

Volund shot me a side eyed look. "More like she's looking for an opening to destroy me. Does everyone in this house have violent tendencies?"

"Yes. So, you should probably agree to my deal and answer my questions. Because I'm your only shot at filling out your wardrobe."

"You're a conniving thing, cousin," Volund smirked.

"Cousin? Wait, are we—"

"Related? Somewhere down the bloodline I'm sure we are. But we're not closely related. I just like the way 'cousin' sounds."

For some reason, his answer had me feeling heavy and...disappointed. For a moment, I'd let myself imagine that my birth family wasn't completely gone. That I wasn't alone in the world as an Elf. And while Volund might be a Nephilim, that wasn't the same as family.

"So does that count as one of your questions?" he asked, reaching for his duffle bag again.

"Of course not," I said. "Does this mean we have a deal?"

Volund sighed and pulled out a hastily stashed sweater from his bag. I wasn't surprised to see him flatten it out on the ground and meticulously fold it. "Fine. I have three full size suitcases at my place, and I want all of them filled with clothes and shoes. As a woman of fashion, I think I can trust you not to shortchange me on my wardrobe."

I hated that he was right.

"Alright, now ask your questions so I can get my clothes," he insisted, waving a careless hand in my direction.

If I were anyone else, it wouldn't have done me much good to just ask him for honesty. But being part Alfar meant that I could read his emotions as he answered me. Volund was about to take a polygraph and he didn't even know it.

"First question, how is it possible that you and I exist? Elves were killed off centuries ago."

"I assume you know the story about the fall of the Shifters?" I nodded and Volund continued. "The Alfar ruled all Shifters, and the Nephilim were their military force. That is, until the Alfar King was killed in the 1300's. By a Berserker."

Volund paused and gave me a pointed look. *He's goading me, trying to see just how loyal I am to the Berserkers. To Morgan.*

"That's the story we've been told," I argued, one eyebrow raised to let him know who's side I was on. Morgan's. *Always Morgan's.* "That the Berserker Chief killed the king out of vengeance. Because he was sick of his people being used as fire power to support the military. But you and I both know that it was a Nephilim who caused the king's death."

"Do we?"

"The Nephilim General had been using the Berserkers for illegal attacks and when the Chief reported it to the Alfar King, the Nephilim General tried to kill the Chief. The king stepped in to save him and was killed by accident in the middle of the Berserker's shift into bear form."

Or so Morgan had told me. And I believed him. Partly because he was my best friend, and partly because he'd shown me some old journals that passed down the story from generation to generation.

Volund smiled and I tried not to let it make me uneasy. "There's one piece of the story you're missing though," he said. "The Alfar Queen saw her husband killed and knew that the General would be after her and her children next. With the Alfar line out of the way, the General would be able to rule with as much violence and authority as he liked. So, the queen sent each of her children off with a spy to protect them. And much like the Romanoff's, only one of the children and their spy got away. Never to be seen again."

"And that's where I come from," I hummed, considering his words.

"That's the legend, anyway. I've seen an old journal entry that's supposedly from the surviving daughter's great grandson, but as I'm not an archeologist, I couldn't tell you if it was legit or not."

"Do you still have the journal?"

Volund smiled. "Is that one of your questions?"

I sighed and rolled my eyes. "No. But someday, if you feel like bringing our trust to the next level, you could always show me that entry."

"Noted. What's your next question?"

Realizing that he wasn't going to give any information away for free, I let the topic slide.

"What's your story? Where did you come from?"

"California. More specifically, my mother's—"

"Volund," I gritted out, tossing a lighter at him from the mantle of the nearby fireplace. "You know what I meant."

"What is it with you throwing things at me?" he demanded, ducking out of the way of the lighter at the last moment.

"What is it with you always dodging questions with humor?" I retorted.

He studied me for a moment and then raised his hands in surrender. "Touché. And as far as my story goes, it's not exactly like yours," he said, continuing to unpack his bag as Daisy ambled over to me and laid down by my feet. "I knew what I was from the beginning. My parents hid nothing from me, raising me themselves, in society but not really part of it. They had regular jobs, and I was homeschooled, each of us participating in life by brushing against it, but never fully engaging. We mostly kept to ourselves for the sake of safety."

Relief flooded through me at the realization that he understood the burden of having to hide. Of never fully participating in life because you couldn't risk being noticed. And then the shame came in.

I shouldn't have been happy to hear that someone had suffered the way I had. No one deserved to be isolated like that; afraid like that.

And yet I was still relieved to know that someone else understood the feeling.

"My parents were good parents," Volund continued. "They wanted only the best for me...but they passed away when I was eighteen. Car accident."

This time, there was no comfort in our similarities. Because while my birth parents were also dead, I still had my adoptive parents. The parents who'd raised me and loved me all my life. In this I was far richer than Volund.

"I'm sorry," I said quietly, meaning the words despite my distrust.

It doesn't matter what kind of person you are or what you've done, losing family is always hard.

"Don't be," Volund scoffed, but he wasn't fooling me. I sensed the sorrow inside him, buried beneath the arrogance. I knew he was in pain, even if he wanted to pretend otherwise. "I was lucky to have them for as long as I did. They've been gone seven years now, and I've managed to make a life for myself in their absence. Found ways to make my life feel full again. So, save your sorrys for someone who needs them. I'm just fine."

Lie. It was the first one he'd told me so far in this conversation, but given the content, I decided to let it slide. I had no more right to rummage through his private life than he had in mine.

"What's your last question?" he asked, setting his now empty duffle bag aside as he stood.

"How did you know to follow me?"

"I knew to follow you because our parents knew each other."

It took a moment for his words to register in my brain, but once they did, I had to hold the doorframe to keep myself upright.

"Explain." My voice came out in a rasp, the emotions scraping my throat raw.

"Your parents and my parents were both Elves," Volund went on, his tone somewhat sympathetic for once. "They kept in touch, warning each other when rumors about Elves would arise or things seemed dangerous. They weren't close, but they looked out for each other."

"Did you know my parents?"

Volund was silent for a moment. "No. Their correspondence eventually stopped and when my parents looked into it, they found you. But they decided not to interfere. They felt they should respect your parents' decision to give you a normal human life."

"So then why did it take you so long to come forward if you knew about me all this time?" I asked, but there was no feeling behind the words. All I could think was that his parents had known mine. And I was desperate to know why God hadn't given me that same curtesy.

"Because although I knew about your parents, I didn't know about you at first. I only found out about you a few months ago from a letter I found in my parents' things. And I know that you may not believe me, but the only reason I looked for you was to offer you what I'd always wanted."

"What's that?"

"The option to not be alone."

I wanted to call him out for lying, but his emotions were stable. He was telling the truth. About my parents, about his parents, and about his intentions toward me. *But none of it makes sense.* If my parents had known Volund's, then that meant they weren't alone. So then why had they given me up? And if Volund just wanted to be friends, why was he being such a cagey jerk?

"I'm not alone," I said after a moment. Volund might not have been lying, but I still didn't trust him.

"No, I suppose you aren't," he replied thoughtfully. And a thoughtful Volund didn't seem like a good thing. "You have your keepers."

"Friends," I corrected, stepping backward into the hall. "They're called friends, Volund. You should try making some. They'll change your life."

Then, with Daisy at my heels, I slipped down the hall. Like a tether attached to my chest, I followed a nearby feeling of concern down the hall. It tugged at me, leading me to open the door without knocking. I was just realizing where the invisible chord had brought me when the door across from me opened and Morgan walked out.

"Care?" he asked, his deep voice laced with worry. He wore only a pair of sweats, his messy hair damp as steam escaped from the bathroom behind him. And at the sight of him, the tether that had been urging me onward suddenly pulled taut.

"Hey, what's wrong?" he demanded gently, slowly making his way toward me. As if he might scare me away.

And in any other moment I might have run. Might have made an excuse or a joke to break the tension and distract myself from his shirtless physique. But right now, I didn't see a man I was attracted to. I just saw a safe haven.

So, without an explanation, I jogged over, and threw myself into his arms. He caught me easily, his body cocooning me with a safety I'd never felt anywhere else.

"You're okay, Care," he whispered, pressing me close as he murmured in my ear, "I've got you."

"Thank you," I mumbled, annoyed as tears began to trail down my cheeks.

"For what?"

"For just...being here."

He nodded, his chin brushing the top of my head. Then, after a few moments, he gently guided me to the floor, sitting us against the foot of his bed, my legs in his lap and my head on his chest.

"What happened, Red?" he finally asked, his fingers rubbing circles on my shoulder. And although his touch was tender, there was a threat in his voice, a protectiveness in his emotions.

"Nothing," I lied.

"Caroline—"

"I sold my house. I just got the email a little bit ago. It's officially not my home anymore."

He relaxed slightly, apparently assured that there was no immediate threat. "How are you feeling about it?"

I shrugged and snuggled closer, too frazzled for the moment to think about our close proximity or his shirtlessness.

Okay, so maybe I thought about it a little. I mean, his pecs were literally *right under my hand.*

"I'm a little sad," I admitted, getting my brain back on track. "That house meant a lot to me, you know? It was the first thing I ever owned by myself, and for a long time, it was my safe place. I'll miss Mr. Finch and the way the bathroom door never closed right, and the old-fashioned doorknobs—all the little things, you know? But...I'm also glad that I moved."

"Yeah?" he asked. It was only one word, but that one word held so much insecurity that I held him tighter to try and snuff it out.

"Yeah," I said, shifting to look up at him. "I was just telling Ariel that although I loved my old house, it never felt like home. I was never going to host a Superbowl party or invite a friend over to hang out or have Christmas dinner there. I loved that house, but it was never really going to be a home."

"And is this?" he asked, his expression so guarded but for the hope in his eyes. "Is this a place that can be home for you?"

I smiled, my eyes finally dry, and held him tighter. "It already is home for me."

"It is?"

"Yeah, it is."

We stared at each other in the light of the bathroom, and in that silence, my magic homed in on him, his emotions wrapping around us like a security blanket. Affection, protectiveness, contentment, and joy curled around my shoulders, and I felt perfectly at peace.

"So, what else had you so upset?" he asked when I broke eye contact, shifting to hide my face and the blush that warmed my cheeks and ears.

"Who says there was anything else?" I evaded, absently picking at the chord of my sweatshirt.

"Care," Mor warned.

"Fine. I was also a little rattled by Volund."

"What did that imp do? If he hurt you—"

I looked up and set a hand on Morgan's cheek, bringing his attention back to me. "I'm fine. You had Merida curse him, remember? He couldn't hurt me if he wanted to."

"Who knows, maybe he found the loophole—"

"He didn't," I argued, sliding my hand down to grasp his chin. "Merida wouldn't make the loophole that easy to guess or accomplish. So, don't worry, Volund is still cursed; he didn't hurt me. He just...He said his parents knew my parents, and it kind of caught me off guard."

Morgan's expression morphed from fierce protectiveness into gentle concern, and he brushed his fingers along my temple, pushing my hair back. "Care, I'm sorry. That can't be easy to hear," he breathed, holding me tighter. "Did he say how they knew each other?"

"Yeah. He said that because they were all Elves, they kept in contact and warned each other of potential threats. Apparently Volund didn't know my parents had a child until he found a letter from his parents a few months ago—they passed away a few years back. He said that when his parents discovered that I existed, they decided to leave me where I was out of respect for my birth parent's wishes."

Morgan was quiet for a moment and despite my desperate need to hear his thoughts, I let him be. He needed more time to mull things over than I did.

"Do you believe him?" he asked after a few beats.

"I don't have a choice. He wasn't lying, Mor. His parents knew my parents and Volund sought me out because he didn't want me to be alone."

"But is that the whole truth, or do think he's omitting something?"

I thought about it, replaying Volund's reactions to my questions and his careful words. I believed he was telling the truth...but was it the whole truth?

"I think there's some other reason he came out of the woodwork other than to just befriend me," I said, the wheels in my mind turning. "But I'm not sure about my parents. Part of me wonders why my parents gave me up if they knew they weren't alone in the world."

"Unless they didn't trust the other Elves," Morgan nodded, empathy pouring out of him at the realization that Volund's family and mine might have been more than just frenemies. "You think they might be the reason your parents are dead?"

"I'm afraid that it's possible," I whispered, grateful when he took my shaking hand in his. "I'm afraid that after all this time of hoping that they died in a car accident on their way back to me, that the truth will be much more brutal. That maybe their deaths weren't accidents at all."

And as if my eyes were on a timer, tears began to cloud my vision again. I wasn't so subtle about it this time, blubbering against Morgan's bare chest. But he didn't complain that I was using him like a human tissue. Instead, he rubbed my back and whispered sweet assurances in my ear.

"I don't know what happened to your parents, Red," Mor crooned, rocking me gently. "But I do know that it's pointless to turn suspicions into facts, because you only end up hurting yourself. Right now, we can only speculate what happened. So, for the time being, we're going to go on believing that your parents' passing was an accident. But there are two things we know for sure."

"What?"

"One, that your birth parents loved you very much. All they wanted was for you to be safe and *happy*. That's why they named you Caroline Felicity. They wanted your life to be bright and full, and only a good parent wishes that for their kid."

"And number two?" I asked, my voice small and insecure.

"That you have a family that loves you," he said, leaning down to swipe the tears from my cheeks. "Your adoptive parents consider you their own and so does your sister. You know they'd go to the ends of the earth for you. And you have this family too. Clint, Mike, Logan and Grey. Even Wallace sees you as a long-lost daughter."

It didn't escape my notice that he'd omitted himself from this list. Unsure what that meant, I met his gaze. "And you?"

"Me?" he smiled, his hand sliding along my jaw. "You will *always* have me, Caroline Felicity Birch. No matter what we find out about your parents or what

Volund does or who tries to come after us, I will always be here for you. I swear it."

And there, in the back of my mind, I saw a version of myself, young and scared, begin to smile. The little girl who wasn't free to have friends or relationships without the burden of secrets. The little girl who'd never had a friend that wasn't family. The little girl who'd never felt accepted, never felt safe. For the first time, she basked in the feeling of being chosen. Of not being alone.

And it felt good.

.

Chapter 11

CAROLINE

"Pringle?"

Morgan glared at me from the driver's seat, and I grinned, munching on another chip. We were driving to west Shifter Haven to Volund's apartment. It was the first time the two of us had been on a mission together in a while and I was feeling nostalgic.

"Haven't we done this before?" He asked in his usual grumble.

"Yes, but you've changed your tune on other things, why not this?"

Mor's eyes widened and a sense of anxiousness came over him. Curious, I turned in the passenger seat and watched him. Morgan was rarely ever rattled, and I wasn't about to pass up an opportunity to watch the show.

"What have I changed my tune on? I still abhor your junk food, even if I'm too whipped to deny buying it for you." I narrowed my eyes at him but didn't reply. "What? Why are you looking at me like that?"

"Because you seem guilty and I'm trying to figure out why."

"I'm not guilty." Morgan shrugged, snatched a chip from my hand and fed it to Daisy, who popped her head up from the back seat. "See? Daisy agrees."

"Daisy agrees to anything if food is involved."

"So do you."

I smacked his arm, a wide grin on my face. Morgan chuckled, and just as I was pulling my arm back, he grabbed my hand. Like a deer seeing headlights, I froze, watching him settle our conjoined hands on his thigh.

Morgan was serene and at ease, like the move was so natural it was mindless. Meanwhile, my heart was pounding out a rhythm so fast it could've kept tempo for one of those Irish stepdance songs.

Morgan is holding my hand. His skin is so soft. Why do callouses feel so nice on a man's hands? Does he like the feel of my hands? Why is he holding my hand? Oh no, can he tell that I like him? Am I sweating? Will that give it away?

On and on my thoughts went, spiraling out of control. For real though, I was pretty sure my palm was sweating.

"Relax, Red," Mor crooned, shooting me an easy smile.

"Who says I'm not relaxed?" I quipped, doing my best to appear aloof.

"My fingers. I think you're about to break them."

Embarrassed, I immediately loosened my grip. "Sorry. I'm just not used to...physical affection." The part that I didn't say was that I didn't think people usually gave this *kind* of physical affection to friends. *Last time I checked, friends don't hold friends' hands, Mr. Touchy Feely.*

"Sorry. Does it make you uncomfortable?" Morgan asked, briefly turning a worried look on me.

All it took was his sweet nerves to boost my confidence. I squeezed his hand and relaxed into my seat. "No. It doesn't bother me, Mor."

Morgan smiled, a sweet, small smirk and I tucked the memory away for later.

"Good. Because I'm a fan of physical affection," he said, flicking on his blinker as we turned down another street.

"Really? Because I never see you so much as hug your brothers."

"Well...that's different. You and I both know that a sibling relationship is just as antagonistic as it is friendly."

"Uh huh..."

"What?"

I shrugged as he pulled into the apartment complex parking lot. "Nothing. It's just interesting."

"What's interesting?"

He parked in front of the correct unit and turned the car off. Then he turned and scowled at me. If he weren't so handsome and I weren't having so much fun teasing him, I might've been scared.

"That you don't hug your brothers or your best friend," I said opening my door to the July heat. "Or bend to their whims when they want something or remind them how much they mean to you all the time."

"They're guys," was Morgan's only defense.

"Yet you touch me all the time, you buy my junk food, take me to Frank's, and you're constantly slipping in a comment about how much you care about me. So, I think," I teased, smiling mischievously at him, "That I'm special."

And while he sat there blushing, I slipped from the car, letting Daisy out behind me. I had her leashed and ready, a red 'careful, I bite' vest secured around her when Morgan finally exited the SUV.

"Care," he said, meeting me on the sidewalk. I paused and looked at him, noting the confident light in his eyes. "You are special."

Then he slung an arm around my shoulders and pulled me into his side. Now it was my turn to blush. I was pretty sure he was teasing me as revenge for my taunting, but the butterflies in my belly didn't think so. Nor did the tingle on my shoulder where his fingers brushed my bare skin.

"Do you want me to hold the door?" Mor and I both turned to see a UPS delivery man standing at the front of the building, holding one of the glass doors open. Because of course Volund's apartment wasn't the kind of place where you walked up some outside stairs to get to your front door. Oh no, this place was fancy, with glass double doors that led into a small seating area. And instead of stairs that were out in the weather, the place had a pair of elevators.

"Why am I not surprised?" I said, looking around at the building as we stepped inside.

Mor thanked the delivery man and walked toward the elevators, his arm still over my shoulder. "What, that Volund's apartment is bougie? Because although we've only known him a day, it's clear that he needs the biggest apartment possible to fit his ego."

"So, what does that say about you and your big mansion?" I teased him, Daisy following behind us into the elevator.

"That I'm generous, obviously. I live in a mansion with five other people. Big difference."

"True, but lately it feels more like you live with four people. I hardly see Logan at all anymore."

Suddenly Morgan's arm tensed around my shoulders. When I looked up at him, his eyes were trained forward, though he worked his jaw back and forth.

"What?" I demanded, sensing a lie. Not because I could feel his emotions, but simply because I knew Morgan. He was hiding something.

"Hm? Nothing," Mor scoffed. But when I continued to stare at him, he caved. "Okay, fine. Logan is on a mission..."

"And? What's so secretive about it that you can't tell me?"

"It's not that I *can't* tell you."

Immediately a little annoyed, I stepped out of his embrace and crossed my arms. "You don't *want* to tell me?"

Morgan quickly shook his head and turned toward me. With his hands on my shoulders, and my back against the wall, he had a captive audience. Although I probably would've been compelled to listen anyway with his grey eyes so sincere and annoyingly earnest.

"No, it's not that I don't want to tell you," he assured me. "It's just that I'm not sure what you'll think. I don't want to give you reason to be afraid."

"Afraid of what? Morgan, I'm confused."

"Logan is on a mission right now," he sighed. "He's serving as a bodyguard. I've never asked him to do it before, but I wanted to make sure I was protecting you. Not just you physically, but the people who matter to you."

And then I remembered Ariel's facetime. The way she seemed to be talking to someone off screen. *A housekeeper my foot.* "Logan is bodyguarding my sister?" I demanded.

"Yeah."

"Yeah? That's all you have to say? How long have you been keeping this from me?"

"Since we took down Eileen."

My jaw dropped and I glared at him with wide eyes. He'd been *lying* to me for weeks!

"Care," he pleaded, moving closer, "I didn't keep it from you to be mean or because I don't trust you. I did it because I was afraid that if you knew I was having your sister guarded, you would think she was in danger."

"Well, isn't she?" I shouted.

"No! Well...yes. Not immediate danger. I don't have any reason to believe that someone's after her or anything. I'm just taking precautions since we still don't know who wanted to buy you from Eileen or how they knew about you. I was protecting her for you." At this, I felt myself soften against my better judgment. Morgan must have realized it, because he came closer still, his hands trailing down to uncross my arms. When he tangled his fingers with mine, I pretty much melted. *So much for being in control.*

"I'm sorry I didn't tell you sooner," he whispered. Somewhere in the back of my mind, I heard the elevator doors opening, but Morgan held too much of my attention to fully register it. "That was wrong. But I really just didn't want to scare you, Red."

"No," I pouted. "No calling me Red."

"Why?"

"Because it does things—" I froze when I realized what I'd said, what I'd insinuated. And judging by the look on Morgan's face, he'd realized it too.

"It does what...Red?"

Was he getting closer? Or was that in my head? I could have sworn his lips were within kissing distance, but a ding broke me out of the trance.

"Oh my," someone said as if scandalized. I turned and saw a pair of older ladies standing in front of the open elevator doors, watching Mor and I with wide eyes and conniving smiles. "Look what we've stumbled on, Irene."

"A clandestine meeting," Irene replied with a giggle. "Maybe we should press all the buttons and close the doors for them so they can have some privacy to finish whatever it is they started."

"Are you kidding?" the other woman exclaimed. "Forget helping the little miss get a good old-fashioned snog in the elevator, I want answers!"

Then, she dragged Irene into the elevator with her and stared at Morgan and I with unabashed curiosity. "So, what's the situation?" she asked, motioning between us.

"Esther," Irene admonished her, swatting Esther's arm. "Leave them be. Just because it's been a long time since we had a good snogging doesn't mean we should ruin theirs."

"Oh, pish posh. Their moment is ruined."

Irene shrugged and turned her bright green eyes on us. "She's not wrong. So, what's the story? Is this your first kiss or just a stolen moment between newlyweds? Better yet, do you happen to have a grandfather who's single?" This she directed at Morgan.

"Oh, maybe the grandpa has a twin," Esther added excitedly.

Glad that the topic had shifted from...whatever moment Mor and I had been having, I slipped away from him toward the elevator doors.

"I don't have a grandfather," Morgan explained with a kind smile.

"Oh, you poor thing," Esther tsked, patting his cheek.

"But I do have a foster father who's probably around your age."

Both women giggled and tittered about the possibility of meeting a man with Morgan's looks in their age range. I didn't think it had yet occurred to them that a foster father wouldn't share Morgan's gene pool.

"You give him those phone numbers," Esther commanded Mor after scribbling their numbers on a notepad from Irene's purse.

"Yes, and ask him if he has any handsome friends," Irene added, eyes sparkling with mirth.

Mor blushed as he exited the elevator, but quickly scowled when he caught me grinning. "What?" he snapped, leading the way down the hall.

"You have a fan club," I laughed, following beside him. "They *loved* you."

"I'm pretty sure they also had no idea who I am, so that helps."

That comment sobered me right up. Latching onto his arm, I tugged him to a stop.

"Hey, don't do that. Who you are cannot be reduced to rumors and gossip. You're handsome, powerful, humble, kind and protective. People don't have to know you to realize it and they don't have to be convinced of it. You show it every time you just be yourself."

He stared at me for a few moments, his gaze intent and searching. Support, affirmation, safety, I wasn't sure what he was looking for, but I hoped he found it.

"Thank you," he whispered, leaning down to kiss my forehead, "Red."

Then, with a smirk, he left me sputtering as he continued down the hall.

"Wha—He just...But I...*Well.*" Blushing and unsure what to think, I chased after Morgan—who had the gall to laugh. "Which door is it?" I growled, looking at the apartment doors with their gold numbers instead of at Morgan's smug face.

"This one," Mor replied. Then he kissed my temple and turned to the nearest apartment.

"Stop doing that," I complained, trying not to look as frazzled as I felt.

"Why? You don't like it?"

"No, I do, I just—" *Shoot.* I flicked my eyes up at him and when he smiled, I snatched the key out of his hand and unlocked the door. "Forget I said that."

"So not happening."

Beet red, irritated and clearly losing control over my tongue, I let go of Daisy's leash and stepped into the entryway. "Dais, do me a favor and go pee on something expensive."

Wagging her tail, my fur child quickly leapt into action and started investigating the space. The apartment was—no surprise—very fancy. With nice brass fixtures, polished wood floors and new appliances, I was beginning to wonder how our Dark Elf friend footed the bill for all of this.

"How much do you think rent costs for a place like this?" I asked, making my way through the living area to the bedroom.

"Probably triple the average," Mor replied, following behind me.

"They probably demand your first born too."

"Which means you can't rent an apartment here."

I glanced at Morgan as I began searching for Volund's suitcases. "Why not? Because I couldn't afford to keep up my clothing addiction and pay my rent?"

"No." Morgan shrugged and began snooping around the room. "Because you already promised your first born to me."

If I'd been drinking, this was the part where I would've choked. As it was, I just tripped over nothing and grasped the bedpost to keep myself upright.

"Come again?"

"That's what she said," he quipped, not even looking up from the desk he was rummaging through. "When I got you a cinnamon roll for breakfast a few weeks ago, you said that you'd give me anything, even your first-born child, if I treated you like that every day."

I stared at him, thinking back to that morning. "Shoot, I did say that."

"Yep, you did."

I glared at his back. "Shut up and search, Bear Man."

Leaving him to his rummaging, I found Volund's suitcases under his bed and went to his closet. No surprise, he had a *lot* of clothes. Maybe even more than me. Of course, his were mostly in black, grey, and other muted, basic shades.

"So, was this why you made a deal with him to get his clothes?" Mor called from the bedroom. "You wanted the opportunity to search his place?"

"I mean technically, it wouldn't have been hard for me to sneak in here. But it did seem like a much more convenient way to do it. Plus, this way whatever we find, I can show him to his face...I also have to respect a man who loves clothes as much as I do."

"Of course, you do," Mor snorted. "So, what exactly am I looking for?"

"That journal he mentioned. He says it was written by the Alfar King's great great great great grandchild—or however many greats it is. Also, if you find anything I can tease him about later, that would be fabulous."

While he snooped around, I worked on packing clothes—and shoes, per Volund's request—into one of the suitcases I'd found. The man had a ton of shoes. Combat boots, tennis shoes, work boots. And of course, he had them all in multiple shades of black and various other 'I'm too dark for the rest of the world' colors. Clearly, he felt the need to prove a point. Although, as a woman who'd found her style by dressing to shock other people, I couldn't really judge him.

"So, who has more clothes, you or him?" Mor called out.

"Hm...Maybe him. He has me beat with tops anyway. But I also have dresses and skirts and I definitely have more shoes than him."

"And that's not including your accessories."

"Hey, are you hating on my accessories?" I argued, popping my head back into the bedroom so I could glare at him properly.

Morgan stepped away from the built in shelves he'd been inspecting and came over to me. "Of course not. I like your ribbons." He trailed his fingers over the ribbon I'd tied to the end of my side braid. "They tell me what mood you're in."

"Oh, do they?"

"Yeah. Like today, you chose mint."

"And what does that mean?"

"That you're feeling feisty but happy. Pink is mischievous. Green is feisty. Bright colors mean you're happy, dark ones mean you're feeling a little negative. And black is either for days when you hate everyone, or for stakeouts."

I stared at him, dumbfounded. That he knew each ribbon meant something different wasn't surprising, but the fact that he knew what every color stood for was...touching.

"I'm impressed," I said as he moved over to the nightstand. "I knew you paid attention, but I didn't know you paid that much attention."

"Only to you," he said offhandedly, picking up a book from the table.

I opened my mouth to ask what that meant—what a lot of the things he'd said so far today meant—but he held up the book for me to see.

"*How to Win Friends and Influence People*?" he said, reading the title. With eyebrows raised, he turned the book over and read from the back. "From the fundamental techniques in handling people to the various ways to make them like you, this book offers insights on how to win people to your way of thinking…"

"There's no way he's read that," I said, thinking back to the few—but unpleasant—encounters I'd had with Volund. "If he had, he wouldn't be so insufferable."

"Volund, you could use this," Morgan read, showing me an inscription written in the front of the book, "Signed 'Dave'. Apparently, Dave agrees with us."

I laughed and Morgan set the book back on the end table. As he turned on the reading lamp above the bed, Daisy trotted into the room, a half-eaten granola bar in her mouth. Somehow, I had a feeling that she probably had the wrapper somewhere in her system. How did I know that? Because Daisy Mae had a habit of stealing food and eating the wrappers when unsupervised snacks were within her reach. The girl was a garbage disposal.

"You are going to be so sick later," I said, crouching down to pet her, "And it's your own dang fault. No, don't lick me with that nasty tongue. I love you, but you're disgusting."

"Care…"

I looked over to see Morgan pulling something out from behind the headboard. In his hands was an old leather journal.

"Oh my gosh," I mumbled, rising to stand beside him. "Is this it?"

"I think so," he said, carefully unwrapping the leather chord that held the journal shut. The pages crinkled as he opened it, their rough brown surface aged and faded. The script was old, and the wording was definitely from another time. As we skimmed the pages, nothing revealing presented itself beyond what Volund had already told me.

"The question is," Morgan said, handing me the journal, "Is it legit?"

"How do we find out?"

"I think I know someone we can trust to verify it."

I nodded, studying the words of someone long gone as Morgan disappeared into the closet. When he came out a moment later, grunting, I glanced up.

"My gosh, how much stuff is in here?" he said, carrying one of the larger suitcases.

"A lot. Although I'm not sure who brought more to your house, him or me."

"You know," Mor hummed, watching me with a bit of mischief running through him, "I'm beginning to wonder if Volund is just a male version of you."

I gaped at him, personally offended. "*Excuse me?*"

"Seriously," he shrugged, moving toward the living room. "You're both obsessed with clothes, you're both snarky as can be, both a little hostile at first. It's like you're the same person."

Angry at the implication that I had anything other than a love of style in common with Volund, I marched after Morgan, seething. "I am *nothing* like him. We aren't even remotely alike..."

But then I remembered my arrogant, glib attitude when I'd first met Morgan and Volund's similar attitude today. Then there was his secretive attitude...*Oh my gosh,* am *I like Volund?*

"Morgan, please take it back and tell me I'm nothing like that annoying Dark Elf," I demanded, following him through the apartment. But he just laughed. "*Morgan!*"

Chapter 12

MORGAN

"Wow, that's a big house."

"Yep," I looked up at the stone mansion that dwarfed Care and I where we stood in the big circle driveway. "The houses for Shifter leaders are always excessive. But in our defense, most of these houses are inherited and very old, so we don't exactly get to pick the size."

Winters House, one of four Witch houses in Shifter Haven, loomed above us, big and imposing. Unlike Berserkers, who had one Sleuth and one Chief for a given area, Witches had multiple leaders and houses. Each house had a Headmaster who was in charge of the education and wellbeing of every Witch that belonged to their house. All Witches had to obey the governing of their Headmaster, but they could choose which house they wanted to belong to in their area.

The downside to being a Headmaster though, was that the people who chose to be a part of your house also had the right to live in it with you. And while most people opted not to live in the mansion, a good chunk of them did take advantage of the opportunity to have their kids live there. Which, I imagined, was part of the reason Merida was always a little overwhelmed, being the Headmistress of Winters House.

"You poor thing," Care sassed, giving me a dry look. "How terrible for you to live in a giant log cabin in the forest. You're such a martyr."

"Hey, remember, you're living there too. So, judge all you want, but you're just as privileged as I am now."

"If I were privileged, then you would have gotten me the milkshake that I begged you for on the way here."

Smirking, I snaked a finger through the beltloop of her jeans and tugged her close. She looked good today, wearing a floral top and a pale blue ribbon in her hair. And when I let go of her jeans to slip my arm around her shoulders, she didn't tense or push me away. In fact, she melted into my embrace. Elated by the progress in our relationship, I let myself give into a victorious grin while she was too busy staring at Merida's house to notice.

She's warming up to me. Granted, she may not be consciously thinking about me in romantic terms yet, but her body certainly wasn't opposed to the idea. *I may not have won the war yet, but at least I'm winning this battle.*

"We were too late to stop, and you know it," I pointed out, enjoying ribbing her and the way her green eyes flashed at me in response.

"Yes, but I'd be in a much better mood if you'd fed me," she smirked.

I shook my head but didn't argue with her as we approached the front door. Merida's house, needless to say, was huge. It was three stories of old stone architecture and diamond paned windows. A manicured garden and a perfect little white greenhouse lay on the right, while well-kept landscaping lined the rest of the house. And a forest surrounded the property, coming right up to the edge of the trimmed lawn.

It felt like a miniature magical university, which was perfect for a group of Witches who spent most of their time studying. Since Witches' ability to cast spells relied completely on their knowledge of spell patterns, research and education were a big deal to the Witch community. And it showed.

"Touché my little spy," I teased, lifting a hand to the giant door knocker. "I should know better than to leave you unfed for more than an hour. My mistake."

"You're just lucky you're cute."

"What?" I snapped my head around and stared at her. It was rare that Care complimented my appearance, and at this point in the game, my love-sick brain was dying to read into it.

But before she could answer, the door swung open, and we both turned to see a stranger standing on the other side.

"Who are you and what do you want?" a young woman demanded rudely. She couldn't have been more than twenty, with dark hair that curled to her shoulders and wide brown eyes that were filled with judgment. She had one of those dead pan kind of faces. The ones that seemed completely expressionless except for a constant look of condemnation. Like that grouchy girl from *Parks and Rec.*

"I'm Morgan," I explained, "And this is Caroline. We're here to see Merida. She knew we were coming."

The girl pursed her dark mauve painted lips and trailed her eyes over us. "Merida," she shouted over her shoulder, "Your weird friends are here." Then she turned and walked away, leaving the door open.

"Okay..." Care said, drawing out the word as she watched the girl disappear.

A little unsure, I led us both through the wide doorway. "Mer," I called out skeptically, "We're here when you're ready."

"Have you never been here before? That girl didn't seem to recognize you," Caroline said, already distracted by the interior of the house.

Just like the outside, the place was huge and very old. Although Merida had certainly put her own spin on it. Different metallic wallpapers stretched across what had probably previously been plain grey walls. Antique furniture was upholstered with soft velvets and rich hues. Old rugs were paired with new ones and all the pictures and knickknacks were a mixture of both antiques and new finds. It was a perfect blend of old and new.

"I've been here a few times, but usually Merida answered the door," I explained, smiling as Care ran her hand over the back of a soft purple chair.

"Can I live here?" she asked with a look of wonder on her face.

"Absolutely not." I shook my head. "But if it'll make you happy, you officially have free reign of our house. I'll even give you my debit card so you can decorate it however you want. You can invite Merida to go shopping with you or do whatever DIY projects you have in mind. Paint it, fill it with florals and pinks, I don't care. But I am not willing to give you up, Red."

"All that just to keep me, huh?"

Her smile was small and shy, but her emotions said she was pleased, and my chest went all warm and fuzzy.

"All that and so much more," I whispered, paying close attention to the way her emotions brightened, filled with joy. And maybe a little bit of nerves.

"Careful, Bear Man. I might take advantage of you."

"Please do."

Her green eyes widened, and her jaw went slack. I was fully prepared to see how much more I could get Caroline to soften toward me, but was interrupted as Merida walked in. "Sorry about Mat," her voice came from behind us. I reluctantly turned to face her, silently cursing her terrible timing.

"Mat?" Care asked, unaware of my devious plans to win her heart.

"It's a nickname," Merida said, waving her hand. "Long story."

Care and I both looked Merida over with mirrored expressions of concern. She was wearing a big baggy sweatshirt that had a big yellow stain on the chest, and a pair of ratty sweatpants. A pair of smudged black reading glasses were perched on her nose, and her dark hair was pulled up into the most haphazard messy bun I'd ever seen. Seriously, the thing looked like it could've gotten cable TV.

"Is this a bad time?" I asked, just as someone somewhere in the house let out a scream.

Merida squeezed her eyes shut and took a deep breath before opening them. "No. Believe me, there have been much worse times."

Caroline looked up at me and we shared a look of worry at Merida's less than encouraging words.

"Come on, let's go in my office where we're less likely to be found," Merida suggested, already turning toward a wide hallway with a carved stone archway above it.

"Do you think she meant to say interrupted?" Care whispered as we followed her down the hall.

"Something tells me the answer is no."

Merida finally stopped in front of a set of wooden double doors that were arched in a cathedral-like style. She turned, looking both ways down the hall, and then quickly ushered us inside like we were sneaking out instead of sneaking in. Once we were safely in the room, she shut the door and leaned against it with a sigh.

"Are you..." Care said, watching Merida like she might pass out at any second, "Okay? You seem a little overwhelmed."

"Huh? Yeah." Merida nodded. "It's just been a busy morning. I have more tenants than any other Witch house in the city, and on the weekends there's no other staff to look after them. So, it can just be...a little much. But I'm fine!" she added brightly, smoothing some wild hairs from her face.

I didn't think Caroline was any more convinced than I was that our friend was okay, but we didn't argue when she motioned us further into the room.

The office was large, with tall, vaulted stone ceilings, and an array of diamond paned windows at the far end. A few chairs and a couch sat in front of the windows while a desk and some other odds and ends like filing cabinets and end tables littered the rest of the space. It was of course updated with nice rugs, patterned wallpaper, and an assortment of pictures and a big acrylic calendar hung on the walls. Except for one wall that was filled with floor to ceiling bookshelves, complete with a rolling ladder.

"So," Merida said, plugging in a strand of Christmas lights that zig zagged across the ceiling, "You said you needed me to authenticate something?"

Care nodded and took Volund's journal from her purse as we all sat by the windows, Merida in a sofa chair and Care and I on the couch. But Caroline hesitated to hand the journal to Merida. "Are you sure you're okay?"

Merida scoffed, blue eyes bouncing between us, seeming a little antsy. "Of course, I'm okay. Why wouldn't I be?"

"Because you seem very frazzled...and you have a bit of bacon in your hair," Care said, pointing to one of the rogue chunks of Merida's hair that hadn't been trained into her bun.

Merida grabbed the bit of hair and inspected it. With a defeated sigh, she popped the bit of bacon in her mouth and leaned back against the chair.

"I'm fine, I promise," she pleaded, and for the first time since I'd met her, my friend seemed close to tears. "I'm just a little in over my head right now. My tenants are...a lot. Most of them are adults—just barely—and they don't all get along. So, weekends can be hard when the rest of the staff isn't here. They're good kids, they're just..." As if to punctuate her point, another scream echoed through the house, followed by muffled shouting. "A handful," Merida finished, rubbing her temples.

"Then there's the other Witch houses," she continued in a strained voice. "We work together on our own council to make decisions for our area, but lately I feel like they're just working against me. They don't take any of my ideas seriously—even though they voted me in as the representative for the region. Well, technically all the Witch leaders in the region did that..." She shook her head. "Point is though, I'm okay. I'm tired and stressed, but I'm not dying and no one's in mortal danger. I hope. Sometimes I wonder if these kids won't end up killing each other."

Care shook her head. "You're not okay, Merida. You're exhausted and you need some help. Surely, we can come help you on the weekends. Or send Clint or Mike. There's no reason that you should be dealing with everything alone. And you're always welcome to come to our house when you need a break—you can even use the home gym if you need to let off some steam."

When Caroline looked for my approval, I nodded eagerly. "Of course. We'll have the boys come over next weekend to help with the kids. It'll be a good exercise for them in patience." At this, Caroline smiled. "And then one day this week you should come over. You can hide away in one of the spare rooms or we can even teach you some hand-to-hand combat."

"Really?" Merida blinked wide eyes at us, sounding small and alone.

"Of course," Care assured her, reaching out to grasp Merida's hand. "You're our friend and we've got your back."

Merida nodded, silently losing a battle against tears. When she regained her composure a few moments later, she gave us both a wobbly smile. "Thank you. Both of you. It's nice to have friends."

I smiled at Care and bumped her shoulder with mine. "Yeah, it is."

"Alright, so let me see what it is you need me to authenticate," Merida said with a sniffle, wiping her cheeks dry.

"It's a journal we stole from Volund," Care explained, relinquishing the book to Merida. "He says it's a diary from the Alfar King's descendant. The book chronicles the events of the Elven civil war as told to them by their family. It also details this descendant's experience hiding as an Elf throughout the late fourteenth and early fifteenth centuries. I stayed up all night last night reading it, but I don't know if it's legit or not."

Merida nodded and took the journal to her desk, where she studied it with a magnifying glass, drawing invisible spells over the pages.

"I guess I'm just trying to figure out if the rest of Volund's stories can be trusted." Care shrugged, watching Merida work. "So, I figure if the journal isn't even authentic, then there has to be some kind of dishonesty about everything else he said."

Surprised, I looked over at my mate. I knew she wanted to be sure that the information in the journal was real. But I hadn't realized that she wanted to use it as a way to discount the rest of Volund's story...

This is about her parents. She wanted to prove that Volund's story about his parents knowing hers wasn't true. That somehow, he'd fooled her ability to read emotions and managed to get away with a lie.

Because deep down, Caroline was afraid that if Volund's parents really did know hers, then it was possible—maybe even likely—that they were at fault for her parents' deaths.

Knowing that there was nothing I could say to ease her worries, I reached for Care's hand and laced our fingers together. She looked up at me, unable to hide the anxiety in her eyes despite her forced smile. Needing to show her as much comfort as I could, even if she was going to pretend she didn't need it, I kissed her forehead and whispered, "I got you, Red."

Her lips stretched and her smile became genuine as she squeezed my hand. "I know. Thanks Bear Man."

Even with my comfort, the stress lingered in her chest, but I felt my worry ease some as a ribbon of affection wrapped around the anxiety, bringing with it a comforting warmth. *I can't do much, but at least I can give her that.*

"Well," Merida said, walking back over to us, journal in hand, "I got a good look at it."

"And?" Caroline asked, sitting up straighter.

"It's real."

Care's shoulders slumped, disappointed. And when I wrapped my arm around her and pulled her close, she didn't fight me, didn't even try to be tough. And that worried me more than anything.

Chapter 13

CAROLINE

I watched the TV above the fireplace in Morgan's living room as Angela, Pam and Karen argued over who's Christmas party would be superior. It was one of my favorite episodes of *The Office*.

"I feel like Volund would be Angela, stealing the power cord to the karaoke machine just to be spiteful," I joked, nudging Morgan.

When he didn't respond, I glanced over to find him sound asleep beside me on the couch. When we'd come home from Merida's earlier, he'd insisted that we should unwind and watch TV. And when he suggested that we make some cookie dough to eat while we watch, I knew something was up.

Morgan never ate junk food.

"He did it for me," I whispered to myself, brushing the hair from his forehead.

He mumbled in his sleep and curled closer to me, his hand finding mine on top of the blankets. Our relationship had been getting more...comfortable lately. But tonight, he'd seemed even more affectionate than usual. He kept claiming to be cold, scooting into my personal bubble and tangling our feet together. Eventually, I'd ended up pressed to his side, our legs twined, and all that body heat trapped under a mountain of blankets. *Cold, my foot.*

Morgan clearly knew how upset I was about Volund's parents knowing mine. So, my big Bear Man—the secret softie—had decided to comfort me to death in an effort to help. *I don't hate it.*

But it did bother me how much this knowledge about Volund's parents was getting to me. So what if his parents knew mine? That didn't mean they'd killed them. Sure, it seemed more reasonable that my parents had been killed on purpose than on accident. Two Elves dying by accident just seemed...anticlimactic.

But part of me knew that I was clinging to this story of my parents being murdered because it would give me someone to blame. Someone to be angry at for making me live alone as an Elf. But the truth was that having someone to blame wouldn't erase the hardest years of my life.

Morgan's breath rustled my hair, and I watched him sleep. I had no idea what Volund wasn't telling me or what part of my fears were true. And it didn't really matter, because I'd never get back all the years I'd spent alone and afraid. But I *did* know that I had a man who was willing to eat food he found toxic and sit in a sauna of blankets for five hours just to comfort me. And that felt nice.

Mor was always doing nice things for me, being patient and sacrificing to make me happy. And for once, I wanted to return the favor. So, I carefully slipped my hand from his and headed for the kitchen to make his favorite protein balls.

"Nasty, tasteless protein balls, but whatever," I mumbled, grabbing the recipe book off the counter and flipping to the right page.

The recipe was easy to make and about fifteen minutes later, I was standing in front of the French doors to the backyard, licking the remaining batter from my fingers while the protein balls hardened in the freezer.

"Ugh, that's just disgusting," I complained, glaring at the mixture on my hands. Why anyone would willingly eat such a concoction, I couldn't understand. It tasted like chalky powder and fake vanilla. "Ew."

I turned for a dishtowel, but paused when I thought I saw a flash of movement outside. The world was quiet out in the dark, the moon covered by clouds and the backyard only vaguely illuminated by the solar lights that lined the grass.

With Daisy upstairs asleep in my bed, I felt a little uneasy as I tiptoed toward the door. Everything was silent around me, the TV in the living room paused and everyone else in the house asleep. But as I stared out through the glass panes, nothing happened.

Everything was still and calm.

"Clearly, I need some sleep," I said to myself, turning back toward the kitchen. "I'm a vigilante for crying out loud, I shouldn't be scared of shadows—"

The sound of shattering glass cut me off and made me stumble. Confused, I whipped around and saw that someone had *plowed through the French doors* like a human battering ram.

"What the heck?" I screeched as a man dressed in black stood to his full height. I craned my neck to look up at him; he must have been nearly seven feet tall. And just my luck, he didn't look friendly.

Rattled and not exactly expecting to face off against an intruder, I wasn't prepared when the man launched himself at me. He tackled me to the ground, and I groaned as my spine hit the wood floor. *That's going to bruise.*

With the man's weight pressed against my chest, I couldn't leverage myself free. I might have been training with Morgan and the guys lately, but I wasn't even close to being as strong as my attacker.

But I *was* pretty clever.

Lifting my hands, I pressed my batter coated thumbs into the man's eyes and squeezed as hard as I could. He screamed as the protein ball batter smothered his eyeballs and ripped my hands from his face. As he fell back to the floor, wiping furiously at his eyes, I scrambled to my feet.

Turning toward the kitchen island, I reached for a butcher knife, but paused when out of nowhere, another body joined the fight.

In a blur, Volund threw himself at the attacker and the two of them fell to the floor in a tangled heap.

Shocked and confused, I stared as the two men battled it out. Wrestling against each other, they each tried to gain the upper hand, but couldn't quite manage it.

The attacker would look like he was winning, but then Volund would flip him over and they'd begin to wrestle again.

Finally, the intruder threw his elbow into Volund's head and crawled away from the fight. When he stood, he shifted his attention to me. But I had no interest in being kidnapped. So, I grabbed the butcher knife and pointed it at him.

"Don't," I threatened, legs braced and ready.

The man eyed the knife, then turned as Volund groaned and rose from the floor. Realizing that he wasn't going to get what he came for, the attacker ran out the French doors and disappeared into the night. Volund moved to go after him but paused when I spoke.

"It's too dark to catch him," I said, setting the knife on the counter and finally wiping my nasty fingers on a towel.

Volund nodded and turned to look me over. If I hadn't known any better, I would've thought he was genuinely concerned about me. But no, the worry I felt inside him must have been directed toward himself. "Are you okay?" he asked.

"I'm fine."

"Are you sure—"

"Caroline!" Morgan shouted, cutting Volund off as he raced into the room, eyes wide and panicked. When he clocked the glass all over the floor and me standing there all rumpled and messy, his expression became dark and threatening. "What happened?" he snarled.

I rolled my eyes as he came over and checked me for injuries, his hands skating along my arms and legs. I wisely opted not to tell him that I'd been nicked by a shard of glass on my shoulder. It was a tiny wound, but to Morgan it would be as if I'd been shot.

"I'm fine, Mor," I promised with a sigh, swatting his hands away. "Someone broke through the door and attacked me. But you'll be glad to know that your disgusting protein balls saved the day."

Mor furrowed his eyebrows but didn't ask me to explain. Instead, he spun and turned his carefully contained rage on Volund.

"You," he roared. "Did you have anything to do with this? Answer honestly, because if I find out you plotted to hurt Care, I'll rip your annoying head from your body without even needing to shift!"

"Easy there, Baloo," Volund pleaded, holding up his hands in surrender. His dark hair was messy from the fight and little bits of glass stuck to his black sweatpants. But he didn't seem harmed. For some reason, that comforted me. "I didn't do anything. I came downstairs for a snack and heard glass shatter. When I came to investigate, someone was attacking Caroline, so I stepped in to help. I didn't have anything to do with the attack and I have no intention of ever hurting Caroline."

"It's true, Mor," I said stepping in front of the furious Berserker Chief before he lost it. "He saved me. He's not lying, I'm sure of it." He was telling the truth and really had nothing to do with the attack—even if Morgan would have loved to blame him for it.

"You," Morgan barked, pointing at Volund, "Sit."

Volund didn't argue, just gave Mor a slightly sassy look and took a seat at the dining room table.

"And you," Morgan snapped, pointing at me. I raised an eyebrow at his tone, and he sighed, his expression crumpling. "Come here," he whispered, already moving toward me.

I obeyed without complaint, letting his arms swallow me in a warm embrace. Neither of us spoke for a while, and I let him take most of my weight since I was finding it harder and harder to hold myself up through my exhaustion. He set his chin on the top of my head, and I splayed my hand over his heart, feeling it beat roughly beneath my palm.

"Not to interrupt, but am I supposed to just sit here and watch while you two get it on?" Volund asked, ruining the moment.

Morgan growled and I felt him tense, ready to pounce on the Dark Elf. Releasing him, I stepped toward Volund, keeping the two men separated.

"You know, if you keep up with this snarky attitude," I said, crossing my arms, "You're just going to increase the chances that Morgan will lose his control and tie your tongue like a cherry stem."

Volund smirked and leaned back against the table. "Well would you rather I have just sat here and watched?"

Morgan growled. "I am going to kill you—"

"Easy, Bear Man," I crooned as if talking to a wild animal, my hands on Morgan's chest to stop him from ripping Volund apart. "We still need to get some answers from our houseguest."

"Fine," Mor bit out, glaring at Volund. "Then can I kill him?"

I glanced at Volund over my shoulder and shrugged. "Sure."

"*Excuse me?*" Volund screeched.

Chapter 14

CAROLINE

"Yeah, that's fine," Morgan said into his phone as he paced the length of his office. "I'll pay triple if you can be here tomorrow."

"Don't you think he's being a tiny bit dramatic?" I complained to Morgan's brothers.

"I mean, someone did try to steal you. Again," Mike said with a shrug, sitting on the sofa beside me. "I can't really blame him for wanting to protect you."

"He's having *bullet proof glass* installed through the entire house. It's a little intense."

"It's romantic," Clint teased, wagging his eyebrows.

I rolled my eyes at the Hohlt boys and listened as Morgan set up an appointment to make our house safer than the president's. *He's totally overreacting.*

"Alright, they're coming tomorrow," Mor said as he hung up the phone. Still pacing. "And you're going to set up a perimeter alarm?" This question he directed at Mike.

Mike nodded. "Yep, I ordered all the stuff I need and overnighted it, so it should be here tomorrow."

"Good. I also think we should set up a guard rotation. We can take shifts so that there's always someone around and on alert."

"I'll set up a rotation schedule," Grey agreed, scribbling on his clipboard.

"As much as I appreciate you guys turning yourselves into my own personal Secret Service," I said, looking from one overprotective Berserker to the next, "Shouldn't we be focusing on finding out more about the attacker?"

"My top priority is your safety," Morgan insisted, pinning me with those danged grey eyes. Curse his attractiveness and its ability to get to me.

"And I appreciate that, but if we really want everyone to be safe, we should be focusing on figuring out who came for me tonight and why."

"Uh, I think the why is pretty obvious," Volund pointed out, reclining in his seat like it was a throne instead of an armchair. "They came for *you*. Duh." I glared at him, but it did me no good. Volund was impervious to the opinions of others. *Heaven help us.*

"He's right," Morgan agreed, still pacing. "They came for you; therefore, we need to protect you."

With a loud, frustrated sigh, I let my head lean back against the couch and patted the empty cushion beside me. "Come here before you burn a hole through the floor with all your pacing. You'll give Grey a heart attack if you get ashes on his nice floors."

Grey nodded, not disagreeing with me. The man was a stickler for a clean house.

Morgan was slower to agree, his posture stiff as he held my gaze. But finally, his shoulders dropped, and he came and sat beside me, stiff as a board.

"Now, let's brainstorm," I said, tugging at his firm, rugged forearm until he finally let me pull it into my lap so I could hold his fisted hand. Obviously, my touch was purely meant to comfort him and not at all for my benefit...*He does have nice forearms though.*

"I'm not trying to figure out what the attacker wanted," I explained, forcing my eyes away from Morgan's manly charms. "As Volt so clearly stated, it's obvious that they were here for me."

I sent my 'cousin' a sweet smile and he narrowed his eyes. "Did you just call me Volt?"

"Sure did. And since nicknames are a rite of passage around here, you should consider yourself lucky."

"Oh, clearly I'm the luckiest man alive," he said with a dry smile.

"So, what is it you're getting at then Caroline?" Grey asked, standing beside Morgan's desk. Honestly, I'd rarely ever seen the man sit. Except for *Bachelor* nights. Those nights, Grey was just as trashy and unrefined as the rest of us.

"I'm saying that we need to be discussing *why* the attacker wanted me. Were they here on the mysterious buyer's behalf? Were they here to kill me? Did they plan to use me as leverage against Morgan?" Mor looked at me, a protective expression on his face as he twined our fingers together. "We can protect me like a jewel all you want, but catching the bad guy is really the only way to keep me—or any of us—safe."

"But he got away," Clint argued. "We can't exactly find out the guy's motive if we can't even question him."

I smiled. "Exactly."

"Exactly?" he parroted. "What does that mean?"

Not quite meeting Mor's eyes, I explained. "I think—"

"Oh no," Volund interrupted, rubbing a hand over his face.

"That we should use me—"

"Terrible idea."

I scowled at him, but he wasn't fazed. He just shook his head like I was an idiot. And maybe I was...

"As bait."

No one said a word as all eyes turned to Morgan, awaiting the explosion we all knew was coming. If me being attacked—and yet coming out unscathed—was upsetting to him, then the idea of me being used as bait to draw in another attacker wasn't going to go over well.

"No," he growled, not meeting my eyes. "Absolutely not."

"But you didn't even hear my plan," I pleaded, turning in my seat to face him.

"Don't have to. It's not happening."

"What if I told you that you'd be with me the whole time? In the same room, breathing the same air, within protecting distance," I begged, using my biggest, most pathetic puppy dog eyes on him.

But instead of caving, he turned and set a stubborn look on me. "Care, let me explain something to you—because everyone else in this room seems to understand except for you. Risking you is *never* an option. If it were anyone else, we could have a conversation about it, but not you. It's not worth it to me to put you in danger like that. Not ever."

I bit my lip, not sure how to argue with him when he was being so freaking sweet. I knew I mattered to Morgan, and I knew that on some level, I mattered to him differently than anyone else did. Because while he loved his brothers, what he felt for me was different. More possessive and stubborn. And when I thought about how I'd feel if the tables were turned and he was the one being used to draw out an attacker, I couldn't help but empathize.

"Morgan, I know how much I mean to you," I whispered, very aware that we had an audience, but too focused on comforting him to care. "Because I feel the same way about you. I don't know what I'd do if you were put in danger like I'm asking you to let me. But the fact is that we need answers, and we can't get them if you keep me in a glass box. We'll be smart about this plan; we'll take every precaution possible...but I don't see any other way for us to find answers. And in order for the attacks to stop, that's what we need. Answers."

He didn't look away as his emotions tumbled from worried to angry to anxious to affectionate and back to the beginning again. "I will not lose you, Red," he insisted, his voice low and threatening. "I don't care what kind of measures I have to take; I'm keeping you safe."

"So..." I said, raising my eyebrows in question.

"We'll use you as bait, but on my terms." I nodded and tried not to look eager, knowing how hard this was for him. "You'll be on coms the whole time, you'll wear protective gear, you will *not* go off on your own, and most importantly," he said, sliding his palm along my cheek and sending a wave of sparks over my skin, "You will stay right next to me the whole time. I want to feel your body heat because you're so close. Do you understand?"

Did I understand? Heck no. I didn't understand how one touch could light my body on fire, or how the look in his eyes could send goosebumps down my back, or how he could look at me like this and feel my pulse beneath his fingers and *not know* how into him I was.

Whether that was a blessing or a curse, I couldn't decide.

"Yes," I finally breathed, trying my best to appear unaffected. "I understand. I'll do whatever you want, stay as close to as you want, and I swear I won't leave your side."

His eyes boomeranged between mine as the beat of my heart continued to speed up like it was racing downhill. The intensity and the fierce protectiveness in his gaze had me struggling to breathe.

But Morgan didn't share my issues. He just dropped his hand to his lap and nodded resolutely. "Okay then. Let's catch an attacker."

Chapter 15

MORGAN

"Was it really necessary to bind me?" Care whined, walking beside me. "Again?"

I flashed her a smirk and she rolled her eyes. But she couldn't hide the bit of attraction I sensed whirling inside her. *I'm winning you over one smirk, one flirt, one touch at a time Caroline Felicity Birch.* And someday I'd work up the nerve to actually make a real move. But here in the darkened hallway of the Shifter Alliance Building with my brothers listening through our earpieces was *definitely* not going to be the time.

The plan was going smoothly so far, but it relied on a lot of small pieces coming together. A few days ago, we had Clint sneak into the building and pull one of Caroline's signature heist moves on a corrupt city official. The next day, word quickly circulated that the vigilante had resurfaced. Which meant that whoever was trying to take Caroline had reason to believe they might find her here.

Which was exactly what we wanted.

"Yes, it was necessary," I insisted, scanning the hallways for either the attacker we hoped would show or a security guard. "Having Merida magically bind you to me again means that no one can take you from me. And I've got the binding on a very short leash, so even if someone tries to kidnap you, they won't get any further than the binding will allow."

"I feel like a dog," Care pouted, looking especially adorable in her black sweatshirt and her hair in two low ponytails with black ribbons around them. "Or one of those kids with a leash backpack."

I bumped her shoulder with mine. "You'd look cute with a leash backpack," I teased. She glared at me, and I gave her an encouraging smile. "I promise I'll drop the binding once this mission is finished. Even if it is tempting to keep you close all the time."

"Swear?" she said, holding up her pinky finger, her green eyes completely serious.

Seeing an opportunity to further solidify myself as a romantic option in her life, I twined my pinky with hers and held her gaze. Then I tugged her hand toward me and kissed her knuckles. "Swear."

Caroline's cheeks went pink, and her fingers trembled slightly in mine. Attraction flared bright in her chest, along with a host of nerves. Which could be a bad thing, or a good thing. *Is she nervous because she's uncomfortable...or because she liked it?*

"So," she babbled, pulling her hand from mine and turning her eyes back to the hall, "Who do you think is behind the attack?"

I blinked at her awkward change of subject. Was she trying to fend me off, or just too flustered to look me in the eye?

"Um," I sighed, trying not to let the feeling of disappointment sink in, lest she sense it, "I guess I'd probably bet on Francine. She's always so hostile and you said she seemed nervous when I brought up those fake Nephilim reports at the meeting."

"She was nervous," Care nodded thoughtfully. "But I almost feel like she's too obvious of a choice. She clearly hates you, so I can picture her working with Eileen to take you down. But something tells me that if Francine were going to make a vicious move, she'd do it unapologetically. She's not one for hiding her feelings."

"Fair enough," I agreed, remembering all the times that Francine had nearly started a fight during a council meeting. It was like a game to her, ticking people off. And if it weren't for all the wards on the council room that make it impossible to use magic, I was sure that she would have shifted and attacked someone already. "So, who do you think is behind it if not Francine?" I asked, glancing down an adjoining hallway to make sure it was clear.

Caroline pursed her lips in thought and I made a mental effort *not* to stare. *Don't be that guy, Morgan.* But my body betrayed me, and my eyes kept flicking toward her. She was wearing lip-gloss—I could tell by the way the dim security lights reflected off her lips, and I desperately wanted to know if the gloss was flavored or not. *Now there's a sure-fire way to get slapped.*

Genevieve had never worn much lip-gloss. She was more of a ChapStick and mascara kind of girl. But despite the two women's differences, I found myself enjoying the more high maintenance aspects of Caroline. She was girly and feminine and yet still strong and fierce. Our relationship was so different from the one I'd had with Gen, but so beautiful and strong in its own unique way. Just like Care.

"I kind of wonder about Finch," she said, and for a moment, I couldn't figure out what the heck she was talking about. Hadn't we just been talking about kissing? *Oh wait.* I had been *thinking* about kissing. Thankfully, I hadn't said any of it out loud. *I hope...*

"Finch?" I asked, surprised at her suggestion now that I actually knew what she was talking about. "The substitute Pixie rep with the slouch and the stutter?"

"Never underestimate those who seem unthreatening," she reminded me, pointing a finger in my face. I grabbed said finger and twined our hands together, dropping them to swing between us. Care said nothing about it, but I did catch a flash of warmth in her eyes. "You of all people should know better."

I rolled my eyes but conceded. "You're right. Underestimating people based on appearance is dumb. So, what is it about Finch that makes you think he might be behind the attacks?"

Care shrugged, mindlessly squeezing my hand a little tighter, like she wanted to make sure I didn't let go. "He's just always so nervous. Like there's so much he's guilty of that every topic puts him on edge. Plus, there's just something about people who appear too intimidated or nervous to be dangerous. I don't trust it."

"Cynical much?"

She gave me a pointed look. "Uh, pot meet kettle."

"Touché." I chuckled.

"So…" she hummed, her nerves seeming to become heavier, more like worry. "What happens if no one shows? What do we do then?"

I sighed, knowing that there was a possibility that this plan wouldn't work. And while part of me didn't want it to work because I didn't like the idea of Care being in danger, I also knew that in order to end these attacks, we had to know who was attacking.

"We'll probably start looking into council members again," I said, wishing I had a better answer. "It's possible one of them is behind it, but catching an attacker would make it a lot easier for us to figure out which one."

"True—"

"Heads up," Mike's said, interrupting Care through our earpieces. "Someone just entered the building through the back entrance. They're headed upstairs…southeast stairwell."

While Clint was pretending to be Caroline in the Alliance Building the other night, he'd also left behind some tiny spy cameras at every entrance and stairwell. That way, even if the attacker jammed the building's cameras, we'd still know when they showed up and where they went.

Care's wide eyes met mine, both of us filled with worry. This was what we wanted, to have an attacker actually show up like we'd planned. But having Caroline in the same space as someone who wanted to do her harm went against every bone in my body, the idea completely at odds with the mate bond. My instincts were screaming at me to get her out of here and to safety even though logically I knew this was what we'd intended. *What was I thinking, letting her talk me into this? She's going to get hurt.*

Without thinking, I dragged Care over to the nearest office and started digging for the electronic lock pick in her backpack. It was too late to leave without potentially running into the attacker, but we could hide until they left.

"Morgan, what are you doing?" Care demanded, turning so I couldn't reach her bag. "You need to hide so we can catch this guy."

"No," I shook my head, setting my hands on her shoulders, "*We* need to hide."

"What? No—"

"Red, this was a bad idea. You're going to get hurt or killed and I just can't..." I tried to catch my breath, but the panic was setting in and I couldn't calm myself down. We'd used Caroline as bait before, but back then she hadn't meant to me what she did now. Back then, she was a reluctant friend that I was still accepting as my mate. Now...*she's everything*. And I couldn't lose her. Just the thought of it had my heart squeezing too tight in my chest and my eyes clamping shut.

"Whoa, hey Mor, easy," Caroline whispered, and I felt her small hands on my cheeks. "It's going to be okay. It's one attacker who doesn't know that you're here. We have the upper hand and I'm magically bound to you this time. Like you said, even if they caught me, they couldn't go anywhere with me."

"But they might threaten you to make me drop the binding. Or they might kill me to get rid of the binding themselves or—"

"Morgan," Care snapped, shaking me gently, "Look at me."

I obeyed, ridding myself of the terrible images as I opened my eyes and focused on Caroline's green ones staring stubbornly back at me.

"You are the only person who has ever successfully kidnapped me, and do you know why?"

Yes, because of the mate bond. But I couldn't say that, so I just shook my head.

"It's because even that first day in the hall when you caught me, I wasn't scared," she said, her touch tender. "I was annoyed, frustrated, and angry, but not scared. I've never once been afraid of you, which was why I didn't fight you nearly as hard as I could have. But whoever's coming for me now, I don't trust them the way I did you. So, no matter what this person does to try and catch me, it won't work because I'm not going to let it. Got it Bear Man?"

I groaned, wishing I could deny her but knowing it was impossible. "Got it, Red."

"Good," she whispered, reaching up to kiss my cheek. "Now, in order for us to get out of this safely, we have to follow through on the plan. So right now, you need to hide."

My instincts drove me to refuse, hating the idea of putting her in danger. But as scared as I was to let anything happen to Caroline, we had to see this through. So, after tugging her into my arms for one last tight hug, I slipped around the corner and hid in the adjoining hallway.

"Alright, I'm in position," I whispered into my earpiece, watching Caroline where she stood in the middle of the hall.

"Ditto," she added, pulling her backpack off her shoulder, pretending to be looking for something. "Hopefully this guy doesn't take too long to attack me."

"So not helping my panic level, Caroline," I growled. Especially because I couldn't see the attacker coming from my vantage point, which left me relying on Care's signal to know when to step in.

Care cringed and sent me a smile without fully turning her head. "Sorry, Mor. Hey Mike, I think I sense someone coming from somewhere far behind me. Is that them or is that a guard?"

"Hm..." Mike hummed, probably checking his camera feed. "Yeah, that's them. They're on your floor now, but still one corridor away from you. They should be there in a few moments though."

My body—already tense with anxiety—went so taut that I thought I might actually snap in half if I had to stand there much longer. The hair on my neck stood on end, my arms prickled with goosebumps and a weight settled in my gut as my mind began playing out the possible outcomes. Caroline being taken hostage, a knife to her throat to get me to drop the Witch binding. The attacker killing me so they could take her, her pained expression the last thing I saw before I died. And worst of all, Caroline dead on the floor, gone before I could protect her...

"Mor," Care whispered, her eyes still on her bag as she pretended to dig for something, "You're panicking. You need to calm down." I nodded but wasn't sure how to do that with a dead Caroline in my mind's eye. "Mor, we're okay. I'm okay, but our attacker is close, so I need you to focus and be ready to move. Okay? Can you do that for me?"

"I've got you," I rasped, my breathing still uneven but my mind now focused on protecting my mate. *Nothing else matters.*

As Caroline's nerves began to climb, I knew the attacker was close. But the hall was silent, neither the attacker nor Care making a sound as she pretended to search for something in her bag. I was just about to pounce, unable to stand the waiting anymore, but then Caroline subtly waved her hand at me.

Taking the signal, I lunged forward and grabbed Care's arm, swinging her over to my hiding spot as I took her place in the hall. The attacker, unprepared for the switch, threw themself at me.

Unfortunately for them, they'd been expecting to catch a small woman. Not an angry Berserker.

Their arm looped around my waist, but I was unconcerned. With very little effort, I pushed us both onto the ground, the attacker's back taking the brunt of the fall. While I flipped around to hold the attacker in place, a masculine grunt came from behind the black ski mask.

"Chief Hohlt," he groaned.

Taken aback by his recognition, I paused for a moment.

Just long enough for him whip a knife from his belt and slam the hilt against my throat. He moved so fast, he had to be a Shifter of some kind. As I tried to regain the ability to breathe, he easily dislodged me, and I tumbled to the floor.

I'd just gotten to my knees when he righted himself, the two of us facing off like we were about to mud wrestle.

"I should've gotten paid double for this," the man complained, tossing the knife from one hand to the other.

"Yeah," I agreed, ready to pounce, "You should've."

Before I could move though, the man lunged at my middle, knocking me back against the marble floor.

"Morgan!" Care shouted, and I blinked up to see her coming around the corner.

"Stay back!" I barked, shoving at the man—who was trying to jab his knife at my chest. "So help me, Caroline, you stay back!"

My fear must have been enough to let her know how desperately I needed her to be safe, because she obediently stayed back at the mouth of the other hallway.

With one final push, I managed to get the attacker off of me and buy myself some breathing room. But it didn't last long. He was fast with the knife, slicing at my arms and trying to hit something vital. But as much as his speed aided him, my strength was better.

He aimed at my throat, but I blocked him with my forearm and threw a fist at his ribs. He cried out and I heard the faint crack of bones splintering. I winced and reminded myself to be careful not to kill him.

Much as I might want to do otherwise right now.

As he fell back, whimpering and clutching his midsection, I rose to my feet. He made a pathetic attempt to swipe me with the knife, but I batted it out of his hand where it clattered to the floor. Latching a hand around his neck, I pulled the man to his feet and glared into a pair of brown eyes.

"You came for the wrong girl," I hissed, careful not to choke him. "She's mine."

The man struggled to breathe, and I loosened my grip ever so slightly. "Not for long," he rasped out.

Deciding that maybe he didn't need to remain conscious anymore, I started to tighten my grip. Just enough to make him pass out. But out of the corner of my eye, I saw him lift a night stick.

And then intense pain radiated across my temple.

"Morgan!" Caroline screamed. I tried to look for her, but my vision had gone blotchy, and an ice-cold sensation was spreading across my head as my body began to weaken.

"Mor, you have to let go," Care pleaded, her voice closer now. Soft fingers brushed against mine and I immediately relaxed my grip. Someone grunted, although I couldn't tell who, my sight turning completely black.

Voices mumbled around me, but all I was aware of was a sudden weightless feeling.

And then I hit the floor. I didn't think I hit my head, an ache instead spreading through my shoulder. "Care?" I mumbled, squinting against the pain.

"I'm here Morgan," she whispered, her voice right next to my ear now. "Mike, the attacker is running. He's limping though, so you might be able to catch him. I didn't think it was smart for me to go after him alone."

"You did good Care Bear," Mike's voice came too loudly in my ear. "What about Morgan?"

"I think he's gonna pass out," Care replied, her voice thick like she was speaking through tears. I blindly reached up to wipe the tears from her face, but all I got was air. "I'm staying with him, but I can't get him out of here on my own."

A hand latched around mine just as I began to drop it, and I held on as tight as I could manage in my dazed state. I tried to keep listening to Care and Mike's words, but it was getting harder and harder to focus.

"Caroline?" I breathed, my consciousness on the fringes now.

"I'm here, Mor," she whispered, a hand stroking my face. "I'm not going anywhere."

Which was good, because my awareness definitely was...

Chapter 16

CAROLINE

Morgan's breath brushed across my collar bone as I watched *The Good Place* play out across my laptop screen. His bed was soft, both of us covered in blankets as he snoozed beside me. Even though I was worried about Mor and the blow he'd taken to the head, it was warm here in bed with him, and I felt content.

Last night, Mike hadn't bothered to chase after the attacker, instead helping me get Morgan out of the building before we could get caught by a security guard. And as much as we both hated to lose the lead, Morgan was more important.

Once we got home, I had the doctor come and check Morgan out. Mor hated that part. But fair was fair. He'd fretted over me plenty both times I'd been injured, so now it was my turn to return the favor.

It turned out that he had a concussion, which we had plenty of experience with. He'd been in and out of consciousness all night and this morning, and I was taking every opportunity to study him like I might never get to do it again.

He was curled against me, his head on my shoulder for a change instead of the other way around. And from this angle, I could see the white of his scar trailing across his eye, then picking back up again on his other cheek. Indulging myself since he was asleep, I let my fingers skate across the mark, recalling the first time I saw it.

"You seemed so angry then," I whispered, smiling at the memory. He'd been so intense, so frustrated with me for complicating his life. At the time, I'd thought he hated me. And between his anger and his reputation, the last thing I'd expected was to find out that there was a big softie hiding under it all.

Even after we'd become friends, after I'd learned to trust him and he'd learned to lean on me, I still wouldn't have expected to feel the way I did when I saw him fall in the hallway of the Alliance building last night. It would have been one thing if I'd been afraid to see him hurt...

But when I saw him go down, his body hitting the floor, his eyes unseeing and his pain echoing out to me through his emotions, I felt like *I'd* been hit. Like our bodies were linked and it was me who'd been injured. I wasn't panicked or upset; I was *distraught*.

The fear and worry were so visceral that I could feel it like a knife in my gut. Because deep down, my body had known what my brain didn't.

I'm falling for him. Hard.

I wasn't sure when it had started—probably because I'd been so insistent on being in the friendzone that I'd diluted myself into believing that I didn't see Morgan that way. But the truth was that I'd *always* seen him as more. More than a safe space, more than a friend, more than a partner. He'd been everything to me for a while now, but I was only now understanding what that meant.

I want him. And the more I thought about it, the bigger the craving got. I wanted Morgan Hohlt *badly*, and I knew now that friendship was never going to be enough for me.

What I didn't know though, was whether or not he would ever want me back.

Suddenly nervous, I fiddled with the blanket around Morgan's shoulders. I'd have to make a move or ask about his feelings eventually—I couldn't live like this forever.

But maybe I could put it off for a while. *I don't need to know* right *now...*

"Don't," Morgan mumbled, making me jump.

"Sorry, I didn't realize you were awake," I said, pressing the blanket around him.

"Don't move please. You're really comfortable."

I laughed and ran my fingers through his hair, indulging him. From the top of his head, around his ear and back again, my fingers trailed. Just like my mom used to do when I was little.

"Hm...that's nice," he hummed, his body fully relaxed against me. "You know, it's been a really long time since I've had a woman in my bed. I think I might be a little out of practice."

"Morgan Gareth Hohlt," I admonished, glad that from his vantage point, he couldn't see my flaming face.

"Oh no, did I make you...Red?" he teased, snickering like a child.

Annoyed that he could get me flustered even in his tactless, half-awake state, I flicked his arm. "You be nice to me, or I'll spike your water with laxatives."

He faked a gasp. "You wouldn't."

"I would, and I'd enjoy every second of it. So don't push me mister."

"But I like pushing you."

My heart melted, a big puddle of sap dripping in my chest. Because I was an idiot. A complete and total idiot for this incredibly frustrating man.

"How do you like the show—or rather how do you like what little of it you've stayed awake for?" I asked, directing the conversation safely away from my pathetic, sappy heart.

"Rough subject change, Care," Morgan tsked, his voice rumbling against my chest and sending a fresh wave of electricity through my nerves. Poor things were overworked with so much time spent lying next to him. "But I'll allow it because I know I'm getting to you."

"Oh, how benevolent," I said dryly, covering my attraction with sarcasm, my old friend.

"In answer to your question, I like the show."

"Better than *The Office*?"

He shrugged. "Eh. I like them both. Really, it's not about the show for me."

"No?"

"Nope. I don't really care what we watch. I just like watching things with you."

Morgannnnn. This boy had no idea what he was doing to me. I was already feeling a little tender having just realized that I was falling for him. And now he was being ridiculously sweet. *Come on Mor. Just this once, I'm actually begging you to tick me off.* It would make it a lot easier to keep my heart from running off with him.

"I'm sorry by the way," he said before I had a chance to respond to his sweet comment.

"For what?"

"For letting the attacker get away. We lost our only chance to find out who's behind the attacks because I couldn't take him down fast enough."

"That's not true, Mor." I shook my head and resumed combing my fingers through his hair. "You didn't ruin anything."

"I did though. Since the attacker got away, whoever hired them will know that it was a trap. They'll know not to come after you the same way. Which means that we can't set them up again."

"That may be true, but it doesn't mean that catching an attacker is the only way to get answers."

Morgan scoffed. "How else are we going to find anything out?"

I thought about it, considering what we'd learned so far. We knew that Eileen had planned to sell me to someone, but we didn't know who. Which meant that somewhere out there was someone who was still in the market to buy an Elf. We also knew that the buyer wasn't found via an auction, which meant that they had possibly known about my existence before Eileen told them about me. While it was plausible that Eileen's buyer was a fellow council member, so far, we had no evidence of it...

"We could just start stalking council members again," I suggested, knowing that we'd only followed a few of them before Volund showed up and threw us off track. "It's been too long since I've ruined the life of a bad guy."

Morgan chuckled. "You know, I never imagined that you would be such a ruthless, stubborn woman."

"What do you mean you never imagined it?"

Mor suddenly stilled; his entire body frozen as nerves flashed through his mind. *What on earth does he have to be nervous about?*

"Morgan?"

"I just mean that when I first saw you, I would never have imagined who you actually are," he stuttered, almost definitely lying. "You looked so different than what I expected a vigilante to look like."

While his words felt false, I couldn't understand why he would be lying to me right now. Then again, he'd taken a gnarly blow to the head not twenty-four hours ago. So, I decided to let it slide. The man wasn't exactly functioning at high capacity today.

"And what about now?" I asked, setting my chin on his head. "What do you think about my personality versus my appearance?"

Mor was quiet for a few moments, humming as he thought. "When I first saw you, I thought you looked like a daydream. But now that I know you, I know you're not a daydream." A little taken aback, I paused my strokes in his hair. "I never could've imagined someone so quick witted and full of light. You're more incredible than my brain could've ever conjured on its own."

Okay...so maybe Bear Man had some game after all. Either that or I was so lost to him that I was enthralled even in his current state. *Such a sap.*

"And when I first saw you, I thought you looked like a nightmare," I admitted gently, feeling him tense against me. "A tempting, dangerous nightmare that looks good, but you know isn't good *for* you...But now that I know you, I know that you're not a nightmare. You're the big bad bear in the woods—pardon the pun," I paused, and he huffed. "At first glance, you're scary and intimidating, but once I got close enough, I realized how beautiful you are. And how safe you make me feel. You're a nightmare to those who might hurt me, but you're my place to rest. My home." Reaching for his hand, I breathed in the scent of him, my face pressed into his hair.

Morgan was quiet. His thumb stroked the back of my hand and I felt him relax, our bodies so right lying next to each other.

"For a long time, I prayed I'd never find you," he whispered, his voice raw and vulnerable, "And I've never been more grateful to have a prayer be denied. I'm glad I know you Caroline Felicity Birch."

I smiled, my grin big and dumb and unrepentant. "I'm glad I know you too Morgan Gareth Hohlt." *So glad.*

Chapter 17

MORGAN

In case anyone was wondering, the definition of a masochist is someone who enjoys an activity that appears to be painful or tedious. *Or you could just look at me, a prime example of a masochistic idiot.*

Here I was, training Caroline in her leggings and tight tank top, her very presence driving me to distraction. It was physically painful to have her so close and yet have to pretend like I *didn't* want to drag her into my arms and kiss her senselessly. But did I hand her training over to my brothers to save myself the pain? No. Because I was actually *enjoying* this miserable time in her presence, pretending to be *just* her friend. *Like I said, masochistic idiot.*

"Good, now make sure when you spin it, you put your thumb here," I said, repositioning her fingers on the pink knife. We'd tried to give her regular black ones, but when she saw the pink ones online and begged me for them, I couldn't say no. *Because newsflash: I'm obsessed with her.* "It'll give you more stability and make your cuts stronger."

"Right," she nodded, her auburn hair all piled up into a bun, a few loose strands stuck to her neck with sweat. *I shouldn't find this sticky, messy look so attractive.* But like I said, obsessed. "Thumb next to the metal piece and keep my motions fluid."

"Exactly." I stepped back and watched as she holstered her knife and faced the self-defense dummy again. Then she walked past the dummy like it was a stranger in a hallway. And at the last moment, she slipped her knife from its holster on her thigh, spun it in her hand, and stabbed the blade into the dummy's side. All in one fluid motion.

"Good!" I exclaimed, proud to see her making such strong progress. Some people had a natural skill for combat, but Care had fought to be good at this. She'd earned it.

"Yeah?" She beamed, and I couldn't resist grinning back. She was contagious like that. "It was pretty good, huh?"

"Easy there, Lara Croft, you're good, but I don't know that you're ready to fight off any mercenaries yet."

"No?" She cocked her head, giving me a challenging look. "Then why don't you teach me, Bear Man?"

God, help me. This woman had *no idea* what she was doing to me; killing me slow and painful with all of these innocent lines that in my caveman brain translated to 'I love you' and 'kiss me now'.

And *this* was why I'd made a point not to train her myself very much. But unfortunately, Mike and Clint couldn't always be around to train her, so I'd had to fill in.

You volunteered, my masochistic side whispered.

"Shut up," I growled back.

"Sorry?" Care asked, arching one eyebrow at me.

Oops. "I wasn't talking to you."

"Okay then, Smeagol," she laughed, spinning the knife in her hand. "So, are you going to stand there talking to yourself all day or are you going to show me how it's done?"

Part of me wanted to squeeze my eyes shut and beg God to please stop this woman from making me crazy. But the other part wanted to see what would happen if just this once, I didn't keep myself in check. *I'm already miserable, what have I got to lose?*

Moving cautiously—watching her face and paying close attention to her emotions—I stepped into her space. She tipped her chin to look up at me, ready for a challenge.

"I can show you how a lot of things are done," I whispered, skating my finger across the tops of her cheeks, "Red."

I held her gaze for a moment, measuring the fire in her eyes. Was it just me, or was there something there under the shock? Something more than just attraction and easy friendship. But just when I thought I saw something, she took a step back.

My hope deflated and I turned under the guise of grabbing my weapons, trying to hide the disappointment on my face.

"Show me what you got," she said, unaffected by the moment, "Old man."

"Did you just call me 'old ma—oof!"

Caroline threw herself at me—literally—and I fell to the floor, unprepared for the impact. Care wasn't a big woman. She was a little on the short side and as I'd pointed out to her before, she was a perfect balance between curves and leanness. Except that I hadn't accounted for her knees, which were now jammed into my back.

It was true what Shakespeare said, 'though she be but little, she is fierce'.

"You just *tackled* me," I gasped. Caroline had completely knocked the wind out of me.

"And you let me," she tsked, sitting on my back and sliding her pink knife back in its thigh holster. "Bad form Bear Man. Don't you—hey!"

She squealed as I twisted onto my side, scooping her up with one arm and pinning her to the floor beside me. "What was that you were saying?" I panted, flicking a lock of hair out of her face. Her adorably pouty, angry face.

"You cheated."

"If I cheated, then you cheated," I pointed out, my arm still slung over her waist. She didn't seem to mind the touch and I tried to gauge what that meant for me.

Did she not notice my arm was even there? Was she just that unaffected by me? Or was she just really good at playing it cool? Every time I touched her like this, be it cuddling or hugging, she wasn't upset, just...hesitant. And I really wished I could tell why.

She smirked. "Yeah, but it's cute when I do it." I had half a mind to kiss that smirk and finally see if it tasted salty or sweet. Because Caroline was definitely both.

"True." Leaning forward, I kissed the tip of her nose. Then I stood and reached a hand down to help her up.

But Care just laid there, staring at the space I'd vacated.

Nerves, bright and buzzing, bloomed inside her. *Hm...*I could only think of two reasons for her to feel nervous. Either I'd just pushed too far, and she was uncomfortable with my affection. Or she was flustered because she *liked* it...

"Let's keep our knives sheathed," I said, pulling her to her feet, "So we don't nick each other."

"What?" She stared up at me, eyes wide and a little unfocused.

"To spar, Red," I whispered, leaning close as if she wouldn't be able to hear me otherwise.

"Oh! Yeah, of course. Duh."

She quickly spun away and stomped over to the large sparring mat in the corner of the gym, and I thought I heard her mutter something like 'Get it together, Caroline'. A smile slipped onto my face as I watched her go, satisfied that I was doing *something* to her.

If I wasn't mistaken, Caroline Birch was more than just attracted to me.

I had to work double time to keep the grin from my face as I walked over to join her on the mat. Once we were both outfitted with thigh holsters and safety sheaths that wouldn't come off while fighting, we both took our places on opposite sides.

"Alright, here are the rules," I said, stretching my arms. "Any blow to the head or the upper abdomen is a kill shot. Otherwise, we keep going. And we'll pull our punches with the head shots—don't want anyone getting *another* concussion."

"Hey, I've only had one more than you," Care sneered, rolling her eyes.

I grinned. "Best two out of three wins."

"Alright. You ready?" she asked, widening her stance and setting her shoulders, ready to pounce.

"Are you?" I winked.

She smiled, that devious, plotting smile that I loved so much. "Go."

In true Caroline fashion, she didn't wait for me to make the first move. She launched immediately, knife already in hand as she snapped it toward my thigh. But this wasn't my first rodeo.

I slid out of the way and stabbed at the back of her neck. But before I could make contact, she dropped to the floor and rolled away.

"Nice try." She smiled, springing to her feet. "But you're forgetting that I've spent my whole life evading capture. I'm pretty good at it."

"And you're forgetting that there's a reason everyone hates training with me," I taunted, pretending to circle to the left. "Because I always win."

Then I pounced. Care squealed in surprise and barely moved fast enough to make my knife graze her elbow instead of her chest. "Okay, so maybe the big bumbling bear does have a few moves," she conceded, blowing a strand of hair out of her face as she mirrored my steps around the mat.

"Bumbling bear?" I demanded, incredulous.

"You're not exactly graceful."

"Excuse me? Who saved you from three attacks? Who—"

Care suddenly bolted forward, plowing her head into my stomach like a bull. Surprised, I went down like a tree, landing hard on my back. "Ha!" She shouted victoriously, sitting on my hips and holding her sheathed knife above my eye, "I win."

Words. I should be using them. But the only ones that were currently coming to mind were 'marry me' and 'I love you'. *Wait, what? 'I love you'??* I couldn't be thinking the L word yet...could I? *Do I love Caroline?*

I mulled it over for a moment as Care still sat on top of me, her hand pressed to my chest and her face hovering high above mine. We hadn't known each other all that long, and half of that time we'd spent hating each other. And even though we were mates, I knew from experience that mate bonds were just name tags identifying 'the one'. They couldn't create feelings. Love came on its own.

"Well, do you admit defeat Mor?" Caroline grinned, her eyes bright with excitement.

Yeah, I love her.

How could I not? She was clever and funny, kind and empathetic, selfless and beautiful and so very complicated. She was Caroline, bright and captivating, and I was the earth. Spinning around her, happy to be in the warmth of her orbit.

But I didn't say any of that out loud. I needed to start with saying 'I like you' before I graduated to telling her, 'I love you and I'd like to marry you next week if you're down with it'. *That would definitely scare her to death.*

Plus, I couldn't imagine Caroline having anything less than a big fancy wedding. A wedding I desperately wanted to be a part of.

"I'll admit defeat this round," I finally replied, covering her hand with mine where it rested over my heart. "But I'm competitive, Red. I won't let you win again."

Her smile softened and she leaned closer. "Good, because when I win, it'll be because I'm better than you."

I opened my mouth to reply, but nothing came out. Well, except for a really awkward hum that I really hoped she hadn't noticed.

I blamed it on her smell. *Has she always smelled this good? Like coconut and sugar?* Or was that just the pheromones tempting me to kiss her?

"Cat got your tongue, Morgan?" she smirked, arrogant.

"No." My eyes dropped to her lips of their own accord. "It's up for grabs." *Okay, so apparently, we're completely taking off the filter today.* Not what I had planned.

Caroline's eyes went wide. Then they fell to my mouth. And stayed there.

Attraction, anxiety, excitement, fear; they all buzzed together like a horde of bees inside her. I couldn't tell for sure if they were motivated by romantic affection or not, but I was starting to feel pretty confident that the answer was in my favor.

But when I took a chance and lifted my hand to her hip, she went tense. And then she leaped to her feet and tucked invisible pieces of hair behind her ears. "You want to do this or what?" she asked, a little out of breath.

I slowly stood, taking in the way her eyes followed my movements, the way she swallowed when I lifted my shirt to wipe the sweat from my neck. *You're not fooling me anymore Caroline. I see you resisting.*

And I was going to find out why.

So I said, "Absolutely, I do," and slowly let my shirt drop.

Care's eyes flicked back up to mine. Then they narrowed.

"Enough tricks, Bear Man. Let's do this."

We sparred again, but this time Care kept all her moves fast and distant. She was so hesitant and unsure, and I hated not knowing why. Was she thinking that I was just messing with her head to win the match? Or was she afraid we'd ruin our friendship if we pushed for more?

Because I was certain now that on some level, she wanted me too—I'd felt her excitement. This wasn't one sided. There was a reason she was holding back. *And I'm going to find it.*

I ended up winning the second round, which ended with her back forcefully pinned to my chest and my knife over her heart. "Should we just call it quits? I don't want to embarrass you when I win round three," I whispered, my lips brushing her ear.

A shiver rippled through her and instead of pulling away, she pressed closer. "Messing with my head won't work, Mor. I'm too smart for that." But the waver in her voice told me she wasn't as indifferent as she wanted me to believe.

I released her, taking a step back. But I didn't speak until she met my gaze. "I'm not messing with you, Care."

She scrutinized me, unsure. "Next round."

"Care—"

"Fight me, Morgan," she demanded, setting her stance.

"Fine."

I didn't wait for the match to officially start before I swiped out at her midsection. She jumped back, glaring at me. "Didn't know we'd started," she snapped.

"Well then pay attention." *To me and all the feelings I'm so blatantly hinting at.*

But Caroline just growled and ran at me. I side stepped at the last moment and tapped her butt with the flat of my knife.

"Morgan!" she shouted, spinning to face me.

"What do you think about the council members?" I asked, distracting her. If she didn't want to talk feelings, then I wouldn't talk feelings.

She narrowed her eyes, both of us taking careful steps around the edge of the mat, circling each other like jungle cats. Care had a feline grace to her movements, lithe and sharp, and I wondered if Grey had spent any time training her. He had a similar grace and finesse—and I wouldn't be surprised if Care had talked him into a few sparring sessions. She could talk a polar bear into moving to the jungle if she wanted.

"I don't like how many people seemed unbothered or overly nervous about the Nephilim," she finally answered, watching me; my own personal human polygraph.

"Me either. Makes me wonder if Eileen was potentially working with multiple people. Like maybe one of them dealt with finding information about your birth parents and someone else was the buyer? I don't know how they all fit together, but I don't like how many pieces there seem to be."

"Agreed." Care ran forward, her knife aiming for my head. But I ducked at the last moment and tapped my sheathed blade against her lower back. Not deterred—because even a fictitious spinal injury couldn't stop Caroline—she whipped around and hit my shoulder.

I reached out to grab her, but she was too fast. She danced a few paces away, watching me.

"But?" I prompted, lunging forward, aiming for her chest.

She blocked me with her arm, hitting her knife against my lower side. "But," she huffed, flushed and sweaty, "I'm almost more worried about those who had no reaction at all. It's unnatural."

"The Wyvern."

I grabbed her wrist before she could pull away, using my grasp to yank her forward. My knife was poised to hit her chest, but she twisted under my arm, breaking my hold.

"He was too unbothered, don't you think?" she asked, retreating to the other side of the mat.

"A little bit, yeah. In all the years I've worked with him on the council, I've never been able to get a good read on Asher. He's just...enigmatic. Always."

"Maybe we should do a little recon."

I shot her a glare, but she wasn't fazed, tilting her head as she gave me a challenging look.

"Care, no."

"Mor, yes," she smiled.

Then she ran forward. Swerving at the last moment, she tried to get behind me. But I was done with this game of catch and release.

Snagging her around the waist, I yanked her close, her back pressed against my chest. But of course, Caroline wasn't just going to let me toss her around. No, she stomped on my foot and threw her elbow into my gut.

Then, in the time it took me to catch my breath, she swung her knife up and tapped it against my neck.

"I win," she panted, grinning as she lowered her weapon.

But I didn't lower my arm.

"Why are you so easily triggered by me going on missions?" she whispered. I tried to focus on her words, but every breath she took pressed her closer against me. The scent of her shampoo filled my nose and the soft glide of her skin against mine sent my instincts into overdrive. 'Protect', they whispered, 'Hold. Touch. Provide. *More.*'

When I didn't answer, Care pushed against my arm just enough to give her room to turn and face me. And now, with our chests pressed together and her eyes staring up at me, the blue ring of the mate bond promising me all kinds of beautiful futures, I didn't know how to say anything without just blurting 'I love you'. Which I was pretty positive she wasn't ready to hear yet.

There was a quiet thud as Care dropped her knife. Then, with a bit of fear in her eyes, she slowly lifted her hands to my face. Her fingers were gentle as they brushed against my skin, pushing my hair from my forehead. "Morgan," she breathed, so quiet I almost didn't hear her, "Answer me please. I need to know why the thought of me going on a simple mission upsets you so much."

"You didn't want to hear it," I reminded her.

Her lips parted and my eyes followed the motion. "You mean you weren't messing with me?"

Confused, I moved my gaze back to hers. How could she seriously not know? I hadn't exactly been subtle. "Care, what did you think I was doing all these weeks?"

"What do you mean?" she asked, being purposefully obtuse. *Alright, I'll spell it out for you Care Bear.*

"The cuddling. The forehead kisses. The flirting. The bribing you with food." She smiled and I couldn't help but mirror it.

"You mean to tell me that every time you've bribed me with food—"

"I was trying to buy your affection, yes," I interrupted, settling both arms around her waist. She didn't seem to mind. "But you're not mad, because you love any excuse to be fed."

"You're not wrong," she replied, mischief in her eyes. "So, we're not actually friends?"

"We're not *just* friends. At least, we haven't been just friends on my end since your second concussion. I knew then that I couldn't lose you, that I was too attached to you to survive the loss. You haven't been *just* my friend in a long time, Red."

But her insecurity reared its head again, and she furrowed her brow. Unconvinced. "I haven't?"

I sighed, my hands flexing on her back. A part of me knew that I could answer her without words. That I could stand here and kiss her until she understood exactly how much she meant to me.

But Caroline had gone her whole life facing off against the rest of the world. Alone. She'd spent years believing that no one would understand; that no one would *want* to. She deserved to hear that I would always be here, fighting to understand. That no matter what, I would always be in her corner. Because that's what love was.

Never giving up.

And I knew because I'd been in love before—real love. I'd loved someone when their hair fell out and they had no more eyebrows to raise at me. I'd loved someone when they were too weak for physical intimacy, their body too sick for me to give into desire. I'd loved someone when she could barely keep her eyes open from exhaustion, an oxygen tube in her nose and a prognosis that meant I only had so much time. I'd loved someone when my optimism fled me, and my prayers became angry and desperate. I knew what love was, and although the desire and the newness were fun, exhilarating and toe curling, it was nothing compared to the contentment I'd found in the sexless, unpolished moments of our life. Because that's what love is really is—not desire or chemistry or attraction—but contentment. The peace and safety of two people choosing to stand beside each other, no matter what.

And that was what I wanted with Care. That was how I was going to choose to love her. Mate bond or no mate bond, I was hers now. And I always would be.

"Caroline—"

"Nothing good ever started with you saying my full name," she teased, but I felt the anxiety underneath. She didn't need to be afraid though. The only way this conversation was going to end was either with her rejecting me or with her against a wall, my hands buried in her hair and our lips fused together.

"Prepare to be proven wrong," I promised, then I gently removed her hands from my face. At first, she looked disappointed. Until I slid my palms along her cheeks, cradling her smooth skin under my calloused fingers. "Because I've got news for you Caroline Felicity Birch, you can be scared or nervous, but I'm not going anywhere."

She raised her eyebrows, giving me a haughty look. "Who says that's what I'm afraid of."

"Is it?"

She held my gaze, watching me, reading me. "Yes."

I couldn't stop the grin from spreading across my face. Don't get me wrong, I hated for her to be scared. But I was thankful she was scared of *losing* me and not scared *of* me.

"Don't look so happy about it," she complained, shoving lightly at my chest.

"But I am happy," I said, my thumbs brushing her cheekbones.

Her eyes fluttered shut and she breathed deep, letting out a contented purr like a kitten. "Me too."

I took a moment to just watch her, memorizing everything. She was gorgeous, and it felt good to be able to openly admire it. To not have to pretend I wasn't checking her out or imagining what our future daughters would look like. *Whoa there. Slow your roll, Hohlt. You haven't even told her how you actually feel yet.* Valid point.

"Care, I—"

"How much longer am I under house arrest?"

I groaned and squeezed my eyes shut, willing *him* to disappear. Leave it to Volund to interrupt my first romantic moment with Caroline.

"If I glare at him hard enough, do you think he'll turn to ash?" she whispered.

My lips twitched toward a smile. "Doesn't hurt to try." I opened my eyes to find her watching me, her nerves eased but still present. "Hey, promise me something?"

She nodded. "Sure."

"Promise me that you're not going to freak out or overthink this," I pleaded, still holding her face in my hands—completely ignoring Volund's impatient presence. "This conversation has been interrupted, but it's far from over. We will talk later Red."

Slowly, Care's smile renewed. "Deal."

"Great, now that we've got your nauseating love life sorted, can we focus on me?" Volund whined. "Because I've been standing here for a minute now, waiting for someone to answer me."

Annoyed, I looked over to see him standing next to the open French doors that separated the gym from the dining room. Why hadn't I thought to put a lock on those doors before? Oh right, because I'd never owned an annoying pet Elf before.

"Huh," Care hummed, still pressed against me, "I forgot you were even there."

"You forgot..." Volt fumed, his dark eyes narrowing. "I'm a very important person. Even if you don't think so. So important that *my people* are waiting desperately for me to return."

Care's eyes went wide, and she slowly turned to face Volund. "Excuse me?"

Volt just shrugged.

Wrong answer.

Care quickly retrieved her discarded knife from the floor and flung it at the Dark Elf. "Explain yourself!" she shouted. Volt ducked just in time and barely missed being hit in the face.

"Are you insane?" he screeched, as if the knife hadn't been sheathed and he'd been in fatal danger.

"No, I'm annoyed," Caroline growled, unstrapping her other dagger from her thigh. "Now answer the question, *cousin*." She spat the word out with a sneer and Volund rolled his eyes. "What do you mean when you say your 'people' are waiting for you?"

Volt crossed his arms, his nose in the air like he was too good to be having this conversation. "Have I not mentioned that other people are involved? Huh, I thought I told you that already..."

"Volt," I warned, taking a step toward him.

A man of self-preservation, he eyed me and took a step back. "I'm not the only Nephilim," he hurriedly explained, "But I am their leader."

Chapter 18

CAROLINE

"Explain," I snapped, perched on the edge of the desk in Morgan's office.

Volund smirked, sitting in the middle of the couch, his arms spread out across the back like he owned the place.

"Touchy," he taunted, "Now be honest, are you mad because I didn't tell you there were more Dark Elves than just me? Or are you mad because of what I interrupted back there in the gym?"

"Both," I growled, standing so I could break his stupid little nose. Daisy Mae, faithful as always, joined me, jumping up from her dog bed in the corner, ready for a fight.

But before I could get far, something caught me around the waist. It took me a moment to realize it was Morgan's arm holding me back and his chest I was pressed against.

"Easy, Red," he whispered, his thumb brushing across my ribs. "Believe me, I want to destroy him just as much as you do, but he's a cockroach; he won't die. He'll just get a kick out of whatever you do to him. Don't give him the satisfaction."

I growled but relented, letting Mor nudge me back to the desk. Honestly, I would've preferred to stay pressed against him, but since we hadn't had a real conversation about our feelings yet, and everyone was watching us, I settled for dragging his arm into my lap. Logan, Clint, Mike and Grey all exchanged looks at the show of affection, and when Mor set his hand on my knee, they all grinned and started exchanging money.

Daisy, appeased but apparently still on alert, sat next to the desk and watched the room like a little sentinel. I made a mental note to order her a new dog toy later. Especially because she seemed to be watching Volund in particular.

The Dark Elf wasn't bothered by her though. He just sat there, smiling like he knew he was right.

And he was.

I'd been worrying about my relationship with Morgan for over a month now. Wondering if what I was feeling was deeper than friendship. Then wondering if he could ever reciprocate it. And *finally,* when I was about to get some answers, Volt *ruined it!*

"You heard Caroline," Morgan growled beside me, his voice low and threatening, "Explain yourself."

Volund pursed his lips, his eyes calculating. "You two have a very power couple-y thing going on," he said, waving a hand in our general direction. "Like Beyonce and Jay Z, Catherine Zeta Jones and Michael Douglas. Oh! Or Hades and Persephone, or Padme and Anakin. Big reputations and lots of alpha male energy. Kind of has some Jaba the Hutt vibes too though, and that's much less sexy—"

"Volt!" I shouted, snatching the nearby pencil holder and chucking it at his head.

Thanks to his Nephilim speed, he dodged it just in time and the cup bounced off the bookcase behind him. But I smiled when a few rogue pens hit him in the chest.

"Dang it, woman!" he snapped. Logan, Mike and Clint all laughed—even Grey cracked a smile. "You really need to stop throwing things at my face!"

"Stop evading questions and I will!" I shouted. These days, I liked to think that I was decently in control of my anger. But Volt had ruined my first truly romantic moment with Morgan. I planned on being ticked for a while.

"Fine," Volund bit out, rubbing his chest. "I meant exactly what I said. I'm not the only Nephilim. There are...a number of us, and I just so happen to be their prince. And as you know, I've been here a while now and I really need to be getting back. So, I'd appreciate it if you would end my house arrest."

"How many?" Morgan asked.

"How many what—ow!"

Volund glared over at Mike, who sat in one of the leather armchairs. And had not so subtly kicked Volund in the shin. Mike smiled. "Don't be an idiot."

"I'm not being an idiot," Volt grumbled.

"So then how many are there?" Grey asked, and I was surprised to sense impatience in the enigmatic Berserker. It was a testament to just how frustrating Volund could be. I'd give the Dark Elf an award if I didn't think he would be so proud of it.

Defiance flooded through Volund, and he glared. "A few."

"Where are they?" Mor prompted; I could feel his patience thinning by the second.

"Somewhere safe."

I sighed, my fingers tightening on Morgan's arm. He leaned closer, squeezing my knee as he pressed a sweet kiss to my temple. It was a good thing I was sitting down because my legs were a little weak.

I'd had a pretty good idea of where that conversation in the gym had been going before it was so rudely interrupted, but it was nice to see that I was right. *Morgan likes me.* I smiled.

"Why are you just now telling us all this?" Clint asked, leaning against the side of the couch. "Clearly, you're not afraid to tell us. So why not say something sooner—maybe even before we bound you to the house?"

Volund rolled his eyes and propped his booted feet up on the coffee table. But his smirk turned to a pout as Mike kicked his feet down. "I don't know if you've noticed," Volt said with a glare, "But my species is thought to be extinct. It didn't exactly seem like the wisest idea to announce that there were more of us."

"So why now?" I asked, exasperated. "Stop with all the riddles and just be straight with us for once, Volt. Why did you save Mor and I in that alley? Why tell us about your people? Why didn't you do it before we had you bound to the house?"

Volund clenched his jaw, but I felt no anger coming from him, only frustration. "I saved you because you needed me," he finally replied, saying each word carefully as if weighing them first. "And if I hadn't stepped in...you might not have survived. I didn't tell you about the other Nephilim at first because like I said, I was still trying to figure out if I should place my trust with you guys or not." I sensed no anxiety in him as he spoke, not a whisp of nerves. "And I couldn't out my people unless I was sure they wouldn't be in danger. I'm telling you about it now, because I've been gone a while, and my people need me. I'm worried for their safety, and I'm hoping you'll let me go."

"How do we know you're not lying?" Morgan asked quietly.

Volt didn't reply. He just looked over at me. Expectant.

I wasn't surprised that he knew I could sense emotions. Honestly, it had been naïve of me to think I could hide it from him. He probably knew everything about me he needed to know before I'd even met him.

"He's telling the truth," I said, annoyed that his honesty didn't give us more to go on.

"Maybe so. But why should we let you go?" Logan asked, crossing his arms as he leaned back in his chair. "Apart from the fact that you have people that need you, why should we risk putting you out into the world when we don't know if we'd ever see you again? Or if you'd betray us all."

Volund leaned forward, setting his elbows on his knees. Raising his eyebrows, he shrugged, unapologetic. "Because you still don't know who came after you in that alley, or why, or which council members can be trusted. All you have is a bunch of questions. But if you let me go to my people, I swear that I'll help you.

You may not know if you can trust me, but it's either trust me, or keep looking for answers in places that you've already exhausted."

Morgan looked over at me, eyebrows raised. He didn't have to speak for me to know that he was waiting for my answer, wanting to know what I thought we should do. *Power couple indeed.*

But honestly, I wasn't sure what to do. Volund wasn't lying, and yet somehow, I still didn't think he was telling us the full truth. I pursed my lips, and Morgan nodded, understanding my hesitation.

He turned back to Volund, looking completely confident. "For now, you're staying," he announced. Volund sighed and collapsed back against the couch. "And we'll see whether or not we need your help."

Chapter 19

CAROLINE

O ne would think that in the last few twenty-four hours, Morgan and I would have found an opportunity to finish our talk from the gym yesterday. Well, spoiler alert: we hadn't.

With Volund's announcement about the Nephilim and his position as their prince, Morgan and I hadn't had time for relationship conversations. We were too busy trying to figure out what to do with Volund.

He hadn't been lying about his people, his position, or even his intent to help us. But I knew there was something he wasn't saying, some lie he was telling by omission. I just wasn't sure what it was.

So instead of talking to Morgan about my feelings, I was sitting in the passenger seat of his SUV, on another stakeout. Granted, it wasn't dark out yet, and the car was moving, but I'd brought snacks, so it still counted.

"Alright, out with it," Morgan said, setting a hand on my wrist to stop me from fiddling with the hem of my black shirt. *See? Stakeout.* "What's wrong? Are you worried Asher will catch us?"

We'd been staking out the Wyvern King's house for two hours when he suddenly left the house and we had to take our stakeout on the road. After last night, we decided to finish off our investigation of suspicious council members. It felt more important than ever to figure out who we could trust.

"No. I'm not worried." Lie. I was very worried. Just not about Asher.

"Caroline Felicity Birch," Morgan warned gently, his grey eyes snapping to me before turning back to the road, "Don't try to hide your feelings from me. It won't work."

I laughed humorlessly. "It has in the past." Too late I realized my mistake, and I saw understanding dawn on his face.

"Care, I know we got interrupted yesterday—"

"May I remind you that your brothers and Grey are listening to this conversation?"

Morgan sighed.

"Hey guys," Clint said cheerily through our earpieces. "Don't mind us, we're playing *Call of Duty*, so we're only passively paying attention."

"Wow, great teammates," Mor said dryly, unimpressed.

"Would you rather we pay close attention while you discuss your feelings?" Mike chimed in, the sound of intense video game music floating through the background.

"Nope!" I jumped in. "Go back to ignoring us please."

The boys dutifully went back to their video game, and Morgan and I sat in silence, following a ways behind Asher's black SUV. Honestly, I wasn't sure if it was even worth investigating the Wyvern. He didn't seem like the type to have worked with Eileen the Dragon Queen, but his lack of emotions in the council meeting had been unsettling. I'd never met someone I couldn't read before, and that made him potentially dangerous.

"So," Mor began, lacing his fingers with mine and causing a host of butterflies to take flight in my belly. "You're not worried about Asher. You're worried about us."

I sighed, dropping my head back against my seat. And just like that, all the butterflies were dead. I wasn't good at conversations like this. I was good at teasing and flirting and being honest about everything *but* my own feelings.

"Care," he began, "I know we haven't had time to talk yet—"

"Yeah, Volund's a dead man."

Mor laughed and I squeezed his hand out of instinct. His happiness was a nice sound to listen to.

"Yes, Volt will pay," he continued. "And I know we haven't had a chance to really have a conversation yet. But I need you to know that we *are* going to have it."

"Yeah?" I asked, turning to look at him.

He met my gaze for a moment and smiled. "Yeah. And when we talk, I plan on doing some revisions to this relationship—if you don't mind."

I grinned, blushing. "I don't mind."

"Good. How about I make you dinner later?"

And just when it felt like Morgan and I were getting somewhere, Clint interrupted. "About time they went on a date," he whispered—loudly—through the earpiece.

"Shut up," Mike said. "You're ruining the moment."

"You're *both* ruining the moment," Grey calmly pointed out. "I swear, it's like you've never watched reality TV before."

And then the three of them then got into a discussion about *The Bachelor*. With the moment now ruined, Mor and I exchanged exasperated looks. And then we burst out laughing.

"So, dinner?" he asked with a chuckle.

I smiled. "I'll be there."

Morgan grinned—*grinned*—and we sat there, both of us buzzing with happiness as we continued to follow Asher. The euphoria started to fade though, as we began to realize where we were.

"Mor, isn't this—"

"Yes." His emotions took a nosedive and his fingers around mine tightened.

We'd been on the outskirts of town for a few miles now, with tall pine trees on either side of the road. And at first the area hadn't seemed familiar, but as we slowed down behind Asher, a large stone mansion came into view. *Merida's house.*

We watched in anxious silence as Asher's car turned onto the long driveway that circled in front of Winters House. The Wyvern King exited his SUV and walked casually up to the front door as if he'd been there many times before.

"How's it going guys?" Mike asked after a few more beats of silence.

Morgan didn't answer, his jaw clenched tight "We followed Asher to Merida's place," I replied. "He just went inside. Seemed like he'd been here before."

"I'm sorry, *what?*" Clint demanded. He didn't even wait for a response before he started going off about Merida being a traitor. Mike was less aggressive in his comments, but still skeptical. And all the while, Morgan remained silent.

"Hey," I whispered to him as the boys kept talking, "Pull over."

Mor glanced at me but did as I said and pulled to the side of the road just beyond Merida's house.

"Let's go see what's going on." I undid my seatbelt, but Morgan just stared at me. "Hey, don't go getting all sad and worried just yet. We're going to go investigate, find some answers, and prove Merida's innocence. There's no universe in which she'd betray you."

"You don't know that," he argued weakly.

"Actually, I do. I can sense emotions, remember? And when I met Merida, I had good reason not to like her." Morgan's lips twitched and I took that as a win. "So, I paid close attention to her. But do you know what I found?" He shook his head. "A good, wholesome, kind person. She wouldn't do anything to hurt you, Mor."

Morgan sighed but eventually he nodded, and we stepped out of the car.

"We're going in," I announced to the boys.

Thankfully, Grey replied before Clint or Mike could say something stupid. "Good luck and be careful."

"This is a dumb idea," Morgan whined as we crossed the street, keeping to the trees. "We're going to investigate a house full of Witches."

"So?" I shrugged, grabbing his hand as we neared the manicured gardens that surrounded the mansion. "You're a terrifying Berserker Chief and I'm a half breed Elf. We'll be fine."

"You know, I usually find your cavalier attitude very stressful in moments like this."

I glanced up at him and smiled. "But today you don't?"

"Nope. Still do."

I smacked his arm, and he smirked.

We were still hidden by the trees that butted up against the garden, but we would have to leave our cover to get to the mansion. Perfectly trimmed hedges, rose bushes and dozens of plants I didn't know the names of would be our only cover from here to the house. But if we stayed low, we could probably pass through it unnoticed.

"Okay, here's the deal," Morgan suddenly announced, stepping in front of me. "This is a recon mission only. We're going to find out why Asher is here, and that's it. We'll listen from the outside, but we're not going in. And if I feel like we're in danger, we're leaving. Agreed?"

Nodding, I stepped closer and set my hands on either side of his face. "Mor, I swear that I will never lie to you." He nodded. "Which is why...I can't agree to that."

Then I ran away.

Crouching low, I darted from bush to bush through the garden, not waiting to see if Morgan followed. The guy was great, but he should know better than to think that I of all people could be convinced to leave when I was told.

"Wait, what'd she do?" Mike asked through the earpiece, more interested in us than their video game now.

"She ran to the house like an idiot," Morgan grumbled. "And all I asked was that we stay safe. How hard would that have been to do, Caroline?"

"Oh no, he's calling me Caroline," I taunted, glancing back to see him close behind. "I'm in big trouble."

"Yes," he snapped, "You are. I literally told you how much you mean to me like a day ago. Would it have killed you to promise me that you'd be safe?"

"Are we talking about the same Caroline?" Mike teased. "Because the Caroline I know is a chaos queen. I've never seen someone cause so much trouble with such little effort. No offense, Care Bear."

"Yes, offense taken," I pouted even though he couldn't see it. "You make it sound like I leave a mess everywhere I go. I am not that chaotic."

Silence met my ears for a moment, and then Clint and Mike burst out laughing. I even thought I heard Grey let out a single chuckle. "You're not fooling anyone Care Bear," Clint huffed between bursts of laughter.

Ignoring them—and their very offensive behavior—I jogged the remaining distance from some arborvitae to the mansion. The windows of the house were set high, so I only had to crouch slightly to stay out of sight.

And now I just had to find Merida.

"Do you know where you're going?" Morgan whisper shouted once he reached me.

"No," I admitted, reaching out with my magic. "But I think I can pick Merida's emotions out of everyone in the house."

We crouched against the stone for a moment, and I sorted through the varying feelings within the house. There was brutal indifference, excitement, arrogance, and peacefulness. But then I felt it, a tangled mess of feelings that could only be Merida.

"I think she's in her office," I announced, taking off to the left.

"And how do you know that?"

"I just assumed that the bright ball of frayed nerves and anxiety was her. I mean, the last time we were here, she was so stressed, she ate breakfast from her hair."

"Fair point."

He said nothing else as we made our way down the side of the house, but I sensed his stress. I wanted to turn and comfort him, but I knew that the best comfort I could offer was to rip off the band aid and see if I was right about Merida or not.

I'd only been to Winters House one time, but I remembered the many arched windows that marked Merida's office. And I sensed Merida inside. 'They're in there,' I mouthed, pointing to the windows just ahead of us.

Morgan nodded and moved around me, pulling out his pocketknife. When he silently wedged it into the seam of the lowest window and wiggled it, I rolled my eyes.

"You really think that's going to work?" I whispered.

He raised an eyebrow and mouthed, 'Watch me.' Then the window cracked open an inch. But it did so with a quiet groan.

Mor and I froze, turning to each other with wide eyes. A few moments passed, and when nothing else happened, we silently leaned toward the window.

"I don't have proof of any of it," Merida was saying, though neither Morgan nor I were willing to risk actually looking inside.

"But you suspect," Asher replied in his deep, monotone voice.

Merida sighed wearily. *Yep, I was right to associate her with stress.* "I suspect a lot of things, Ash," she said, "But I don't have proof of them, and that's what we need—proof."

"Which is why we're working together. I've done this before; I can do it again."

"You've been very successful in the past, but you also had a much less obvious way in. Things aren't so easy here."

A beep broke through the quiet, and I patted my pocket to check my cellphone out of habit. But the sound had come from inside the room.

"Well, we don't have the proof we were hoping for, but I do have proof about something," Merida announced.

"Well?" Asher asked impatiently. "What is it?"

Merida didn't respond at first. A few silent moments passed, and then her voice was right above our heads. "That my idiot friends are listening outside the window."

I turned wide eyes to Morgan, but then suddenly the window was open, and Merida was leaning out of it, her hair pearly white and her eyes glowing gold as she wove a spell to keep us frozen.

"Okay, you were right, I was wrong," I mumbled, glancing at Mor. "This was a bad idea."

Chapter 20

CAROLINE

Five minutes later, we sat silently on the couch in Merida's office, her and Asher watching us from their armchairs.

Well, everyone actually present was silent. Morgan's brothers...not so much.

"Guys, what's going on?" Mike's voice came through our earpieces.

"Did Merida catch you?" Clint chimed in. "Also, do you know if she's single?"

Mike scoffed. "Really?"

"What? It's a fair question."

"But right *now*? Our brother and Care Bear might be dead or captured."

"Morgan's not dead," Grey argued, "I can hear him growling."

Morgan sighed and rubbed his forehead, completely exasperated. Amused as I was by his irritation, I knew that I needed him to behave for the time being. So, I bit back my smile and spoke into my earpiece. "Hey guys, I think we're safe, but I'm gonna have to shut you off for now. Okay, bye."

Then, before Mike or Clint could complain, I took out my earpiece. And without bothering to ask, I took out Morgan's too and stuffed them both in my pocket.

Morgan immediately relaxed. "Thank you."

"No problem, Bear Man." I smiled and patted his knee, then turned to Merida. "So, what's the deal? Are you a traitor or are we crashing some kind of romantic clandestine meeting?"

Merida's blue eyes went wide, and I sensed her shock and embarrassment. "No! We're not together. We're just friends."

Feeling how genuinely appalled she was, I knew she was telling the truth. Granted, I couldn't read Asher's emotions, so it was possible he was interested in Merida. But the important thing was that she wasn't into him. Because if she had been and he got in the way of Fitz and Merida's as of yet nonexistent love affair, I would have had to do something drastic. But Mitz still had sails! *My ship is sailing!*

"Funny, I thought *we* were friends," Morgan snapped. All humor left me at the sense of betrayal that rolled through him. He was hurt, and I hated it. "But apparently, you've been lying to me."

"We are friends, Morgan," Merida sighed, sinking back against her chair. "And I didn't lie. I haven't told you anything about my situation with Asher because, like you, he's my friend. And I don't betray friends. Which is why I haven't told him anything about my situation with you either." At this, Morgan flinched, properly chastised. "Now it's your turn to be honest. Explain to me why five minutes ago, I saw the two of you on the security feed, crouching outside my window."

Puffing out my cheeks, I looked at Morgan. Who was watching me expectantly.

"Oh, come on, this wasn't all my idea," I whined. But he just raised an eyebrow at me. "Okay, fine, it was my idea. We'd been following Mr. I Have No Feelings over there and saw him come here. Which of course made us suspicious."

"You watched way too much *Spy Kids* growing up," Merida said, shaking her head.

"True, I did. But in my defense, it was a great movie."

Meanwhile, Asher leaned forward in his seat; his eyes so dark they were almost black. "Why were you following me?"

Morgan scooted closer to me, setting arm an along the back of the couch, his hand resting possessively on my shoulder. The move didn't escape Asher or Merida's notice, and Merida smiled.

"You first," I insisted, trying to brush off the round of butterflies Morgan's touch induced. Now that he and I had opened the door to talking about feelings, every time we touched seemed extra charged and extra distracting. "What are you doing here?"

Asher the great and terrifying didn't seem phased by me and my directness. He just watched Morgan and I with an enigmatic expression on his face. And even though I could feel a very vague sense of curiosity coming from him, it was so faint that I couldn't be certain I felt it correctly.

"You might not know this about me, but I worked for the Shifter Alliance of the Midwest region when I lived there," he finally replied. "The council was a mess, and I spent my time cleaning it. By the time I left to come here, the Midwest region was functioning properly for the first time in decades."

"You want to get rid of all the corrupt representatives on this council," Morgan hummed thoughtfully. "That's the proof you were talking about."

Asher nodded. "I've spent the last two years watching every council member, trying to discern who's trustworthy and who's not. But unfortunately, as Merida has pointed out to me multiple times, my position here is too high profile to accomplish much. Back in South Dakota, I worked undercover for the Shifter Unit as a clerk in the Shifter Alliance building. So, it was much easier for me to access information without people taking notice of me. Here, it's not so simple."

"Maybe Fitz *should* start auditing council members," I mumbled.

At the mention of the mayor, Merida's cheeks went a little pink and I felt a little bit of embarrassment fly through her. *Yep, my ship is definitely sailing!*

"So now you know why I'm here." The Wyvern King clasped his hands and looked between Morgan and me. "Your turn. Why were you following me?"

Sensing that Morgan still wasn't totally convinced he could trust Asher, I decided to answer myself. "Because I can't sense your feelings. When Morgan presented the fake report about the potential Nephilim sightings and you didn't react, it seemed suspicious."

Asher opened his mouth. Then closed it. Then turned to Merida. "I assume you know what she's talking about?"

Merida gave an exasperated sigh and glared at me. "Yes, but I was under the impression that we weren't revealing that information to *anyone*."

I gave her an apologetic smile, ignoring the irritation I could feel coming from Morgan at my unplanned announcement. "We weren't. But you trust him, right?"

Merida rolled her eyes but nodded.

"What do you mean you can't sense my feelings? And why would you two make up a fake report about Nephilim?" Asher asked, sounding the slightest bit exasperated. It was the first emotion I'd seen him express so far.

"Well, that's the crazy part," I explained, deciding to just rip off the band aid, "I'm an Elf. Actually, I'm part Alfar and part Nephilim. And I'm sure it goes without saying that my identity is a secret. But over the last few months, I've been hunted. So, we're trying to figure out which council members might be involved—"

"By making up fake reports to test people's reactions." Asher nodded. "Makes sense. And you can feel emotions...but you can't feel mine?"

I shook my head. "I can get a very vague sense sometimes, but not enough to really know what it is you're feeling...Why is that?"

This time, I didn't have to sense his feelings to know that Asher was anxious. His expression became so smooth, so neutral, a perfect mask. He went completely silent, and I began to wonder if he would ever answer.

"You don't want anyone to know that you're an Elf," he eventually replied. "Because you would be hunted. I don't want anyone to know I'm different, for the same reason."

I wasn't completely satisfied with his answer, but I couldn't deny the empathy that took root in me. I'd lived my life on paper-thin ground, always afraid the next step would be the one to finally make it rip. So, from one hunted to another, I wouldn't pry. For now.

I nodded my understanding and Asher relaxed. "Thank you," he said, pausing as he seemed to consider something. "You know, you're putting an awful lot of trust in Merida's opinion of me, by assuming that I'll keep your secrets. And it's not like you're gaining anything by being honest with me. So why do it?"

Morgan's hand flexed on my shoulder, and I instinctively pressed into his side, offering silent support. "Because allies are made with honesty...Plus, now that we've shared with you, I'd imagine that given the chance, you'd return the favor."

Asher didn't respond, just inclined his head in agreement.

At the Wyvern's assent, Mor turned to me. It was a look he'd given me many times over the course of our relationship. But with the progress we'd made recently, it felt more intimate now than it used to. He was asking me if I trusted him, and just like every other time, the answer was easy.

I nodded, and he gave me a small, private smile before turning back to Asher. "You've shared sensitive things with us. And regardless of whether or not you help us now, we'll keep everything you've said private."

"I appreciate that." Asher narrowed his eyes at Morgan, suspicious. "But I don't like owing people things...and truth be told, I don't have a lot of allies in this town. I could use a few more. What can I do to help?"

Morgan relaxed, and I grasped his hand and gave it a squeeze. "Well, until recently, we thought Caroline was the only Elf alive."

"Until recently?" Asher parroted.

Merida, who'd been contently listening until now, shot us a panicked look. Poor girl deserved a spa day after all the stress we were putting her through. Asking her to keep secrets and then blowing them ourselves.

Morgan wasn't looking at her though and continued on. "We found a Nephilim. He's been in our custody for a while now, but yesterday he told us that there are more Nephilim, and that he's their prince. He's not lying, but he is being cagey. We're hoping to find some answers before we decide whether to let him go or not, but we're spread a little thin and honestly, I don't know where to start."

"So, you want me to find his people—if they exist?" Asher surmised. I couldn't tell if he was surprised, appalled or offended by the idea, but he didn't *seem* angry.

"They do exist," I chimed in. "As someone who can sense emotions, I'm basically a human polygraph. I've been wrong before, but it's very rare. I'm positive that he wasn't lying."

Asher seemed to mull this information over, silently rubbing his chin. But Merida was much less controlled. She fidgeted in her seat, running impatient hands through her black hair.

"You know," she said with a nervous laugh, "My life used to be a lot simpler before all of you came to me with all your issues. The most stressful part of my life used to be managing the obstinate young Witches in my charge. Now I'm a part of a coup, and if we get arrested, I look terrible in jumpsuits."

"I'm sorry, Merida," Morgan grimaced. "I know I've brought a lot of stress on you these last few months. I didn't mean to, but...I don't trust a lot of people. But if we do get arrested, I swear I'll make sure they know you weren't in on it. And once this is done, I'll never involve you in anything shady ever again—"

"Yes, you will," she interrupted with a rueful smile. "You'll keep dragging me into your business, and I'll keep letting you. Because you're my friends. I've got your backs, just like I know you'll have mine when I get into my own trouble."

"Absolutely we will," I assured her. Morgan smirked at my reference to *The Office* and nodded his agreement.

"Of course, we will," he said.

Asher sighed, deep and heavy, and set his hands on his knees. "So, now that we're all friends who may or may not get arrested together, what do you have to go on for me to find these missing Nephilim?"

"Uh..." I turned to Morgan, and he shrugged. "That they're missing?"

"And the prince's name," Mor added. "It's Volund. Volund Nilsen."

Chapter 21

CAROLINE

"Will you grab the garlic?"

Morgan's voice snapped me out of my thoughts. Thoughts about how sexy he looked working the stove like a man who knew his way around it. *Chicken alfredo has never looked so good.*

"Care?"

I ripped my eyes away from his hands stirring the sauce—who knew hands could be so attractive—and immediately spun around to search for the garlic, hoping he didn't see my blush.

I should've known better. "Am I distracting you, Red?" Morgan teased. I didn't have to look at him to know that he was grinning like the devil. But I looked anyway. *Can you really blame me?* The man was a full course meal himself.

"What, you? No. Why would I find you distracting?" I gave him as unbothered an expression as possible, passing him the jar of garlic powder.

He took the jar, making sure our fingers brushed. Then he leaned close, his free hand skating along my side. "I don't know, Care. You tell me. Why do you find me so distracting?"

I swallowed—loudly—and met his heated stare, aware that we were blissfully alone. Somehow, he'd convinced the guys to keep Volund out of our hair for the evening. So, while they were playing video games upstairs, Morgan was cooking me a private dinner so we could discuss our relationship. We hadn't actually talked about our feelings yet, but something told me it wouldn't be a long talk.

Or maybe I was just interested in other things than talking right now.

"Maybe..." I whispered, resting my hand on his chest. He was wearing his grey Henley tonight—my favorite. But I'd decided to wear something he'd never seen, banking on him being a sucker for a black dress like every other man on the planet.

It was cute and tasteful, but flirtier than I normally wore. It had a cinched waist and flared to my knees, with little raised black flowers all over. But the sheer sleeves and semi-low back added a little bit of a sexier spin.

"Maybe, what?" he demanded breathlessly.

"Maybe I'm distracted, because...I'm hungry, and you're the one who's supposed to feed me." I grinned victoriously as Morgan rolled his eyes.

"That was mean, Red," he groaned, turning back to the stove. "You're a cruel, heartless woman."

"But I look good doing it."

Right on cue, Morgan glanced at me over his shoulder, his grey eyes smoldering as they skimmed over me. Again. He'd looked more than his fill already tonight, but I didn't mind. I'd worn the dress for him. It felt good to know he appreciated it.

"Yes," he said, pausing to bite his lip, "You do."

Suddenly feeling a tiny bit shy, I turned and leaned against the counter beside him, watching him work. *Why is this so difficult?* Touching him was easy. Flirting with him was easy. But putting my very vulnerable emotions into big kid words was *so* hard.

"You're thinking awfully hard over there," Mor hummed, eyes focused on his pasta.

I thought about denying it, but in the end, I decided to get it over with and just be honest. "I'm just wondering how we're supposed to go about all of this...feelings stuff."

Morgan looked up, studying me carefully. Then, without saying a word, he moved the pot and pan off the burners, stepped in front of me and took my hands in his. "We go about it however we want. Would it be easier to just say it all now instead of waiting for dinner?"

I shrugged one shoulder, unsure what I wanted. *Well, that's not true.* I knew what I wanted: Morgan pressing me against the counter, giving me the kissing lesson of a lifetime. But what my heart *needed* was words. To hear and share affirmations and explanations so that the kissing would be a confirmation, not a question.

"I just wish it wasn't such a strange thing to share like this," I whined, slipping one of my hands free from his to push my hair from my face. "I'm the most honest person I know—"

"I can vouch for that," Mor teased, smiling.

"And yet I'm having a severely hard time verbalizing my emotions. I feel like I'm in high school, all awkward and unpracticed."

"You're not awkward—"

And as if I'd choreographed the whole thing, I dropped my hand to my side, accidentally knocked off the jar of garlic powder, and watched as it shattered on the wood floor. *If this is an omen of my ability to be in a romantic relationship, I'm doomed.*

"Shoot," I mumbled, dropping to the ground to clean up my mess. But of course, I knelt right on a shard of glass. "Ow!"

Without even pausing to realize that I wasn't gravely injured, Morgan picked me up like a toddler and set me on the counter.

"Where all are you hurt?" he demanded, his voice low and gravelly. "Did the glass get you anywhere other than your knee?"

"No, Mor, I'm fine. And it's not even that big of a piece of glass. See?" And because I was double stupid, I yanked the glass out. And then proceeded to cry. "Ow, that hurt."

"I'm sorry, Care," he whispered, wiping my cheeks with his thumbs. "I'll clean up the wound, but it's probably going to sting some."

I nodded and he pulled a first aid kit out of a cabinet and got to work. As it turned out, Morgan was a very diligent wound caretaker. He was gentle as he cleaned my injury, coated it with antibiotic and bandaged it. It wasn't deep enough for me to have to go to the hospital or get stitches, but it hurt like the dickens.

"Here," Mor said, handing me a few pills and a glass of water. "Tylenol. It'll help with the pain."

I obediently took the pills, my knee still throbbing. And as I sat there, waiting for the Tylenol to start working, Morgan began to clean up his first aid supplies. At first, I thought he was just being thorough, but after all the supplies were put away and he still wasn't making eye contact, I knew something was off.

"Morgan, what's wrong?"

"Hm?" he hummed, still looking at the first aid kit like he planned to rearrange everything in it. Anything to avoid looking at me, apparently. "Nothing's wrong."

"Don't lie to me. I know something's wrong, but we can't fix it if we don't talk about it. Morgan, please look at me," I commanded gently.

He sighed heavily but turned toward me, his gaze piercing and intense, like he was looking for something. Whatever it was, I desperately hoped he found it, because I wasn't willing to lose us before we even started.

"I'm just scared," he admitted quietly.

Not liking the hesitance in his voice, I tugged him toward me. He came easily, stepping close so my legs brushed against him. "Why?"

"Because you seem nervous about us, and I want to be honest. I want to tell you how I feel. I've been bursting to tell you for months now—"

"Months?" I couldn't help the way that one distinction sent my heart fluttering. I'd assumed his feelings had developed slowly like mine. I hadn't realized they'd been fully developed and waiting for *months*...

"See, I'm scaring you already and I haven't even said it all yet. I'm not saying you shouldn't be scared or that you have no right to feel anxious. But I've waited so long for you to want this, and I don't want my feelings to scare you off."

"Mor..." I breathed, my heart breaking at the fear coursing inside him. My big, intimidating, closet-cinnamon roll was scared because of me. I wanted to slap myself for it.

"It's okay, Care. Really. I'm just realizing that I should probably go slower than I intended to."

But I didn't want him to go slow. That's all we'd done is go slow. And in the beginning, that was fine. I'd never trusted another person the way I trusted him, and it took time to build that. But the trust was built now. We had a base, a foundation to build an entire new relationship on. And I didn't want to press pause on that.

"No," I insisted, grasping his hips to pull him closer. Surprised, he stumbled forward, standing between my legs, his hands on the counter to brace himself.

"Excuse me?" he asked, even as desire flashed in his eyes.

"I don't want to slow down. We've already done slow. I'm ready for more now."

"But—"

"I'm scared to be honest about my feelings because I don't have experience vocalizing them like this, but I'm not scared of *you*. I want you, Morgan."

The fear that had been clouding him finally parted, and a flash of joy and excitement lit inside him. Slowly, he lifted his hands from the counter and slid them along my jaws, his fingers brushing heat along my neck and my cheeks.

"In that case, I'm gonna go ahead and jump the gun, then," he said, almost like he was asking my permission. I eagerly nodded. *Let's get this show on the road baby.* "I don't remember if I told you, but I haven't dated since Gen died. I'm not a serial dater, it's just not my style. I'm more of a penguin kinda guy."

"Adorable in a tux? Because I'm going to need visual proof." I smiled, the image of Morgan in a tuxedo now taking up space in my mind, rent-free.

Morgan smirked, but the expression quickly faded, and he grew serious.

"No...I mate for life." It may be cliché, but you could've knocked me over with a feather. My head went light and floaty and I felt every inch of my body buzz like a hornet's nest, vibrating like thunder as heat flooded my face. "I haven't dated since Gen because I don't want something shallow. I have no interest in getting to know someone under a romantic pretense, only to find out that we don't gel."

"Did you just say gel?" I knew I was ruining the romantic moment, but I couldn't help it. He'd just declared that even though he'd already loved someone and lost her, he wanted to be just as committed to me as he had been to Genevieve. *I think my heart might explode.* That had to be why it was beating so fast.

"Shut up, I'm being romantic," he commanded, smirking.

I grinned, thankful that my immature tactic of dealing with my emotions by infusing humor into the moment didn't bother him.

"Sorry, go on. You were talking about gel."

"Woman," he growled, exasperated even as he ran his tongue over his bottom lip and failed to hold back a grin.

"I'm sorry. I'll shut up, just please continue."

I offered him a sweet smile and my most apologetic puppy eyes. He tried to hold out but eventually sighed, pressing his forehead against mine. I closed my eyes, soaking up the innocent intimacy of this moment and this touch.

"I don't want to date a bunch of women only to realize that none of them are you," he insisted, as if I were going to argue with him about it. *Don't worry sweetheart, I'm at your mercy now.* "I don't want anyone else. Not now. Not ever. I was so blessed to have Genevieve, and I never imagined I'd get the chance to have that a second time—yet here you are."

His thumbs skated tenderly along my cheekbones, his grey eyes marveling like I was some kind of miracle. Little did he know that he was mine.

"So," he continued, taking a fortifying breath, "What I'm telling you, Caroline Felicity Birch—the woman who's been a thorn in my side since I first saw you, who's clever whit keeps me on my toes, who's quick temper annoyed me at first before I realized just how readily you forgive and how passionately you dole out affection, and who's unholy love of unhealthy food is still a point of contention but something I'm willing to overlook because it's you—" he paused, pulling back just far enough to look at me, "Is that I don't want to date you and see if I like you. Because I already know I like you more than any other person on the planet.

So instead, I want to date you, because it's the required step between friends and forever partners."

Wow. That was all I could think. Just 'wow.'

Morgan had just given me the speech of a lifetime and my alphabetic knowledge had dwindled to just two letters.

After a few moments of my silence, his forehead began to wrinkle, and his expression shifted into one of concern. "Care? Was that too much?" he asked, panicked. "Please talk to me."

I shook my head, unable to find the words to describe what I was feeling. Well, other than 'wow'.

"No?" he guessed. "Are you shaking your head because you don't reciprocate or because I didn't scare you? I can't tell; you just seem shocked."

"I am," I rasped, staring up at those infuriatingly gorgeous grey eyes. "I mean, I was hoping that you liked me back, but...I didn't expect..." And then, the stupidest words I've ever said came out of my mouth, serving as the declaration of my feelings—a moment which would be carved in my mind forever. "I'm a penguin too."

Morgan was only confused for about two seconds before he grinned, a laugh escaping his lips.

"Don't make fun of me," I complained halfheartedly, shoving at his chest. "You know what I mean."

"No." He shook his head, stepping closer until he'd not just invaded my space, but claimed it for his own, planting a proverbial flag. "I think I need you to say it, Red. All of it."

Dang him. *Although, it's only fair considering that he just* bore his soul *for me.* Fine.

"Okay, here goes." I took a breath, squaring my shoulders. "I feel the same way you do. I mean, I haven't loved; therefore, I haven't lost, but I do know that I've never felt this before..." Then I faltered, chafing against the rawness of this much vulnerability. But the brush of Morgan's fingers against my cheeks gave me courage.

"The thing is, I don't find any enjoyment in meeting guys or letting them buy me dinner. In fact, I hate it. And to be honest, I've been pretty careful not to let anyone get close enough to make a move anyway," I admitted with a shrug. "Because trust is hard. I've been pretty stingy with it because I'm afraid that people will break it...But that fear feels worth moving past—for you. *With* you. I don't want to get to know anyone else or learn to tolerate anyone else, or build a bridge with anyone else, because I've already found the right person to do it all with. I already found someone who makes trust easy, not scary. So, while it's early and we haven't even defined the relationship yet...I know I only want you."

Morgan's eyes had gone soft and heated about two seconds into my speech, but they were practically searing now. His hands on my face were gentle but firm as he leaned closer.

"Care, that was a terrible confession of affection." He was teasing me, but I didn't care. Because that smirking mouth was getting closer to mine.

"Yeah? What are you gonna do about it?"

"Really?" He rolled his eyes. "What are you, four?"

"You like it," I smiled, loving the ease I felt with him now that all the words were out. Turns out, getting them out wasn't the problem, keeping them in was.

"I like just about everything you do," he breathed, his eyes dipping down to my lips. I swallowed as I felt my stomach drop, a pleasant kind of nervousness flooding my body. "Even when I don't want to." He was so close now, his eyes almost out of focus, but then they flicked back up to mine. "Care, I...Can I?"

I nodded hurriedly, eagerly—I was practically begging him as he leaned down. And because I was impatient and desperate for him, I tugged on his shirt to help him reach me faster.

It might not have seemed like the hottest thing to do, asking for consent before he kissed me, but it had me sweating. The sheer need I'd seen in his eyes, and the eager way he'd asked, like it took all his restraint not to devour me on the spot, were undoing me completely.

By the time his lips met mine, I could've stamped 'property of Morgan Hohlt' on my forehead, because that man just about owned me. And if his emotions were anything to judge by, the feeling was mutual.

He was gentle at first, tentative and sweet as he pressed his lips to mine, both of us tilting instinctively to get better access. Then his hands shifted, one leaving my face to find my hair, while my own hands explored his neck and shoulders. And all the while, his lips remained tender and soft, the sweet innocence of a first kiss somehow protected even in the midst of so much heat. It was perfect, and I melted into him.

He responded to my every shift, hanging on my every sigh. And slowly, the kiss grew deeper and more passionate as he loosened the reins on his self-control. With every moment, I held him tighter, pretty sure my entire skeletal structure was going to liquify and leave me a limp string of fiery nerves.

I hadn't realized it could feel like this, kissing 'the one'. The fireworks in my veins, the tingles across my skin and the butterflies swooping in my stomach. Whether it was just so new or just that good, I didn't know. Didn't care either. *Just don't let it stop.*

And almost like I'd manifested it with my own thought, Morgan abruptly pulled back, staring down at me with eyes half glazed and fully wild.

"What?" I gasped, my breaths a little uneven. But as I took in the wide-eyed look on his face, I began to panic. "Oh no, did I do it wrong? Please, tell me if I did it wrong."

Morgan shook his head, looking a little bewildered. "Wait...was that your first kiss?"

Embarrassment flooded through me as a blush warmed my cheeks. My lack of experience with men wasn't something I broadcasted. Mostly because people had one of three reactions. Either they thought I was lying, that I was naïve and immature, or that I was weird. And none of those options ever made me feel good.

"Yes," I sighed, trying to find the words, "It's not something I really tell people about. And if I do, they usually think I'm ignorant and naïve, or that I'm weird and awkward. Which just makes me feel ashamed, so...I don't usually try to explain it. But it's not that I don't want to be kissed or held—because I do. I just never met anyone that I wanted to do with it...until you."

I wasn't sure how Morgan would take this news, but instead of looking at me with pity or judgment like so many people had, his expression had gone all soft and melty. Every bit of him was filled with affection, and I was warmed just by being near it.

He cupped my face again, his hands slowly sliding back into my hair, his eyes drinking me in like I was precious.

"Don't *ever* feel like you have to explain your choices to anyone," he whispered fervently. "Not even to me. No one has any right to judge the choices you've made. And of all the things for someone to make you feel bad about..." He shook his head, a murderous look in his eyes. "I hate that people made you feel bad for not kissing anyone. It's disgusting that someone would treat you like that. Here you've been valuing your physical affection enough not to squander it on just anyone, while half the world tosses out touches and kisses and sex like they're meaningless scraps of confetti. I just—"

"Morgan," I interrupted him, grasping his chin between my fingers, "Thank you."

"For what?" he growled, clearly still angry with the world for hurting me.

Feeling braver now, I leaned forward and pressed a kiss to his lips. "For not judging me. For not looking at me with pity like the only reason I'd never been kissed is because no one wanted to kiss me." At this, he scoffed. "Thank you for defending me and making me feel safe. But what I really need to know right now is if I did anything wrong in the kiss. Because I will not have you suffering through bad kisses because you're afraid to tell me."

Morgan sighed, his hands dropping to wrap around my waist. Then his eyes lit like twin torches, scathing me down to my bones. "You did *everything* right, Red."

Stomach clenching with pleasant anticipation, I smiled at him. "Everything?"

He didn't reply, just hummed as he swooped in and kissed me again, the noise vibrating pleasantly against my lips.

Where his first kiss had been gentle and tender, this one was insistent and fervent, all about the culmination of so many moments coming together in one explosion.

Eager, I followed his lead. And in case anyone was wondering, my lack of experience didn't seem to bother either of us. On the contrary, every effort I made to customize the kiss only made him groan and tug me closer.

Turns out, physical affection is a chemical thing; instinctual and quick to learn when you're willing.

And the bonus to this being my first kiss was that every sensation was so new and exciting, my nerves pleasantly shocked by every touch. His lips teasing mine, playing and chasing and coaxing. His hands finding my hair, skating along my shoulder and slipping around my waist. The gentle pressure of his lips on my neck making me gasp in surprise. And the growl rumbling through his chest as I tangled my fingers in his thick hair.

A few more precious moments passed when he suddenly pulled away, taking a big step back until he was grasping the island behind him.

"I need a break," he rasped, breathing so hard that I could see his chest rising and falling.

Confused, I looked at him dumbly. "Why..."

Morgan licked his lips, and my eyes tracked the movement of their own accord. "Because we weren't exactly leaving room for Jesus over there, and I'm honestly losing my mind—the part that houses my self-control in particular."

Ah. Now that he mentioned it, I wasn't really in full control of my will power either. *It's those danged lips.* And the hands. His scruff was nice too, the way it lightly scraped against my cheek and my neck...

"Caroline," he warned, and I snapped my eyes back to him, realizing that they'd been wandering.

"Sorry. But...I guess I can take this to mean that the kiss was good?" I asked shyly, running a finger along the countertop, too self-conscious to meet his eyes.

I sensed him move closer—his hulking presence was hard not to notice. His body brushed my legs, and then he was standing between them, his arms banding around my back to slide me closer.

"Care," he whispered. Feeling braver with him so close, I looked up and set my hands on his chest.

"Yeah?"

"That kiss," he said, his breath brushing my face, "Could win awards. And I'm not talking about a Dundee. I'm talking about world records, Grammys, Oscars, all of them. Because of your kissing prowess, I'm going to have to keep at least three feet between us at all times if I'm going to have any hope of keeping my hands off you."

"Who says I want your hands off me?"

A rumble echoed in his chest and his arms tightened around me.

"Don't tease me, Red. I'm a good man, but I'm still a man. My desire is stronger than yours and I can only draw boundaries by myself for so long. You gotta help me out here."

Sighing, I leaned up and kissed him one more time. He was quick to respond, deepening the kiss immediately to something more passionate. But this time, I stopped focusing so much on what I felt and really let my magic home in on him. So, when his desire began to skyrocket, and I felt his control slipping, I pressed a closed mouth kiss to his lips and gently pushed him away.

"Back to dinner?" I asked cheerily, hopping off the counter, careful not to upset my knee. Which was feeling 'miraculously' better. *Huh. Imagine that.*

When I turned to Morgan, he was watching me. Not with desire this time, but just a sweet affection. Leaning down, he kissed my forehead and slipped his hand into mine.

"You're incredible Caroline Felicity."

And to my surprise, tears sprung to my eyes. Morgan, concerned, swept me into a hug. I clung to him, trying to figure out where my emotional reaction came from. Was I crying happy tears? Was I just grateful I'd found Morgan? Or...was it that after twenty-two years of having to build a mote around myself, pull up the drawbridge and threaten anyone who came near, I'd never even dreamed that anyone would ever adore me like this? *I've never even let myself want it.* But now that Morgan offered it so freely, I didn't intend to ever let it go.

Chapter 22

MORGAN

"**I**s there anything else anyone needs to discuss now that we've come to the end of the agenda?" Fitz asked from his spot at the circular table. Today was our monthly council meeting, and by some miracle, it hadn't taken nearly as long as I'd thought it would.

I held my breath as the mayor glanced around the room. It was rare that someone didn't have some kind of—mostly unnecessary—question or comment to make at the end of these meetings. And the fact that no one was speaking seemed too good to be true.

"Alright then," he said after a moment of silence, "This meeting is adjourned, and I will see you all next month. If you have anything to add to the next meeting's docket, please send me an email!"

I launched from my seat and raced for the door, having no desire to get stuck in the mosh pit of whining council members. Being around the group for a few hours once a month to talk about business, I could survive. But getting stuck talking about our weekend plans and what we had for dinner last night, I *refused* to survive.

"Got a hot date? Or maybe some new crimes to cover up?"

I ignored Francine, the Minotaur representative, wishing she'd just up and retire already. She was in her fifties, and although Gerard the Hunter representative was older than her, he didn't tick me off like she did. He could stay; she could go.

"Oh, go guard your labyrinth, Francine," Brooks, the young Fenrir rep warned her lightly in his easy going way as he fell into step beside me. "The meeting's over, and we all want to go home. Let's not start something."

For a moment, she looked like she might press the matter. But then she glared at us and walked ahead to the door.

"I'm not much of a hater," Brooks said with a lopsided smile, his messy hair partially hidden beneath a beanie, "Takes too much energy to be bitter. But man, I hate that woman."

I chuckled, allowing myself to engage instead of walking away with a grunt. Brooks had never been someone I spent a lot of time talking to, but he also wasn't someone that necessarily irritated me. He was one of the younger reps, but he had a good head on his shoulders, and he was always willing to find a solution. He was practically a unicorn amongst all the liars we worked with.

"I'd love to disagree with you..." I paused dramatically as we reached the door, and smirked. "No, I take it back, I don't want to disagree with you. I hate Francine."

Brooks laughed and we walked through the short adjoining hallway and through the single door at the end. The second we stepped out into the rest of the building; I felt a weight lifting from my chest. Though the marble floors and smooth tiled walls were the same here as they were in the council room, this space felt free of the oppression that seemed to haunt the council room.

"I knew I liked you, Hohlt," Brooks said as we made our way down the hall. "Even if you are a cantankerous old man."

"Old?" I demanded, mostly teasing. "I'm only like ten years older than you."

"Exactly. Old."

Brooks' smile was cheeky, and I let myself laugh, glad there were at least a few council members I didn't have to hate.

"So, what's up with you and your secretary? You brought her last time, but she didn't come into the meeting."

I stumbled a bit at his question, my instincts instantly on edge as my emotional walls went right up like a fortress.

"Oh, is Morgan being grilled about his lady friend?" I sighed as Merida's voice floated up from behind me.

"She's not my lady friend," I lied smoothly. Technically, I hoped that after our kiss, she was now officially my girlfriend. But I had yet to ask Caroline if she saw it that way or not.

Merida gave me a knowing look and smiled at Brooks. "She's his lady friend."

I growled. "Merida—"

"Yes, dearest friend?" she taunted; arms crossed. Normally I would chastise her for being friendly to me in public. We tried to keep our friendship off people's radar for Merida's safety. But with Brooks standing here, I figured it wouldn't be particularly damning for Merida to be seen with me in a group.

"We're..." I sighed and rubbed my temple. "We're dating...kind of."

"Kind of?" Brooks smirked, taking Merida's lead and pushing my buttons. "How you do kind of date a woman?"

I glared at him, but he was unmoved. *Sometimes, I really wish I could just fan the flames of my bad reputation instead of trying to eliminate it.* At least then people wouldn't dare to tease me.

"We've flirted and...stuff." I hedged around telling them about the kiss. I was already shocked at myself for telling them this much. It probably goes without saying, but I'd never been much of a sharer. But I hadn't had a chance to share this stuff with my brothers or Logan or Grey yet, and apparently, I needed to tell someone.

"Stuff?" Merida mocked, grinning. "Does this stuff include hand holding?"

"Lip puckering?" Brooks added with a wink.

"Shut up, the both of you," I snarled, turning toward the lobby. "I'm sorry I ever said anything about it."

"Wait, Morgan! We're sorry," Brooks said, keeping pace beside me. "We won't make fun of you anymore."

"Speak for yourself," Merida snickered from my other side. I glared at her, and she rolled her eyes. "Okay fine, I'll stop teasing you—for now. But the next time I see you outside of this building, your relationship with your lady friend is fair game."

While I appreciated Merida omitting Caroline's name from the discussion since I hadn't disclosed it to anyone on the council, I did *not* appreciate the ribbing. "Such a charitable soul you have," I quipped, only slightly annoyed.

"Listen man, it sounds like your girl likes you," Brooks added. "Now all you have to do is keep her. And one piece of advice that's stuck with me for years is to always chase the woman, no matter how long you've had her. Because the minute you treat her like she's caught is the minute she doesn't feel valued anymore."

Huh...It actually wasn't bad advice. And knowing Caroline, she'd want to be chased until we were old and grey. *Fine by me.* She was well worth the effort.

"He's right," Merida nodded as we neared the double doors that led outside. "Women like to be pursued, no matter how long you've been together or how established your relationship is. And we *hate* guessing about your feelings. So just be straightforward and honest—even if it feels uncomfortable."

"Thank you...I think," I hummed as we stepped out into the warm sunlight. "That was actually really helpful. It's been a while since I've been in—" I stopped myself just before I said 'love'. I hadn't told *Caroline* that I loved her yet. There was no way I was about to tell these two about it. "A relationship with someone. It's good to have a refresher."

Merida smiled. "Our class is open any time for enrollment."

"Yeah," Brooks agreed. "I know you and I don't know each other well, but you're one of the few good ones in there, Morgan. I think us honest council members need to stick together."

I nodded, slowly realizing that through my last few years spent in grief and hatred for all the people who judged me, I'd hated the good people too. People like Brooks and Asher. But maybe it was time that my inner circle started getting a little bigger...

I felt content as I walked to my car, hopeful even. It was a beautiful day, I had an amazing woman at home, and it turned out that I didn't hate everyone. *Not bad for a Monday.*

But as I reached for the door handle, a strange pang of panic flared to life inside me.

Panic that wasn't mine.

At first, I didn't react. I was no stranger to feeling Caroline's feelings. I sensed them all day, and sometimes she panicked over small things like a ruined shirt or a lack of Pringles in the kitchen. But as I started driving and the feeling didn't fade, I started to worry.

Then, when the feeling intensified, now mixed with shock and anger, I called Mike.

"Where's Caroline?" I asked before he could so much as utter a 'hello'.

"She's here," he replied, and I detected worry in his voice. "She's...having a bit of a hard time."

"I'm on my way home now. I should be there in ten minutes. What's wrong? Is she hurt?"

"She's not in any physical danger, but we're not at the house."

I couldn't help it, I knew she wasn't in danger, but my blood went cold, and I felt the sudden need to strangle someone. "*Mike, where are you?*"

"We're at the courthouse," he said, and I could practically hear the flinch in his tone. "She wanted to come and request her birth certificate, but things have gotten a little complicated and—"

"I'll be there in two minutes."

Mike let out a breath of relief and I hung up before I went all caveman and blamed him. I knew it wasn't his fault, but my mate was in emotional distress, and I was too far away to help. The mate bond seared through me, begging me to be near her, to comfort her or protect her or be whatever it was she needed right now.

So, I drove faster.

After running two yellow lights and crossing two lanes of traffic in an intersection, I finally arrived at the courthouse. By the grace of God, I did it in one piece.

Stressed as I was, I didn't take the time to put change in the meter after I parked. I'd probably come back to a ticket, but Care was worth far more than the money they'd charge me.

I bolted inside without a thought and headed for the main lobby.

"Where would I go to get a birth certificate?" I asked as I strode up to the little window where a receptionist sat.

The middle-aged woman eyed me like I might be a threat to national security, and I half expected her to press some secret button under her desk. "Are you requesting a birth certificate for yourself?" she asked cynically.

I sighed, willing myself not to lose my cool. But with Caroline's anxiety prodding at the back of my mind, it was proving difficult to remain calm.

"No, I'm actually looking for someone and she's here for a birth certificate."

The woman began to shake her head. "I'm not sure I can help you—"

"Listen, the girl I'm in love with is having a panic attack right now and I *need* to be there," I begged, clinging to the counter the woman sat behind. "So please tell me where to go, or so help me, I will run through these halls screaming for her at the top of my lungs."

I couldn't tell if the receptionist was offended by my threat or moved by my admission of love. She just continued to stare at me with narrowed eyes, either judging me romantic or crazy. Maybe both.

Finally, she sighed. "To your right, take a left at the first hall, and it's the second door on the right," she said, shooing me with her hands. "Now get on, go find your lady. But so help me, if you shout in these halls, I will call security."

"Yes ma'am," I nodded, taking off down the hall at a dead run.

I almost missed the correct hallway, skidding past it and then nearly falling over as I turned back to take the turn. But it turned out that I didn't need the receptionist's directions anyway, because I could both feel Caroline's panic intensifying as I drew nearer and hear her shouting.

I barely paused as I shoved the correct door open. I winced as it slammed back against the wall, but no one seemed to notice. They were all too busy staring at a young woman with tears on her cheeks and a frayed edge to her shouting voice.

Caroline.

She was standing at a counter, yelling at another young woman who clearly worked here.

"No, it cannot wait," Care shouted through her tears, slamming her fist on the counter. "You can't just drop a bomb like that and then tell me I have to wait!"

"Miss, as I've already explained several times," the woman behind the desk said calmly, clearly empathetic to Care's reaction, her face drawn in sympathy, "I don't have the information here, and I can't control how quickly you receive it. All I can do is request it. I put a rush order on it, but that's all I'm able to do. I literally don't have any other options for you."

As the two women argued in the small office with framed certificates on the walls and file folders stacked on the desk, Mike stood off to the side. When he caught my gaze, he gave me an apologetic look. "I tried to comfort her, but she shoved me away and refused to listen."

I nodded, understanding the hurricane that was my mate. Even *I* could barely calm her down sometimes, and I had the advantage of the mate bond. I could hardly blame Mike for not being able to accomplish the task.

"Care," I said, stepping further into the room to touch her arm.

She spun around, eyes a little wild like she expected to fight off a stranger. But when she realized it was me, her anger turned to sorrow and her lip quivered, fresh tears clouding her eyes. "Morgan?"

"I'm here, sweetheart" I assured her, gently squeezing her arm. "Now tell me what's wrong."

"I came to get my birth certificate," she blubbered, holding a large manila envelope in her hand like she wanted to rip it to shreds. "I thought we might find something helpful about my birth parents that might lead to Volund or the buyer. But then *this woman* told me that I had an inheritance that was never given to me."

"What?" I demanded, looking to the woman behind the counter.

The girl sighed, clearly tired of being the target of Care's wrath. I couldn't blame her. The wrath of Caroline was no joke.

"As I told your girlfriend," the girl explained, still managing to maintain a kind tone—God bless her, "The inheritance had been logged incorrectly because her first name was spelled wrong. Which unfortunately means that she was never notified of it. Although I can see she has an inheritance, I'm unable to see who it's from or what's in it as those files are private. All I can do is put in a request for the files to be sent to her immediately. I put a rush on it, but it could take up to a month."

"It's my parents, Mor," Care insisted, grasping the front of my shirt, the blue ring in her eyes a physical reminder of my need to fix this. To ease her pain somehow. "They gave my adoptive parents money for me when they first gave me up, but what if this is more than money? What if it's a letter, explaining why they left? Or a warning about what happened to them? Morgan, what if I have a chance to finally meet them?"

I opened my mouth, somehow hoping to gently remind her of their death, but she shook her head.

"I don't mean literally. I know they're gone. But what if..." she paused, struggling to speak as her tears came faster. "What if whatever it is they left for me is the only window I have into who they were? Into how much they loved me? I never got to meet them, Mor. I never even got a real picture of them. But maybe this is my chance to know them, even a little bit."

"You might be right," I assured her, setting my hands on her shoulders. "Maybe this is your chance for closure. But that closure isn't going anywhere. It'll still be there, even in a month."

"No!" Care shouted, stepping away from me. "I can't wait, Mor. I've waited twenty-two years to find out if they loved me. I can't wait another day. I just can't..."

*Ah...*This outburst wasn't about a letter or a hope for closure. It was about a little girl who never got to hear her birth parents say 'I love you' before they died.

My heart broke for her as I envisioned a young Caroline crying over the parents she never met, while simultaneously loving the parents she had and not knowing what to do with either of those feelings. My sweet girl had been carrying this around for the better part of a decade, and I had a feeling she'd intentionally carried it alone. *Oh, Care.*

Slowly, watching the wariness in her eyes, I closed the gap between us and took her hands in mine. When she didn't fight me, I moved closer, setting my forehead against hers.

"Caroline *Felicity*," I whispered. "I've never heard of a more loving name for a parent to give to a child. They didn't name you Hope or Charity, they named you Felicity because above all else, they wanted you to be *happy*, Red. That's all any truly loving parent wants for their kid. And that's how I know they loved you. Because they didn't just leave you with a bank account and a new family, they left you with the hope that you would be happy."

"Intensely happy," Care corrected, her hands shaking in mine. "I know that they loved me...but I want to see it. Just this once, I want more than a name to tell me they cared."

"And you'll have it, Red. But until it gets here, just hold onto Felicity, okay?"

She nodded against me, her breaths deep as she fought against her tears. "I donknowhaIdowoutyou," she blubbered—which I interpreted as 'I don't know what I'd do without you'.

"You'll never have to find out."

Then, because I couldn't stand to be inactive when she was so distraught, I leaned down and swept her up into my arms. She didn't complain, instead she latched one arm around my neck and buried her face against me.

"Does she need to do anything else, or did you already finish the request?" I asked, leaning over to speak to the woman at the counter.

"I already put it through," the woman smiled gently, eyeing us tenderly. "When it comes, it'll arrive in her mailbox."

"Thank you, and I'm sorry about all of this."

"Don't worry about it," the woman said, swiping at her eyes. "It's actually very touching to see a man be so tender. You be good to her."

"Always," I smiled.

The woman waved goodbye as she sniffled, and I let Mike open the door so I could get Caroline out without jostling her.

"Morgan, I'm sorry. I didn't know what to do—"

"It's okay, Mike," I cut him off, heading back the way we'd come. "There's nothing you could've done. When Care gets set on something, there's no stopping her."

"Right here," she mumbled against my neck, and I chuckled, liking the way the sound vibrated where her face pressed against me.

"Sorry, Red," I whispered, gently rubbing her arm with my thumb.

She mumbled something unintelligible, and by the time we made it back to the lobby, she'd fallen asleep against me. I couldn't blame her. Big emotional bursts like this were exhausting, and if I could help her rest, then I was satisfied for the moment.

"Oh, my goodness, is she okay?" the receptionist asked as we passed, standing up swiftly at her counter.

"She will be," I assured her, speaking quietly so I wouldn't wake Care. "I think she's pretty exhausted from being so upset, but I'm taking her home to rest."

The woman's lips puckered, and she watched us like one might watch an injured puppy. "Oh, sweet thing. I hope she'll be okay."

"Me too."

The woman watched us leave, a sympathetic look on her face. But my attention was focused solely on the girl in my arms. With Mike's help, I was able to get her buckled in the front seat of my car, the ticket on my windshield well worth it to see her safe and resting.

"I'm sorry you were scared," Mike said as I stood there watching Caroline sleep.

"It wasn't your fault, it's just...I feel like I'm too protective of her, too possessive. But she's not just my mate, Mike. She's my *second* mate. Something I really never thought I'd have..."

"I know," Mike nodded, no doubt remembering my days of grief and reclusion after Gen died. He and Clint and the rest of the guys had all lived through those rough years with me, watching me drown in her absence. Losing a mate was something I'd never wish on anyone. Something I sometimes felt surprised to have survived at all.

"I can't lose her," I admitted, my voice quiet as tears built in my eyes. "It would kill me."

"Hey, you're not losing Caroline," he assured me, clasping my shoulder.

"You don't know that. I never thought I'd lose Gen either, and look where we are."

"Exactly," Mike said, forcing me to turn and face him. "Look where you are now. After all that pain you went through, did you think you'd ever be genuinely happy again?"

I shook my head, unable to put into words just how miserable I'd been and how hopeless I'd felt.

"Exactly," he went on. "Your whole world went dark after Gen, and we were all terrified that we'd lose you. Then once you recovered, you weren't...*you* anymore. But then Caroline happened."

I let out a short laugh that was quickly swallowed by tears as I recalled the first time I saw her. It'd been dim in that office, but even before I knew she was my mate, I was intrigued. And then I'd seen those eyes and realized who she was—*what* she was to me—and I knew, even when I tried to deny it, that trying not to fall for her would be a losing battle.

I'd never been so happy to lose in my life.

"Morgan, you're happy again," my brother went on, squeezing my shoulders, "And that's proof that there's joy after pain. So even if the worst happened and you lost Caroline, you would survive. And eventually, you would find a way to be happy again. So don't let this paranoia steal the joy you've found. You and Care Bear both deserve more than that."

I wasn't a man who had anything against crying, because I knew tears were healthy, but I'd rather not have cried them in the middle of the street. Still, I let them fall and clasped my brother in a hug, letting him support me in ways he shouldn't have had to.

"I'm sorry," I mumbled as we stood there hugging. "You guys should have been enough for me. It shouldn't have taken finding my mate for me to finally be happy again."

"I don't care how it happened, bro. I just care that you're happy."

"But I need you to know it," I insisted, pushing him back so I could see his face, surprised by the tears I saw in his eyes. "You guys were enough, and I'm sorry that I was too entrenched in my grief to see it."

"You're forgiven," he said easily, sniffing back a few tears. "But honestly, you don't have to apologize. We all deal with grief differently, and I think that with a little more time, you would have remembered how to be happy, even without Caroline."

Moved by my little brother's confidence in me, I gave him one last tight hug before I stepped away. "Thanks Mike. You've always been the most discerning of us all."

"It's the golden child syndrome," he shrugged humbly.

I chuckled, and as I drove off with Caroline safely beside me, Mike waved, smiling.

He was right, I was happy again, both with my family and with Caroline, and it was high time I started basking in it.

Chapter 23

CAROLINE

I shifted on the couch, my body way too exhausted for someone who'd spent half the day crying and the other half sleeping. My body felt like I'd run a marathon. And emotionally, I supposed I had.

"You comfortable?" I asked, wiggling against Morgan, who was currently serving as the big spoon to my little spoon.

"Red," he murmured, his arms tightening around me, holding me closer, "I don't remember the last time I was this comfortable, so please stop wiggling."

I smiled, and burrowed deeper into our fortress of blankets. I didn't remember the drive home from city hall, but by the time I woke up, Morgan had me bundled up on the couch, watching me like a hawk. I tried to assure him that I was fine, but he wasn't buying it. So, it was no surprise that when I asked him to stay with me, he hadn't exactly been a hard sell.

For a few hours now, we'd fluctuated between napping and watching TV, tucked together under bunches of blankets and a snoring Daisy Mae. Even though it was July, the fireplace was roaring, and I felt cozy and content in my Morgan cocoon.

Well, mostly.

With a pair of worried eyes boring into my head, my sense of peace was slightly dampened.

"Care..." Morgan hedged.

"Can't you just enjoy this lovely binge session and cuddle me like a good Bear Man?" I whined, rolling over onto my back, knowing exactly where this was going; an interrogation of my wellbeing was about to begin.

"I know you hate this," he said, grabbing hold of my hand and keeping it hostage, warm and cozy between us, "But I had my heart pummeled with a meat tenderizer when I saw you falling apart in that office. So please just humor me and tell me how you're doing."

I glared at him, annoyed that his affection was so pure. Why, just this once, couldn't he be negligent when it came to my feelings? "That's not fair," I pouted. "But fine, for you, I'll be honest."

He kissed my forehead. "Thank you."

I blew out a loud breath, trying to figure out how to explain my feelings in a way that made sense. Challenging since *I* didn't even fully understand my feelings. "I was fine until the woman at city hall told me that I had an inheritance that had never been given to me," I sighed. "And since my birth parents had already left money with my adoptive parents to give to me when I turned eighteen, I knew that whatever this mysterious inheritance was, it probably wasn't money. Which meant that it was probably sentimental. Something personal..."

"But then the woman told you that you would have to wait to get the inheritance," Mor added, seeing me struggle with the words.

I nodded silently, recalling the sudden panic that had come over me. It was like, out of nowhere, I was awash in grief. Like they'd just died all over again and I was being told I had to wait to say goodbye.

"I can't explain it in a way that doesn't sound stupid," I said, clutching a blanket beneath my fingers. "But when she said I had to wait a month to find out what they'd left for me, I just felt so insecure. I'd never met my birth parents. I had no letters from them, no mementos other than a single photo. I had no evidence that they cared, and here was an opportunity to—I don't know..."

"Hear them say they loved you?" Mor prompted, dropping my hand to wind his arm around my waist, his body warm against my side. "That's okay, Care. It's okay to want to know that your parents loved you."

"But that's the thing. I know how obvious it is that they loved me. I know that they chose my adoptive parents carefully and they left me money—"

"But unlike most kids who hear their parents say the words 'I love you', you had to wonder," he interrupted gently, "People need affirmation, Red. They need to be told they're important. That's not just a Caroline thing." He smiled and I rolled my eyes. "It's okay to be upset that you never had the chance to feel loved by the people who gave birth to you."

"But it's silly to be so upset when I know I'll get the inheritance within a month."

"It's not silly. It's okay to be angry or sad that you have to wait. This whole thing drudged up a lot of feelings and now they're unsettled."

"Yeah, I guess..."

"Hopefully when your inheritance arrives, it can give you the comfort you need. But even if it doesn't, you'll be okay. Because you're not going to do any of it alone."

I looked at him with misty eyes, awed by God's sweet generosity in giving me Morgan Gareth Hohlt.

"Have you always been so wise?" I whispered, setting my hand on his cheek.

"No. That's the effect of a good woman."

I laughed, but the sound quickly dried up as I remembered his own panic from earlier. I'd scared him with my breakdown, and I hated that even now, he was worried because of me. "I'm just sorry I worried you earlier," I whispered. "I know you don't mind supporting me, but still. I scared you over something silly and I'm sorry for that."

"I don't want you to be sorry, Care. Your feelings are valid," he murmured gently, covering my hand with his large one, his calloused fingers warm against me. "I just want you to always be honest about them. And if that means that I worry about you, then so be it. I've been in love enough to know that I can't fix everything for you. I can't make everything better out of determination and brute strength. But I *can* be here for you. And that's all I need, Care, is to be what you need. So don't apologize for being upset—no matter the cause—and don't you ever hide it from me to keep me from worrying. I want to be your partner, which means lifting you up when you need me. So please let me."

I desperately wanted to pay attention to his incredibly sweet speech, but all I could think about were those four little words in the middle of it. 'I've been in love'. Did that mean...*No, it couldn't be.* Morgan couldn't love me...But what if he did? Did I even want that?

Yes. Because somehow, I'd fallen in love with my best friend without fully realizing it until right now. *Huh. You'd think I would have noticed that.*

"Mor?" I asked nervously, wiggling onto my other side so I could face him. "What did you mean, just now?" He gave me a confused look and I dropped my gaze as I fiddled with the top of his shirt, avoiding his eyes. "Did I hear you right? Did you say...love?"

I couldn't see his face, but I knew he understood what I was asking. But then I began to panic, because *he understood what I was asking.* Which meant that he probably gathered that I wanted his answer to be yes. *Maybe I can just change the subject and pretend this never happened.*

But before I got the chance, he set gentle fingers on my chin. "Caroline, please look at me."

I was reluctant to obey—what would he see in my eyes? What would I see in his? Could I survive a rejection from him? Would I have to? But when I finally raised my gaze to his, I saw only affection and loyalty reflected there. And suddenly a little burst of hope lit inside me.

"Yes," he said, his voice barely louder than a breath, "I said love. Because I've known for a while now that I love you, Caroline Felicity. For a long time, I didn't think I had the capacity to love again, or that I was worth loving at all...until you."

Even though I'd already cried plenty over my birth parents today, I began to cry *again*. Because apparently the human tear ducts knew no bounds.

But this time, they were happy tears.

"Really?" I asked in wonder, realizing that I recognized this look on his face. I'd seen it a lot lately. And this warmth in his chest that slid like a warm blanket over my soul wasn't new either. And now, I understood what they were.

Love.

Morgan loves me. Morgan loves *me.* I repeated the words like a mantra in my mind, but still it felt surreal. For a while now, I'd been so afraid to lose the precious friendship we had, to lose this closeness that I'd never had before. And here my best friend loved me back and it turned out that my safe space and my adrenaline rush were bound up in the same person.

"Really," he nodded, trailing his fingers along the edge of my face before diving them deep into my hair. "I think I've been in love with you since the moment you said you trusted me. But I've been wanting to say it for a few weeks."

I couldn't help the stupid grin that stole across my face. "Well, I guess I'm a late bloomer, because I didn't realize it until a little while ago..." I paused, flattening my hand against his raging heart. "But I love you too, Morgan."

Now probably would have been the right time for a big romantic speech, but I never got the chance to make one. Because no sooner had I finished speaking, than Morgan swooped in and kissed me.

I felt fire in his lips, his desire big and powerful. But my joy ruined the moment because I couldn't stop smiling long enough to really kiss him back.

"Caroline," he growled, grey eyes glaring at me.

"I'm sorry," I giggled—yes *giggled.* Because love made me twelve years old. "I'm just really happy."

His expression immediately softened, and he pulled me tight against him. "Me too. Makes me wonder how I survived so long *not* being this happy."

"They do say ignorance is bliss," I hummed, snuggling my head under his chin.

"True."

"Thank you, by the way."

"For?"

I shrugged, closing my eyes as I listened intently to his heartbeat. "For loving me. I know it had to be scary, taking the chance to love someone again after losing

Gen. So, thank you for taking that chance on me. I'm honored to be your second love."

"You know you're every bit as important to me as Gen was, right?" he asked, and I lifted my head to meet his eyes. "Because I may have loved Gen—and I always will—but you're my future, Care."

I nodded, a delicate smile on my face to match the delicate emotions inside me.

"I know. You're my future too, Mor."

Smiling, he kissed me again, and this time I managed to return it. This kiss was different from our first. It was surer, braver. Instead of being a curious exploration, this kiss was possessive and strong. A metaphorical brand to mark us both as belonging to one another, because I was Morgan's now, wholly and completely, and he was *mine.*

Chapter 24

CAROLINE

"What are you doing?" I asked, watching Morgan stare intently at his computer screen.

"Plotting," he growled.

I leaned forward from my perch on the edge of his desk and peeked at his computer's idle home screen. He was supposed to be looking up council members so we could start making a list of who else we should be looking into. We were kind of out of leads at the moment, so this was the best idea we had. "No. You're brooding. Plotting involves making a plan, brooding is just staring threateningly into space."

Mor lifted his grey eyes to me and glared. "You know, you're not doing great at this whole girlfriend thing."

Despite the fact that I was a twenty-two-year-old woman in love with a thirty-two-year-old widow, my heart went all dumb and fuzzy at the word 'girlfriend' like I was seventeen.

"I didn't know I was officially your girlfriend," I said with a nonchalant shrug, toying with a stack of post-its.

But my fiddling ceased as Morgan's hand covered both of mine, his expression warm and teasing. "Liar."

"You never said we were officially together."

"Yes, I did. I just happened to be speaking in tongues."

He winked and I gaped at him, my ears and cheeks catching fire.

"Morgan Hohlt!" I squeaked, surprised by the taunting heat in his gaze. "I can't believe you just said that."

"You liked it."

He tugged on my hand, and I let myself tip to the side, leaning closer to him.

"I like a lot of things about you," I murmured, our lips a breath away.

"Like what?" he whispered, eyes alight with affection.

"Like the fact that I can call you 'boyfriend' from now on." Then I kissed him.

But when he began to lift me by the waist like he intended to move me to his side of the desk, I pulled back.

"Huh uh, Bear Man," I protested, tapping him once on the chest before I retreated too far away for him to reach. "None of that."

He gave me puppy dog eyes, feigning innocence, but I wasn't buying it. "What? I wasn't going to do anything other than kiss you."

"You were going to move me closer."

He smiled, wide and dopey. "I like you closer."

"And so do I. But once you pull me closer, I'm betting that it would take about fifteen seconds for my self-control to crumble and then I'd be in your lap. And while I'm very fond of your lap, I don't trust myself getting that close to you when we're alone like this. You're too tempting for your own good, Hohlt."

"Mm...I think it would only take ten seconds," he said, a mischievous look on his face. "Shall we bet on it and find out?"

Rolling my eyes, I smacked his chest. "Morgan—"

"Yo, did you check your email?" Clint asked—loudly—as he stepped into the room, completely ignorant of our adolescent flirting.

"What are the chances that someone would adopt my idiot brothers?" Morgan groaned, laying his head on the desk.

I looked over at Clint as he took a seat on the couch. He smiled and tossed me a wink, the picture of humility, clearly. "Zero. You might be able to get someone to take Mike, but Clint is a lost cause."

"Rude!" the youngest Hohlt brother exclaimed, wide eyed with false innocence.

"You have an annoying knack for ruining every romantic moment I have with Caroline," Morgan mumbled against the desk. "So, forgive me if I'd rather you didn't exist right now."

Clint shrugged. "Fair enough. Although in my defense, I didn't know what I'd be stumbling on when I walked in here. I assumed that in a workspace, you'd be doing *work*. Silly me."

Morgan lifted his head and glared at his baby brother. "Leave now or I'm selling you to the circus."

"I don't think there is a circus anymore. Plus, don't you want to know why I came in here and ruined your nauseating love fest?"

"No."

Clint ignored Morgan and continued on anyway. "I came to tell you that you just got an email from Mayor Fitz announcing that he's starting a Shifter task force that will be assigned to do a full audit of each Shifter group and their leader. Including you."

Like magnets, Morgan and I turned toward each other. The city auditing Morgan wasn't necessarily a bad thing. But an investigation like that would probably lead to...

"They'll find you," Mor said, speaking my own thoughts aloud. "If they look into me, they'll check my financials, interview my Sleuth, check the house. They'll know you've been living here, and they'll look into you too, Red."

He was right. Even if we told the task force that we were dating and that's why I was so engrained in Morgan's life, they'd still probably look into me too. As the significant other of a regional representative, I was bound to be limited in my ability to maintain privacy. And if the task force dug deep enough and asked the right questions, they might discover that I wasn't my parent's child, and that I was neither human nor Berserker.

"What exactly does the email say?" I asked, needing to calm the anxiety in my chest.

Morgan immediately turned to his computer and pulled up his email. While he searched, I peered over at Clint. "How did you know about this email anyway?"

"I have Morgan's account on my phone," he shrugged simply.

"Excuse me?" Morgan barked, scowling at his brother.

With one finger on his jaw, I pushed my boyfriend's gaze back to the computer. "Sh. Focus on the email, Bear Man." He grumbled at me but complied and continued reading.

"He's totally going to kill you later," I warned, looking at Clint.

"Nah," Clint rolled his eyes. "I'll just stick you in front of him and he'll be distracted just like that." He snapped his fingers.

I gave him a pointed look, but it was ruined by the blush that worked its way across my face.

"Okay I found it," Mor interrupted, tapping my knee. I glanced at the screen and balked at the sheer number of unread emails he had in his inbox.

"How on earth do you do your job with your inbox that full?" I demanded, appalled at the unending list of emails.

"Hey, I do my job just fine," he defended, giving my knee a gentle squeeze. "Now listen to what Fitz said." I obeyed and listened as he began to read the email. "As we all know, Eileen is now safely locked up in Niffleheim, and many of you I'm sure believe that the buck stops there. But I disagree. While I don't have any concrete evidence that there was anyone else involved in the crimes perpetuated by the Dragons on Eileen's orders, I'm not convinced that we should let the matter die."

"In fact, when one considers the evidence accumulated by our vigilante, this city—this region—is infected with a coldness and a greed that's been left unchecked for too long. City officials have been caught and imprisoned for things such as trafficking Shifters, working the magical black market, plotting against regional representatives, setting up city wide disasters for the sake of personal gain, and much more. But the real shame in all of this is that we weren't the ones who caught these transgressions. A vigilante—a citizen with presumably less resources and connections than our governing body—has proven over forty-three people guilty of heinous crimes in the last three years. A citizen shouldn't have to step up and do the hard job of keeping us safe. As regional and city officials, that's *our* job. And the willful ignorance and selfish silence ends today."

Mor paused and glanced at me. I tried to blink away the mist in my eyes, but he saw it and kissed my temple.

"You deserve that," he whispered, so much pride swelling inside him. He'd told me before about the meeting where Agent Johnson had defended me to the council, but to hear *Mayor Fitz* stick up for me like this...I was surprised at how moved I felt.

I hadn't taken on the role of vigilante because I wanted a thank you or a pat on the back. I did it because I saw an injustice that no one else was doing anything about. But to have the highest-ranking city official semi-publicly give me credit felt nice.

Mor watched me for a moment, and I gave him a nod to go on.

"I've spoken with Agent Johnson," he continued reading, "As well as the city police and a few other mayors from the other regional Shifter councils, and with their help, I've come up with an idea. Starting next month, we'll begin utilizing a new task force. This task force will be comprised of volunteers from each of your species. You may select these volunteers yourself, but each group must supply at least two. In just a few weeks, this task force will begin being trained and be briefed on their new assignment, which is to investigate each regional Shifter representative and their people. From your financials to your laws to your people's behavior, everything will be scrutinized, and if anyone has any secrets, we'll find them. If this news makes you uncomfortable, then I urge you to consider if perhaps your time on the council should come to a close. Until the next meeting, Mayor Fitz."

Surprised by both the email itself and the accurateness of Fitz's words, I sat silently staring into space. Shifters had been an open part of society for well over a hundred years and for most of that time, we'd been our own worst enemies. Fighting with each other, selling each other, betraying each other. It was about time that someone called us out on it.

"Is anyone else shocked that Fitzy boy had the nerve to send an email like that?" Clint asked, spreading his arms out along the back of the couch. "I never thought of him as a particularly combative guy before."

"I didn't used to either," Morgan agreed. "But lately he seems to be gaining some confidence. He's been a little less lax in meetings, and much more direct than he used to be."

As the guys continued talking about Fitz and the task force, I pulled out my phone to text Merida.

Me: Did you see Fitz's email?

Then I sent another text.

Me: Are you blushing?

And another.

Me: Let me guess. You're imagining being alone with him in the council room. He walks up to you, tells you he means business, and then you two start making out on the council room table. *GIF of Blanch from *The Golden Girls* misting herself with a squirt bottle*

Merida texted back almost immediately.

Merida: Do you want me to jinx you a microwave that perfectly reheats French fries that actually taste good? Or do you want me to curse you with an intolerance for processed food instead?

Me: *eyeroll emoji* Okay, fine. Please just tell me one thing...

Merida: What

Me: Is daydream Fitz a good kisser?

Merida: ...

Merida: Very authoritative.

I snickered and Morgan gave me an incredulous look. "What are you doing?"

"I'm texting Merida," I defended, sending her a whole line of kissing emojis before I put my phone away. "She's likewise impressed with our mayor's authority."

Morgan sighed. "You and the matchmaking, I swear."

"You know you love me," I grinned.

"Questionable," he quipped.

I smacked his arm just as Mike walked into the room.

"I have bad slash good news," he announced.

Mor, Clint and I all sat up straighter and anxiously faced the middle Hohlt brother. "Rip the band aid off, dude," I said, not excited for whatever this news was.

"I got a hit on the website," he said, sounding a lot less enthused than I thought he would.

"Why is that bad?" Mor asked, eyes narrowed skeptically. "It means the Sleuth is on the lookout like I asked them to be, and they trust us enough to report it on the site."

"Yes, in that respect, it's good news," Mike nodded, not quite meeting Morgan's eyes.

"Mike?" Mor pressed.

"Someone reported a gambling den member, and it turns out that they're linked to Caroline," Mike blurted.

Morgan and I both tensed and turned toward each other, the same look of dread on both our faces. *Well, that doesn't sound great.*

"Explain please?" I begged Mike, trying to keep Morgan from Berserking out in his desk chair. Lord knows he'd break the thing in his bear form.

Mike, looking very apologetic, nodded. "You see, there's been a few hits since we set up the site, and I've had a few guys looking into them. For the most part, people have either been reporting things that aren't actually dangerous, or things that we already knew. But a few days ago, someone reported the identity of a gambling den member who was supposedly in the leader's inner circle. I had my guys look into it and it's true."

"As they were looking into him, they also discovered that a few months back, he was paid a lot of money by a shell account. And thanks to the info Care Bear stole from the Dragon Queen's computer, we know that the account belonged to Eileen. Which means that she hired that gambling den member. And the kicker? The payment he received was just a week before the first attack on Caroline."

"Which means?" Clint prompted.

Mike crossed his arms, looking bleak. "I think that this is the guy Eileen hired to find that safety deposit box from Caroline's birth parents. The one that gave Eileen all her info."

I saw Morgan go rigid, and I reached for his fisted hand, rubbing his fingers until they relaxed, allowing me to lace our fingers together. I knew he was scared, but *I* was scared that in his fear, he would do something stupid. Like barge into the closest gambling den member's house and snap their neck. And then he'd end up in prison. Or dead.

"So, you're telling me that the entire Berserker gambling network might know about Caroline?" Mor demanded, seething in his seat.

Mike looked between Clint and Morgan before setting sympathetic eyes on me. "...yes."

"Meanwhile, *you're* telling me that Fitz is starting a task force that might lead to Care being outed as the vigilante or an Elf," Morgan said, scowling at Clint.

"Unfortunately," Clint winced.

Sensing that Morgan was beginning to spiral, I walked around to his chair and set my hands on his shoulders.

"They're going to catch you," Mor mumbled, shaking his head.

"Bear Man, I love you, but you need to chill," I said, kneading his shoulders. "The task force hasn't even been assembled yet, and there's only a one in twelve chance that you'll be the first council member they investigate anyway. We have time to figure out what to do about it."

"I know," he said with a moan, tilting his head forward as I massaged away the tension at the top of his neck. "But what about the gambling dens? If they find out you—"

"They won't. Now let's think, if Eileen is the one that hired that guy, then it's possible that he's told his coworkers about me. But since Eileen is a Dragon, and Dragons have the ability to make people believe their lies, maybe Eileen convinced him that I wasn't noteworthy or that the documents about me were fake. It's possible that the den member doesn't actually know anything about me. Although, we'd be stupid to count on it..."

"It's more likely that the gambling den knows and they're the ones who've been trying to kidnap you lately," Clint suggested.

Morgan raised his head, and I didn't have to see his face to know that he was scowling at his brother. "Seriously?"

"What? I'm just saying..."

"You know what, I think I'll go ahead and volunteer you for the task force," Mor growled. "That way you'll be Fitz's problem."

Clint swatted his hand through the air disinterestedly. "Eh. The task force kind of sounds boring. Lots of research and record keeping. I'm more of a hands-on kinda guy."

Morgan sighed. "Ugh, you're right. They'd probably fire you and then investigate me immediately for suggesting you. Maybe I'll send Mike instead. He likes researching and logging and all that. Plus, he gets along with people better than you do."

"I get along with people!"

"Single female people," Mor corrected, deadpan.

"I could join the task force..." Mike offered thoughtfully, seeming a little excited by the idea. But Clint and Mor were too busy arguing to listen.

As they continued to bicker, my thoughts turned around and around in my head. We needed to find a way to check into the gambling dens and see what they did and didn't know. It was possible that the guy Eileen hired didn't know about me if she'd used magic to convince him otherwise, but maybe he knew who else Eileen had been working with.

But we don't have the manpower to look into it. There were five of us—four if you considered the fact that Logan was busy bodyguarding my sister. And it wasn't like Morgan could afford to go sneaking around getting intel on the gambling dens. He had a reputation to mend and a task force to deal with.

"Wait a second," I exclaimed, my hands freezing on Morgan's shoulders, "That's it."

"What's it?" Mike asked, confused by my interruption.

"The task force. Their job is going to be auditing every council member to see what they've been hiding," I explained excitedly, the idea in my mind coming into focus.

Clint turned a lost expression to Morgan. "...Okay?"

"No, you don't get it! The task force is going to be doing to council members what we want to do to the gambling dens!"

"Sweetheart," Morgan said tightly, tapping my hand, "I think I know where you're going with this, and I want to be excited, but you're kind of cutting off the circulation in my shoulders."

"Oh, sorry." I gave him an apologetic smile as he turned in his chair to look at me.

"Don't be," he smiled, tugging me over to sit on the arm of his big office chair. "Now if I'm understanding you correctly, you want us to start our own task force to look into the gambling dens?"

I nodded. "Yes. We need more information, and none of us can really afford to get our hands dirty right now. Not with everything else that's going on. What we need is a small group of people that we can trust to research and spy and log what they find out—not only with the man Eileen hired, but also what they find about with the gambling groups in general. I know you want to squash them," I said, turning my attention to Morgan, "But you can't if you don't know where to start. Therefore, we need a group to provide intel. They'll be like a little group of vigilantes! Oh, I could even train them myself!"

Mor rolled his eyes, but I saw the way his lips twitched like he wanted to smile.

"That's not a bad idea," Mike hummed. "We've always been a step behind with the gambling dens. But if we had a crew that could help us investigate, we might be able to get the upper hand."

But even though the boys seemed to agree with me, Morgan just sat there brooding.

"We need help, Mor," I prodded gently. "We can't fight on both fronts by ourselves."

"I know..." he met my gaze as I took his hand and gave it a reassuring squeeze. "But if I have people look into the guy that Eileen hired, then they might find out about you too. It's a good idea, but it's dangerous, Red."

I opened my mouth to argue with him, but Clint beat me to it. "That's not entirely true." Mor glared at him, but Clint was unfazed. "You could ask the Sleuth for volunteers to be on your task force. You and I both know they would do anything to protect Caroline."

Morgan stared at his brother in shock. "You mean you..."

"Yep," Clint said, although it was unclear what he was saying yes to. "We both do." Mike nodded along, smiling. "The Sleuth loves her; it wasn't hard to realize why."

"Huh," Mor grunted, watching his brothers curiously.

Completely lost, I looked between them. "I'm confused. Why would the Sleuth do anything to protect me? And what are you being so cryptic about?"

The boys all nodded to each other and then Mor looked up at me on my perch. "You remember when I told the Sleuth that what they do to you, they do to me? Well, they believed me. They'll protect you because you're important to me."

"And what was all that just now with the cryptically unfinished sentences?" I insisted, watching all of them with narrowed eyes.

"It's a brother thing." I wasn't sure I believed that, but we had bigger fish to fry.

"Alright whatever," I said with a wave of my hand. "You focus on gathering a task force of Berserkers to look into the gambling dens, and Mike and I will go take care of the rest."

I hopped off the chair and headed for the door, dragging Mike with me.

"Wait, what?" Mike sputtered; my hand latched onto his arm.

"What do you mean, the rest?" Mor called after us, confused.

Pausing by the doors, I smiled at him over my shoulder. "Mike and I will take care of legitimizing my backstory so that when the task force comes calling, there won't be any dirt on me to find. Remember Bear Man, just because I'm pretty doesn't mean I'm not smart."

Chapter 25

CAROLINE

C lint's paw soared toward my head, but at the last moment, I ducked under his arm and reached up to slash at his paw with my sheathed dagger.

"Not fatal!" he shouted at me.

"No, but you'd be in severe pain and distracted right now," I argued, dancing out of his reach. Then I threw my dagger at his neck, where it bounced off him harmlessly. "And now you'd be dead."

He roared at me, but I wasn't fazed. I'd seen the worst of the Berserker boys in these practice sessions, and I knew they were all bark and no bite.

But apparently, Morgan didn't agree.

He slammed his own furry bear form into Clint's, the two of them both falling to the ground in a heap of limbs.

"Your boyfriend is really something," Mike taunted, nudging my arm. I reached out and petted his shoulder, his black fur soft to the touch.

I rolled my eyes. "My boyfriend is a child. A big, fluffy bear child."

"I'm getting evidence on video to blackmail him with later," Volund said, his phone pointed at Morgan and Clint's wrestling match. "He's denied me a trip to the hair salon for too long, when the least he could do is let me hire someone to come out here. I mean, can you believe that it's been almost seven weeks since I had a blowout?"

Mike and I exchanged annoyed looks. Volund had begged us to let him join in on our training session, but he quickly came to regret it when the boys decided to use him as a target for their practice fights. Volund was actually sweating, his hair all flat and damp for once instead of perfectly styled like usual. *Serves him right. I can't even get my hair styled as perfectly as he does.*

Feeling vindictive, I shot a smirk at the Dark Elf. "Mike, I think Volt wants to do another practice run of that two on one fight you guys did earlier."

Mike, enjoying himself immensely, growled as he stepped toward Volund. Volt let out a high-pitched squeal and scurried a few feet away, eyeing Mike like he might snap Volund in half at any moment. *Pansy.*

It wasn't as if the boys had been harming him, they just had him stand in as an attacker and mimed how they would fight in that situation...And sometimes Volt mysteriously ended up on his backside. It was a completely unexplainable phenomenon...

"I haven't said anything rude in at least an hour," Volund huffed, crossing his arms over his black workout shirt. "There's no reason to be hostile."

"Oh, there's plenty of reasons to be hostile," I pointed out. "You insulted my wardrobe earlier, made fun of Morgan's bear form, locked Clint out of the house yesterday, and you ate all my chips."

"Okay now hold on," Volt argued as I plopped down and laid back in the grass. "That shade of pink doesn't flatter you nearly as much as the mint shirt you wore yesterday. That's not me being mean, it's just fact. And I didn't make fun of your boyfriend's furry body—I just said the grey made him look old. As for locking Clint out of the house," Volund shrugged, "He shouldn't have chased me around the yard with his fangs like I was a squirrel."

"And the chips?" I demanded as Daisy Mae trotted over and tried to lick my face.

Volt checked his nails. "How was I to know they were off limits? They're good chips, you should have known that you needed to hide them if you didn't want to share."

I growled and glared at the blue sky above me. "Morgan, come kill Volund. I'm sick of his annoying personality. Then, when you're done, come sit with me. We have business to discuss."

Volund sputtered complaints and Morgan and Clint ignored me for the moment, still too busy wrestling to pay much attention. So, I closed my eyes as Daisy laid down beside me and let the warm July sun warm me down to my bones. *What I wouldn't give for a pool and an ice-cold drink right about now.*

"What business do we have to get down to?" Grey asked, walking up to me with his trusty clipboard in his hands. He flipped through the papers, frantically looking for any indication of the business I was referring to.

"That's what I'd like to know." A shadow suddenly blocked out my sunlight and I blinked up at Morgan in his human form. "Are you plotting something that I don't know about?" he asked, sitting down in the grass behind me, his legs sprawled on either side of my body.

I started to sit up, but he gently pressed me back down and began to play with my hair. *A pool would have been nice, but this works too.*

"Happy?" he teased, smiling down at me.

"As a clam."

Morgan chuckled, and Mike and Clint joined us in their human forms, taking a seat in the grass.

"So, what is this business you have?" Grey asked, sitting gingerly on the ground, like he couldn't understand the appeal. "I don't have anything on the schedule."

"Relax Grey," I teased, watching him check the papers on his clipboard again. "It won't take long; I promise I won't ruin your very detailed schedule."

Grey rolled his eyes, his cheeks now dusted with a faint shade of pink.

"What's on your mind, Red?" Mor asked, his fingers brushing across my scalp down to the ends of my hair.

I tried not to purr like a kitten, but based on Clint and Mike's teasing looks, I was unsuccessful. "I think Mike and I have tightened up my background enough that no one should ask much in questions about me, but we did run into one teeny tiny snag."

Morgan turned an icy gaze on Mike. "Oh? And what snag is that?"

Mike bit his lip and I felt his nerves flare. *Poor guy.* It wasn't his fault that my history as a vigilante was hard to hide. "The fact that even though Care jammed the security footage during her heists, the exterior footage from the building across the street is intact. No one's looked at it yet, but if anyone gets curious about the timing of her move to Shifter Haven and the start of the vigilante heists, they might think to look there. And since she only changed her hair and not her face, they could identify her."

"So how do we fix it?" Morgan growled.

Trying to calm the anger I could feel building inside him, I set my arms on his legs and squeezed his knees. "It's really not that hard," I explained on Mike's behalf. "We'll just have to go in and alter the security footage. Mike has already made some kind of bug or software or something that will delete me from the security tapes. So, all we have to do is install it."

"All?" Mor clarified, not impressed with our solution. "And how exactly do we install it?"

"Um..."

"*Caroline.*"

"Ugh, I hate when you call me that." I rolled my eyes. "It means you're frustrated with me."

"Then answer the question," he prodded, his hands somehow still tender in my hair even though his emotions were taught and ready to snap.

Blowing out a loud breath, I looked up at met his penetrating stare. "We'll sneak into the security office to change the tapes."

"Caroline, you were attacked the last time we broke into the Alliance building—"

"But we're not going in the Alliance building."

"But it's *across the street.*"

"Yes, but last time we baited the attacker," I argued, not willing to let him swat this idea down. We needed to prepare ourselves for the day that Morgan was eventually investigated, and this was our best option. "This time they won't expect us."

"We've been lucky, Care," he said, his voice quiet and pleading. "We've taken a lot of risks and been fortunate to make it out of most of them relatively unscathed. But I don't think we should try sneaking in right after a failed attempt."

"Morgan—"

"Your safety is my priority, Care. Nothing else matters. We're not going."

I sat up and turned so my glare would be at eye level. "You don't get to decide that. You're not my father."

"No, I'm your mate."

At first, I thought I'd heard him wrong. But as everyone else went suddenly silent, refusing to meet my eyes, I knew I heard him right.

"*Explain,*" I whispered, confused and angry as I realized that everyone else seemed to know what he was talking about.

Everyone except me.

Morgan's face remained calm, but I knew better. I sensed his fear. His panic. But that only made me angrier as I felt the first pricks of betrayal. "Do you know what mates are?" Morgan asked.

"They're like magical soul mates," I answered in a monotone as the rest of the guys stood and went to the other end of the yard. Although they had to drag Volund because he delighted in watching our drama. "But Shifters are pretty private about it, so I don't know the details, but I thought mates were pretty rare."

Morgan shook his head. "Every Shifter has a mate. There's a lot to it..."

"So talk fast."

Mor flinched. "You're right that mates are like magical soul mates. But there are some extra side effects that go along with it. For one thing, mates have a mark that only their mate can see—"

"Your eyes," I breathed, recalling the question I'd asked him months ago about why there were blue rings in his eyes. At the time, he'd told me it was because he was Chief. Well actually, he just hadn't argued with me about it...

"I'm sorry I didn't tell you the truth when you asked," he pleaded quickly, lifting his hand and then dropping it again as if he was going to touch me, but then thought better of it. "It's just that at first, I lied to you because I didn't want another mate. I didn't want to love like that again and risk losing it. But the more I got to know you, the more I realized that I did want you as my mate. But by then, I was in so deep with the lies that I just...kept it going..."

Even though empathy prodded my heart as I sensed his pain, I told it to go kick rocks. Anger was safer than heartache; less hurtful. So, I clung to it.

"What else?" I asked, softer this time, but still detached.

"The mate bond is activated by close proximity," Mor explained patiently, heartbreak in his grey eyes. "So when I tried to catch you that first time, the bond was activated. It's why I felt strange for the following month. My emotions were off because they weren't all my emotions—they were yours."

I flinched as if smacked, leaning away from him, staring with wide eyes. This time, I was certain I'd misunderstood him. There was no way that Morgan had gone *months* being able to sense my emotions and not told me about it.

"Can you..." I paused, forcing myself not to cry. "Can you feel my emotions?"

Morgan hesitated, and in that tiny pause, I felt my trust begin to crumble. "Yes. The minute the mate bond is activated, mates begin to feel each other's feelings. And if you aren't aware of the bond, it can be disorienting because you don't realize the feelings you're feeling belong to someone else."

"And let me guess, with a mate bond, there's no limit to how far away you can sense each other?"

Morgan cringed, no doubt recalling how he'd tricked me into believing that the reason I could sense him over any distance was because of my attraction.

"I lied about that too, because those are the signs for the bond," he explained, "And I didn't want you to guess that we were mated before I told you myself. The bond is also the reason you trusted me not to hurt you when we first met.

It prevents us from harming each other, that way we can't accidentally kill each other before realizing we're mates."

"Is there anything else?"

"That's it," he insisted, this time reaching out to clasp my hand in both of his. Part of me wanted to shove him away, but the other part never wanted to let him go. *Freaking mate bond.* "But I need you to know, Care, that the mate bond is just a sign—that's all. It allows us to sense each other's emotions, and it gives us the assurance that we won't physically harm each other, but that's it. At its core, it's really just a supernatural name tag that tells us who 'the one' is. A gift from God to all animal Shifters to help us see past our sometimes-impulsive natures and find the right person. It doesn't create anything or manipulate anything; it just points us to a connection that already exists."

Tears pressed against the back of my eyes, but I held them at bay, determined to keep it together until I was alone.

"Is that it?" I asked coldly.

Morgan sighed and I nearly broke as his eyes grew watery. Very few times had I seen Morgan Hohlt cry, and it killed me to know that I was the cause of it.

"Yeah, that's it," he replied quietly; defeated.

Sensing my own emotions begin to seep out of me, I snatched my hand away from him and stood, heading for the house. I'd made it all the way to the stairs in the dining room when a warm hand grasped mine, stopping me in my tracks.

"Red, I—" Morgan's voice was wobbly and broken, and I closed my eyes against the urge I felt to comfort him. Was that the mate bond? Or was it my own feelings for him that were pushing me? Because I couldn't tell anymore.

He said that the mate bond was only a sign, that it didn't affect us or our relationship, but how could we know that for sure? How could we be certain that the bond hadn't messed with our feelings...messed with *his* feelings? And why hadn't he told me? We'd been together for over a week and friends for months before that. He'd had so much time to tell me the truth, and yet he'd kept all of it to himself.

"You lied," I said, the words nothing but a breath as I turned to face him, my tears unrestrained and streaming down my cheeks. "For months you kept it from me."

Mor hung his head, ashamed. "I know. And I can't tell you how sorry I am, but I need you to understand why I did it." He watched me as if waiting for me to argue, and when I didn't he took a step closer. "At first, I hoped that we could just ignore it. I'd already lost Gen, and I didn't want to go through that again—I *refused* to go through it again. So I tried to put space between us." With a sigh, he squeezed my fingers, his expression tender. "But then I started to like you and I realized that fighting the mate bond was a lost cause. Because I was already into you. At that point, I considered telling you about the bond, but I was afraid that it would only push you away or scare you. So, I kept quiet, but the longer I said nothing, the more afraid I was that you wouldn't forgive me for keeping it a secret. It became this deep pit of secrets that I didn't know how to dig myself out of. I'm sorry, Care. I shouldn't have kept it from you."

"No," I agreed, glaring at him through my tears, "You shouldn't have."

Morgan studied me, his expression slowly becoming less and less apologetic as confidence flashed in his eyes. "But that's not why you're upset," he said, standing close enough now that I could feel the heat of his body.

"*Excuse me?*" I demanded, vacillating between anger and betrayal, hurt and fear. "Then why don't you tell me why I'm upset, *mate*."

Even though I was baiting him, Morgan didn't get angry or frustrated. Instead, he hummed with patience and persistence as those grey eyes bored into me. "You're upset because you're scared."

"Of course, I'm scared!" I shouted, my face contorting with my tears. "How could I not be scared, Morgan? For once, I thought someone had *chosen* me. That I was special. That out of all the girls in the world, you chose to love *me*."

Morgan stood there, stricken and silent as he watched me cry. His hand was cold against mine now, a sad reflection of the icy pain in my heart.

"I've been alone for *so long*, Mor. No one has ever made me feel safe the way you do. And to find out that it's all because the magic chose me..." I shook my head.

"I'm not scared—I'm *terrified*. The one person in the world who *saw* me, who knew me and understood me and chose me, only did it because of some freaking mate bond! I wanted *you* to choose me, not for some magical bond to *tell* you to choose me. How could that not scare me?"

Then suddenly I was enveloped in warmth, Morgan's arms cocooning around me, holding me close. Holding me safe.

"The mate bond told us to pay attention to each other, but *we* fell in love, Red. *We* built this," he whispered, his arms strong and comforting around my back. "I love you Caroline Felicity Birch, for no other reason than that you're *you*. Frustrating, impulsive, stubborn, clever, funny, brilliant, and the brightest spot in my life. I love you because it was empathy that made you become a vigilante. I love you because you called me out when I needed it, and you didn't take me at face value like so many others have. I love you because you see the world with bright eyes and clever ideas—something I don't have." He placed his hands on my cheeks, gently pushing me back so he could see my face. "I love you, Red. Not because a mate bond told me to, but because you saw me and took the time to understand me. You're special, and I didn't need magic to tell me that."

My mind tumbled with thoughts, but no words came out of my mouth. I believed him, and yet...

Insecurity reared her ugly head, and deep in my chest, I wondered if he would have chosen me with no magic involved. *You were the one person to see through me.*

But instead of saying my doubtful thoughts out loud, I reached up on my tiptoes and place a tender kiss on his lips. He held me tight but scarcely moved, like he was afraid he'd spook me if he seemed too eager.

"I believe you," I whispered, eyes still closed. "But the fear—"

"I know."

"I need time."

"Take it," he nodded, his thumb stroking my waist. "I'll be here."

When I opened my eyes, his were locked in on me. Sure and patient.

"I..."

"I know," he replied, and I remembered that he could sense my feelings. He felt the love, even if I didn't voice it. "I love you, Red. And I'll be here whenever you're ready."

As I walked away, I felt guilty. I was making him pay for a fear that wasn't his fault. But fear is a powerful thing, and love, while resilient, is also so fragile. Because as stubborn as it can be, always refusing to give up on those it chooses, it's also so quick to believe it's been abandoned and unreciprocated.

Chapter 26

MORGAN

"Oof! That makes one for Morgan, four for Clint, six for Mike, and six for Logan," Volund called from where he lay, reclined in a lawn chair that I didn't remember owning.

"Did you pay for that?" I shouted, bypassing Logan's attempt to run me over as I bolted toward Mike, who was busy fending off Clint.

"Your Amazon account did," Volund shrugged, a legal pad and a sharpie in his lap, and a glass of lemonade in his hand. "You know, you really shouldn't leave your account logged in on your laptop if you're going to leave it unattended in common spaces."

I scowled at the Dark Elf, but then a big furry body knocked the wind out of me.

I was heartbroken and discouraged after my talk with Caroline yesterday, and how did my family attempt to make me feel better? Bear fights.

And yes, it was exactly what it sounded like.

The four of us Berserkers were in our bear forms in the backyard, playing a version of tackle football. But without the football. Whoever got tackled the least was the winner, but as far as I knew, the winner didn't get anything other than bragging rights.

And as for how any of this was supposed to make me feel better, I honestly wasn't sure it was.

"I think you're getting a little too comfortable here, Volt," I said, grunting as I dislodged Logan from my back.

"And I don't think you're understanding the point of this exercise," Volund tsked. "Seven for Logan."

I roared and slammed my front paws against the ground. "And what is the point of this? To literally beat me while I'm down?"

"The point is to distract you," Clint said, shaking his head, his rusty brown hair reflecting the sunlight.

"Well, you guys failed epically," I snapped, plopping myself on the ground, my back legs spread out wide with my front legs in between them.

All I could think about was the heartbroken look on Caroline's face last night. I hadn't seen her since our talk by the stairs—I'd been giving her time like she wanted. Now if only I knew how *much* time she wanted...

"Hey, don't get all doom and gloom on us," Mike urged, laying down on the grass next to me.

"Yeah, it's too soon to start giving up," Clint added as he dropped to the ground with a grunt, Logan settling down on his other side, all of us still in bear form.

What could have been a nice moment was somewhat dampened when Volund walked over, and sat crisscross on the ground, squeezing himself between Logan and Clint. He looked around at the group, his dark eyes too eager and his smile too happy for my taste.

"What are you doing?" Logan asked, his expression scrunched up like he was talking to a parasite.

"Helping to fix Morgan's love life," Volt shrugged innocently. "Now first please explain to me why you kept the mate bond a secret from your *mate*."

I dug my claws into the ground, pulling up chunks of grass as I glared at Volt. "I don't owe you anything."

"No, but I'd also like to know the answer to this," Mike argued gently, his expression much more sincere than the Dark Elf's.

"I..." I sighed. "I was scared. In the beginning, I was afraid to open myself up to that kind of love again after losing Genevieve. So I thought that maybe if I kept Caroline at arm's length until we could separate, that we could just ignore the bond. But Caroline's not one to be ignored." At this, the guys chuckled and nodded. "Then after I realized I liked her, I thought that if I told her about the bond, it would scare her away. She hasn't had that many people she felt safe enough to be open with, and I didn't want to ruin what we already had. But then as time went on and I hadn't said anything, I was scared that she'd never forgive me for lying for so long."

Clint tsked and shook his head. "You really made a mess."

I smacked him on the shoulder. "Believe me, I know. Caroline isn't speaking to me now. She thinks that the mate bond made me choose her. Because of this freaking bond, she's scared and insecure, and it's my fault because I wasn't honest."

"But the mate bond doesn't create feelings," Logan argued, sprawling his legs out a bit further in the grass.

"I know. And I tried to tell her that, but this whole thing was like throwing a match on a puddle of lighter fluid. Care already had these insecurities—fears that she thought I had bridged. And now she thinks the mate bond is responsible, not us."

No one spoke for a few moments, none of us really knowing how to deal with the situation. Care's feelings weren't wrong or invalid, but she was wrong about the mate bond. The mate bond hadn't created our feelings, we did. *We'd* made the choice to fight for each other and *we'd* made the effort to build our relationship. But insecurity was a funny thing. It didn't need any ground to stand on or any logic to make it feel valid. Which made it really challenging to get rid of.

I should know. Because the truth was that Caroline wasn't the only one who was scared. I was scared too. What if I loved Caroline and lost her just like Gen? What if my reputation got worse and she was caught in the thick of it? Care was incredibly resilient, but would she really be able to love the beast that everyone claimed I was?

And yet even in the face of all those thoughts, I felt *her*.

Caroline was up in her room, and I could feel her fuming and angry. Underneath that was the pain she was trying to push down. But buried beneath all of it was the love I'd been sensing from her for a while and only recently learned the name for. I knew life would be hard—especially for us—but I also knew that our love was strong enough to live through it. Because we were both too stubborn to ever let go.

"Is this the part where you do the whole grand gesture thing?" Logan asked, tapping his snout with one claw. "Or is that only when you've done something really bad like lied about who you are?"

"What are you talking about?" Volund asked, staring at Logan with a confused expression.

"You know, in those girly books and movies, when the guy does something stupid like lies about his identity or fails to defend his relationship with the girl or whatever?" Logan explained excitedly. "And then the guy has to go and do some kind of grand gesture. Like he writes her a hundred letters, or buys her a house, or gives up his dream job—some big romantic gesture or sacrifice."

Silently, we all stared at my best friend, unsure what to think. Logan had never exactly been a paragon of romantic wisdom, so why was he so full of good advice now?

"Dude, what kind of books and movies are you watching?" Clint taunted, tossing a handful of grass Logan's way. "And please tell me you at least didn't watch them willingly."

"Ha ha." Logan rolled his eyes. "Laugh all you want, but I'm the one who's wooing the girl."

"What girl are you wooing?" Mike taunted, pushing one of his rear paws at Logan, who batted it away. "Could it be—"

"Doesn't matter," I quickly interrupted, not trusting Volund enough to talk about Caroline's sister in his vicinity. He might be joining our heartbreak pow wow, but I still didn't trust him with sensitive information. "Point is, Logan has now cashed in his man card for a *girl*."

I grinned at my best friend, and he shrugged, becoming very interested in the grass at his feet. "Well, what's the point in a man card if all it buys you is loneliness? I'll gladly give up my man card if I get—" he paused and glanced at Volt, "*Her* out of the deal."

I was happy for my best friend, but I had to admit that my pride was also a little wounded. Here the man with the least relationship experience was successfully wooing the woman of his dreams, and I was pouting on the grass like a child, potentially losing the woman of mine. *He's right. Time to man up.*

"Logan's right," I nodded. "I'd rather have Caroline than my man card."

"Well jokes on you, cus right now you don't have either," Volund said matter-of-factly.

"Nice one!" Clint laughed, raising a paw to Volund, who readily high fived it.

"Now, about this whole grand gesture thing," Volund continued, "What kind of grand gesture does Caroline need?"

"None."

We all turned to look at Mike where he laid in the grass, looking much more knowledgeable on the topic than I'd have anticipated. As far as I knew, Mike didn't talk to girls. Ever. Logan could at least interact with women. Mike just avoided contact altogether.

"Think about it, this is Caroline we're talking about," Mike explained, motioning a hand back toward the house. "She's not going to be impressed by one big gesture. You said she's scared because she thinks you didn't choose her, that the mate bond did. So instead of doing one big gesture, you should do a bunch of small things. Reminders that show her that *you're* choosing her, not the bond."

*Hm...*It wasn't a bad idea. Care had told me she needed time, but what she wanted was assurance. Reminders that I wasn't going anywhere. That *I* wanted her, not the bond.

"I think you're right," I hummed. "Now I just have to figure out what that looks like. What should my small gestures be?"

"How should we know?" Mike said, laying his chin on his paws. "She's your girlfriend."

"Just think of all the things that Caroline is insecure about when it comes to you," Logan suggested, more helpful than my brother. "And think of ways to push back against them. It doesn't matter how small the gestures are. The goal is not to win her over by tomorrow, but to eventually earn her trust in your feelings again. Which will take time."

I pushed myself up onto my back legs and tapped into my magic to shift back into human form. The transition happened quickly, completely painless and silent. Within moments, I was a man again, free of fur and claws. "Got it," I nodded, feeling my despair fade in favor of determination. "I'm gonna go brainstorm."

"I'll help!" Volund volunteered, standing with too much enthusiasm.

"You want to help?" Clint grinned, showing off his sharp teeth. "Use your Nephilim speed and run around the yard and we'll see how long it takes us to catch you."

"There is no—*Ah!*"

Volund shouted as Mike launched himself at the Dark Elf, and Volund took off at faster than normal run across the yard, screeching as he went. The sight made me feel a fraction less sad.

Chapter 27

CAROLINE

My converse tapped across the hardwood floor as I headed toward my office, Taylor Swift's 'This is Why We Can't Have Nice Things' playing in my head. With my black shirt, black jeans, and darker eye makeup, I definitely felt like I was in my *Reputation* era. Sure, my shirt had sheer sleeves and frills around the cuffs and my converse were my usual pale pink, so there was still a Barbie tinge to my aesthetic, but my soul felt black and vengeful.

Okay, that might be a little extreme. I wasn't angry per se, but I definitely wasn't feeling like myself. It had been four days since I'd found out that Morgan and I were mates, and I was still feeling...discombobulated. Fear, insecurity, and anxiety all hung around like squatters in my head. And since anger and frustration were much less intimidating emotions to feel, I latched onto those instead.

"Oh, that blue in my eyes? Don't worry about it," I whined in a pathetic imitation of Morgan's voice. "It's just because I'm Chief. And don't ask me why you can sense my feelings no matter the distance, because I'll just insinuate that it's because you like me and not because we have a mystical *mate bond.*" *Ugh, I could just strangle him.*

But all my angry thoughts fled as I stepped into my office and found a sticky note on my desk.

Reason #9 that I love you!
the way you roll your eyes whenever
you disagree with me — so pretty much
all the time. I love you.
Love, Morgan

Fury burned in my chest, and I snatched up the note. Fume was practically spiraling from my ears as I stomped my way to Morgan's office. Without bothering to knock, I shoved both doors open and stormed inside. Morgan—no nicknames for him until I decided what to do with all my unpleasant feelings—looked up from his desk as I entered the room.

"You have to stop," I demanded, slapping the sticky note on his desk.

He'd left me nine little notes in the past few days. On the can of pringles, under my door, in my office—they were everywhere. He'd written sweet things like 'reason #3 that I love you: how selfless you are, giving up your own safety to make sure that others don't have to suffer in fear the way you have.' Then he'd also written flirty things like 'reason #5 that I love you: you're a *really* good kisser.' But the notes had to stop. They were too thoughtful, too mushy and they made me think way too much about my feelings, which were still a big ball of icky.

He studied me for a moment and set his forearms on the desk. *Ugh, those forearms...* So strong and big and masculine. And now that I'd been wrapped up in them, I knew how delightfully cozy they were. How nice it was to feel that light dusting of hair across the top. *So masculine...*

"Red?" His voice shocked me out of my stupid thoughts and I blinked to find him watching me with a smirk.

Funny how easy it was for me to glare now. "Stop leaving me notes."

Morgan propped his chin on his folded hands and pursed his lips. "No."

"I'm sorry, did you just say 'no'?"

"I did," he smiled. "I'm not going to stop leaving you notes. I'm doing the small gestures thing."

"The *what?*"

"You know how guys in books and movies do a grand gesture to get the girl back? Well, I'm doing small gestures...Wait, shoot. I don't think I was supposed to tell you that."

I bit my lip to keep myself from giggling. The big idiot was acting like we were in a romcom. And he was right, he wasn't supposed to tell me that part. Part of the magic of a big gesture was the surprise and the inevitable romantic speech. *He's wooing me wrong, and it's the most adorable thing I've ever heard.*

Dang him, I was trying to be mad! Anger was my first line of defense against the horrible doubtful, sad feelings that were lurking on the edge of my mind. I had to stay vigilant.

"You're right, you weren't supposed to tell me," I snapped, putting my hands on my hips to let him know I meant business. Unfortunately, all that did was distract him.

His eyes skimmed down my body, an appreciating light in his eyes as they took in my curves.

"Hey," I said snapping my fingers in his face, "Eyes up here. I'm still mad at you."

He obediently looked away from my figure, but when his eyes met mine, they took on a studious look that had me wanting to squirm. It was that special Morgan-gaze that always saw through my veneer to the deeper, vulnerable levels. Levels that were full of turbulence and turmoil right now.

"No, I don't think you are," he said with too much certainty.

"Of course, I'm mad," I scoffed, crossing my arms. "Why do you think I look like Wednesday Adams today?"

A slow smirk spread across his face, and he raised an eyebrow, the light in his eyes bringing heat to my cheeks. "Because you look good in black."

Even though my chest fluttered at his attraction, I forced myself to scowl. "You can't flirt your way out of this, Morgan. I'm mad. End of story."

Morgan slowly stood from his chair and came around the desk to stand in front of me. Then he lifted a hand to graze the tail of my black ribbon, and I nearly combusted.

This was the longest we'd gone without physical contact since we met, and I hadn't realized until now just how desperately I wanted it. Because having him stand close, in my space but not invading it, was not enough. *It'll never be enough.*

"You're not mad, Care," he whispered, his breath fanning my face. "You can pretend that you are, but I know better."

Freaking mate bond. I'd forgotten that he could sense my feelings the same way I could sense his.

"You told me that you're scared," he continued, letting go of the ribbon. "And I get that. And I'll give you all the time in the world to get past this doubt. Because when you're ready, I'll be right here waiting. And in the meantime, I'm going to starve your fears."

I was too confused by his words to stop him when he reached for my hand. And then it just felt too good to pull away.

"You can't just starve fears until they go away," I argued, my voice growing softer as his thumb rubbed the back of my hand.

"I think I can," he insisted, stepping closer, our chests barely brushing. "I think if I face down every one of your insecurities and doubts, they'll fall."

"It's not that simple." I tried to tug my hand away, but he wouldn't budge.

"It can be. Boy meets girl, boy waits for girl. It doesn't have to be complicated, Red."

I stared up at this perfectly imperfect man, unsure what to say without it ending in a make out session. Thankfully, I was saved from my own stupidity by a loud knock at the door. Eager for a distraction, I looked around Morgan and saw Asher standing in the doorway to the office.

"Asher? What are you doing here?" The Wyvern raised an eyebrow at my words as he stepped into the room. "I didn't mean it like that, I just meant that I didn't even know you knew where we lived."

"I know what you meant, Caroline. I didn't come for a social call," he said. And then he turned and shut the double doors behind him.

Well, that can't be good. I looked up at Morgan and he turned to face our guest, still holding my hand.

Asher didn't bother to take a seat, just crossed his arms like he was barricading the exit.

"What's going on?" Morgan asked; I could almost sense him bracing for bad news.

Asher sighed, seeming slightly reluctant. "I think I might have found a potential address for your Dark Elf's people."

"I'm sorry, *what?*" I exclaimed. Even thought we'd asked him to search for Volund's people, I honestly hadn't expected him to have any success. "You found an address?"

"A *potential* address," he corrected dryly. "I don't know for sure if it's the right place, because I can't tell just by looking at the people if they're Nephilim or not."

"Maybe *you* can't…" I thought aloud, looking up at Morgan, who was already shaking his head.

"No," he said immediately.

"Oh, come on! I can make myself look like Volund and the Nephilim will never know the difference."

"Heck no."

"Morgan Gareth Hohlt, stop being a big butthead," I complained, yanking my hand from his. This time he let me.

"Caroline, we have no idea what Volund is up to," he argued, that stubborn, impassive look on his face. "Sure, I trust him a little more than I did when we met him, but I sure as heck don't trust him that much. The man's been keeping an awful lot of secrets."

Now it was my turn to cross my arms and raise an eyebrow.

Morgan glared. "Not the same thing. Volund lied about hiding an entire group of people who are part of an extinct species, and we don't know why. For all we know, he could be planning to wage war on the other Shifters. The secret I kept, I kept out of fear, not with the intent to hurt you. There's a very big difference."

"Should I step out?" Asher asked, already reaching for the door handle.

"No!" I insisted, only sparing him a glance. "Because we're going and we're doing it now."

"Care—"

I cut Morgan off, stepping so close that he had to tilt his chin to look down at me.

"Stop me, Bear Man. I dare you."

Morgan let out a long, frustrated sigh. Then he turned to Asher, an angry fire in his eyes. "I guess we're going now."

Chapter 28

CAROLINE

"This is a dumb idea," Asher sighed. I turned in the passenger seat of Morgan's SUV and glared at Asher in the back seat. The Wyvern King wasn't fazed. He just stared back at me and shrugged, dark eyes deep and unimpressed.

"I just want to be on record as saying that this idea is not one that I condone. That way when one of you dies, I can't be sued." Since his emotions were too blurry for me to read, and his expressions were always so enigmatic, I couldn't tell if he was joking or not.

"Why did we bring him?" I demanded, turning to Morgan.

Mor just smiled patiently at me. "Because you have a track record of getting injured on missions like these. And as we've established, I'm completely smitten with you, which means that I'm very invested in your safety."

My initial instinct was to argue with him and insist that he didn't care the way he thought he did. To lie and tell him that I was still mad even though we both knew otherwise. But the sincere look in his eyes gave me pause. It's hard to find reason in your fears when the other person is completely impervious to them.

And when they keep leaving you reassuring notes. I'd found one this morning in my back pocket when I put on my jeans. It read:

Reason #10 that I love you!
You never take no for an answer.
While it also drives me crazy, I love
+ admire your fire. Don't ever let it
burn out. It's what keeps me warm.
              Love, Morgan

Yeah, I was having a bit of a hard time not melting when I read that one.

"I have a better question," Asher said, interrupting the confusing moment. "Why is *she* here?"

Morgan and I both turned and looked at Asher, who sat as close to the door as possible, while Daisy Mae sat in the middle seat. Staring at him. When he gave her a sideways glance, her tail started banging and she did her best to lick his face off.

"Seriously, why is she here?" he whined, shoving her away. It was the most emotion I'd ever seen him show, and it was all because he was afraid of a forty-pound dog with a kissing problem.

"I figured we might need her as backup," Morgan explained, fighting valiantly against a chuckle. "She's really good at espionage."

"Yeah, she's a genius," I said, snapping a few photos of the two lovebirds on my phone. "Great for distractions and the occasional attack when necessary."

Asher just glared at me as he shoved Daisy to the other side of the car, only to have her wiggle back over and try to lick him again. "Ugh, can we get this show on the road so this 'genius' and I can part ways?" he pleaded, sighing as he gave up and let Daisy crawl into his lap. She finally stopped trying to kiss him though.

Snickering, I turned and looked out the front window at the apartment complex we'd parked down the street from. It was a newer one, with copper accents, nicely trimmed grass and sweet little balconies. But I could see why it had caught the Wyvern's attention in his search. Because as we watched the various tenants going about their business, it was very apparent that they all knew each other much better than new neighbors should.

"No one's a stranger here," I said, watching two women talking like they were old friends. Someone walked past and the ladies talked to them the same way. Like they were family. Then they did the same with another person. And another. And another...

"It's possible that the reason they all know each other is because they're all Nephilim." Morgan pursed his lips thoughtfully, his worry rising. I knew he hated this plan, and I couldn't blame him. But we needed answers, and I didn't know how else to get them.

"It'd be nice if we could have had Paul look around here first," I said, wishing I'd thought to ask for his help.

Morgan nodded. "He would be useful in moments like this. We should bring him on staff, but something tells me he'd say no."

"Oh definitely...but maybe he'd eventually say yes if we started with baby steps."

"Like?"

I mulled it over silently. I'd been working with Paul since I came to Shifter Haven, and he'd never liked accepting money from me or help of any kind. But he did like being useful...

"Maybe we could buy him a burner phone to start with," I suggested. "Include him more on our plans like he's part of the team. Then we start having him come to team meetings—"

"Team meetings?" Mor asked incredulously. "We don't have team meetings."

"Sure, we do. They're the ones we do in your office all the time." He shrugged but didn't argue. "So, we invite Paul to team meetings and start including him, and then eventually, I can just start putting him on payroll and he won't even notice."

"He won't notice a paycheck?" Asher argued from the backseat. "I don't think anyone would be that oblivious."

I rolled my eyes and prepared to defend myself, but Morgan spoke first. "We'll stop on the way home and get him a phone."

"Really?"

Mor looked over at me, offended by my disbelief. "Of course. He's a good guy, he deserves to have a full life. Plus, he's important to you, so he's important to me."

I said nothing, not sure what *to* say. My two halves were at war, one of them wanting to leap across the console and kiss him, while the other wanted to keep as far away as possible.

It wasn't that I didn't trust him, but what was a girl supposed to think when it turns out that the love of her life chose her in part because he was told to? The mate bond had shown him that I was the one for him. But would he have come to that conclusion on his own if not for the bond? I wasn't sure.

Which was why I put away my kissing fantasy and stayed put in my seat. Confusion and desire don't mix. So, it was best not to try.

"I was able to do some more in-depth checks on a handful of the residents," Asher said, interrupting the moment, one hand tentatively on Daisy's back like he was petting a cobra. "All twenty-three of the people that I looked into moved in during the same week. Not the same month, but the same *week*. How many neighbors do you know that all moved in at the same time?"

Hmm..."Alright, time for my plan," I announced.

"Your plan?" Morgan scoffed. "Your plan consists of you walking over there with Volund's face on, hoping that someone says something informative and praying that no one finds it suspicious that Volund has suddenly shown up after being gone for so long. That's not a plan, Caroline."

"Of course it's not." I rolled my eyes. "I'm also going to be wearing his body because wearing just his face would be dumb."

He glared. I grinned. The world shifted back onto its axis. Somewhere a hometown quarterback won a football game. An author used another em dash. A McDonalds worker dipped the fries into the grease for a second time, and an angel got its wings. And all was right with the world.

"So, what are you going to say when they ask you what you're doing here or why you're not staying?" Morgan pressed, and even though he was acting like the caveman he'd been when we first met, I could feel the intense panic that pulsed underneath. "Do you even know?"

My heart ached for him, and I grabbed his hand on the console and gave it a reassuring squeeze. "Yes, Mor. I know what I'm doing. I promise. Do you trust me?"

He tilted his head, eyes silently begging me to take pity on him. But I couldn't. We needed answers, and this was our best bet. "If anything happens to you, I'm burning the place down," he growled.

I bit back a smile.

"As sweet as this moment is," Asher complained, Daisy wagging her tail at the sound of his voice, "We should probably get this over with. Something's bound to go wrong, and I really don't want to deal with getting either of you out of jail."

Chuckling, I stepped out of the car, and before my feet even hit the pavement, I'd already shifted into the most annoying Dark Elf that ever lived.

"Well," I said, smirking back at Morgan through my still open door, Volund's voice coming out of my mouth. "What do you think? Do I pull it off?"

Morgan cringed, but Asher slowly rolled down his window and cocked a vaguely impressed eyebrow at me. "Cool," was all he said. And coming from Asher, that was a huge compliment.

I beamed at him and squared my shoulders. "Alright, I'll be back. Shouldn't take me long."

But as I turned to leave, Morgan leaned across the console and caught my hand. His expression was heavy with worry, his emotions clouded and anxious.

"I'll be right back, Bear Man," I promised him.

He held my gaze for a long moment before he finally nodded.

"This is weird," Asher complained emotionlessly from the backseat. I glared at him through the window.

"He's not wrong," Morgan admitted, releasing my hand. "I really don't want to have a sentimental moment between us ruined by the fact that you look like your annoying non-cousin. And I'm definitely not kissing you with that face on."

I shrugged. "Fair enough." But just as I was about to shut the door, I leaned back into the car, grabbed Morgan's face and kissed him on the cheek.

"Caroline!" he barked, shoving me away. "That was disgusting!"

"Rude," I said, doing my best imitation of Volund's classic pout. Morgan glared and even though Asher didn't smile, I sensed a tiny bit of amusement coming from him.

With a smile and wave, I turned and headed toward the apartment complex. But the closer I got to the buildings, the more my amusement faded. For all my glibness, I knew Morgan was right to be nervous about this mission. All it would take was one little slip up for these people to realize that I wasn't Volund. And even though I was a competent fighter now, I had zero confidence that I could get away from an entire compound of Elves if they decided to grab me. And the last thing we needed was for Morgan to run over here in bear form and rip everybody apart. The man was finally getting some positive publicity for once in his life and I wasn't going to let anything ruin that.

Pushing the nerves from my mind, I did my best to focus on confidence and calmness, trying to mask my worry from Morgan. The more at ease he thought I was, the less likely he'd be to charge in and get himself in trouble.

As I walked down the sidewalk in the apartment parking lot, I saw a woman standing by her trunk, unloading groceries and speaking to another woman who stood nearby. Pulling out my phone, I pretended to be texting and walked toward them, hoping it would be a good enough excuse not to have noticed them if they recognized me.

I let my magic uncurl as I drew closer, silently brushing up against their emotions to test them. I knew the moment they recognized me, shock and relief pinging inside them, and I braced myself to lie.

"Prince Volund," the woman with the groceries exclaimed, her eyes wide.

I stopped on the sidewalk, pretending to have only just noticed her. I wasn't sure if I—or Volund—was supposed to know the woman's name or not. *I should have thought this through.*

"What are you doing here?" the other woman asked. "We weren't expecting you yet. Has something gone wrong?"

Yet. She wasn't expecting him *yet.* But they *were* expecting him. *You have some splaining to do Volt.*

"Yes, everything's fine," I assured them with a smile. "Technically I'm not back yet."

"Oh," they both nodded.

"So don't worry," I added. "Everything's still on track."

The woman with the groceries smiled and shifted the bags in her hands. "To be honest, we thought you might have her with you when we saw you again."

Her? Her who? *Oh.* They meant me.

When I didn't respond right away, the other woman spoke up. "Or did you decide that it was safe to leave her?"

Wait, what? What exactly was Volund planning to do with me? Was this whole thing just a ploy so he could watch me? Him showing up in the alley that day and us putting him under house arrest, it all felt too convenient now. *What the heck is he plotting?* But just as I was about to ask the question and blow my cover, my phone rang.

I answered it without thinking, still a little shocked.

"Care? Are you okay?" Morgan's voice came through the other end.

"Sorry, I have to take this," I said to the two women, stepping away. But I could feel their gazes on my back and with every step I took, my heart raced.

"Caroline, talk to me," Morgan demanded.

"I'm okay, Mor." I glanced back over my shoulder and smiled weakly at the women. Sure enough, they were watching me.

Desperate to escape now that I'd discovered more than I planned to, I widened my eyes and pretended to see something alarming behind them. When they both predictably turned around to check, I shifted myself into one of the other people I'd seen earlier from the apartment complex. Then, using my Nephilim speed, I swiftly bolted behind one of the buildings.

"They were expecting him, Morgan," I whispered into the phone, moving quickly along the backside of the building toward our car.

"What?"

"They were expecting him to show up but they thought he was early. They said that they'd expected him to bring 'her' with him. Then they asked if I left her because I thought it was safe not to bring her."

With every step, I felt his emotions drawing nearer to me and I took comfort in it. But only when I could see his black SUV waiting by the sidewalk did I start to feel any semblance of calm.

"Slow down, Care," Morgan pleaded, but I ignored him, my emotions still high.

"No, Morgan. Volund is planning to escape somehow in the near future, and these people are expecting him to bring *me* with him."

The line went silent, but I could see Morgan now, still sitting in the front seat of his car. And I'd hate to be the one on the other end of the murderous look on his face.

"Not if I have anything to say about it."

Chapter 29

CAROLINE

It took us an extra fifteen minutes to get home. Morgan had made a pit stop so I could get a phone for Paul. And no, I was *not* melting about the sweetness of the gesture...

But unfortunately for Asher, that meant that he had to sit in the car with Daisy Mae while we were in the store.

He wasn't happy about it.

"Couldn't you have done that at another time?" he complained as we walked into the dining room from the garage. The Wyvern King's tone was just as enigmatic as usual, but he'd been complaining for a solid five minutes now. It was the most emotional I'd ever seen him. "Like maybe when I wasn't stuck in the backseat with your tongue obsessed dog?"

"She likes you," I taunted, smiling at Morgan. But he was still too anxious about Volund's plans to find Asher's whining as entertaining as I did.

"Volund!" Morgan shouted—loudly.

"Ow!" I pressed a palm to my ear. "Bring it down a notch, would you?"

Ignoring me, he headed for the stairs. "I want to see that little snake!"

"Mor, I get that you're mad, but—"

"Mad?" He spun on the step and glared down at me, thunder in his eyes. "You think I'm *mad*? I'm not mad, Carline. Volund has officially threatened the safety of *my mate*, the woman I *love*. I'm not mad. I'm *murderous*."

I blinked up at him. *Oh.*

I liked to think that I was a mature, self-respecting woman who had enough dignity and awareness to know that extreme possessiveness or violent behaviors in a man were *not* attractive. Abuse isn't hot, manipulation isn't sexy, and domineering, disrespectful forms of masculinity are unacceptable. But *this* was something else. This was a respectful, gentle, kind, loving, supportive man who felt an innate need to protect his girl. Not because he owned me, but because he cared. And it was really hot.

No, bad Caroline! This is not a make out moment. Stay focused!

"And while I appreciate that sentiment—you have no idea how much," I felt myself flush, "Well, actually you probably do know since you can feel what I feel...Anyway!" I shook my head, really wishing Asher weren't listening to all of this. "The point is that I want answers too, but if you kill Volund, we won't get them. So, I need you to promise me that you won't touch him."

Morgan stared, unblinking.

"Okay, fine, you can punch him once." Morgan didn't reply. "Twice?"

But Mor just leaned down, grasped my chin between gentle fingers and gave me a quick kiss. "I promise that I'll let him maintain the ability to speak."

Then he turned and stomped up the stairs. I glanced back at Asher, but he looked just as emotionless and broody as usual, so I raced after my idiot mate.

"Volund, you little rat, get out here!" he yelled, swinging Volund's bedroom door open without bothering to knock.

"Volund," I called out a little less aggressively, "We need to talk."

"No, there will be no talking," Mor hissed, scowling at me. "He'll be *squealing*."

"Would you relax? I'm trying to get him to come out here. Which he's not going to do if he's afraid you're going to murder him."

Morgan gave me a slightly reproachful look, but we both swung our gazes toward the door as a cellphone rang. Asher took his phone out of his pocket and answered the call, stepping out into the hallway.

"Where's he at?" Morgan growled, looking around the empty bedroom. The *very* empty bedroom. *Actually...*

"Does this room seem strangely empty to you?" I asked, walking over to a nightstand. It was bare except for the lamp and clock that came with every room. Curiously, I opened the drawers, but they were empty too.

I met Morgan's gaze, and he must have felt my anxiety, because he clenched his jaw and disappeared into the bathroom. A few moments later, he came out looking grim. "It's empty. Not even so much as a shampoo bottle or toothbrush."

"Those women said that they hadn't expected to see Volund *yet*," I reminded him, thinking back to the ladies at the apartment complex. "But they *were* expecting to see him."

"With you," Mor pointed out. "They expected him to have you with him. So why would he leave without you?"

"Better yet, *how* would he leave? He's bound to the house."

"Apparently not." Morgan and I both turned as Asher entered the room, his cellphone still in his hand. "That phone call was from the spy I had watching your house."

At that, Morgan's anger flared and he stepped forward; fingers gripped into fists. "You had someone watching my house?"

Oh boy. Moving quickly, I stepped in front of him, blocking his path to the Wyvern. As epic as a battle between a massive bear and a Wyvern might have been, we really didn't have time for testosterone fights right now.

"Asher, why don't you go ahead and explain yourself?" I suggested as Morgan moved closer, pressing himself against me. "Preferably very fast and speaking with a soft tone."

"I'm not an animal that's going to spook," Mor rumbled, his chest vibrating against my back.

"You sure about that Yogi?" I quipped.

I could feel his frustration mounting, but thankfully Asher started speaking before Morgan could start yelling.

"I had someone watch your house in case Volund ever had a visitor or managed to escape," Asher explained, though he didn't bother to use the hushed voice that I'd suggested. *Probably wise.* Morgan might've snapped his neck if he had.

"Really good job your friend did since Volund *got away*," Morgan sneered behind me.

"Ow," I growled, glaring at him over my shoulder, "Stop yelling."

"I'm not—"

Turning, I clamped a hand over his mouth. "Yes, you are. My broken eardrums are the evidence, and if you don't stop, I'm going to sue you for making me go deaf. And since you don't have millions of dollars at your disposal, you'll have to give me this big house as restitution. And once I own it, I'll kick you out and take your room. Then every night you can cry yourself to sleep knowing that I'm in your bed without you. Got it?"

Mor stood there for a moment, my hand on his mouth and his grey eyes narrowed. Slowly, inch by inch, I felt his fingers slide around my waist. Then, with gentle fingers, he removed my hand.

"Quite the vision you painted," he said. And then he kissed my palm.

"I'm a very imaginative threat-maker."

"I noticed. I promise I'll behave now, just please don't sleep in my bed without me."

I bit my lip to kill the smile that threatened to stretch across my face. "Promise," I said, holding up my pinky.

Morgan twined his around mine and tugged my hand closer so he could kiss my knuckles. "Promise."

Ignoring the butterflies in my belly and the simultaneous warning bells in my head, I turned back to Asher. But Morgan's hand, still on my waist, and his chest against my back made it difficult to maintain my indifference.

"So, what happened?" I asked, trying to pretend I wasn't completely affected by Morgan's proximity.

"He saw Volund leave the house," Asher replied, unfazed by Morgan and I's behavior. "He said he followed him down to the street where he got in a ride share car and left."

"Did he follow the car?"

"He did. And he got an address for the house the Elf was delivered to. My guy is stationed nearby, waiting to give me updates on where he goes next."

I let out a deep breath and settled back against Morgan more out of instinct than intent. "Okay, so we know where Volund is. Now we just need to decide—"

I paused as my phone started ringing. I pulled it out and barely glanced at the screen before moving to ignore the call. But I froze as my sister's name flashed across the screen. *He wouldn't...*

"Ariel?" I said warily, answering the call.

"Sorry, Ariel can't come to the phone right now." At the sound of Volund's voice, my blood ran cold, my body rigid with fury.

"Where is she?" I demanded, my voice so calm and icy that I almost didn't recognize it.

Morgan came around to stand beside me, worry etched on his face. And even Asher looked marginally concerned as I put the call on speaker.

"Oh, I think she's with her bodyguard," Volund goaded, his voice bloated with arrogance. "Although he was unconscious last time I checked."

Morgan went taut beside me, and I didn't have to sense his emotions to know that he was fully prepared to break the Dark Elf in half once he found him. Now, I just might let him.

"How did you even leave? You're bound to the house," I said, setting a hand on Morgan's chest to remind him not to beast out right here in the bedroom.

"Ask Morgan. He's the one who kept leaving his laptop signed into his Amazon account. It's not my fault you never inspected any of the packages I had delivered for contraband."

I closed my eyes, feeling an oncoming headache. "You had someone send you a Minotaur artifact." Minotaurs were impervious to magic, and objects imbued with their blood could counteract things like Witch bindings. Although they were very much illegal.

"A keychain, actually," Volund bragged. "It seemed fitting. And since Minotaur artifacts can counteract bindings, I'm a free man now."

Getting to the end of my patience, I snapped my eyes open clutching the phone tighter. "What do you want?"

"Well, you're all business, aren't you, cousin?" Volund sneered. "You know, this will all go a lot smoother if you can have an open mind."

"Says the man who abducted my only sister." Now it was Morgan's turn to put a hand on my shoulder to try and keep me calm as I my shoulders bunched and my face burned hot with rage. "You don't get to speak to me about open minds or forgiveness or working together or whatever image you've concocted in your mind. We aren't family, Volund. We aren't even friends. You lost that opportunity the moment you put someone I love in danger! Now *tell me what you want.*"

Volund sighed, and I felt gratified to know that I'd ruined his fun. "You really know how to kill a moment. But fine, I want you to meet me tomorrow night at my house. Midnight. Show up and I'll give you your sister and Logan."

Morgan growled beside me, but I shook my head. I had this covered.

"You know what Volt? No."

"No?"

"No. I don't need you to give me my sister and Logan back. Because I'm not worried. You know why, Volund? Because you're cursed." The other end of the line went silent, and I smiled maliciously, plowing ahead. "Even a Minotaur artifact can't interfere with a curse, which means that you still can't hurt me. And since Merida never specified what kind of pain you couldn't cause, I'm assuming emotional pain is included. And we both know that if you hurt or kill Ariel, you hurt me."

"...You're not wrong." The fire was gone now from Volund's voice and he just sounded tired. Like if he couldn't maintain an air of pageantry, then he wasn't interested in the conversation. "But you're forgetting something, Caroline. I may not be able to hurt her, but I can keep her from you indefinitely. And can you go the rest of your life without seeing your sister?"

Anger boiled in my chest, rising through my body as my muscles coiled, ready for a fight. How dare he threaten me? Didn't he know who he was crossing?

"I have a better question," I said, confidence permeating my words, my mind made up. "Do you know who I am? I'm not your cousin, Volund. I'm Caroline, mate to Morgan Hohlt, daughter of Henry and Lisa Birch, vigilante of Shifter Haven and Alfar Queen. I am a force to be reckoned with, and you've just royally ticked me off. The next time you see me, *run.* Because I won't be showing you any mercy."

Without waiting for a reply, I smashed my thumb on the screen and ended the call.

Morgan wound his arm around my waist, his body warm and comforting against my back. I felt his anger, still bright and burning, but it was coated now with empathy and concern.

"We'll get them back," he whispered, holding me tight.

I closed my eyes and nodded. "I know."

"Volund's not going to get his hands on you, Red."

"No, he's not." I'd make sure of it.

Chapter 30

CAROLINE

"Of course, he picked the gaudiest house in the neighborhood to squat in," I complained, looking over at the big two-story house. It had to have at least seven bedrooms, with a gigantic set of double doors at the front and a meticulously perfect yard. We were hiding in the shadow of the garage next door, but Volund's chosen hideout easily eclipsed this one.

"You have to give him credit though. He was smart enough to squat in a foreclosure where no one would notice," Mike shrugged, two guns holstered at his hips and a few knives strapped to his thighs.

He, along with the rest of the group, had all worn black to blend in with the night—a failed attempt for Mike. The man was just so big and broad that he immediately stood out, even when dressed to match the darkness. One thing was for sure, he was going to be a hot commodity on the task force.

Morgan had officially asked him a few days ago to be one of Morgan's two volunteers, and Mike readily agreed. I had a sneaking suspicion that he saw the task force as his opportunity to prove himself.

"Oh please," I scoffed, crossing my arms. "He totally stole that idea from *The Vampire Diaries*. Volund is nothing more than a Ryan The Temp who wishes he was a Damon Salvatore."

"Mixing your TV show metaphors there?" Mor teased, rubbing my shoulders.

I swatted his hands away and glared. "You gonna stop me?"

He lifted his hands in surrender, a smirk on his face. Rolling my eyes, I turned to the rest of the group, who could've been mistaken for a supernatural swat team. Merida looked like a kick-butt vampire assassin with her long black hair pulled up in a high pony, and her dark clothes a stark contrast to her pale skin and bright blue eyes. Asher looked like a very bored werewolf with his messy dark hair, eyes that were nearly black and his scruffy beard. Meanwhile, Mike and Morgan just looked like undercover superheroes, all muscles and strong jaws.

And then there was me. The Pixie who looked like she was dressed for a funeral. *Super menacing.*

"Are we ready?" Asher asked tiredly. He was the only one of us who hadn't brought a single weapon. When I'd asked him why, he said 'I'm not worried. If I'm in danger, I'll know it before anyone gets a shot at me'. And since Wyverns can sense when anyone—including themselves—is in danger, I figured he was probably right.

"Yeah, we're ready," I nodded, stepping closer to the group. "So just to recap, the goal is to get—"

"Caroline?"

Everyone stiffened, drawing their weapons, but when I saw my homeless friend Paul walking up the sidewalk, I waved everyone down. "Relax guys, he's one of us." Tonight, Paul was dressed in jeans and a T shirt to combat the warm July weather, all his belongings stuffed in the backpack on his back.

Paul warily eyed the group beside me, and I couldn't say I blamed him. He'd met Morgan before, and Asher was with us when we gave him the prepaid phone earlier today, but we were still an intimidating group.

"Hey Paul," I greeted him warmly, drawing his attention away from the more formidable group members. "You didn't need to come tonight." Volund's temporary hideout was in one of the neighborhoods downtown, so it wasn't far from Paul's usual stomping grounds by the Shifter Alliance Building. But I still didn't like him to be this close to danger.

"Yes, I did," he insisted. "You texted to tell me you were breaking in here—"

"I only told you where we were in case something happened to us. That way you'd know that I didn't just disappear for no reason."

He shrugged, not persuaded in the least. "Do you have a lookout?"

I sighed and looked at Morgan. Silently, he reached out and took my hand, understanding my concern.

I knew Paul had seen a lot of ugly things during his time in the service, but I really didn't want him to be triggered by anything that might happen tonight. *He's already been through enough.* "Actually," I said, looking back at Paul, "I don't know how rough tonight is going to be—"

"I understand the risk," Paul insisted. *Stubborn man.* "You're going into a fight—most likely outnumbered—against a bunch of Elves. I know you're worried, but I promise you I've endured worse. So, you can give me that pleading look all you want, but I'm not going anywhere, kid. You need a lookout and I need to know you're okay. So, I'll stay out of sight, and I won't get involved, but I'm not leaving."

I shook my head, but any real annoyance was softened by the knowledge that he was worried about me. "You're incorrigible."

"Pot, kettle," he sassed.

I laughed, Morgan snickering beside me. "Fine, but you have to promise to keep your phone on you at all times and call if you need us. Remember, both mine and Morgan's numbers are in there."

Paul pulled his new flip phone from his pocket. "I know, I've got it. Now you go get the job done and call if you need me to call the police or anything."

I tried to bite back my grin, but I couldn't help it—it was either that or hug the poor man. And I knew he wasn't ready for a breach of boundaries like that yet.

"Don't smile at me," he warned, but there was no bite to his tone.

"Aw Paul, you care about me," I teased, genuinely touched by his affection. The two things Paul and I had always had in common were that people's assumptions about us were often wrong, and that we cared for and were cared *about* by very few people. I was honored to be one of those people to him.

"Don't let it go to your head kid. Now get on with it. I've got places to be and people to see." Then he gruffly waved goodbye and trudged off to find a hiding place.

I pulled my eyes back to the group, ready to get this show on the road. "Alright, now that that's settled, let's get down to business. Remember, the goal is to get in, get Volund, and take down anyone who gets in our way. Oh, and don't die."

"Inspiring words, team leader," Asher sassed dryly. Then, without another word, he turned and began making his way toward Volund's house.

"Lovely man," Mike joked, smiling as he followed after the Wyvern.

I rolled my eyes and watched Merida join the two men, keeping close to the house and out of sight. But just as Morgan started to move toward them, I tugged on his hand. He paused and glanced down at me, concern etching his face.

"What's wrong?"

I didn't answer. Instead, I shook my head, reached up and pulled his mouth down to mine.

Morgan required no explanation, immediately dropping my hand to wrap me in his arms. Thanks to his Berserker strength, he lifted me from the ground like I weighed nothing, my toes dangling over the grass. And now that I didn't have to crane my neck to reach him, I kissed him with all the longing, fear, and love that I'd been suppressing—making up for lost time.

My fingers tunneled through his hair as he held me up, and he hummed, pleased, when I let my nails trail across his scalp. "I love you," I breathed against him, not bothering to pull away to speak.

He growled and took control of the kiss, making a declaration of his own. And I welcomed it, letting him guide me, chase me and claim me. 'I'm yours', I wanted to whisper. But that would've required that I stopped kissing him. So, I kissed him again. And again. And again.

But finally, when my lips were warm and deliciously swollen, he pulled away and pressed his forehead against mine. "Do you feel that?" he whispered, still out of breath. "Do you feel that warmth, that affection in my chest?"

I nodded, sensing his emotions through the mate bond. They were strong and loud and unyielding.

"That's me choosing you, Red. Whenever you sense that feeling in me, I want you to remember that it means that I chose *you*. That I want *you*. Got it? I love you, Red."

Pushing back the tears that threatened to overwhelm me, I nodded. "I love you too. And I'm sorry I didn't trust your feelings. I was just so scared that it was the mate bond that wanted me, not you. And that's not your fault—"

"Care—"

"No, I need to say this. Morgan, I love you, and I know that you love me. But there's a part of me that's always afraid. The little girl who had to keep secrets and hide herself away and be careful to never get too close to anyone because she couldn't be honest with them. Before you, that little girl was terrified that no one would ever choose her or see her or understand her. But then I met you and fell in love with you and that changed. But when you told me about the bond..." I shrugged helplessly. "It gave my fear room to grow. It's not an excuse, but it's the reason I pulled away from you. Not because I don't trust you or love you. But because the girl who's been alone for twenty-two years was afraid that she hadn't really been chosen after all. And honestly, even without the mate bond, I would have eventually gotten scared. Because there's a part of me that doesn't believe you'll ever love me as much as I love you."

Morgan's expression broke as he watched me, a raw, vulnerable pain in his eyes. "I get it, Care. The truth is, I felt the same way." When I furrowed my brow at him, he sighed. "I'm the beast, remember? The evil Chief who murders people. I've been the big scary boogie man since I was a pre-teen. I never thought anyone would be able to look past that. Gen did it, but after she died, my reputation just kept tanking and I never even considered that someone could love me now. So, when you said you did, I was happy...but I was also terrified. Because what if something happens? What if I'm accused of something else or what if one day I shift and lose control and hurt someone? Would you be able to love me then?"

Hurting on his behalf, I held his face in my hands. "Of course I'd still love you. I'll always love you."

Morgan grinned and kissed the tip of my nose. "I know Red. But for a moment, I let the fear get in. But then I reminded myself how strong we are, how constantly I feel the love in your chest. We have to put our faith in that. In each other."

"You might have to remind me sometimes."

"That's what the notes are for."

I smiled and gave him a quick, sweet kiss. "Thank you for those, by the way. I lied when I said I wanted you to stop."

"I know." He winked and kissed my temple before setting me back on the ground. "I love you, Care."

"I love you, Mor."

Morgan smiled, kissing me once more before he laced our fingers together and tugged us toward the house.

"Aww," Merida smiled as we reached the group. Apparently, they'd waited for us. Which meant they saw everything. *Lovely.*

"Aww?" Asher parroted incredulously.

"Yes, it's romantic. We're about to go potentially to our doom, and they had a sweet moment to express their feelings. I'm honestly a little jealous."

"Oh? Should I call a certain dark-haired—" Merida cut me off by punching me in the shoulder and I was surprised how much the hit hurt. "Don't worry, my lips are sealed," I smiled, pretending to lock my lips together and throw away the key.

"They weren't a moment ago," Morgan mumbled, pride swelling in his chest. Embarrassed, I shoved at his shoulder, but he just shrugged.

"What? They all saw it."

"Yeah, but it's dark," I complained, whispering now that we were just outside Volund's house. "No one saw it in detail."

Morgan wasn't the least bit sorry, and when he kissed my cheek, I really didn't know that I cared.

"Mike, are we good on security cameras?" Merida asked, already beginning to shift. Her black hair went white, her eyes shifted from blue to gold, and her skin took on that pearlescent gleam. As if she didn't look intimidating enough already.

Mike nodded, pulling out his phone. "Yep, they're all looped, so we're good."

And that was my cue. With a ripple of magic, I altered my appearance. I didn't know what any of the Nephilim looked like, so I couldn't imitate them. Instead I took on the appearance of a random woman.

"Impressive," Merida commented, studying my new face. "I've never seen anything like it."

"Thanks." I smiled. "But we're about to go into a home with who knows how many people that can easily do what I just did. So, remember, while they can imitate your appearance, if you don't speak, they *can't* imitate your voice. It's still going to be hard to tell each other apart if they decide to mimic us, so, no kill shots just in case it's the real one of us you're fighting. The goal is to knock them all out and get to Volund. We ready?"

Everyone nodded and I stepped up to the small door on the side of the garage. I opened it easily with my electronic lock pick and slid the tech back in my pocket as we slowly walked inside. The space was dark, the streetlight outside illuminating the room just enough for me to make out a single black car parked on the concrete.

Morgan nudged my shoulder and motioned toward the room around us, silently asking if I sensed anyone nearby. I nodded, pushing my senses out and feeling for the emotions of everyone in range. My magic brushed against varying degrees of focus and anxiety, but to my surprise, I felt no aggression.

I held up two fingers to indicate the number of people I sensed in the garage and Morgan nodded. I'd just turned to motion everyone forward when someone jumped out from behind the car.

A woman dressed all in black stood in front of us. Wearing my face.

As a Nephilim, I was usually the one pretending to be another person. So, I'd never seen someone pretend to be me. *Can't say I'm a fan.* It was disorienting, looking at my own face on another person. The woman had even shifted her outfit to match mine, but she didn't speak.

With everyone momentarily frozen in disturbed shock, the woman launched out at us. And though she moved quickly, Merida was somehow faster. The Witch seemed to have a spell ready, because she motioned to the woman like she was tethering her to an empty space of air, and then the fake me fell to the ground, her eyes closed.

I turned to Merida; my mouth open in awe. 'Wow', I mouthed, thoroughly impressed. Merida smiled and shrugged, her hands already drawing another spell in the air.

A few grunts snagged my attention, and I looked back to see Morgan and Mike lowering a man to the ground. He was a perfect replica of Asher.

The Wyvern King looked down at the unconscious man and wrinkled his nose in disgust. Tapping his arm, I mouthed, 'Why didn't you warn us?' Since he could sense danger preemptively, he should have been able to alert us to the coming attack or intervene.

Asher shrugged and pointed at the unconscious Nephilim. 'There was no danger', he replied silently.

Taken aback, I looked at Morgan. Why would the Nephilim attack without meaning us any harm? What would they gain by not hurting us? More importantly, how did they expect to win if they didn't intend to actually hurt us?

Feeling uneasy now and somehow out of the loop, we moved slowly to the next door, all of us on edge. There was no electronic lock this time, and when I turned the handle with no resistance, we all shared shocked looks.

First the guards weren't interested in harming us, and now the door wasn't locked. *What the heck is going on?*

Despite the trepidation building in my stomach, I held up all ten fingers, letting the group know how many people I sensed in the house. But since more could show up at any moment, we would need to move fast.

As planned, Asher stepped to the front of the group, his hands weaponless but no less dangerous than the knife in mine. Merida walked beside me with Mike and Morgan directly behind us, and we stepped into the house.

The place was completely silent, but unlike the garage, all the lights were on. Confused and wary, I followed close behind Asher. Everything felt off, from the unlocked door to the attackers who didn't intend to harm us.

A flash of black to my left jolted me out of my thoughts and I spun around to face—Mike? I shook my head. No, it wasn't Mike. It was a Nephilim pretending to be Mike. And as confusing as it was to face off against someone wearing my friend's face, I pressed my magic against him, comforted when I realized that his emotions were too placid to be the real Mike.

The Nephilim might be able to imitate our faces, but they can't replicate our emotions.

Assured who I was fighting, I lifted my pink dagger to lunge at the attacker's shoulder. But Morgan beat me to it.

I would've been annoyed with him for taking my shot, but then more Nephilim popped out of the rooms connected to the hallway, and my annoyance was eclipsed by panic.

Morgan, Merida, Asher, Mike and me all began to replicate as more Dark Elves stepped into the hall wearing our faces.

As we fought, it became increasingly difficult to tell who was real and who was fake. Even with my ability to sense feelings, I found it hard to identify my friends. There were just too many emotions all jumbled together with so many bodies in the tight space.

Confused by the chaos, I turned and saw Merida facing off against a fake Morgan a little further down the hall. Dagger in hand, I ran to her and raised my knife to strike at the fake Morgan. But then his eyes widened, and he shook his head mouthing 'it's me'.

I hesitated for just a moment to test his feelings, but the fake Merida took advantage of my pause and tried to rip the knife from my hand.

Angry that I'd been duped, I yanked my hand back and slammed the hilt of my knife against her temple. She stumbled back a step, right into Asher.

He was busy fighting a fake Mike—at least I thought it was a fake Mike—but he instinctively wrapped his arm around the fake Merida's neck until she passed out.

Her face would turn back into her natural one soon since she wasn't conscious to hold the magic, but for the moment she still resembled the Witch who was stringing people to spells down the hall like Wonder Woman and her magic lasso.

Now that the fake Merida was taken care of, I reached out for the mate bond, needing to latch onto Mogan's feelings for the sake of comfort. He was anxious and...furious? I glanced up at him, but too late I realized that the emotions weren't tethered to the man in front of me.

Before I could move to fight back, he'd grasped my wrists in his big hands and my knife clattered to the floor. I tried to shove him off, but he was too strong, dragging me down the hall away from the fight. Looking back, I saw Morgan—*my* Morgan—trying to follow, but he was hindered by more Nephilim, each of them imitating one of us.

The man holding me hostage suddenly let me go and I stumbled away from him. But he didn't attack, he just stood there, blocking my way back to the hall. Then he silently motioned to the cased opening on my right.

Wary, but curious, I turned and saw a large, fancy kitchen attached to an empty living room. And standing between the two spaces, was Volund.

He was dressed—you guessed it—all in black. But like Asher, he held no weapons.

"Welcome, cousin," he smiled. "Glad you could make it."

My anger roared to life again, and I looked back down the hall where my friends fought off more Dark Elves. Some of the ones they'd already knocked out were regaining consciousness and rejoining the fight, thickening the throng. But when my eyes met Morgan's, I squared my shoulders and nodded.

Morgan glared, and I knew that if he hadn't been afraid to hurt one of our friends by mistake, he would have shifted there in the hall and torn the place to shreds for me. But when I mouthed the words 'I can do this', he visibly softened, and I felt his stubbornness fade into pure anxiety.

This was the part I had to do alone, and he knew it.

'I love you', he mouthed. 'Come back.'

'I promise,' I nodded. 'I love you.' Then, forcing myself to push my fear aside, I turned and walked into the room to face Volund.

He was calm, his expression patient and as arrogant as ever. But there was a subtle anxiety inside him, and I clung to that. Reminding myself that this fight hadn't been won yet.

"Why are we here, Volund?" I asked, letting my irritation grow, letting it fuel me. "What's with the game of cat and mouse? What do you want with me?"

Volund hesitated and then smiled. It was just a moment, a tiny blip, but for just a second, his insecurity had shown. "I'd think you would be more concerned about your sister's safety than my motivations. Or do you not care if she survives the night?"

"Oh, I'm not worried. In fact, I'm willing to bet that by now, she's out of danger." His brow furrowed and I smirked. "Go ahead, Volt. Check and see how she's doing."

A beat of silence passed, and he pulled out his phone, tapping away on the screen. A moment later, his expression cleared, and I could've sworn that I felt a tiny bit of relief inside him. But then he flashed with annoyance.

"So, you sent part of your troupe to rescue her, and the rest of you came on an ill begotten mission to what—capture me?" he taunted, back to his usual arrogant self.

"You never answered my question, Volt," I said, slipping my remaining knife from its sheath on my thigh. "What do you want with me?"

"Can't tell you. At least not yet."

Frustrated, I spun the pink knife in my hand. "So how exactly did you think this would go down then? A Minotaur artifact may have combatted your binding, but they don't work on curses. You can't hurt me, which means you can't fight back. So how do you expect to kidnap me when you can't even beat me?"

Volund grinned, a child enjoying a game, and I growled.

"You're right, I can't fight back," he said, not stepping away even as I began to approach him, "But I can wear you out."

I smirked, not intimidated by his false confidence. "We'll see."

Then I ran at him, knife drawn and prepared for battle. Volund, true to his word, didn't try to fight me. He focused on evasion, slipping away and forcing me to fight harder. But I wouldn't be worn down.

I attacked with more ferocity, more aggression. But every time, he outmaneuvered me, ducking, bending and dodging out of the way at the last moment. I had to admit, he was good.

But I had to figure out a way to be better.

"Come on, cousin," Volund taunted, watching me with cat-like intensity. "Take me down. Stop playing and give me your best."

"You want my best?" I gritted out between clenched teeth, taking in his every move. The way he always stepped with his left foot first. The slight lean to his shoulders right before he ducked to the side and the glint in his eyes before he darted out of reach.

Then I stepped toward his left, and just as I'd anticipated, he curved to the right. *Big mistake.* Quick and efficient, I stabbed at his right side, and he let out a small cry.

Stepping back, I cringed as I saw the blood coating my blade and fingers, warm and slick.

My stomach turned.

"What? Can't you handle the sight of the blood you drew?" Volund called out, smiling even though I sensed his pain. "My blood is quite literally on your hands, cousin. Own it!" he shouted.

Angry that he could make me feel so small when *he* was the one who was bleeding, I lunged at him again. He jumped back to avoid being stabbed in the stomach, and I hated that I felt relieved. That I didn't *want* to hurt him. "You don't know me!" I yelled. "You don't know what I'm capable of!"

"Care!" I whipped my head around at the sound of Morgan's voice. He stood in the hallway just beyond the living room, fighting off a few Nephilim. I could hear the sounds of the fight behind him, but he paid them no mind. He only had eyes for me. "You can do this."

I nodded even though I wasn't sure if I believed him. Could I do this? I was a spy, not a fighter. And even though I was equal parts Nephilim and Alfar, I'd never felt dark. Blood lust just wasn't in me, and the bile that rose in the back of my throat every time I looked at my knife just confirmed it. *I'm not cut out for this.*

"Caroline," a strange voice called, and I turned to see a burly man in Volund's place. He had sandy brown hair sprinkled with grey, and green eyes that felt familiar. *No.*

I froze as recognition dawned.

"Change back," I croaked, emotion clogging my throat.

"What's wrong?" Volund asked, his voice different, deeper in this new form. "You recognize this face?"

"I said change back!"

I sprung at him, but it was messy and slow, and he side stepped me easily.

"Why? Who am I Caroline?" he asked, taking two measured steps toward me.

My emotions surging like a tidal wave, I resisted the urge to squeeze my eyes shut, not willing to let him jump me. Yet the shock in my body and the hurricane of emotions that rushed through me demanded that I drop my weapon. So, I did.

"Caroline, you don't have to do this," he whispered, and my brain rejected it. *It's not real.* "You don't have to fight me."

"You're not him," I hissed, snapping my foot up and kicking him hard in the chest. "My father is *dead.*"

I'd never seen my birth parents' real faces. But before they gave me up, they took a family picture with me. I'd spent countless nights staring at it, crying over it, hating them for never coming back. I knew those faces—the face Volund was using. It wasn't my father's real face, just the one he'd worn when he gave me up. But it was the one I'd dreamed about for twenty-two years, imagining a life where they came back and loved me right alongside my adoptive parents.

A life that would never happen because my birth parents were gone.

"I know," Volund said gently, and I might have believed that he was suddenly feeling empathetic if not for the way he began to approach again. Careful and calculated. "But aren't you curious how I know this face?"

"Because you went through my things and saw that picture," I spat out, swinging my fist at his face.

He ducked it, expression still set in fake kindness. "No." He shook his head. "I know what your parents looked like because I met them once as a child."

"Liar!" I screamed, punching him the jaw.

He took the hit, stumbling back a step. "Caroline, I can't tell you everything right now," he said, pausing to spit out a bit of blood. "But I *can* tell you that if you trust me, I can give you what you want."

"Oh, and what's that?"

"A home. A place where you won't be the only one like you. A place where you'll be accepted and understood. Don't you want that?"

My instinctive answer was yes. I'd always wanted that. To be a part of a community that understood me instead of hiding from one that would hunt me. To be wanted and accepted instead of alone...

But that was before I met Morgan. And Mike and Clint and Logan and Grey and Merida and even Asher. Before, I'd isolated myself, afraid to trust because not trusting people is what kept me safe. I'd had to alter myself into someone dangerous and cunning in order to stay alive. *But now...*

I glanced back at Morgan. He and the others were gaining the upper hand. He was fighting off a fake Asher, but as if he sensed my gaze, he looked up and we locked eyes.

And then I recalled the words he'd said to me months ago. 'You spend so much time trying to prove to others that you're enough...but I don't know that you believe it about yourself, and I wish you would.'

Morgan loved me not because I was enough. Not because I was the vigilante, but because of *why* I was the vigilante. He didn't love me because I dressed like a Barbie or because I pretended to be tough and callous. He didn't love the veneer that I showed to the world, he loved the girl underneath it all. I'd never had to suppress myself for him or alter my appearance to please him. For Morgan, being me had always been enough.

And finally, I think it's enough for me too.

"I don't need you to accept me, *cousin*," I said, turning back to Volund. "I don't need anyone to tell me I'm enough. I have people who've done that for me without asking anything in return. And most importantly, I can do it for myself." My confidence gaining, I stepped closer to him. "I don't need you," I paused, grinning, "I never did."

And starting today, I was going to be enough for me. Because using magic wasn't a weakness; it wasn't a cheat. It was part of me, and as Morgan said, I was worth loving.

I braced myself as I coaxed my magic forward, knowing that it would require every ounce of strength I could muster. Bit by bit, the magic multiplied, strengthening even as my body grew weaker. Finally, when it was strong enough for what I intended, I sent it out into the room.

It sought Volund out, searching his feelings. Nerves and frustration brushed against me, and just like with the attacker who gave me my second concussion in the alley by the Shifter Alliance Building, I didn't encourage Volund's emotions where I wanted them.

I *yanked* them.

One moment he was frustrated, and the next he was completely compliant.

"Kneel," I commanded. He obeyed, dropping to the ground without question. There was a faint resistance in his eyes, but it wasn't enough to fight me off. I was too strong for that. "You will surrender, and you won't fight."

"I won't fight," Volund replied, a little doe eyed.

I sensed Morgan's approach before he even came into my line of sight. He stood beside me, panting and tired.

"Is anyone—"

"No one's injured," he assured me, shaking his head. "But all the Nephilim got away. One moment we were fighting, and the next they just fled."

"They're gone?"

Morgan nodded and I turned back to Volund.

"Something's wrong with all of this," I mumbled, my muscles fatiguing the longer I held my magic in place. "Why did your people flee?" Volund didn't answer. "You want me to trust you, Volt? Then explain to me what's going on."

I reined my magic in, just enough for him to speak, and Volund's eyes cleared. "I can't," he replied, still under my control—although my strength was growing thinner. "But you can trust me, Caroline. It's other people you can't—"

Suddenly his head snapped to the side, and he fell to the floor like a sack of potatoes. *Hmm...* Must've had something to do with the fact that I kicked him in the side of the head.

"Atta girl!" Morgan shouted, pulling me into his arms, and lifting me in his exuberance.

"Okay, easy there, Bear Man," I laughed, holding onto his shoulders as he set me back on the ground.

"I'm so proud of you, Red," he said, grasping my face in his hands.

I thought he said other words, but they came out half-muted and unclear.

"What'd you say?" I asked, squinting as I tried to focus harder on his voice.

His lips moved again but all I heard was a mumble. I opened my mouth to tell him, when suddenly the room began to tilt.

"Why are there two of you?" I breathed, watching as Morgan's brows furrowed.

And then I fell over.

Chapter 31

MORGAN

Caroline's eyes grew dim, and I caught her just as her body crumpled. Lifting her into my arms, I carefully cradled her body against my chest.

A flash of red caught my eye, and I felt myself begin to panic as I registered the blood on her hand. But a second, calmer perusal showed that she didn't bear any injuries, although I was sure she'd be black and blue in the morning.

"She okay?" Mike asked as he walked into the room, holstering his bloody knife.

"No," I growled. "Do me a favor and zip tie him?" I nodded back to Volund and Mike was only too happy to tie up the Dark Elf.

"Here, let me see her," Merida said as she ran over to me, her hair back to normal now that she wasn't actively using magic. She bore a gash along her shoulder, but she'd already assured me that it wasn't deep. We'd been lucky to get out so unscathed.

"She used a lot of magic on Volund," I explained as Merida began drawing invisible patterns in the air above Caroline's body. While I couldn't see the magic, I could see Merida shift, her hair turning white again as she drew her spells. "I think she over exhausted herself, because I can't find any injuries."

When Merida's hair turned back to black, she blinked up at me, a little more tired than she'd been a moment ago. "I can't tell if she's injured or not, but I charmed her body. If she's hurt, it should help her heal a little faster. And if she's just taxed herself too much, it should help her come around faster."

"Are you sure that was smart? You don't look so good."

Merida punched my arm, and I was surprised how much power she managed to put behind it. "I'm a little tired, but I'll be fine. Let's just focus on getting your girl home."

"Thank you."

She nodded and pushed me toward the cased opening. I passed Asher, who was already rifling through the room, looking for things the Elves might've left behind. It was probably a lost cause, hoping to find answers that way, but I just thanked him.

"Don't worry, I'll be cashing in on a favor of my own someday," he said, a microscopic smile on his face. "Now take care of your mate. We'll meet you at the house once we've swept the place for clues."

I tried to chuckle or smile, but I just couldn't quite manage it. Not with my mate unconscious in my arms.

"Don't worry, Red," I whispered as I headed toward the car, "You're going to be fine."

I'd make sure of it, no matter the cost.

Chapter 32

CAROLINE

Had someone dropped me in a vat of concrete? Because my entire body felt heavy and tired. *So tired.* Even my eyelids felt like they had weights attached. I'd been trying for five minutes now and still couldn't quite get them open.

"Are you awake? Because so help me, if you've been awake this whole time, I'm going to kill you, Caroline!"

Ariel? Tapping into every ounce of energy I had, I finally pried my eyes open. But then I shut them.

For some reason, someone had thought it was a good idea to open all the curtains in my room so I could be blinded by searing sunlight the moment I woke up. So thoughtful.

"Care?" Ariel screeched, and I felt the weight of her hopping on the bed next to me. "Are you awake?"

I slowly peeled each eye open, one at a time. When I could finally see past the brightness, my gaze focused on my sister. Who was just staring at me, grinning.

"Listen, I'm sorry about threatening to kill you," she said, bouncing on her knees. "But in my defense, you've been out of it for two whole days! And a sister can only take so much panic before she feels the need to resort to threats."

Then she threw herself at me and I grunted under the weight of her. She was short little thing, but she could pack a punch. "Oof! I'm sorry did you say that I've been unconscious for *two days?*"

Ariel shrugged, straightening the Marvel T shirt under her cardigan. "Technically, it was about forty six hours, give or take."

"Oh my gosh."

I flopped my head back against my pillow, letting my eyes wander around my bedroom. Everything looked as it usually did, except for the tray of untouched food at the foot of the bed, a chair next to me where I assumed Ariel had been sitting, and a vase of peonies on my nightstand.

"Who—"

"Morgan," my sister replied to my unfinished question, wagging her eyebrows suggestively at me. "This is the second batch. The first one had a few flowers that were barely wilted—honestly, a florist wouldn't have even noticed—but he went and got a second bouquet to replace it. He insisted that you deserved to wake up to happy flowers, not half dead ones."

I hated to fuel my sister's antics, but I had to know how Morgan was doing. I could sense him at the other end of the mate bond, but other than anxiety and frustration, it didn't tell me much. Plus, I owed her a *lot* of gossip. She didn't even know about Mor and I saying the 'L' word yet.

"How how's he doing?" I asked, unable to hide the desperation in my voice.

"Worried about you," she said, surprisingly devoid of teasing. Instead, her expression was thoughtful. It seemed that my sister was feeling sentimental. "He's sat in this chair the entire time you've been asleep. I had to physically force him out of the room to get him to shower. He's been holding your hand, wrinkling his forehead in the most adorable worry, and leaning over you as he prayed fervently for you to wake up..." Then Ariel narrowed her eyes to slits and squeezed my hands. "What have you not told me??"

I laughed and shook my head. *Here we go.* I really hoped Morgan was far enough away that the inevitable screaming from Ariel Birch wouldn't completely destroy his eardrums. Because I would not be so lucky.

"I told him that I love him," I admitted, a little shy. "And he said it back."

Ariel's big blue eyes stared at me for a moment. Not blinking. Just staring. Then the screaming started.

"Oh my gosh! You're in love! This is amazing! I told you he was into you," she gloated, pointing a finger in my face.

"Yeah, well...he's also my mate."

I waited for her to be confused, but instead, understanding stretched across her face. "You're mates? Wow. That's huge."

"Wait...how do you know about mates?"

Now it was Ariel's turn to be shy. I watched as her cheeks turned pink, and wondered why she would be embarrass—

"*You and Logan?*" I demanded. Loudly.

She nodded, failing to hold back a grin. "I'm sorry I didn't tell you immediately after I found out," she pleaded. "But it got complicated and then we were kidnapped."

"Do you love him?"

Her smile widened—freely this time. "I do."

I gasped, and then we broke into a fit of squeals and giggles. But we both jumped a mile high when the bedroom door burst open without warning.

Morgan stepped into the room, already smiling, but when his eyes met mine, his expression became warm and tender.

"Hi," I said lamely.

He stepped further into the room. "Hi."

For a moment we just stared at each other. Pining like idiots.

"Well..." Ariel said, drawing out the word as she skittered off the bed and went to the door, "That's my cue to go. Morgan, you might be in my sister's bedroom, but no funny business until you ask for my permission to marry her."

Morgan quirked an eyebrow at her. "Isn't that the dad's job?"

"Ariel's scarier than Daddy," I explained. "Which is one of the many reasons that I like him better."

"Rude!" Ariel gasped. "And here I was going to give you all the details on me and Logan later."

"Okay, fine. I'm sorry," I hurried to amend. "Please tell me everything!"

"Apology accepted. I'll fill you in after you get in a good long make out session with Beast Boy."

Then, with a wink, she let herself out. Leaving Mor and I alone.

"How long have you been awake?" he asked, coming to sit on the edge of my bed.

"Only about ten minutes. Well, I was technically awake a little bit before that, but I was still too tired to open my eyes."

I'd said the words as a joke, but when Morgan's gaze grew dark, I regretted it. Fear clenched in his chest and his hand fisted in my comforter. There were dark shadows beneath his eyes and a haunted look on his face. *Genevieve.*

"I'm alive, Mor," I whispered, taking his clenched hand in mine. With every stroke of my fingers, it gradually loosened until I could thread our fingers together. "I know I scared you, but I'm okay now."

"I know." But he still studied me as if I might disappear at any moment. "But I could have lost you so easily. You used so much magic that it completely drained your body of energy, and when you collapsed..." He shook his head, tears gathering in his grey eyes. "I can't describe the pain of losing someone so important. I would have given anything—a limb, my health, my home, my life—*anything* to keep Genevieve. And although I'm grateful that I had the opportunity to find love and happiness again with you, I have no desire to do it a third time." His tone darkened, a stubborn, immovable quality to it now. "But there will be no third mate. Do you hear me, Red? You're it for me. I'm only tying ribbons to one more person in this life and it's you. So, I forbid you from dying, understand?"

I nodded, tears building in my eyes. "I'm not going anywhere, Bear Man," I assured him, squeezing his hand. "By death or by choice. Not until we're really really old and more wrinkled than a Shar Pei." Swiping the tears from his cheeks, I watched the love in his eyes. Trusting it now in a way I hadn't before. "I'm sorry that I've been confusing with all my insecurities lately. I know we already talked about it, but I just want you to know how sorry I am—"

"Care," he interrupted, grasping my face in his gentle fingers, "You never have to apologize for being scared. It's okay, I understand the fear."

"But you got over your doubt so much faster than I did," I argued, despising the fact that I struggled—even now, though not nearly as much—to believe that I could have this. That Morgan would want this. With *me*.

"And that's okay," he insisted gently, "Relationships aren't fifty, fifty. Sometimes, one person only has ten to give, so the other one comes ninety. Then it switches. There are going to be times when I need you to come further because I can't give my whole half. But the point is that it doesn't matter how far I have to go for you, it only matters that we each give it everything we have. And right now, I have more than you do. So be scared, Care. Just be scared *with* me."

Wow. Good speech. Somehow, I managed to smile even as tears streamed down my face. Morgan was unbothered by my ugly cry, brushing the tears away as he pressed a sweet kiss to my lips.

"I love you," I whispered, wishing I had more to give him. That I had a grand speech or some kind of big vow I could make that would compare to the one he'd made me. But instead, I gave him all I had. "I can't promise you a lot, but I can promise you that loving me will be a challenge." He chuckled. "And I can also promise that I will love you until the day I die. That I'll give this relationship my all, and that you—*us*—will always be my highest priority. You're my mate and my partner, and I'm going to choose you every day until forever, Morgan Gareth Hohlt."

His eyes bright with adoration, Morgan kissed me again, deeper this time. I might have been tired, but there was nothing like a Morgan Hohlt kiss to wake a girl up.

When we finally had to come up for air, he brushed my hair from my face and kissed my forehead. "I love you, Red," he whispered, crawling into the bed beside me and scooping me into his side.

"How much?" I murmured, perfectly content with my head on his shoulder.

"A lot...why? You've got a nefarious smile on your face."

"How far would you go to assure me that you love me?"

He hesitated. "Far..."

"Would you do a flashmob?"

"No."

"What? Why not? You can't tell me that the guys wouldn't *love* to do a dance to 'That's What Makes You Beautiful'."

"I think I'm saving us all from a very traumatic experience that we'll never be able to recover from. And besides, you getting to see how terrible of a dancer I am is definitely not going to improve my sex appeal."

"You don't know what I find sexy. Maybe I'm into crummy dancers."

"Not a chance, sweetheart," he whispered, his voice close to my ear as I began to drift off to sleep again. "But maybe I'll consider it when I propose."

"If you did, I'd say yes..." I mumbled. And then I fell asleep, completely at peace.

Chapter 33

CAROLINE

"Really?" I sighed, shaking my head as I walked into my office a few days later.

Clint was sound asleep on my velvet couch, and Mike was snoring in one of my plush armchairs. "Big babies."

I knew they liked my furniture, but this was taking it a bit far. Although I did love that their obsession with my office annoyed Morgan. It had become a bit of a battle, seeing whose office everyone wanted to meet in most frequently. I was pretty sure Mike and Clint were taking advantage of our little battle, but I didn't really care. I just liked beating Morgan at things.

Mostly because it usually resulted in a banter match that almost always ended with a kissing match. And in that, we were always tied.

"Hm..." I hummed as I sat at my desk, pulling out my phone to call my mom. I'd kept her semi-apprised of things here in Shifter Haven, but I'd left out a few of the more dangerous details. Telling her that I was in love would be fun though.

Glancing around the office, the boys sound asleep and a new picture of Morgan and I framed on my desk, I felt my chest fill so tight that it could almost burst. "I'm happy." It was a strange feeling to be this content, especially in the midst of so much continuing chaos.

Volund was locked in a cell, and although we assumed he was behind everything that had happened lately, he wasn't giving us any answers. Yet even with so many unanswered questions, life was good in the ways that mattered most, and I wasn't going to look that gift horse in the mouth.

Just as I began to dial my mom, Grey knocked on the open door.

"Hey," I smiled.

"This was in the mail for you," he said, handing me a large manilla envelope with my name on it.

"Thanks."

"Overgrown cubs," Grey chuckled quietly, shaking his head at Mike and Clint. "Maybe we should start baby proofing your office."

"Ha. That'd be fun! How long do you think it would take them to figure out how to work a baby proofed door handle?"

"I'd bet on forty minutes."

"I say twenty-five."

The older man gave me a mischievous look. "Ten bucks?"

I smiled and nodded as we shook on it. Why this family was so obsessed with betting, I didn't know, but it made for a lot of interesting situations.

"Should I let Morgan in on the bet?" Grey asked, but I barely heard him. I was too busy looking at the return address on the envelope. *The courthouse.*

Grey said something else, but I didn't catch it, still staring at the envelope.

I should have rushed to open it. I should have been excited. But I wasn't.

What if whatever was in this envelope wasn't what I wanted it to be—what I *needed* it to be? What if all my hopes of finding something sentimental were let down? What if it wasn't something that could give me peace after all this time? *What if I got my hopes up, only to have them dashed?*

"Care?" I jumped as large fingers covered mine, but relaxed when I looked up and saw Morgan kneeling in front of me. "What's wrong? Grey said you're acting strange. And your emotions feel...dark."

I glanced at the door, but Grey was gone, leaving Morgan and I alone with his sleeping brothers. "I just..." I sighed, the envelope crinkling beneath my tight grip. "I don't know what to do."

"With your inheritance?" Mor's hands were warm on mine, easing some of the tension from my fingers.

"I'm afraid of what it is," I whispered, embarrassed by my own fear. "What if it's something unemotional like money?"

"They already left you money though."

"Yeah, but...I'm worried that whatever's in here won't fix this." I put a hand to my heart. "That I'll open this envelope and just feel empty."

Morgan set his hands on my thighs and gave them a gentle squeeze. "I think that whatever is in that envelope is something they desperately wanted you to have. And that's all that matters."

I nodded. He was right. I'd never had any kind of contact from my birth parents. Even the revelation that I was an Elf came from my adoptive parents. For twenty-two years, I'd longed for some kind of connection to the people that gave me up. And now was the moment that I would either feel connection or closure.

Whatever the case, I needed to know.

So, with a gut full of trepidation, I opened the envelope. Inside was a smaller, sealed envelope with one name written in beautiful cursive. *Felicity.* Inside was a letter.

"To our dearest baby girl," I read aloud, "Leaving you was never part of the plan. As we're sure you're aware, plans often don't turn out as we like, and although we wish we could've kept you, raised you, and taught you about where you come from, we rest easy knowing that you're deeply loved where you are..."

My words broke off as I began to cry, and I handed the note to Morgan. He watched me, concerned, until I nodded for him to continue.

"Please know that we love you more than life," he read, "But we had to give you your best chance. And as much as it breaks our hearts, that chance wasn't with us. Your new parents are good people who can give you the love, safety and stability that we want for you. Please be good to them and be patient. They weren't prepared to raise an extraordinary daughter like you. And should the time come that you have questions about what you are or where you come from, there are people you can ask. People like you. Whether or not you seek them out, the other Alfar are out there, ready to help you if you need it. But sweet Felicity, whatever you do in life and whatever choices you make, know that we love you, and above all else, we want you to be safe and happy. Forever, Mom and Dad."

Morgan stared at the note for another few heartbeats before meeting my eyes. "There's an address." When I said nothing, Mor handed me the paper. Sure enough, at the end of the letter was an address for the Alfar. "What do you want to do?" he asked patiently.

"I..." I stared at the page. Grief, relief, love, peace, anxiety and curiosity all pounded through me in one big tangle. What did I want? "I want to call my mom. Tell her I'm in love and thank her for being my mom."

Morgan smiled and I grabbed his hand, giving it a squeeze. "I want to buy a headstone for my birth parents. It's time that I move forward and set the pain to rest. And this way I can visit them and bring flowers."

"I think that's a great idea." Mor lifted my hand and kissed my knuckles. "What else?"

I took a deep, fortifying breath. This was the million-dollar question. And the answer could potentially change my entire life. "I want to go meet the Alfar."

Morgan smiled, although I felt an anxious twinge in his chest. "And I'm sure they want to meet their queen."

Or so we hoped.

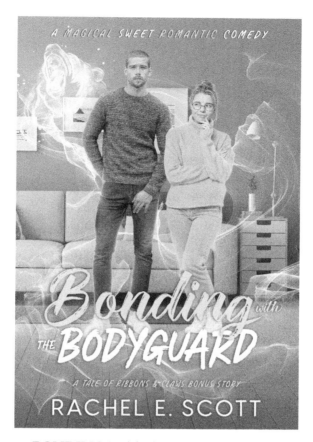

BONDING WITH THE BODYGUARD

Want to know what happened while Logan was bodyguarding Ariel? You're in luck! They're standalone book is coming next after Morgan and Caroline's final book. If you want to stay in the know about its release, you can either subscribe to my newsletter or follow me on Amazon by clicking on my name on this book's Amazon page!

(Blurb to come!)

Hi! Thank you so much for reading the second installment of Morgan and Caroline's story! And if you're hoping to find out what happened between Logan and Ariel, keep on the lookout because their book is coming after the final book of Morgan and Caroline's story (*Check-Mate*) comes out this winter. And if you want a fun sneak peek at the first chapter of Ariel's story, you can join my newsletter.

And if you're attached to any of the side characters from this book, chances are, either a trilogy or a standalone is in the works for them. **BUT** if there are any specific characters you want to see get their own story, please feel free to send me an email or send in your suggestion on my website! I have lots of plans for the Shifter Universe, but I always want to keep reader's preferences in mind!

And for those of you who like short stories starring characters you know, extra scenes, and fun behind the scenes things, you can always check out the newsletter! And if you're interested in chatting with other readers (or me), you can join my private Facebook group. There's also my Instagram page and YouTube channel. Or if you just care about the books, that's fine too! I'll see you in the next one!

Thank you for reading,

Rachel

When you join my newsletter, you get my novella *The Grinch Next Door* for FREE! You also get access to short stories, extra scenes and more!

Join at rachelescott.com

Also by Rachel E Scott

Contemporary

The Grinch Next Door

Fantasy

Legends of Avalon: Merlin

Legends of Avalon: Arthur

A Tale Of Ribbons & Claws

Stale-Mate

Bond-Mate

Check-Mate (coming SOON!)

Plot Twist

Bonding With the Bodyguard (coming 2024)

Acknowledgments

Somehow, writing a 100k word book is much easier than writing my acknowledgments. But we're going to give it a shot!

Thank you to my family for always supporting my crazy dreams. Maybe they just realized that like John Locke, Rachel doesn't like being told she can't do something. Wise of you all. But regardless, you've carried so much of my load, and my poor back would've broken without you!

Also, a huge thank you to my friends, Beth and Melody and so many others! And to my friend Leigh who was my awesome beta reader! These books wouldn't be the same without you!

And thank you of course to the One who gave this passion to a child (kind of irresponsible really. This creative streak got me into a lot of trouble as a kid). But really, thank you God for storytelling, it's my truest love in the world.

And last but not least, thank you to my babies Daisy Mae and Marshall Moose. Am I really thanking my dogs right now? Absolutely, I am. They're my joy and the best part of my day. I love you guys.

And thank you reader for reading this book! If you get a chance, please leave a rating or review (especially on Amazon)! Reviews mean so much to a self-published author like me!

Until next time,

Rachel

About the Author

Rachel is an author of both contemporary and fantasy stories. She's a *The Office* enthusiast, a *The Lord of the Rings* superfan, and a sucker for all things geek. She reads anything with some clean romance—bonus points if there's some snarky MCs, funny side characters, and a happy ending. Rachel is dog obsessed, and two of her series even include her dogs (Daisy Mae appears in *A Tale of Ribbons & Claws* and Marshall is in *Legends of Avalon*). This hobbit author and her dogs spend lots of time writing, walking, and of course, watching *The Office* and *The Lord of the Rings* and *The Hobbit* appendices.

Where to Find Me

All info, including my Facebook page, Instagram, Newsletter and Podcast can be found on my website rachelescott.com

Made in the USA
Las Vegas, NV
01 November 2023

79850030R00213